GW00402126

IN THE FAC...

Not a bird could b[...]
reigned over the jungle. Occasionally, a groan
would rise from the humanity heaped on the
bridge, making itself heard over the constant
murmur of fast-running water. A flock of
vultures gathered in the high trees near the
bridge. Every so often, they fluttered closer to
the corpses strewn below — growing bolder,
but none yet venturing to commence the feast
that waited.

Since noon, the stench of rotting flesh had
risen from the bridge and permeated the
upper slopes of the bluff, making the
Australians retch at the results of their own
handiwork. Now, in the heat of high afternoon, it seemed to foul the valley for miles
around. There was no escape from it.

Woody had no expectation that the lull
would last. He took advantage of it to wrest
the Lewis from its position and heft it ten
yards to the right. One more attack would
finish the ammunition.

"You OK, sport?" he called out softly to
Rich, who was crouched a few feet below his
new location, idly toying with a grenade.

IN THE FACE OF THE ENEMY

Douglas Scott

Hamlyn Paperbacks

A Hamlyn Paperback

Published by Arrow Books Limited
17-21 Conway Street, London W1P 6JD

A division of the Hutchinson Publishing Group

London Melbourne Sydney Auckland
Johannesburg and agencies throughout
the world

First published in Great Britain
by Secker & Warburg 1982
Hamlyn Paperbacks edition 1983
Reprinted 1985

© Douglas Scott 1982

Printed and bound in Great Britain by
Anchor Brendon Limited, Tiptree, Essex

ISBN 0 09 940990 9

Contents

Man has three ways of acting wisely:
    Firstly, on meditation, this is the noblest;
    Secondly, on imitation, this is the easiest;
    Thirdly, on experience.
    This is the bitterest.

Confucius

One

The Sea Captain

As a means of keeping in touch with the wider world beyond the horizons of the Java Sea, the ancient six-valve radio receiver in the saloon of the steamship *Machiko* left a good deal to be desired. Its function seemed to be in no way governed by the known scientific laws of communication by radio waves. On those days when reception was good – that is, on those days when the only obtainable sound was not a crackling rage of atmospherics – the *Machiko*'s saloon radio could pick up London, Tokyo, Singapore, Darwin, San Francisco and a variety of short-wave morse transmissions, simultaneously and all at the same spot on the dial. Very occasionally, a single station could be heard crystal-clear and without interference from other stations. Even this could be freakish, because the broadcast heard could be coming from another hemisphere while the output from a local station only a hundred miles away was unobtainable despite frantic twiddling of the tuning condenser. Perversely, of course, a local radio station could come in at maximum volume to the exclusion of all else while the station tuner was rotated throughout its entire compass.

No single piece of apparatus could have been more cursed and vilified by those for whose entertainment it had been obtained. A consequence was that it lay neglected for weeks on end, and the officers and small complement of cabin passengers diverted themselves by playing checkers or poker.

In December 1941, however, the *Machiko*'s saloon radio suddenly became the most carefully nursed and cosseted instrument on the small ocean trader – because it became the only means by which the officers and crew could glean any information of the war that had erupted throughout the Orient.

An English-language broadcast from Tokyo had provided the

1

first numbing news of the Japanese attacks on Pearl Harbor and Malaya. By then, the *Machiko* was clear of the islands and on the final leg of her perambulating westward itinerary from Honolulu to Singapore.

The ship had been without a radio – other than the saloon receiver – since September, when the radio cabin had been gutted by fire. She had also been without a radio officer. The sole occupant of that office had been severely burned trying to quell the flames and he had been hospitalised in the Carolines.

Travelling at reduced speed to conserve her dwindling supply of coal, the *Machiko* was still some days out from Singapore when the New Year of 1942 was ushered in. By then, the ancient radio was receiving Batavia with some regularity and good clarity – but this was of little comfort to the news-hungry inhabitants of the *Machiko*, whose combined knowledge of the Dutch language was infinitesimal. Much greater effort was exerted to pick up the asthmatic tones emanating from Singapore and giving news in English against a competition of high-pitched morse signals and fierce atmospherics.

No one was more bewildered by the news coming from Singapore than the *Machiko*'s master, Robert Ross. The bulletins suggested that the forces of the British Empire were whipping the impertinent Japanese in Malaya – an assertion which didn't quite seem to tally with the speed of the Japanese advance down the Kra Isthmus.

A rage of sorrowing frustration had built up in Ross from the day he had learned of the attack on Pearl Harbor. It was not simply because he had a young wife in Honolulu and he worried for her safety. It was much more than that. It had more to do with the certainty growing within him that he was irretrievably trapped by the follies of a world on which he had largely turned his back.

He had not become a hermit. Nor had he rejected all the conventional values of his kind. He had, however, not always conformed to expatriate attitudes in the East, with the result that he had repeatedly come into conflict with them. Time and again, his independence of mind had found him in a minority of one. So he had gone his own way, carving a way of life for himself which brought its own measure of happiness and owed nothing to external values. He had realised early that one man is a puny force in opposition to attitudes entrenched by centuries of arrogance or ignorance, so he had rejected all those standards –

whether Western or Eastern in origin – with which he could not live comfortably. Now, perhaps, he belonged neither to the West, where he had been born and brought up, nor to the Orient, where he had spent most of his adult life. Yet he clung to what he admired in both worlds and, at the age of thirty-three, believed he had come to terms with life on an imperfect planet.

Until Pearl Harbor.

For Robert Ross, the day of Japan's entry into the war was the day when all his hopes and expectations of life were tipped right off the balance scales. There was no consolation for him in the knowledge that he had seen the war coming for years. He had read the signs and raged in his impotence as the opportunities of avoiding the inevitable had not been seized by the influential and the powerful to steer Japan away from war.

Now the war that Ross had dreaded had come. And with it, he knew, would come all the other things he had secretly dreaded but were too fearful to contemplate. All that he had built and gained for himself – and some might say that was precious little – was about to be snatched away from him. This was the consequence that crushed down on his mind more than any other.

There was a terrible irony in it. He had walked a lonely road because he had refused to let himself be corrupted by the false values of fools and rogues. Now, the account for all the folly and all the roguery was going to have to be paid in full. And it would be the innocent who paid the lion's share – not the guilty. That was the terrible irony. That was the great injustice.

Ross brooded on those things as the *Machiko* steamed steadily towards Singapore. As she completed her westward run through the Java Sea, Haraldsen, the First Mate, had a recurrence of his periodic malaria. Ross stood the morning watch for him as the ship began her sedate north-westward passage to the Karimatas.

Watching the dawn come up, the tranquil multi-coloured beauty of sea and sky touched some emotional well deep in the *Machiko*'s captain. He found himself willing the sun to delay its appearance so that he could savour that glowing moment when the horizon was shot with an opaque light of green and gold and pink and mother-of-pearl. But the sun's rim appeared with its inexorable power; bathing the horizon in fire and burning crimson into the more delicate tints, forcing them to flee from its fiery path.

Ross watched the spectacle with a sadness of acceptance. The East had endowed him with a more pronounced fatalism than he

3

would have admitted. It was working in him now. His mind was accepting the fact of war as it had accepted the sun's rising. He had wanted neither to occur at precisely the moment they had occurred, but nothing he could have done would even have delayed their happening. He would have to face up to the fact of war as he would have to face up to the fact of a new day.

He acknowledged in his heart that he had allowed himself to be lulled into a false sense of security by what he had won from life: a pleasant home in Honolulu, a wife who loved him, a way of life (voyaging among the most exotic islands on earth) that suited him. He had believed it could go on forever. He had thought the hard part of life was over: that from here on in, it would all be downhill. But the hard part hadn't even begun. Had he any right to be resentful of the bloody stupidity of war just because it was catching up with him? In Africa, in Europe, in the icy Atlantic, men just like him had been dying for over two years – so what right had he to think he was immune? That he could escape just because it hadn't touched him so far?

For almost a month now, the forces of Imperial Japan had been bringing war south from their homeland in a tidal wave of aggression that was sweeping towards the Equator on a front 5000 miles wide – but, so far, not even a ripple of war had reached the *Machiko*. Here, in the calm solitude of the western Java Sea – without having seen a ship, friendly or hostile, in weeks – it was almost impossible to imagine that battles raged anywhere on the earth.

Ross savoured the peace of the morning, girding himself for whatever lay ahead. And a kind of serenity did come to him – a calmness, a resignation, a resolve to endure what had to be endured. It was as if, for the past few weeks, he had dreaded the reality of whatever awaited in Singapore and had wanted to postpone his arrival there indefinitely. But, now, he was ready and almost anxious to be there.

The reality, though, was to prove a far greater ordeal than his wildest imaginings conceived possible.

In the dawn of a new January day, the *Machiko* arrived in Singapore.

This day had begun for Ross two hours before sunrise, when the ship was in the Durim Strait. She had been challenged to identify herself by a Royal Navy patrol vessel. Ross had gone to the bridge and exchanged information with the patrol ship's

4

skipper by loudhailer . . . He had remained on the bridge until the *Machiko* was safely at anchor in Singapore Roads.

The city looked peaceful enough in the light of breaking day. Smoke, wisping up from smouldering fires in the heart of Chinatown, hung about in the still air: a lingering reminder of a Japanese air raid the previous day. Officers from the port's Customs and Health authorities came and departed before seven. Little time was wasted on the inward clearance of Ross' little island trader because of a troopship convoy's imminent arrival.

The speed of these entry formalities pleased Ross. A good omen, he hoped. With luck, the *Machiko*'s stay in Singapore would be short and the ship would be loaded, bunkered, watered, stored and outward bound within the week. The only disappointment of the morning so far had been the non-appearance of the Honolulu, Hong Kong and Islands Shipping Company's Singapore agent. Normally, he boarded as soon as the hook was down.

Ross ordered an early breakfast in his cabin and was just sitting down to eat it when he heard the shouts and deck noises that announced the arrival of a launch alongside. He assumed it was the agent, but it was a stranger who was shown to his cabin – a naval officer from the governmental department responsible for shipping control.

Rather than postpone his breakfast, Ross invited the RNR two-ringer to join him. Lieutenant Jimmy Hamill quickly accepted. He, too, had been on the go since 4 a.m., and his only sustenance in that time had been a mug of tea which he had allowed to get cold while he shaved. He tucked in with relish to the speedily produced feast set before him by Ross' Filipino steward: piping hot flapjacks and molasses, followed by corned beef hash with poached eggs on top.

"You know you've caused a hell of a flap ashore?" Hamill asked Ross cheerfully as he ate. "Signals flashing back and fro between us and the Yanks. Our boys have been beating the air waves for you for weeks. And, lo and behold, you turn up in the middle of the night from nowhere and get one of our ships to radio ahead for berthing instructions. D'you not realise, my dear chap, that your ship has been officially posted missing since Christmas? If it's not a rude question, just where the bloody hell have you been?"

Ross did not know whether to be amused or annoyed.

"Where have I been?" he echoed. "The same places we always go. Why should there be any panic? Anyone wanting to know roughly where the *Machiko* is at any given time has only got to contact our Singapore agents, Asiatic Oriental. A phone call to Mr Yasheda there is all that's needed. He might not always be able to say precisely where the ship is – but he knows every scheduled stop on our run and always has a rough idea of our whereabouts."

Mention of Yasheda's name brought a grimace to Hamill's face. He shrugged.

"You obviously haven't heard about Mr Yasheda?"

"What about him?" asked Ross.

"He was interned. The same day as the Japs landed at Khota Bahru. And, like all the other Japs who were rounded up, he's been bundled off to Ceylon out of harm's way. The Asiatic Oriental office was closed down by the police."

Ross frowned. Perhaps he should have expected something of this nature. Why did he feel so shocked? Was it because old Yasheda, now well into his sixties, had always been such a kind and courtly man? Ross couldn't imagine him harming anyone.

Some of the lead-heavy sadness that had weighed on him since he had heard of the Pearl Harbor attack returned to his shoulders. There was no anger – just a burdening sorrow. Yasheda's internment was the first hurtful reality of the war he had not wanted to happen.

He made no outward show to Hamill of the distress he felt at the other's news – a sign, perhaps, of how much life in the Orient had made him assimilate oriental attitudes. Instead, he enquired if Hamill knew of alternative arrangements for the companies represented by Asiatic Oriental and, in particular, for the HHK & I shipping line.

"God knows we're not the Blue Funnel, but we've got a right to exist," he told Hamill. "You can't just close down our agent and let us go hang."

Hamill plunged his fork into a poached egg and spread the oozing yolk into the potato mixture on which it rested. He waved the fork recklessly.

"A Mr Bishan Singh is looking out for Asiatic Oriental's customers, as far as I know. He is the Sikh gentleman with the office next door." Hamill waved his fork at Ross with an almost conspiratorial air. "You realise, of course, that Mr Singh will have precious little business to worry about on Yasheda's behalf. His customers were all Japanese. That goes for your own company, Captain Ross."

"Correction," said Ross. "HHK & I is a British-American company."

Hamill was unperturbed. Again, he waggled his fork; this time in a good-humouredly reproachful manner.

"The owner is Japanese, a Mr Matsumishi. I've done my homework, Captain."

"If you had done your homework, Lieutenant Hamill," Ross said patiently, "you would know that Mr Matsumishi is an American citizen and a resident of Honolulu. He's my boss. He is also my very good friend."

Uncertainty flickered in Hamill's eyes.

"That could make things awkward. An American citizen, eh?" He did not explain how it could make things awkward. Instead he asked, "Why does your ship fly the red duster, Captain Ross? Why not the stars and stripes?"

Ross replied by sketching a potted history of the Honolulu, Hong Kong & Islands Shipping Company for the RNR lieutenant. "The founder was a Captain Bell, an Englishman who made his home in Hong Kong. He had been trying to go independent for years but, although he had the ideas, he didn't have the money. Then a couple of ships came on the market cheap during the Depression – and he found a backer: Mr Matsumishi. Mr Matsumishi put up nearly all the capital – something like ninety-eight per cent. He supplied the finance and Captain Bell supplied the shipping know-how and a knowledge of the China Sea and South Pacific that was second to none. It was really rather brave of Mr Matsumishi to risk all his money the way he did. He was prepared to invest just about all he had at a time when other speculators were jumping off sky-scrapers in Wall Street. But he believed old Bell knew his onions and he had faith in him."

Ross went on to tell Hamill how the two men had named the ships after their respective daughters – the *Laura* and the *Machiko*. Ross had served as a second mate under Bell and had been offered command of the *Machiko* after a chance encounter with the old sea captain.

Matsumishi had given Bell a free hand with the running of the ships and the engagement of crews. As a result, the HHK & I's fleet of two had been registered in Hong Kong and flew the British flag. Bell had died in 1938.

"OK," said Hamill when he had heard Ross out, "I accept that the *Machiko* is not Japanese-owned, as we were led to believe. That may, for the time being, save your ship from being seized and a prize crew put aboard – but you are still going to have to answer a lot of questions ashore."

Cold shock ran through Ross at the other's bald, almost throwaway statement about the possible seizure of his ship. But, again, he concealed the emotion he felt.

"Questions?" he asked. "Such as?"

"Your complete radio silence. Honolulu station has been putting out calls to you since mid-December. So have we. You were to return to Honolulu or, alternatively, make your position known to the nearest shore station or friendly ship of war."

"We've had no radio since September, two days out from Honolulu," said Ross with a shrug.

"What happened to it?"

"The radio cabin was completely burnt out – an electrical fault. It was pretty antiquated, mind you. Must have been one of the first sets Marconi ever built. We shovelled up what was left of the equipment and gave it a sea burial."

"But where have you been?" persisted Hamill. "You were due here four weeks ago. Four weeks is a hell of a long time to be overdue."

Ross smiled at the RNR man's obvious bewilderment.

"Four weeks is nothing," he declared. "Good heavens, we don't run to a timetable like a London bus." When Hamill continued to stare at him without any sign of comprehension, Ross said, "You want to know where we've been, Lieutenant Hamill? OK, I'll tell you. We've been taking the necessities of life to just about every island and atoll between here and Hawaii. If you know anything about the islands, Lieutenant, you'll know that that's the equivalent of making a voyage to Jupiter or Venus. You expect to be out of touch for indefinite periods. Coming here is like arriving from another planet. You and your high-powered Navy people are going to have to make allowances for us ocean-going gypsies."

Hamill made a limp, indeterminate gesture with his hand.

"We're not bogeymen, Captain. I'm sure you can explain things perfectly. It has been pretty desperate here, you know. Communications can get fouled up. To be frank, I thought your only ports were Moresby and Rabaul. I didn't know you were island-hopping."

Ross smiled. "We go to places that never see a ship from one year's end to the next. How fast or how slowly we get to Singapore – which is the end of the line – depends on the trade we find and the needs of the islanders. A five-hundred-mile detour to collect fifty tons of copra or deliver forty tons of rice is nothing – the rule rather than the exception. We make the run from Honolulu

8

through the islands to Singapore once a year. It can take five months or it can take eight. There's no way of telling in advance."

"I think I get the picture," said Hamill. He gave a lopsided smile. "Bit like the old country postman, eh? Never pass a farm gate without stopping to chat about the crops?"

"We're a lifeline to the outside world," agreed Ross. "The people out there *depend* on us showing up once a year. Even if we'd got those orders to return to Honolulu, I'm not sure we would have taken any notice of them. It would have meant letting too many people down. Our owner knows that. I just can't believe that any recall order originated with him."

The Filipino steward arrived to clear away the breakfast crockery.

"An excellent breakfast. Thank you," Hamill beamed. To Ross he said, "Those islands could be in the front line before long, you know."

"They know it," said Ross. "They've known for some time. But how are things here? The only news we've had is what we've been able to pick up on the saloon radio. For a time we were wondering who was going to get to Singapore first, the *Machiko* or the Japanese Army."

Hamill regarded Ross solemnly. "We'll hold out *if* we get reinforcements in time. The trouble is that the Japs are having it all their own way in the air, murdering bastards that they are."

Hamill's words knifed at Ross, aggravating the weary sadness inside him. He winced mentally if not physically.

"Some Japanese may be murdering bastards. But it's a great pity, don't you think, that we Westerners haven't exactly spent much time trying to understand the Japanese?" He saw Hamill's eyes widen and quickly added, "Oh, we've taught them a lot . . . How to jump into the twentieth century from the Middle Ages – but if we'd given a damn for what happened to them in the process, maybe it wouldn't be the warlords and generals who would be running their country today, and running it straight to hell."

Hamill's stare was icy. "They're barbarians!" His eyes challenged Ross to dare contradict him. But Ross' eyes did not reflect the other's anger. They held only sorrow.

"Barbarians?" he asked softly. "That's how the Romans saw our British ancestors, wasn't it? Yet it was the Romans who went around crucifying people. They also had fratricide, regicide, even matricide and infanticide, down to rather a fine art."

9

Hamill's fierce glare now combined outrage and plain hostility. "The Japs butchered our people in Hong Kong. They've raped nurses in the north. You may call that civilised behaviour, Captain Ross. I call it barbarian."

Ross conceded a point but not the argument. "I'm not condoning any crimes that Japanese soldiers may or may not have committed. All I am saying, Lieutenant, is that there's a hell of a lot more to the Japanese than an insatiable appetite for murder and rape. I've always found them to be the very opposite to barbaric – people of great personal charm and humility, a very gracious people, and kindly."

"Well, you'd better keep bloody quiet about it in Singapore," said Hamill fiercely, "or you could get yourself lynched!" His eye fell on a framed photograph on Ross' desk. Ross intercepted the look and the sudden glint of surprise.

The photo was a full-length studio shot of a young woman in traditional Japanese dress: kimono and obi, her raven hair piled high and held with a decorative comb. The face – lit by a half shy, half mischievous smile – was a perfect oval shape and there was no question of the woman's stunning beauty.

Hamill's smile was robbed of any sincerity by the distinctly acidic tone of his voice.

"You obviously have a great admiration for the Japanese," he commented.

"My wife," said Ross, and there was pride as well as challenge in the way he said it. "Her name is Machiko, the same as this ship. She is the daughter of Mr Matsumishi, who owns this ship."

Hamill was silent. The only sound in the cabin came from the brass wall-clock on the bulkhead above Ross' desk. It clicked forward to 8.30.

Ross glanced at his watch and gave a sigh of impatience as he left the driveway of the big house in Cluny, some miles out of Singapore city. The day was half gone already and nothing had been achieved. A sizeable queue – predominantly female and many with young children – had formed in the driveway of the mansion-sized house. They were queueing for liner tickets to take them away from Singapore and the war that was ravaging Malaya.

The house in Cluny had been taken over by officers engaged in shipping control and administration. P & O staff had moved out from the shipping line's premises on Collyer Quay to handle and co-ordinate all sea passenger traffic out of the port – a move that

10

enabled the crowds of civilians to assemble in more safety from bomb attack than was the case at the sea-front.

Although considerable uncertainty now surrounded the future movements of the *Machiko*, Ross had taken a taxi out to Cluny to register details of his ship's capacity to ferry away evacuees in a worsening of the emergency. He still retained a hope that, war or no war, the *Machiko* would be outward bound to Port Moresby inside a week.

The closure of the Asiatic Oriental offices had, however, caused all manner of problems. The cargo for Moresby had not been booked or, if it had been, no one knew where it was. Even more serious was the discovery that the HHK & I's bankers had, on American Government instructions, frozen all moneys belonging to the shipping company. Ross was completely without funds to buy bunkers, stores, cargo, labour or anything else. On top of all this was the very real threat that the military authorities might commandeer his ship and take it away from him. One way or another, a day that had started well was becoming progressively more disastrous with every hour that passed.

Ross' meeting early in the day with Bishan Singh, who had been appointed by the government to act as caretaker agent for Asiatic Oriental's clientele, had done little to inspire confidence. As a ship supplier he might have been excellent, but he was clearly out of his depth with chartering procedures and seemed not to have the foggiest idea about the funding of shipping operations. He had been given his caretaking brief, it seemed, on the strength of having an office adjacent to Asiatic Oriental, and Ross suspected that his duties had been seen as likely to be more janitorial than commercial. However, armed with appropriate letters of authority, Mr Singh had gone off to the bank to seek a lifting of the sanctions on HHK & I money. And that was something. Ross was now on his way to meet the Sikh.

As the taxi took him back towards the city, Ross sagged back in his seat and allowed the fan of air from the open windows to work its cooling therapy. The impatience and frustration which had built up in him throughout the morning dropped away as he allowed himself to think of the woman he had left behind in Honolulu the previous September. As always, he had only to picture Machiko in his mind and the magic worked. Her serenity enfolded him, enveloped him – enclosed him in a capsule of such enchanted detachment that all the troubles and torments of the world could not intrude.

11

It was strange that he never thought of her as "my American wife", or "my dear wife", or even just "my wife". It was always "my Japanese wife". It was not that he had a plurality of wives of different nationalities, nor that he was so racially sensitive that he placed her on a different plane of humanity from himself. It was simply that her Japaneseness gave so much and was so essential to the quality of their relationship that it could not be excluded from any thought of her. The fact of her ethnic origin and the fact that she was his wife had become so inseparably fused that neither fact on its own could do justice to the uniqueness of the whole.

Machiko had brought to her marriage more than just her womanhood. She had brought to her loving and honouring of her partner a style and tradition that Ross knew he could never have found in his own race. Initially, he had fallen in love with a lovely face and a sweet nature, a personality that sparked with the promise of hidden springs of delight – but it was not until after marriage that Ross discovered the seams of gold, the untapped wells of happiness that far surpassed his imaginings and expectations.

At first, Machiko's father had been opposed to the marriage. He had not wanted Ross as a son-in-law, in spite of a strong liking and respect for the young sea captain. Two things had made him change his mind. The first was his cherished daughter's quietly borne heartbreak in her filial obedience to his wishes. Her unhappiness distressed him deeply and he hated being its author. The second was his deep friendship with his English business partner, Captain Bell, whom he had come to love as a brother. Ross was a younger edition of his friend in many ways. If, the father reasoned, he could feel family-type bonds for one foreigner, why should he not extend them on his daughter's behalf to another? So, the old man had relented.

Ross recalled with a smile how the old man had taken him aside on the eve of his wedding to instruct him how he should behave to Machiko on their wedding night.

"Machiko is great treasure to ageing parent," the old man had said. "Must now learn to be treasure to honoured husband. Husband must be lord always. Must *command* wife. Must show that love in heart has not turned blood to milk. Husband must show face of tiger."

The old man had actually growled and made fierce sounds to emphasise how Ross must snarl his dominance the moment the couple were alone on their honeymoon. Machiko would be offended, the old man had insisted, if Ross did not immediately proclaim in the gruffest possible way that he was her lord and master.

For old Matsumishi's sake, Ross had said that he would do as tradition demanded; but without any real intention of coming the Victorian heavy with his bride. Perhaps it was the ritual drinking of *sake* before a shrine of Shinto gods that had begun the process of changing his mind. Perhaps it was the awe of the moment when the white silk headband was removed from Machiko's bowed head during the ceremony. The final doubts had vanished, however, in the privacy of the honeymoon bedroom. From the moment of their arrival there, Ross had detected an expectancy about Machiko that was more than just anxious anticipation of the physical consummation of their marriage. She seemed to be *waiting* for some kind of proclamation from him and appeared to be more and more disappointed at its non-utterance.

He had made up his mind as she had completed her toilet in the bathroom of their suite overlooking Waikiki beach. After his shower, he had donned the same kind of night attire as he had worn since first coming to the east: a gaily coloured sarong gathered at the waist. She had emerged shyly from the bathroom, her long hair down: hanging in a single cascade over her right shoulder to her waist. There was still about her that discernible air of disappointment. Ross had found it vaguely irritating, this playing of games, but it helped him summon sharpness to his tongue.

"Wife! Come here! I have something to say to you." He had barked the words in his best ship-to-shore voice, doing his utmost to keep his face straight as he maintained a glowering severity. She came in a dignified scurry, head cast down – but not before he had glimpsed the look in her eyes. Excitement. Pleasure. She stood demurely before him. He had felt his own excitement rise. With it had come an instinct to play his expected role to the full.

"When you were in your father's house, it was your duty to obey him. Now, you are my wife . . . You will obey me! It will be your duty to please me in all things. Is that understood?"

The upward look she had cast him was adoring.

"Yes, honoured husband."

He had warmed to the role, beginning to enjoy it: encouraged by the mischievous lights sparkling in her adoring eyes.

"In marriage, it is the husband's duty to command. The wife must submit to her husband in all things. I want you to know that

13

although I love you I have not turned soft like a woman. You will honour me with respect at all times, as you would respect a tiger whose wrath is only sleeping."

"Yes, honoured husband."

In hindsight, the theatrical nature of the ritual amused Ross and he wrily acknowledged that his share of the dialogue owed a lot to his conversation with Matsumishi Senior. At the time, however, he had been surprised and excited by Machiko's enthusiasm for her charade and her obvious approval of it. This, in spite of her education at a modern American school and exposure to the matriarchal trends in American society. As a forerunner to lovemaking, the ritual had certainly proved unexpectedly exciting and had undoubtedly led to a casting aside of all inhibitions.

For it was in lovemaking that it had ended. Machiko had asked, in that way of hers that was both respectful and mischievous, how she might demonstrate both her complete obedience and great love for her honoured husband. He had glanced towards the bed. Her answer had been the 1000-watt gleam in her wide, understanding eyes. She had shed her kimono, displaying her body proudly for him with almost childlike pleasure. There was no feeling of shame or false modesty, Again, her Japaneseness. Nor was there any reserve about the passionate abandon and acute awareness of his desires that she brought to the marriage bed.

Ross sighed. He came back to the present with a jolt as his taxi shuddered to a halt outside the building where Asiatic Oriental had their offices. The shipping agents' doorway was shuttered up and a handwritten notice directed all enquiries to Singh & Co. Ltd. next door.

Ross picked his way through the jumble that was Singh's front store. Drums of paint vied with coils of manila rope for floor space and paraffin lamps hung in clusters from hooks on the wall. "Everything from a needle to an anchor" was the boast of most ships' chandlers and, in Singh's, it seemed possible. The place was stacked from floor to ceiling.

A tall figure in a dark suit, neat white collar and blue tie emerged from a cubbyhole office to greet Ross. Bishan Singh wore a turban which matched his blue tie. His face had a worried look.

"Oh, Captain, Captain, so many misfortunes are befalling that it is not knowing where to begin that I am finding myself. Great calamities have fallen."

"You've been to the bank?" If no money was available, Ross

14

wanted the bad news first. "They're still stopping our credit?"

"The bank manager was very helpful, Captain," said Singh morosely, "but all our affairs are in a frightful kettle of fish."

"Are they going to let us have any money?"

"No, Captain. No money, they are still saying. No money for Honolulu, Hong Kong and Islands Steamingship Company. Their credit is not being good."

"But why?"

"It is orders, Captain. From persons in American Government. All properties of Honolulu, Hong Kong and Island line is being frozen up. Court is having to decide who is owner of your ship."

"But Mr Matsumishi's the owner. Surely to God they haven't interned *him*!"

"Mr Matsumishi is dead, Captain."

Ross stared at the Sikh without seeming to comprehend.

"Dead?"

"What I am saying is true, Captain. At bank, they are showing me cable message from bank in Honolulu. It is saying that Mr Matsumishi is being deceased on same day Japanese bomb Pearl Harbor. His daughter also. Same name as your ship . . . Machiko . . . That is why American Government must decide . . ."

His voice trailed away as he caught sight of the look on Ross' face. The sea captain looked like someone who was about to collapse in a dead faint. The Sikh took a step towards him, but the arm he extended to aid Ross was gripped by a hand that pinioned him above the elbow like a steel claw.

"You said 'his daughter also'. What the hell did you mean?" Ross' words were snarled and his eyes were savage. The Sikh staggered back a pace, alarmed by the other's look and the fierce grip on his arm.

"Please, Captain. I am only saying what is in the cable message. Both Mr Matsumishi and his daughter are being deceased on day that Japanese are bombing Pearl Harbor. They are believing at bank that bomb hit Matsumishi house, but is not saying in cable. Only that Matsumishi and daughter are being deceased on same day." He threw Ross a beseeching look. "Please, Captain, my arm."

Ross dropped his hand. Only a day or two ago, his thoughts had circled ominously on the share of pain that this war would bring him. But not this. Not the death of his beloved Machiko. A terrible calm gripped him – another mark, perhaps, of how orientalised he had become. Grief could not be shared with stran-

15

gers, lest the impression be given that their sorrow was solicited. The obligations of such a debt could not easily be repaid – so, the debt was avoided.

Ross' calm was simpler than that. He knew and had long ago learned that death was an immutable fact. But to accept the fact that Machiko was dead, he wanted desperately to be on his own.

He left Singh's as quickly as the rest of his business with the Sikh permitted. He took with him a small bundle of mail for the *Machiko*. For a time, he walked aimlessly. Finding himself in Raffles Square, he turned into the hotel bearing the name of Singapore's founder. The bar was crowded with army officers whose talk filled the air with a great hee-hawing of sound. He ordered a large whisky and soda at the bar and went in search of a quiet corner.

Seated alone at a table, he opened his briefcase and took out the bundle of mail. There were eight letters from Machiko, the last one dated 30 November. He read them one by one. Then he read them again.

Her words caused him a sweet pain. Her joy and love for him leapt up at him from every page, as if she were still alive. The letters sang with her happiness at the prospect not only of their reunion in the spring of 1942 but of a special event in February: the birth of their firstborn. She promised him a boy.

So, three persons had died when a bomb had hit the Matsumishi house, not two.

"Mind if we share your table, old boy?"

Ross looked up from the depths of his thoughts to see two young army officers standing with drinks in their hand. The one who had spoken looked very young. He had a wisp of blond moustache, silky soft and scarcely visible. It occurred to Ross that its owner could not have been shaving long.

"You can have this table," he said. "I'm just leaving." He bundled the letters into his briefcase.

"Letters from home, eh?" asked the young officer.

"Yes," said Ross. "Letters from home."

But he had no home now. No, that wasn't true. His home was out there in the Roads – a fifteen-year-old steamship with no cargo and nowhere to go.

Two

The Australians

In late January 1942, with the Japanese Army advancing towards its gates, Singapore was like an overcrowded madhouse in which the inmates preserved the illusion that they were residents of some Alpine holiday hotel cut off by avalanches but not seriously threatened by the crumbling mountain on which they lived. Despite constant bombing, there was a determination that, although some inconvenience must be accepted, life must go on as usual. Tiffin at four – but bring your tin hat.

As the days slipped by, Ross battled with a seemingly indifferent officialdom to resolve the problems surrounding the fate of his ship. At night he lay sleepless in his bunk, the prisoner of a grief that could only be endured in private. Time and activity would blunt the sorrow but, for the moment, the open wound had to be borne without analgesic. The future was a black, uncharted sea. In the past he had tracked his own path across it. But, now, he felt a strange helplessness in fighting the currents. He had the feeling of having no more control over his destiny than a cork in a mill-race.

But, for all that he was wrapped up in his own problems, Ross was not so preoccupied with war's effect on himself that he was unmindful of the effect it was having on others much more directly involved. He had lost his wife and it hurt – but there were still some blessings to count. And, in the dark of his sleepless night, he enumerated them: he was in good health, he ate well, he had countless comforts he should be thankful for. Above all, he was thankful that his occupation did not require him to fight gun in hand in the jungles of Malaya. He had seen enough of the Malayan hinterland to feel a desperate pity for the soldiers who were struggling and dying amid its swamps and fetid darkness in an attempt to stop the Japanese. He was acutely aware that, as he

17

lay in his comfortable cabin feeling sorry for himself, others were preserving his comfort by enduring horrors more terrible than anything he had ever known.

Corporal "Woody" Woodhouse – who, at that moment, was wishing he was anywhere in the world other than Johore State – would not have disagreed to exchanging places with Ross had the option been available. He did not like the Malayan jungle, even though he was getting used to it. After north-west New South Wales and its wide, treeless plains, Woody hated the strangling abundance of vegetation that clung to the earth of Malaya and hid it from the light of the sun, suffocating the land.

A month of war had not made the jungle any more endearing to Woody. Yet, his attitude now was not one of total hostility. The forest, he had learned, was neutral. Warring man could treat it like an enemy or use it as an ally. The Japanese had known this from the start of their push down the Kra Isthmus – and that was why they were winning.

Woody moved his body to ease the cramped feeling in his legs. He kept the dark shadow of the bridge in view. It was no more than a shape, lit by a scattering of stars visible above the trees.

The animal inhabitants of the forest were enacting their nightly ritual. The cries and calls of the hunters and the hunted rent the air like banshees: distant cries, starting suddenly and rising before the dying, strangulated cadence; medium-distance cries, flaring eerily; and cries so close that the shock of them curdled the blood of the alien intruder – man.

Woody became instantly alert at a sound from the direction of the bridge. He rolled over on his belly and widened his view from the dugout by moving a decay-stinking stem of epiphyte creeper. The rotting creeper fell away in front of the dugout and dropped on to a bank covered in tangled roots twenty feet below. It scarcely made a sound. But it was heard by the creature near the bridge. It had loped on to the path to the bridge, brushing against the fronds of shrubbery massed like a hedge along the side of the path. The gentle slap of the disturbed fronds springing back to their original position was the sound that had alerted Woody. He, in turn, had made the animal aware of his presence by causing the gentle fall of rotting creeper.

A head turned in the direction of the dugout. Woody could see only two red eyes burning like coals in the dark. They stared at him for just a moment. He heard a low warning snarl from the throat of the hunting feline. Then the eyes disappeared, as did

18

their owner. There was only a gentle rustle of disturbed leaves to indicate the direction she had taken along the river bank.

Woody gave a sharp exhalation of breath. His relief was two-fold. Those big jungle cats were fine in Tarzan movies. He had no desire to get closer to them than the front row of the stalls, nor to put to the test the possibility that they might not disdain raw Australian for supper. His prime relief, however, came from his realisation that the nocturnal prowler was not in human form and wearing the uniform of a Japanese infantryman. He and Big Rich, it seemed, had the forest to themselves.

Big Rich – Private Desmond Richardson, to give him his full title – was sleeping soundlessly at one end of the dugout they had fashioned for themselves and the Lewis gun. Woody rolled over on his back and, stretching out a leg, dug at the recumbent body with the heel of his boot. Big Rich came alive slowly. He never did anything in a hurry.

He blinked, cursing softly to himself as he swatted insects from his face.

"Damn these bloody mozzies," he complained. "They got a bite like a dingo. What didye wake me up for, sport? What time is it?"

"Nearly four. You've had your head crashed down since midnight."

Big Rich sat up.

"Nothing'll happen before daylight," he said. "Let's have a ciggie."

They lit cigarettes, pulling their poncho capes over their heads to screen the flare of the matches. Then they smoked, the cigarettes cupped in their fists. Woody spent three matches before his cigarette was alight. His matchbox was damp and soggy – like just about everything else in this green wilderness.

"Think we'll ever see the boys again, Woody?" Big Rich's question was calmly speculative.

"Nope," said Woody. "Not this side of hell."

"The lieutenant wasn't a bad sort – for an officer." Big Rich was unaware of using the past tense, as if the lieutenant was already dead.

"He was all right," agreed Woody, also using the past tense unconsciously.

"There were some good lads in the outfit," Big Rich went on thoughtfully, his voice tinged with regret. "Christ, that Norm from Kalgoorlie! He was wild, wasn't he? And that Pom, Whitey, was OK once you got used to that funny accent of his. Even old

19

Big-Wheel Bellamy was all right. Tougher'n a jarra plank. Never thought I'd see the day when I'd have a kind thought for a sergeant – particularly him, the old bastard."

"I once met old Big-Wheel in Sydney," said Woody. "We got drunk as dukes. Before that, I'd always thought the old sod was a right wowser. Kind of lonely old duffer in his way."

"Maybe they'll make it back," said Big Rich without conviction.

Woody did not reply. He knew, and the lieutenant had known, that the remnants of their once-proud company had drawn the short straw. Forty men counter-attacking north of the river wasn't going to stop the Japanese tidal wave – but, of course, it wasn't expected to stop it. Just delay it. The entire Brigade was pulling back towards Johore Bahru and the Causeway, and it was along the main Singapore road that the heaviest Japanese thrust was expected. The Japs, however, had split their forces and sent a column into the forest to strike for the Kerbau River crossing. The intention was to get round the rear of the retreating Australians and cut the road. The Brigade was in danger of encirclement.

Brigade had decided that the Japanese push to the Kerbau crossing had to be slowed up by "aggressive defence". Battalion HQ had been ordered to send a company north of the river and engage the Japanese in the hilly jungle ridges five miles to the north of the Kerbau bridge.

"They've got to be stopped there for twenty-four hours at least," the Battalion Commander had been told. "Stop them before they reach the bridge."

The Battalion Commander had counselled against moving north of the river, wanting instead to dig in round the bridge and wait for the Japanese. He had been overruled. The Japs were to be ambushed north of the river and their progress delayed. After that had been done, the delaying force could fall back on the bridge, blow it, and then catch up with the forces retiring along the main road.

The Battalion Commander's dilemma had been acute. He had few enough men for the rearguard action along the main road without detaching a company across country to the Kerbau. A Japanese Guards Division, with armour, was spearheading the drive along the road and this surely posed the main threat. With great reluctance, he had delegated the company he still thought of as Bull Ballantyne's for the Kerbau diversion.

But it was neither a company nor Bull Ballantyne's. Ballantyne had been killed up near Gemas and, in almost two weeks of continuous fighting, his company had been reduced to about a third of its original strength. Only one officer, a lieutenant, had survived.

It had been the sergeant, Big-Wheel Bellamy, who had broken the news to Woody why the outfit had suddenly been bundled off through the jungle along what was little more than an animal track.

"They want somebody to buy twenty-four hours for the Brigade," he said. "We're the lucky jokers."

It was Bellamy who had suggested to the lieutenant that the ramshackle bridge over the Kerbau should not be left unguarded. "Just in case anything goes wrong, sir. It's the only way out of that tiger country over there. A couple of sections with bows and arrows could hold up an infantry division here for a week. It's also the only way we're going to get out."

The lieutenant had agreed. Neither he nor Bellamy were enamoured with the idea of trying to stop the Japanese north of the river. They had been fighting the Japs long enough now to know that they had a better chance of stopping them at the river than on the forested high ground further north. The Japs were adept at infiltration and could be through their lines in no time. The brass hats, it seemed, still had a trench warfare mentality – which was OK if the terrain was open and the other side played it that way, too. But this was the jungle – and a man could pass within five yards of you without you even knowing.

Woody and Big Rich had been dismayed when they had been ordered to stay behind at the bridge with the Lewis. The company of your fellow-men – even when walking into certain death – is sometimes preferable to segregation from the herd and the uncertainties it brings. Both Woody and Big Rich would rather have taken their chances with the outfit than been left alone in the middle of nowhere waiting for God knew what.

Their comrades had filed north of the bridge just after midday, making choice comments to Woody and his companion.

"So long, you bloody bush bums," Norm from Kalgoorlie had called. "With your kind of luck, you could go through the card at Randwick and finish with enough dough to buy Sydney Bridge!"

"Or buy out BHP," a former miner from Broken Hill had added.

"It's baik-lah for some lucky jokers," another mate had shouted, using the Malay term for OK, which had been adopted as their own idiom.

"Just you watch out for little yellow men," Woody had retorted, with a forced smile that had nearly cracked his face. In truth, watching them go, he had felt like weeping.

The lieutenant had stopped briefly for a final word with Woody. "You know what to do, trooper?" (He called everybody "trooper".)

"Yes, sir. We blow the bridge at fifteen hundred hours tomorrow. Regardless."

"Just remember that, then. The bridge goes. Whether we're back here or not." Then, in a louder voice, so that the whole column could hear: "See you tomorrow, trooper."

Two men had remained in addition to Woody and Rich. They were sappers and had spent the next two hours placing explosive charges under the bridge and running cable to a plunger which they located on the bluff close to the site Woody had chosen for the Lewis gun. The machine-gun on its tripod was concealed from view above a bend in the trail but pointed straight across the bridge to the north. On the north side of the bridge, the trail ran quite straight for about two hundred and fifty yards and then bent away out of sight.

When the two engineers had finished their task, they showed Woody how to operate the plunger. They made it plain they did not want the device returned. They had no idea where their outfit would be. They were from a British RE unit on loan to the Australian battalion and their orders were to mine the bridge and get back to Battalion Command.

"Better get on your running shoes," Woody had advised them, with a smile big enough to let them know that the remark was not meant with bitterness. The sappers had laughed but had not lingered.

When they had gone, Woody and Big Rich had spent some time searching around for empty cans: debris from the unit's meal-break before departure. Then, on the north bank of the river around the bridge and on the bridge itself, they had laid tripwires which they connected to pairs of cans hung in shrubs and on the branches of trees. When darkness fell, they would have their own early-warning system of any approach.

Supper had consisted of a tin of sardines apiece, with biscuits and lemonade made from crystals and river water. They had scarcely started the repast when, from the north, had come the sound of rifle and machine-gun fire. It had continued until well after dark.

They had said nothing, exchanging looks when the sound of mortars and light artillery drowned out the small arms fire. Someone was getting the hell knocked out of them. Their mates. They were glad they weren't with them but they both felt they should have been. So, they said nothing; finishing their meal quickly.

Darkness came on them with its usual bewildering rapidity. They had settled down to watch the bridge and wait. It was a long, long night.

Woody had wakened Rich at four, not because he wanted sleep himself but because he wanted company over the longest part of the night: the last hours before dawn. He knew that he was past sleep now. It would have been a waste in any case. Nothing wakens the senses like the knowledge that the day you have is possibly your last on this earth. There was all eternity left to sleep in.

"Do you think we'll get out of this, Woody?" It was Big Rich thinking aloud.

"Too right we will," said Woody.

"We've had some beaut times."

"There'll be plenty more."

"It's kinda like old times this. Just the two of us. We humped our blueys across a lot of miles. Remember the two sheilas at Watson? The blonde one was real set on marrying you."

Woody smiled.

"That was more than old Watson was. Gee, that old fellow was a tartar! Chased me half-way to Queensland with that rabbit gun of his. I've never seen anyone so mad."

"Well, if you'd kept your mind on your work instead of that daughter of his, you wouldn't have tipped him into that tank of sheepdip."

"It sure as hell cleaned the ticks outa his whiskers." Woody grinned at the memory. "Remember that time in Melbourne, Rich? That slave job humping beef in the fridge store?"

Big Rich laughed softly.

"Six weeks' hard labour. Worse than cutting cane. But the money was good. We coasted for three whole months after that. Then it was back working for our scran. Yeah . . . We had some beaut times."

"It could be tough tomorrow, Rich. Today, I mean . . . when the sun gets up."

"I know, Woody."

23

"She'll be right, though."

Woody wanted to tell Rich that, whatever happened, it had been good knowing him. But he couldn't bring himself to say what he wanted to say. It was sloppy to come right out and say to a grown man that he was the best cobber a guy could wish for. These sentiments were understood, not spoken. Woody's mind did not go so far as to frame the idea that what he felt for Big Rich was love – but that's what it was, in the purest and noblest sense of the word. They had shared so much. Hard times as well as good. They would have died for each other gladly – and had come close to doing so on several occasions. The Bible had a word for that kind of fellow-feeling – even if it was a word that neither Woody nor Big Rich would have used in the context of their own relationship.

It was Big Rich who broke a long silence.

"There's one thing, Woody . . . One thing I'm glad about. Just the two of us being here, I mean. If one of us goes . . . Well, hell, I wouldn't like to be left around if anything happens to you . . . What I mean is – if they get you, they're going to have to get me, too."

Woody's teeth gleamed white in the darkness.

"I know what you mean, Rich. I know what you mean. The same goes for me, too."

The silences between them became longer but somehow easier. It was as if the last formal rites had been disposed of. Formalities made them both uncomfortable. They had not needed to reaffirm their friendship with fancy words, but both had acknowledged that they valued it above life itself. They drew strength from the acknowledgement.

"Not much of a bridge," said Woody, nodding in the direction that the Lewis was pointing.

"Just planks and wire," said Rich. "Not really much of a river, either. What's it called?"

"The Kerbau."

"The 'Cowboy'?" queried Rich, his vowel sounds mangling the Malay word.

Woody spelt it out.

"It's the local word for water buffalo," he enlarged.

"I haven't seen any water buffalo around here," said the big man. He seemed vaguely disappointed. Woody grinned.

"Just as well you haven't. Or sure as hell we'd be having fresh milk for breakfast and grilled steaks for supper."

Birdsong – varying from sweet trilling to harsh parrot-like squawking – heralded the dawn. The night creatures fell silent. The day creatures awoke. A rattling of tins sent the two Australians to readiness behind the gun. But it was a wild pig. It scurried across the trail near the bridge, skidding on its haunches as it changed direction by ninety degrees before disappearing into the undergrowth.

The Australians heard the Japanese before they saw them. They were chattering away noisily as they came up the trail. The chatter died so suddenly that it was like a half-heard radio being switched off. The reason for the sudden silence was that the leading Japanese had come within sight of the bridge.

Woody worked his tongue round inside his mouth. His throat had gone awfully dry. He watched the silent pantomime being enacted beyond the bridge. The leader of the group was making motions with his hands, silently detailing his men into the forest on either side of the trail. He signalled to one man to move ahead towards the bridge.

This man advanced cautiously, keeping to one side of the trail. As he neared the bridge, he suddenly froze. Woody saw him bend and fumble at his ankle. The man had spotted one of the trip-wires. He withdrew his foot gingerly. Then he stepped over the wire and kept coming towards the bridge, eyes casting around for more snares and glancing forward anxiously at the bridge and its surrounds. He knew he was there to be shot at. But it did not stop him moving forward.

The soldier saw and stepped over more tripwires. His friends off the trail were less observant and one triggered a tintinnabula-tion of sound which made the scouting Jap turn an alarmed face in the direction of the sound. It was as if, in that instant, he had expected the volley of rifle fire signalling his death. But it did not come. He was to have a moment or two more to feel the heat of the morning sun.

Now, he had reached the bridge. He advanced across it, confidence growing. Reaching the south side, he did not relax his caution but some tension went from the muscles of his face, changing the expression. Triumph? Relief?

He was now almost under the Lewis position, where the trail bent away to follow the river upstream. The two Australians could see him quite clearly. The heavy face beneath the twig-decked scuttle helmet was all but invisible now from their elevated position. He carried a light pack on his back. A water bottle hung

25

at his right hip from a strap over his left shoulder. Below the twin pockets on each breast of his khaki shirt, two grenade pouches were fastened to his belt. His unevenly bound puttees were tied so that they were held by two diagonally crossed tapes with a knot showing at the ankle.

When it seemed that the Japanese scout would pass out of sight below them, Woody – in answer to Big Rich's querying look – nodded towards the rifle beside the big man and then made a motion with his head. Rich nodded understanding and slid the weapon into his hands.

Woody made more dumb-language signals with hands and head. Rich got the message. It would be his job to account for the lone scout but he was to take his cue from Woody opening fire with the Lewis. Rich moved stealthily on his belly into a position where he could keep the Japanese soldier in sight. He froze as the Jap decided he had explored far enough and began to retrace his steps to the bridge.

He did not recross the bridge. Remaining on the south side, he called out to the far side of the river. Half a dozen Japanese cautiously emerged from cover. The leader, a sergeant, grunted an order and the men crouched in ready positions on the bridge approach. They did not cross.

More Japanese had halted at the far bend of the trail. They were led by an officer wearing a sword. He advanced alone along the trail to meet the sergeant. There was a brief consultation midway between the bridge and the bend of the trail. Then the officer and the sergeant advanced towards the bridge together. The officer spoke as he reached the group at the bridge. It seemed that he was reserving for himself the honour of crossing the bridge at the head of his men.

The officer was unusually tall for a Japanese. Woody noted that, unlike his shirt-clad men, he wore a tunic. On the collar was a red and yellow patch with two stars. The patch had three yellow bands over a base of red. A lieutenant, guessed Woody. The Australian corporal's finger tightened round the trigger of the Lewis.

The lieutenant, disdaining even to draw his revolver, strode across the bridge. His men followed, their rifles at the ready, the sun glinting on the wicked-looking single-edged bayonets. The entire advance unit was on the bridge when Woody pulled the trigger.

With the first blast of sound, flocks of birds rose in squawking clouds from the trees of the riverside. The Japanese on the bridge went down like ninepins. Only one man at the rear was left on his feet as Woody's bullets raked the bridge. This man charged forward alone over the bodies of his comrades but his strangled "banzai" was cut off with a short second burst from Woody. His charge was halted in mid-stride: his chest torn open by a pattern of pulverising hits. He spun and fell. His long Arisaka rifle flew from his hands and clattered against the side of the bridge, where it teetered momentarily before falling into the swift-running stream below.

The solitary Japanese who had scouted the bridge had been briefly petrified into immobility at the first bark of the Lewis. He had looked upward, mouth open with shock – locating the source of the sound – before throwing himself for cover at the jungle's edge. But Big Rich was lining him up in his sights even before he had moved. The man's left leg was flung forward, left foot six inches from the ground, when Rich's bullet hit him. The stride was never completed. An unseen hand seemed to jerk the man round by the shoulder and throw him to the ground.

The Japanese, one shoulder shattered and arm trailing, tried to lever himself along the ground on his good arm. With a grimace of distaste at what he had to do, Big Rich resighted and fired a second bullet. The sprawling shape on the trail convulsed once and lay still.

In the immediate aftermath of the firing, several sharp commands in Japanese echoed from the bend in the trail where, now, no one was to be seen. Then a quiet fell on that part of the jungle. Birds, disturbed by the firing, continued to circle and make a din. But, soon, even they settled again in their treetop perches and an uneasy silence filled the morning.

Woody looked at his watch. It was fifteen minutes after eight. Nearly seven more hours yet before the bridge was to be blown. It was going to be a long day.

At precisely 8.30, although the two Australians could see nothing stirring in the forest across the river, a ragged volley of fire erupted from the far bank. Bullets gouged passages through the thick foliage of trees cloaking the ridge where the Lewis was concealed. Some were perilously close but the Japanese fire was haphazard and dissipated along the breadth of the bluff.

"They're trying to draw our fire so that they can get a line on us," Woody called softly to his friend. "Do you see anything, Rich?"

"Not a bloody thing," came the reply. "Can you manage that meat-grinder on your own, Woody?"

"Sure."

"Good. I'll move along the ridge a bit and get a different angle of fire. I'll have to pick my targets."

"Good on yer. I'll watch the bridge."

A second volley of speculative fire blazed from the far side of the river. As a third started, a dozen Japanese poured out of the undergrowth beyond the bridge and careered towards it emitting blood-chilling battle-cries. They stood no more chance against the Lewis than had their predecessors. Once on the narrow confines of the bridge they made targets that were impossible to miss. This time, when the Lewis stopped barking, the far side of the bridge was blocked by a mound of squirming bodies.

When the Japanese tried yet another frontal attack, the soldiers engaged in the charge had to climb over their dead comrades in order to get a footing on the nine-feet-wide bridge. Grim-faced, Woody continued his carnage, his head swimming with nausea at the destruction to human life he caused. It reminded him of a time he had gone on a 'roo shoot as a youngster with a group of older boys and had been appalled at the mindless massacre of these living things. Others had laughed and joked at the sport – and he had laughed and joked, too, for the sake of appearances, but inside he had been sick.

Looking down at the bodies heaped on the bridge, Woody felt no sense of triumph. He felt only a strong desire to be many thousands of miles away, engaged in some less unsavoury activity. Holiday time would be over back home now. The New Year celebrations in Melbourne and Sydney would be long past. He thought of other summers and the long lazy holiday season – a Test Match at the MCG with Larwood coming in like a train to hurl his thunderbolts at the squat, stocky figure of Don Bradman. Bradman was all the Sydneysiders could talk of. Our Don. Our Don and, of course, Our Bridge.

Well, Sydney Bridge would be a far better place to be than this bloody Kerbau bridge!

Another crashing volley erupted from across the river. Woody heard the bullet that ripped his arm and shirt-sleeve as it sliced through branches screening the Lewis. A lucky shot or not, he did not know. He was aware only of a red-hot pain in his upper arm and the warm trickle of blood running down to his elbow. It could have been worse, not that he was enjoying it. The flesh had been gouged, as if by a bull whip, down to the bone. For a moment, he thought he might be sick. But the wave of sudden giddiness and nausea passed quickly. A cloud of insects descended on the wound. He brushed at them ineffectively. They were lapping at his blood, swelling up to three times their size as they became bloated on it.

Woody could hear Big Rich sniping away but had no idea what his friend could see to shoot at. It was Big Rich himself who slithered back into the dugout a few moments later to tell him.

"They're trying to cross the river downstream of the bridge." He saw the bloody shoulder and arm. "Hey, are you all right?"

"It's nothing. What are you doing back here if they're crossing the river?"

"These!" said the big man. He held up a grenade before stuffing it into a haversack that was already bulging. When the haversack was full, he belly-crawled out of the pit and disappeared with a rustle into a shaded tangle of greenery where the sun never reached.

Swampy high grasses flanked the river where the Japanese were trying to cross from slightly higher and drier ground. This swampy ground on the south bank drained and filled according to season. Now, as the river rose rapidly with the monsoon rains, the ground was flooding anew. Within a week, it would all be part of the river. It was a dangerous place to cross, not just because it was a broadish part of the river but because of the deceptively calm surface of the swift water. If the river had been drained, a great S-shaped underwater canyon of rock would have been revealed. Two great shelves of rock protruded from below each bank, nearly but not quite interlocking with each other: like monstrous teeth in two jaws that never quite closed.

The surge of water flowing into this basin of deep underwater passages created undertows and counter-currents, unrevealed except for slight swirl effects on the surface.

The Japanese soldier who – stripped to a loincloth and with one end of a rope round his waist – entered the water to swim the river, soon discovered its treacherous nature. But he was a brave and powerful swimmer. He made it to the other side, albeit some distance downstream from his intended landing-point. He stretched himself out on the bank near the long grasses of the south side, utterly drained of energy.

By the time Big Rich had fought his way along the top of the jungled bluff to a point looking down on the long grasses, the swimmer had recovered his breath and had made the rope fast to the stunted stem of the only tree on that part of the bank. It bent in an arch, its branches in the water.

Already, on the far bank, the swimmer's squad-mates were edging out chest-deep in the river. Each man was endeavouring to hold his rifle high, and at the same time propel himself along the rope with an arm crooked round it. The first man out did not make it. The moment the fierce undertow took his legs, the shock of it caused him to lose his hold on the rope. He was swept under.

The lifeless bundle that was his body reappeared far downstream, just a shape and barely distinguishable from the other driftwood and flotsam of the river.

Big Rich slipped from the cover at the top of the bluff and inched his way through the twisted masses of roots which interwound in profusion across its steep breast. The move brought him into view of the lone Japanese on the far side of the river who guarded the secured north-bank end of the rope. A shot rang out and a bullet chewed into the earth, inches from Rich's head.

The Australian glowered across at the far bank. The Jap who had fired at him was standing, having fired from the shoulder. Rich smiled grimly to himself. That helped the odds, he thought. Two weeks of combat had taught him that the Japanese rifleman was a much more dangerous proposition when he did not have to fire from the standing position. It was not that the Japs were poor marksmen – their snipers, with a monopod and a telescopic sight on their Meiji 38s, were deadly. It was more the fault of their standard issue rifle. It was long and unwieldy and had a clumsy straight bolt handle that was the very devil to operate without lowering to recock. Rapid fire from the erect position was an impossibility. The rifleman had to lower his rifle, cock it, raise it again, and then resight.

Big Rich knew, therefore, that the infantryman on the far bank of the river would provide him with vital seconds after every round he fired. Provided, of course, that he did not hit him.

Rich made a few yards before he decided it was time to flatten. Crouched low and breathing hard, he heard a second shot splinter into a heavy root a good ten feet above his position. His descent of what remained of the slope into the shelter of the tall grasses was precipitate rather than graceful. Leaping and slithering, he tumbled down a muddy bank to come to rest knee-deep in stinking stagnant water, but out of sight of the rifleman. A third shot whistled through the long grasses as he splashed into the morass.

Now, he waded as quickly as the terrain would allow, setting a course for the lone tree on the river's edge. The near-naked Jap who had swum the river heard his splashing approach. He was looking round fearfully when Rich stretched to his full height to get new bearings. Rich ducked quickly again. A grenade was already in his hand and his fingers were drawing on the ring. He counted, measuring the seconds. Then he threw. He heard the squelchy thud of the grenade landing in soft mud. It was followed almost instantly by the thunderclap of its explosion and an acrid stench filled the air.

Rich stretched up again to peer through the grasses. There was no sign of the Japanese who had swum the river. The tree to which the rope had been attached was a black smouldering skeleton. In the river, Rich got a glimpse of bodies being washed away downstream: an arm desperately clawing the air here, frenzied but futile splashing there, three or four heads trying to rise clear of the water as the ferocious undertow sucked at the bodies to which they were attached.

Only the rifleman on the far bank remained. Rich knew he would have to take his chances with him. He splashed back through the marsh of the tall grasses and, then, with a deep intake of breath, began the ascent of the root-entangled slope of the bluff. He prayed that his enemy across the river was ignoring him and had gone to the assistance of his comrades in the river.

In fact, the Japanese soldier could do little to help his friends. There was no way he could go downstream along the bank of the river because of the impenetrable vegetation skirting the water's edge. He turned his attention and his anger on the Australian soldier who, with a single grenade, had robbed him of the best friends he had ever known.

The Japanese soldier rested his long rifle along the bent trunk of a tree which leaned over the river. He sighted it carefully towards the far bank, his eyes searching for a movement in the tall grasses where he knew his enemy was concealed. He had made a complete sweep of the area from left to right when Big Rich broke cover at the extreme left of his angle of vision. The Australian had left the protection of the tall grass and was climbing the root-entangled slope of the bluff, legs and arms working in feverish urgency as he negotiated the muscle-tearing obstacles in his way.

He had reached to within fifteen feet of the top – where a profusion of intergrowing trees and thick bush offered safety – when the Japanese fired. A tightening of the lips, no more than a

31

wince of satisfaction, creased the rifleman's face as he saw the Australian halt in the action of pulling himself higher and then swing right round to face the river, his free left hand clutching at his neck. The Australian let go his grip on the elbow of exposed tree root above his head and sagged slowly back against the slope in a sitting position.

The Japanese marksman recocked his Arisaka and took aim again. Even as he did so, the figure on the bluff was moving again. He fired. The rifle's recoil caused the long barrel to leap slightly against his grip. Perspiration rolled from the Japanese soldier's forehead into his left eye, causing him to blink. When he squinted again along the alignment of the barleycorn and open vee-sight, the enemy across the river had vanished.

Big Rich was cursing the thick bush of the bluff, even though it had been his salvation only moments before. Blinded by his own sweat, he hacked at the undergrowth like a man demented as he tried to find his way back to the Lewis position.

The first bullet fired from the Japanese across the river had caused a freak injury. It had nicked into the bone of his left shoulder, striking at such an angle that it had carried on and upward through the lobe of his left ear. The second bullet had been only a cigarette's length away from his heart, grazing the rib cage and hurting like hell.

Rich knew he had been lucky. But for a slight movement on his part as he climbed, he could have died there and then on that leg-breaking maze of a hill. The thought of dying filled his mind. The appalling certainty seized him that this was the day ordained for it and that the hour and minute were nearly upon him. He wanted to cry out. He did not want to die here – alone. Please God, not alone. He wanted to be in sight and sound of his best friend. There was a comfort in that. That was all he asked from whatever God there was. If this was the day it had to be, then let it be the day. But not alone. Not alone in this green hell of a jungle.

Blindly, he hacked at the labyrinth.

A shattering explosion from the direction of the river pulled him up short. He stood, staring about him, the turmoil of his crazed mind subsiding. He shook his head in the manner of one emerging from sleep, clearing a fog of stupor from his mind. The movement of his head sent blood showering from his torn ear.

"Keep the lid on your old brainbasket, old sport," he admonished himself aloud. "This bloody place is getting to you." He felt a gnawing of shame that he had momentarily lost control

32

of himself. He had been flapping through the bush like a joey with its tail on fire.

He took stock of his half-dark environment – this world of damp, creeping, strangling growth and clinging fungus. That explosion? What was it? Rich's first thought was that Woody must have blown the bridge. But it hadn't been that kind of a bang somehow. Too sharp. And it seemed to have come from beyond the river – or from beyond where he reckoned the river ought to be.

With more deliberate calm, Rich began anew to hack his way through the green wilderness of the bluff. Now, he worked methodically: noting the direction in which the ground sloped, mindful of the direction of the briefly glimpsed sun where the rays penetrated the chinks and openings in the jungle canopy, eyes open for signs of his earlier passage through the forest to the marsh of the long grasses.

He gave a grunt of satisfaction when he finally stumbled back across his former trail. Now he knew exactly where he was. He shut off his mind from the searing pain he felt below his armpit at his chest and from the burning nip of his mangled ear. He worked his way steadily towards the Lewis and Woody.

He encountered Woody sooner than he expected. The corporal had abandoned the original dugout and hauled the Lewis to a new position – slightly higher than before but still commanding a good view of the bridge through the shade of a tree's lower foliage. The leaves were long ovals with a surface like shiny rubber. Woody was bathed in sweat, concentrating fiercely on settling the Lewis' tripod so that it stood firmly.

"If I'd been a Jap, you'da had a bayonet up yer backside," Rich announced his arrival, grinning. Woody didn't even look round.

"I knew it was you. Ye're breathing like a sow in labour. I can tell your snort a mile off." He sat back on his haunches, judging his handiwork. "Besides, I could hear you hacking trees down with that Gurkha tomahawk o'yours. You musta cleared a track wide enough to take a St Kilda tram."

He turned, and recoiled with surprise at Rich's bloody appearance.

"Christ!" he breathed.

The big man grinned at him.

"The Nips won't try swimming the river again."

"I heard some shooting – and one grenade."

"The grenade was mine. It got the Nip who swam the river –

33

and the rope he'd got round a tree on this side. When the rope broke, the rest of the Nip squad got swept away."

"Any of them land on this side?" asked Woody.

Big Rich shook his head.

"Two miles downriver maybe. But I doubt it. I take back what I said about it not bein' much of a river, Woody. It's nasty. It just sucked them Nips right under."

"It's rising with the rains. It'll get nastier. What happened to your ear? One of them Nips take a bite out of you?"

"It's not much. Gimme a hand, will you? I'll put a field dressing on it."

They bound each other's wounds, anxiously eyeing the bridge for Jap activity as they did so.

"I heard a loud bang . . . When I was on my way back here. What the hell was it, Woody?" Big Rich spoke through a muffle of field dressing which Woody was trying to tape over his ear.

"Some Nips committing hara-kiri," said Woody, moving the dressing away from Rich's mouth. "I saw them dodging over the trail over there with what looked like a mortar. I reckon they tried to set it up in the trees."

Rich pulled a face.

"I thought they woulda been pasting us with mortars long before now. What do you think's been keeping 'em?"

"My guess is that they've got mortars over there all right but they don't have the right ammo. That bang you heard was a mortar crew going to meet their ancestors. At least, that's what it sounded like. Did you hear the screams? Somebody over there was hopping around looking for a leg or something."

"I didn't hear any screams. You think they blew up their own mortar?"

"Almost certain. Maybe they've only got impact ammo . . . which is OK if you've got space to fire the stuff off. The only clear space over there is on the trail and they've got more savvy than try that. My guess is that they tried through a gap in the trees and hit a branch about three feet over their skulls. End of experiment."

"The Nips we tangled with up near the Gemencheh River didn't use impact ammo in their mortars," said Rich. "It was all time-fused stuff, remember? Gave me a right dose of the jim-jams."

"Too right I remember," said Woody, a memory of the night attack by the Japanese on their lines still vivid. They had heard the Jap mortar bombs thudding and crashing into the bush all round them and then had agonising seconds of waiting for the explosions to come. When the explosions had come, the whole of the forest seemed to blow up around their ears.

"I hated those bloody night attacks," said Big Rich, also reliving recent memories. "The little devils didn't use their rifles much up there on the Gemencheh. Just softened us up with mortars and then crept up on us like bloody ghosts with their grenades."

"They won't wait until night to have another go at us here," said Woody. "That's why I moved the Lewis . . . and the box of tricks for blowing the bridge." He pointed. "It's over there, under that tree with yellow flowers all over it."

"Why don't we just blow the bridge right now, Woody?"

The corporal gave a sad kind of smile.

"Fifteen hundred hours, the lieutenant said. Some of the boys could still make it back to the bridge. You're not suggesting we make them swim for it, with all them Nips over there?"

"No. 'Course not," said Rich sheepishly. "It was just a thought. They're mighty quiet over there. If the Nips are gonna come, why don't they come?"

The next Jap attack did not come until the sun was astride the zenith. The attack had undoubtedly been delayed because of the impenetrable nature of the forest around the north side of the bridge. Bringing forward even light automatic weapons to sites where they could be effective against the Australians meant hacking through dense undergrowth for distances of well over a hundred yards. Progress which enabled one man to travel fifty yards in an hour was good going.

Woody and Rich heard the steady chop-chop-chop of axes and jungle knives long before the attack started. It began with a fierce crossfire from two Nambu light machine-guns, blazing bullets across the face of the bluff at a rate of eleven hundred rounds a minute.

Other Japanese exposed themselves to view on the far bank to hurl grenades across the river. The grenades fell well short of the Lewis, exploding harmlessly. Rich's counter-attack, also using grenades, was much more effective. From higher ground and without having to show himself to the enemy, he was able to bombard the far bank with ease. He removed one Nambu gunner with his third grenade and then, stalking through the less dense bush of the river's south side, he gauged the position of the second Nambu gunner and accounted for him at the second attempt.

While he did so, Woody did not give away the Lewis' position by firing at single targets or spraying bullets indiscriminately into the bush beyond the river. He had decided that the Lewis and its dwindling supply of ammunition had to be reserved for any Japanese attempt to cross the bridge. He did not, however, remain idle. Never moving far from the Lewis – in case its firepower was wanted in a hurry – he took his rifle and concentrated on the Japanese grenadiers, who showed a suicidal disregard for their own safety.

The Australians held a considerable advantage in the nature of the terrain on their side of the river. It had height and it allowed far greater freedom of movement, without any loss of cover to its defenders. The Japanese, on the other hand, had to contend with an approach to the bridge over flatter ground that was almost impassable – except for the trail – for some distance up and downstream. They, too, were clearly under orders to make sure the bridge was not damaged by their grenades. It was wanted intact.

To Woody's eyes, there had been nothing cautious about the earlier Japanese rushes at the bridge – but he reasoned that these first attempts to cross the river had instilled a certain caution in the enemy. They could not know that they were faced by only two men. And the longer they could be kept guessing in this respect, the better.

Big Rich's mobile role had helped to keep them guessing. Woody ranged far less freely, maintaining quick access to the Lewis at all times – but he had aided the deception by judicious sniping from locations close to the machine-gun. It encouraged the Japanese to believe that the Australians were far more numerous than was the case and that they were using their positional advantage with maximum effect and a remarkable economy of their resources.

Chastened by the loss of the two Nambu gunners in addition to their other losses and uncertain still about the strength of an enemy who remained an unseen and unknown quantity, the Japanese retired to lick their wounds. Woody guessed that the troops across the river were probably the light probing scouts of a much larger Japanese force. They had probably encountered the Australians who had been sent north of the bridge only twenty-four hours before but had by-passed them during the night, leaving the main body to deal with the Aussie force. Unable to cross the river, the Japanese would now wait for the main body to catch up.

Woody's assessment was correct up to a point. In fact, he over-estimated the size of the infantry flying column that had reached the bridge – and he underestimated the damage that he and Rich had inflicted upon it. It was now all but decimated. Only eleven men, including the captain in command of the scouting party, remained alive. It was for this reason that no attempt was made to rush the bridge during the abortive grenade attack.

The respite which the Australians had won ended shortly after two in the afternoon. That was when the first shell came whining across the river from a location nearly a mile to the north. It exploded high on the bluff. It was the first of many.

"Battalion gun," said Woody through clenched teeth. "This is it, Rich. You know what to do."

The big man nodded and slithered on his belly to a ditch-like defile that skirted the Lewis position and wound for forty yards or more along the face of the bluff. At four places along its length, Rich had already stacked in piles of six the two dozen grenades they had left.

The big man had no sooner gone than the Japanese mortars opened up. There were four of them and they were operating from the extremity of their 700-yards range. The bridge became all but obscured from view as a wall of smoke and flame leapt from the trail and its hedges of green below the Australians.

This was the kind of attack Woody had expected with some dread from the break of day. The mortars the Japanese were using scarcely merited the name "mortars". They were light easy-to-handle weapons which more correctly would have been described as grenade-launchers. And their missiles were time-fused. Ideal for close quarters in the jungle, where long-range weapons and pinpoint accuracy were relatively unimportant. They depended on blast rather than shrapnel fragments to kill.

Woody's instinct, as explosions shimmered on the air between him and the bridge, was to burrow a hole deep in the ground and crawl into it. He acknowledged the instinct by crouching lower, digging into the butt of the Lewis with his chin. But he kept his eyes steadfastly on the bridge as its timbers came back into view through the wafting smoke. It remained partially visible as more and more mortar bombs came peppering down, saturating the area of its southern landfall.

In the meantime, the 70mm Japanese "battalion" gun kept booming away, overshooting the Australians by four to five hundred yards. Terrifying as the bombardment was, the

37

Australians' luck was holding good inasmuch that they were within a ribbon of territory between the two arcs of exploding missiles. They were saved, for the moment, by the limitations imposed on any artillery by the jungle – in particular, that imposed by the inability of the bombarding battery to observe the results of its labour.

Suddenly the mortar fire stopped and the booming howitzer fell silent. A strange silence hung over the jungle for a little over a minute. This silence was shattered by a blood-curdling cry as many voices took it up: "Banzai . . . Banzai . . . Banzai . . ."

The trail to the north was suddenly filled with figures. They came running from the bush on either side of the muddy track, flourishing their long rifles; the size of these weapons made to appear more elongated and terrifying by the twenty-inch bayonets attached to them. They came rolling like a wave at the bridge. An officer, drawn sword waving high above his head, spurred on the khaki tide.

Woody waited until the first rank reached the bridge before squeezing the trigger. The human wave faltered and bodies fell, but still it rolled on. The bridge now seemed to be filled with Japanese, elbowing past comrades as they fell. On they came. On and on. There seemed no end to the pressing mass. They reached the south bank and spilled over on to the Australian side.

The Lewis kept up a remorseless fire until it seemed there were more dead and dying on the bridge than living. The press of advancing Japanese seemed to thin in swatches, like wheat flattened by rain. The mass trying to reach the bridge faltered and finally halted. Its number seemed to dwindle away, progress marred by a wall of grotesquely sprawled bodies where, here and there, an arm or leg moved, a voice cried out.

Less than a dozen men reached the Australian side of the river. It was for these intruders that Big Rich was waiting. His first grenade erupted in their midst before they could dive for cover at the side of the trail. The survivors split two ways. Those who ran right were impaling themselves on a spiky bush that defied them entry to its depths when the big Australian's second grenade made their desperate haste unnecessary. Two more grenades and a salutary burst from the Lewis removed any threat from the Japanese who had broken left from the track.

Not a bird could be heard in the silence that reigned over the jungle. Occasionally, a groan would rise from the humanity

38

heaped on the bridge, making itself heard over the constant murmur of fast-running water. A flock of vultures gathered in the high trees near the bridge. Every so often, they fluttered closer to the corpses strewn below – growing bolder, but none yet venturing to commence the feast that waited.

Since noon, the stench of rotting flesh had risen from the bridge and permeated the upper slopes of the bluff, making the Australians retch at the results of their own handiwork. Now, in the heat of high afternoon, it seemed to foul the valley for miles around. There was no escape from it.

Woody had no expectation that the lull would last. He took advantage of it to wrest the Lewis from its position and heft it ten yards to the right. One more attack would finish the ammunition.

"You OK, sport?" he called out softly to Rich, who was crouched a few feet below his new location, idly toying with a grenade. The big Australian rolled over on his back and looked up. Woody was hidden in shade but Rich addressed himself to a gap in the foliage where the sounds of the Lewis' tripod being bedded firmly down indicated Woody's presence.

"I'm being eaten alive and that stink makes me want to vomit. How long to go now?"

"We blow the bridge in exactly twenty minutes."

"If we live that long." A silence followed Rich's unhappy comment. Then he said, "See them deathwatch kites up there, Woody? I'd rather kill them than Nips. It makes me sick to my stomach to think they're just sitting up there waiting to fill themselves to the craws with dead men's flesh."

"Better not to think about it, Rich. They could be sizing you up."

"I hope they choke on me." He made a snorting sound to show his disgust. "Stone me, Woody, I ain't got no love for the little yellow devils but I don't like the idea of them being eaten any more than I like it for myself." He gave a sad, ruminative shake of the head. "Did you see the way that them Nips came over that bridge? They came at us like they all wanted to die and we was doin' them a good turn by knockin' 'em off. I can't make up my mind whether they're a hell of a lot braver'n I'll ever be or just plain downright stupid."

"It's a big honour for them – the biggest glory they can get. Dying for the Emperor!"

"Dying for them vultures, most like!"

"Yeah," agreed Woody, "that's the trouble with war. Only the vultures get fat."

Rich brushed away insects swarming in the vicinity of the bloodsoaked dressing over his ear.

"And the bloody flies!" he said with feeling. He grinned up in the direction of his friend. "Hey, Woody, chuck me down an iced beer, would'ye?"

"Sure thing, cobber. D'ye fancy a bottle of Toohey's best?"

"A Carlton, please. I've always been a Carlton man."

"We're fresh out of Carlton."

"Forget it then, I'll . . ."

Big Rich never completed what he was going to say. The air suddenly reverberated with flat thunderclaps of sound as a fresh rain of mortar grenades began to fall on the bluff. This time, the range was better. The position which Woody had recently vacated became a black charred hole on the face of the bluff. Similar smoking black holes appeared as a pattern was extended across the north-facing slope. One missile fell near one of Rich's stock-piles of grenades, causing the lot to go off with a resounding treble-thump. The blast seemed to rush along the natural trench where Big Rich was crouching low. Woody saw it lift his friend bodily and throw him several feet. Rich lay terribly still.

In that moment, Woody ignored the need to man the Lewis. His one thought was for his best friend. Disregarding any danger to himself, he plunged from his leafy cavern and leapt into the dip where Rich lay.

Woody rolled him on his back, searching for fresh wounds. But there was none that he could see. He groped at his friend's chest for a heartbeat. A flutter of pulse gave him hope. In the mean-time, the mortar barrage from across the river was continuing without respite. Woody threw himself across Rich's body as he heard a dart-like grenade strike the canopy of trees somewhere above him and make its branch-lopping descent. It exploded ten yards away. The scorching heat of the blast ran across Woody's back, tattering his shirt and singeing the hair of his neck. He was aware of a shadowy shape passing over his head and landing like a spear only feet away. He glanced up to see the Lewis gun embed-ded by its nose in soft earth only a short distance from his own nose. The Lewis would never fire again, he realised. It did not occur to him that only his anxiety for his friend had saved him from sharing the fate of the machine-gun.

A fresh volume of banzai cries from the bridge wakened him to the desperate nature of the new situation. Abandoning Rich for a moment, he stole a look at the bridge from the brow of the dip. A new wave of Japanese soldiers was advancing on the bridge. This time, it was not a headlong charge. The bodies littering the path made this impossible. This time, the Japanese were advancing more carefully, crouching and dropping flat: using the bodies of the dead as cover.

Woody slipped along the narrow defile, his eyes fixed on a bushing tree covered with yellow flowers. He found the box with the plunger where he had propped it between two stout roots. Sweat ran down his face in streams as he manoeuvred the box from its resting place in the near darkness of the tree's shade. He found enough space to operate the detonator, checking the cable which snaked away from it to the bridge. He offered a silent prayer that the circuit was still intact.

At last, all was ready. He took a deep breath and pressed down the plunger.

The rush of sound which came as a clap on the eardrums knocked him off balance and caused him to fall sideways. It was followed by a sighing sound like the whisper of a great wind. Then came the crashing rain of debris falling on the forest.

Woody returned to the trench-like defile and observed the river from its lip by belly-crawling under a bush with sabre-like fronds. The scene was transformed. Nothing remained of the bridge. It was as if it had never been. There was only the river rushing between its two banks.

The explosion had seemed to signal a brief halt in the mortar barrage. Now it resumed. To Woody, it seemed that the grenades were falling all around him. He slithered back into the sheltering dip and, lying flat on his face, tore at the ground with his fingernails as if the only escape from the pulverising sound was to burrow into the warm womb of mother earth. Tension and fear made him oblivious to all else.

The mortars had been silent for fully two minutes before the fact dawned on his mind. He became aware of large drops of water splashing his flesh. It was raining. The raindrops splattered down slowly at first. Then the tempo and quantity increased until they were beating down on him in rapid tattoo. He looked along the ground at his hands, watching them clench and unclench. He wondered why they were behaving in that way, as if they did not belong to him. Water gathering in the ditch began to trickle through his clenching knuckles. He willed the clenching to stop. And it did. Memory of where he was and what he was doing there streamed back to him. His head cleared, although a humming semi-deafness remained.

Rich? He had to get to Rich. A feverish anxiety for his friend stirred him. He pulled himself to his knees and, obeying a strange animal-like instinct, began to crawl along the floor of the dip.

He found Rich sitting with his head in his hands, slowly recovering from the shock of the blast that had knocked him senseless. The big man was shaking like a leaf.

"Hell's bells, Woody," he said ruefully, "I've had this bloody war. I want to go home."

"There's nothing to stop us here now," replied Woody. "No orders. No officers. Nothing. I reckon they wrote us off with the bridge."

"You blew the bridge?"

"Yep." Woody blinked at his watch, stared at it hard and then held it up to his ear. "Damned thing's stopped," he said, looking at it again. "Right on three!"

"Is three o'clock the same as fifteen hundred hours?"

"As near as doesn't matter a damn," said Woody forcing a grin. "We did our duty, old sport. Blow the bridge at fifteen hundred hours, the lieutenant said. Well, there ain't no bridge there now and the only Japs south of the Kerbau are dead ones."

"There ain't many live Aussies this side of the river neither," said Rich with a sad weariness. "What the hell do we do now?"

"We get the hell out of it," said Woody. "There'll be plenty of transport back at the road. The Brigade was being pulled back to near Johore Bahru, maybe to Singapore itself. So, we're going to get back to the road just as fast as our legs'll take us. We'll report to Battalion Command and tell 'em we want to go the rest of the way in style – riding in a truck. It's the least they can bloody do for us."

They stopped only once during the night, resting for three hours. It was nearly noon the next day when they reached the road. They were dog-tired, scarcely able to move one leg after the other. Only the thought of the trucks they would find at the road had kept them going.

But the road was deserted. Nothing moved on it. The two men had been uneasy for the last half mile to the road. Their hearts had sunk when they had reached the Chinese-owned tin mine which, forty-eight hours previously, had served as Battalion HQ. It had been deserted and was as still as the grave. But they had still expected to find traffic on the road. Two days before, it had been busier than Pitt Street on a Saturday. Now it was empty for as far as the eye could see.

"The whole bloody army has just pissed off and left us," said Rich bitterly.

"And the Japs'll be along any minute now," said Woody. "D'you get the feeling, Rich, that we just don't bloody well count? Wouldn't it bloody cake yer? Well, from here on, we start looking out for ourselves! Come on."

He started walking, his limbs stiff with pain and fatigue.

"Where are we going?" asked Rich, limping behind him.

"Well, it isn't going to be to any infantry mustering point, because no bastard told us where to find one!" He pointed down the road ahead of him. "Singapore's down this way."

"How bloody far is it to Singapore?" asked Rich, shuffling to catch up with Woody.

"I dunno. Fifty miles. Maybe a hundred. Who cares?"

The groan that escaped from Rich suggested that he cared.

"Are we going to walk all the bloody way?"

"If we have to," said Woody. "Hell, what's a hundred miles? You've got me for company. And be honest . . . That's something you wouldn't change for anything."

"Oh no? That's what you think, mate."

Woody turned his craggy face towards Rich and eyed him with an expression of pretended outrage.

"Now what in the world would you sooner have to help you over the miles than your old cobber?"

Rich lengthened his stride.

"A horse, old buddy," he said. "A horse!"

Three

Last Twilight

The police launch pulled away from the *Machiko* and took a wide turn before setting course towards the distant city skyline. Singapore lay under a pall of black smoke.

The smoke came from burning oil tanks on Pulau Ubin, a small island half a mile off the Changi peninsula in the middle of the eastern mouth of the Johore Straits. The fuel was being destroyed by Singapore's defenders so that the Japanese would be denied its use. A light breeze from the north-east pushed the billowing smoke across Singapore island and carried it in thinning streamers out across the clusters of southern islands towards distant Sumatra.

Two men sat in the forward part of the police launch as it cleared a foaming path through the smooth waters of the Roads. The *Machiko*'s master was one of them. He had a preoccupied air: staring at the great smoke clouds but without any sign that they held his interest. His mind and thoughts were far away. Beside him, an older man in his early forties held a blue uniform cap in his hand and was mopping the leather lining band with a handkerchief. The curling grey hair at the side of the man's head was flattened and damp with sweat where the cap had been.

Inspector Jock Webster was unhappy at the task he had been given out of the blue on this humid February morning. He had known the captain of the *Machiko* off and on for a number of years and liked him. Executing the order of some government wallah for the arrest of this man, who was more friend than acquaintance, had been the most distasteful job he had had in his years with the Straits Settlement police. He felt the need to apologise.

"You realise that it's probably some damn-fool misunderstanding," he told Ross. "I don't want you to hold it against me. I just

44

have to do what I'm damned well told."

Ross was miles away. He turned, having only half-heard what Webster had said but getting the gist of it. He managed the glimmer of a sympathetic smile.

"It's OK, Jock. I know you're only doing your job."

"Have you no idea what it's about?" asked Webster.

"None at all." Ross grimaced. "Unless it's to put me in the debtors' prison. I've been signing IOUs all over Singapore on the strength of a letter of credit from the Hong Kong and Shanghai Bank. Maybe they've had second thoughts about me. The *Machiko*'s going to leave a hell of a pile of unpaid bills in Singapore."

"You would think – with the Japs sitting across in Johore waiting to wipe us all out – that the powers-that-be would have a damned sight more to worry about than unpaid bills. It must be more serious than that. Are you sure you don't have a hold full of contraband? All I was told was that the *Machiko* had been refused outward clearance and that the master was to be apprehended and brought, forcibly if necessary, to the HSO's office." He threw a sly glance at Ross. "You weren't thinking of skipping without getting clearance, were you?"

Ross smiled ruefully.

"Don't think the temptation hasn't crossed my mind."

"The mandarins of the Harbour Board wouldn't like that," said Webster. "They thrive on red tape. This whole bloody island is strangling with the stuff." He leaned forward and lowered his voice to a conspiratorial tone. "Mind you, from what I hear, you needn't worry about the Harbour Board. The buzz is that the whole bloody lot have got their bags packed. They're clearing out and leaving everything to the Navy."

Both men looked up at the sound of aircraft engines, lots of them. The aircraft were coming from the west – a tight formation of twenty-seven Kawasaki Ki-54 bombers – a diamond of dark airborne shapes visible fitfully through the streamers of smoke drifting across the sky.

Steadily they came: across the south-west tip of Singapore island; across the island's western artery, the Jurong Road. AA guns began to pump shells at the Japanese bombers but the aircraft maintained height and formation.

Ross and Webster knew what was going to happen next because the Japanese had been following the same unvaried bombing routine day after day for several weeks. It was to be no different today. At a signal from the leading aircraft, all twenty-seven Kawasakis released their bomb-loads simultaneously – causing a blanket of explosions which sent a booming drum-roll of sound rippling out from the target area. It seemed to ripple on and on and then, suddenly, the noise died. Now, the drone of the engines could be heard again and, with it, the flat clump-clump-clump of anti-aircraft guns firing from sites on the roof-tops of the city.

The raiders flew out across the Roads to seaward and then wheeled north in unbroken formation, well to the east of the Changi peninsula. Behind them, they left great dust clouds rising from the flattened godowns of Keppel Harbour.

"They come and go as they please," observed Webster bitterly.

Two ambulances, travelling at speed, hurtled west along Collyer Quay towards Keppel Harbour as Webster and Ross came ashore from the launch. Ross waited at the top of the landing steps for the police officer.

"No paddy wagon, Jock? I thought you would have at least provided transport to the cells." Ross' eyes gleamed with mischievous reproach.

"We walk," said Webster. "It's not far. The guy you have to see at the HSO's office is Burra Sahib Moorhouse. He only recently moved in, so don't ask me what he does there. Do you know him?"

"Never heard of him."

Webster curled a lip.

"Randolph Moorhouse. From what I hear, he is God's gift to the British Empire. That's his opinion. As far as we working coppers are concerned, he's just another government desk pilot from Empress Place. They say that his minions round there had their own name for him – the Honourable Whorehouse."

Outside the Fleet Post Office, a trishaw lay upended in the gutter. Its rider, who had apparently been unseated, was sitting against the wall of the building holding his head. The trishaw-man moaned softly to himself as Ross and Webster came abreast of him. Webster would have walked past but Ross stopped.

"Are you all right, chum?"

Ross stooped over the man and touched an emaciated wrist. The Chinese looked up at Ross with impassive face. Blood was oozing from a three-inch-long gash at the man's temple.

Although Webster hovered impatiently, Ross would not be hurried. He took a clean handkerchief from his pocket and gently pressed it against the trishaw-man's cut, indicating to the man that he should hold it against the wound.

The man nodded gratefully and told Ross that he had taken a tumble when the Japanese planes had dropped their bombs. He had taken his eye off the road and the wheel of his trishaw had caught the edge of the deep monsoon drain.

Ross offered the man a cigarette and then gave him a light. He told him to keep the handkerchief.

"OK now?" he murmured.

"OK now," the man replied.

Ross straightened and rejoined Webster, who was standing shaking his head in wonder.

"That your good deed for the day?" he asked.

"I hope you'd do the same for me, Jock," Ross said. They continued walking.

"I keep forgetting you have a soft spot for our yellow brethren."

"And what the hell is that supposed to mean?" snapped Ross.

Webster gave a shrug.

"No need to get shirty, Skipper. I'm not being critical. You know me better than that."

"It was the way you said it as much as what you said. What did you mean?"

"You know what I meant." Webster's face flushed with embarrassment. "Maybe I should have said yellow sisters. Damnit, man, you did marry a yellow girl. And it's nothing to be ashamed of. I admire you for it. It shows you have some moral crust. Which is more than I can say for some of the sods out here who'll bed yellow and brown and every colour in between but would kick you out of their club if you walked into dinner with an Asiatic."

"Forget it, Jock," Ross said wearily. "I know you don't mean to sound patronising but that's exactly how it's coming out. Let's change the subject, eh?"

But Webster would not let go.

"How is she? Your wife? Did she stay in Honolulu this trip?"

Ross sighed.

"She's dead, Jock."

The police inspector halted and stared at Ross, eyes wide with shock.

"Oh, God! I'm sorry . . . I'd no idea."

The last thing Ross wanted was pity, but Webster's contrition was real and, in spite of himself, Ross was touched by it.

"You weren't to know, Jock. I didn't put a notice in the *Straits Times*. The first I knew of it myself was when we arrived here in Singapore."

Webster was shaking his head with chagrin. Normally, his lack of tact did not trouble him. He interpreted his forthright manner of speaking on the most delicate of subjects as honesty. But, now, he would have given an arm to have taken back his remark about "yellow brethren". He had met Ross' wife only the once, back in '39, and it had been plain as a pike how devoted they were. As if the pair had discovered some special ingredient for happiness that was kept secret from other mortals. He had admired Ross' refusal to apologise for marrying outwith his race. Some of the Anglo-Saxon community had made their disapproval known in the crudest possible manner but Ross had stared them in the eye, pitying them, and gone his own sweet way. There was nothing artificial now in the compassion that Webster felt for Ross in a loss that he knew must be deep and private. It glittered in the moist eyes in the craggy policeman's face.

"If there's anything I can possibly do . . .?" Webster spoke barely above a whisper. "Anything. Anything at all."

"I know, Jock. I know." He brushed a hand against the other's shoulder. "I know you mean it, Jock. Thanks."

"It sometimes helps to talk about it. Do you know what happened?"

"I do now. It was the same day as the attack on Pearl Harbor. I was told a bomb had hit the house. But I cabled Honolulu for details . . ."

"And?"

"She was burned to death. Her father, too."

Webster stared at Ross, grim-faced.

"An accident?"

"Yes and no. The fire was started deliberately. The people who did it may or may not have known that there was anyone in the building."

"It's murder just the same," said Webster vehemently. "I hope they caught the bastards!"

"I don't know," said Ross. "All I was told was that some crazy idiots got drunk and decided to revenge Pearl Harbor by setting fire to Japanese property. My wife and her father were working in an upstairs office at the back of the building. The whole of the ground floor was alight before they even knew about it. They didn't have a chance."

A look of pain crossed Webster's face. He shook his head.

"I don't know what to say."

"There's nothing you can say, Jock. Nothing can bring them back."

48

They walked on in silence.

Outside the pillared entrance to a four-storeyed office block with a handsome stone front, they paused briefly.

"Your ship," said Webster, "isn't it called after your wife?"

Ross confirmed that it was.

"Machiko," said Webster, savouring the word. "It's a nice name."

Ross gave a sad little smile. It *was* a nice name. Many Japanese names had a poetic quality. He sobered. One could say there was a poetic quality about the name, Kawasaki — but twenty-seven Kawasakis had just tried to blast Keppel Harbour off the face of the earth. It was a safe bet that precious few of the three million souls now crowded on to Singapore island saw anything lyrical or lovable in things Japanese, names or otherwise.

This was borne out within minutes when Ross was shown into a first-floor office where two men in civilian clothes were waiting for him. One, tall and bespectacled and with a military moustache, was in his late fifties. He took up a stance near a window, leaving the stage to a younger man seated behind a desk. This younger man, Randolph Moorhouse, studied Ross through pale blue eyes and with an expression of thinly veiled contempt.

Life in the tropics had not darkened Moorhouse's skin. It retained a soft fluffy pinkness. Heavy jowls accentuated a general tendency towards overweight. This flabbiness and thinning fair hair made him look older than his thirty-eight years.

"Ah, yes. Ross, isn't it?" Moorhouse thumbed through some papers on the desk. He looked up and his stare was malevolent. "Got quite a reputation for letting the side down, haven't you? You're the fella with a Japanese master in Honolulu. And a Japanese woman, too, I believe. Do you know who I am, Ross?"

Ross controlled the quick burn of anger he felt. It flamed through him but he gave little outward sign of its passion apart from a hardening gleam in his eyes. He stared at the other man with a half-smile of such innocence that the insolence of his reply struck home like the blast from a double-barrelled shotgun.

"You must be the Honourable Whorehouse?" he said with calculated affability.

The pink face behind the desk turned a bright crimson. An explosive snorting sound erupted from the direction of the window where the man with the military moustache nobly tried to stifle laughter. Webster, who was standing impassively at the door like a disinterested sentinel, hands behind his back, winced visibly

49

at Ross' temerity and seemed to be waiting for the man behind the desk to go up in smoke.

He did not go up in smoke but fury smouldered in the look that he directed at Ross.

"The name is Moorhouse," he enunciated coldly. "Since you were ignorant of that, you are also probably ignorant of the fact that I have been appointed by the Governor to co-ordinate civilian security on the island and spearhead the drive against fifth columnists and enemy subversives."

Ross shrugged his shoulders.

"I can't see what that's got to do with me."

"Can't you, Ross? Well, I'll tell you. Two days ago you spent a morning making enquiries in a certain neighbourhood on the Bukit Timah road. You visited a bungalow there."

Surprise showed in Ross' eyes.

"You're remarkably well informed. I was looking for an old friend. May I ask how you came by this information?"

"It was reported to me, Ross. By a patriotic citizen. Someone who was disturbed that an Englishman like yourself should be consorting with Japanese. It was just your bad luck that the same someone ran into me in the bar of the Sea View last night. Naturally, in my position, I felt impelled to investigate the matter further. What I have discovered about you so far has done nothing to diminish my suspicions that you have all the hallmarks of a traitor to your country."

Ross stared at the other man in disbelief.

"You mean that that's what this nonsense is all about? You think I'm a spy? A fifth columnist?"

"That's precisely what I think," snapped Moorhouse. "Does it surprise you? What else am I to think when the first port official I turn to for information tells me you've been creating merry hell trying to get clearance for your ship in spite of considerable irregularities in the papers you have presented. Why are you in such a tearing hurry to get out of Singapore, will you tell me? Is it because you have an assignation at sea with the Japanese Navy? Or is it because you're a coward, another rat who just can't wait to get off the sinking ship?"

Ross could only stare at Moorhouse. It was all so ludicrous. All such a monumental waste of time. The man was a lunatic. He surely didn't expect to be taken seriously. Ross threw up his hands.

"Looks like I'd better make a clean breast of things," he said

50

with solemnity, and noted with satisfaction how Moorhouse's eyes widened in surprise. "That bungalow out the Bukit Timah road . . . You'll know that the ninety-year-old woman who lives there goes under the name of Mrs Yasheda and that she's an invalid. You probably know, too, that her son was interned. He was the Singapore manager of Asiatic Oriental . . ." Ross leaned forward confidentially and Moorhouse bent eagerly towards him, smug triumph and expectation in his eyes. Ross lowered his voice. "You would have found out sooner or later . . . Mrs Yasheda isn't who she says she is . . . She's . . ."

"Yes," breathed Moorhouse.

". . . the long-lost sister of Emperor Hirohito."

No pin dropped to break the silence that followed. It lasted for fully thirty seconds before a guffaw from the window signalled that the military type could contain himself no longer. Now he laughed without restraint. By the door, Webster was racked by half-stifled giggles.

Moorhouse looked from one to the other, his face suffused with fury. Then he glared at Ross with pure venom.

"Don't think you've heard the last of this!" he snarled. He got up from behind the desk and strode to the door. There, he paused and glowered at the man by the window. "You'd better take over, Rawlings. If you can control yourself, that is. I've got to be at Fort Canning in fifteen minutes. I'll want a full report first thing in the morning."

"Yes, sir," said Rawlings, doing his best to maintain a straight face. Moorhouse went out and slammed the door behind him. Rawlings gave a little snort of disgust.

"Arrogant bastard! He knows bugger-all about security. Why they have to keep saddling us with bloody amateurs, God only knows!" He frowned at Ross as he took Moorhouse's vacated seat. "You made the Burra Sahib lose face, Captain. He'll make us all suffer for it – and he'll never forgive you."

"I'll survive," said Ross.

Woody and Big Rich had survived. Not only had they survived, they had contrived to arrive in Singapore in some style.

The first part of their journey had been utter misery: on foot and in teeming rain. They had travelled only a few miles south when they had come upon what was left of a convoy: a dozen or more burnt-out vehicles abandoned at the side of the road.

The Japanese Air Force had done a first-class demolition job on the mixture of civilian and military vehicles littering the roadside, with the exception of one. It was a short distance away from the others and appeared to have skidded off the road and become bogged down axle-deep in thick mud, where it sat, relatively undamaged.

It was a hearse, complete with a plain mangrove-wood coffin in its curtained interior.

The two Australians cranked the engine and found to their astonishment that it ticked over sweetly. When they tried to get the hearse back on the road, they made two more equally astonishing discoveries.

Deeming it essential that they must first lighten their transport of non-essentials such as its cargo, they pushed the coffin out through the rear doors. It slid down a bank and burst open to reveal not a corpse but several dozen bottles of Scotch whisky. A search of the hearse's gloomy interior had uncovered an even more useful haul: several jerrycans filled with petrol and more than ten thousand cigarettes.

The two Australians had tried to imagine what set of circumstances had forced the hearse's owners to have abandoned the hoard with such alacrity that they had not even bothered to close the driver's door. But Woody and his companion wasted no time trying to solve the mystery. It was neither the time nor the place to look a gift-horse – or as Woody put it in his own wry way, a gift-hearse – in the mouth.

They had bullied the vehicle out of its mud-trap and back on the road. Then, fortified by Scotch and chain-smoking to keep themselves awake, they had continued south in much greater comfort than they had dreamed possible.

Their journey had not been without incident. Only a mile or two further on – with heavy rain beginning again and the tropic night falling fast – they had run clean through a bicycle-equipped contingent of fity or more astonished Japanese who were making camp at the roadside.

Woody had simply put his foot down on the accelerator and kept going. Not a shot was fired but, from that point on, the Australians had braced themselves for whatever might face them round every bend in the road.

Some miles outside Johore Bahru, they had encountered rear-guard lines of the Australian 22nd Brigade and had been ordered to keep going right through and on for the Causeway and Singapore. The entire army was leaving the Malayan mainland and long lines of trucks were drawn up for the evacuation.

Reaching Singapore island, they had been directed to a military hospital where they had been stripped, bathed and generally repaired. With clean white bandages over their wounds and sundry jungle sores and in freshly laundered clothes, they were deposited by ambulance with other walking wounded at a transit camp close to Kallang airfield.

It was here, at about the same time as Ross and Webster had watched the air attack on Keppel Harbour, that a British major had arrived at the camp looking for two volunteers for special duty. Much to Big Rich's horror, Woody had stepped forward in response, dragging his companion with him. They were told to draw side-arms and ammunition and report to the Adjutant's office in thirty minutes.

"What the bloody hell did you go and do that for?" Big Rich complained bitterly at the first opportunity. "They're probably looking for a couple of lunatics to swim the Johore Straits and lay booby-traps all round Yamashita's personal field latrine."

"Lay off, Rich. It won't be anything like that. This way, they won't split us up, don't you see? I tell you that two-man jobs are the ones to go for. A Pommie sergeant told me they drafted fifty men out of here yesterday to go and dig defence works up at Kranji. Is that what you want landed with — penal servitude?"

Woody's instincts proved right. The "special duty" involved no hard labour, had motor transport and a driver provided, and turned out to be the most bizarre job that either of the Australians had ever undertaken.

The pair were entrusted to be the armed guard of a government official collecting crates of banknotes from outlying banks and taking them to a cellar furnace below Empress Place for burning.

Woody and Big Rich could not believe their eyes when they delivered their first consignment from a city bank — a mere hundred thousand dollars in five and ten notes. Fondly believing that the money was being placed in some impregnable vault for safekeeping, the Australians were appalled when they discovered what *was* happening to it.

Chinese labourers unloaded the first two crates of dollars from the closed van and, with the two Australians escorting them, the crates were carried into the cellar of the government building. There, each batch of money was checked by the Acting Federal Secretary and the serial numbers noted.

The money was then unceremoniously cremated in the fiery depths of the furnace.

Parker, the government employee whom Woody and Big Rich had to guard – as several banks were visited and fresh loads of banknotes were collected – was a nervy individual who seldom spoke to the Australians and seemed preoccupied with secret thoughts and dreads of his own. A certain unease that the Australians harboured about Parker's demeanour hardened into suspicion during one call. It was in a bank that had been badly damaged by a bomb. Parker went to great pains to go into a private huddle with the manager. This individual seemed as sweaty and nervous as Parker was.

"They're up to something," Big Rich confided to Woody.

"Creaming off a little percentage for their old age, d'you reckon? Maybe they don't like burning all that stuff any more than we do." Woody nodded at the two men, who were talking urgently to each other in a corner of the main office where stout timber props shored up a damaged wall. The men kept their voices low and kept glancing over their shoulders to make sure no one was within earshot. "They're both sweating like pigs and closer'n two fleas on a dingo's tail."

Parker and the banker broke up their confab to supervise the removal of a single crate from the strongroom. Woody and Rich escorted the money, borne by two Chinese, out of the bank and into the van. Parker followed them out alone. He carried a leather attaché case. He stowed it in the front of the van under the passenger seat.

"That your share of the swag, Mr Parker?" asked Rich with a broad grin.

Parker's face was a study. He did not exactly turn green but a pallor started across his face from the eyes, a chalky greyness which crept over his cheeks and mouth and seemed to set his lips twitching as it spread. He managed to speak.

"No such luck," he stammered. "It . . . It's Lawson's . . . the manager's. Lucky blighter's being evacuated . . . I said I would drop it off for him in town. He . . . He's shutting up shop here."

Parker was dissembling like a schoolboy who had been caught sticky-fingered with a hand in the sweet jar. Rich said nothing and joined Woody in the back of the van.

"What do you think he's up to?" he whispered to Woody.

"I dunno. But you or me would get twenty years for it."

"What are we going to do about it?"

"Nothing," said Woody. "It's none of our bloody business. It's his conscience, not ours."

The air raid sirens were whining as the van turned into Orchard Road. In the dim sweaty interior of the van, the two Australians heard the ack-ack guns opening up before the last wail of the sirens had died. They knew little about what happened next. The whole world seemed to explode around their ears. There was an angry screeching of tyres as the van seemed to career sideways. Then there was a rending of metal as the sideways movement ended suddenly and their tiny, dark, encapsulated world seemed to somersault. They were thrown against each other and the sides of the van as the flight ended with a thunderous crash and the oblivion of unconsciousness.

From the back of his taxi, Paul Newton saw the closed van lose control in the seconds after the bomb bursts. The first bomb hit the roadside right alongside an ancient rattletrap of a truck in which Chinese workmen were crowded against the high sparred sides. The truck and its human cargo disappeared in a showering eruption of flame, smoke, wheels and bodies. More bomb bursts flared, running in a line away from the road like a monster firecracker, but it was the closed green van that caught Newton's eye. It had been sixty or more yards ahead of the coolie truck and its driver lost all control of it. It careered across the road and into the path of the taxi. Newton saw the front wheel of the van hit the open monsoon trench. The vehicle skidded for a few yards and then did a slow, lazy turn before coming to rest on its side.

The taxi braked to a halt alongside the overturned van. The taxi driver slumped over his wheel with a huge sigh. When his hands had stopped shaking, he turned to face his passenger.

"No good this way," he said, shaking his head. "No want to go to docks now."

"You'll go," said Newton in a tone that did not invite further discussion of the matter. He pushed open the taxi door and got out. Swaying gently, he waggled a finger at the taxi driver. "Come on, Chiang-Kai-Shek, get off your fat backside. We'll see if we can give a hand here."

Newton lurched a step, then gathered himself and walked with a steadier gait towards the van. The taxi driver debated with himself what his next move would be. The deciding factor was the large fee that the tipsy American had promised him to get him to the docks. Reluctantly, he followed the American to the van.

A glance through the smashed windscreen was enough to tell

55

Newton that the Chinese driver and the white civilian beside him were dead. The civilian's face was a mask of blood. Newton turned away with a grimace of revulsion.

"Nothing we can do," he said to the taxi driver. "They're both dead as mutton." He was about to climb back into the taxi when there was a sound from inside the van.

Newton, aided by the unenthusiastic taxi driver, lifted Woody and Big Rich out into the road. Neither of the two Australian soldiers seemed seriously hurt. Both seemed liberally bandaged under their shirts and one had a white earphone of a dressing on the side of his head but, apart from dazing, their only fresh injuries seemed to be cuts and bruises. They sat in the road, lamenting their sore heads and bruised bodies in language that the American found colourful. He offered them first aid from a silver flask which he drew from an inside pocket of his rumpled panama jacket.

Woody and Rich took swigs from the flask in turn and gazed up at their benefactor with interest.

"Thanks," said Woody. "That's good medicine."

"It's addictive," said the American with a tired smile. "I've gotten through a case of it since last Tuesday."

Woody cocked an eye up at the tall, sad-faced stranger: a handsome man, aged about thirty, but gaunt-eyed, with dark pockets under the eyes.

"Do you just like it or are you drinking yourself to death?" he enquired.

The American laughed.

"Well, I did think about putting a bullet in my brain. Or somebody else's. But I settled for the whisky way out. It takes longer — but it's not so messy." He gazed down at the two Australians with an air of apology. "Look, if you two guys are OK, I'll be on my way. I got me a liner ticket out of this hell-hole and I gotta be at the docks before six . . ." He paused, making a decision. "You guys keep the whisky." He handed the flask to Woody and added with a grin, "The cripple throws away his crutch, eh? I guess it's time I got along without it."

He turned on his heel and walked over to the taxi.

"Come on, Chiang-Kai-Shek," he called to the taxi driver, who needed no second bidding. "Let's get this goddamned show on the road again."

As the taxi pulled away, Newton saw that a dun-coloured army car had stopped on the other side of the road. The driver wore

56

the red cap of the British military police. A British major in a steel helmet got out of the back seat and walked across the road towards the two Australians.

Newton hoped that the officer did not intend to confiscate the silver flask, which the Australian corporal was hastily stuffing into the breast pocket of his shirt. He wondered if he should have waited to explain that the gift of the flask had been genuine and quite spontaneous. He turned his back on the scene. To hell with it. That ship down on the docks wouldn't wait. He intended to be on it.

Having made up his mind, Paul Newton reached absently in his inside pocket for his flask with the intention of fortifying his resolve. Then he laughed out loud as he realised what he had done. His laughter caused the taxi driver to throw a desperate look over his shoulder. He thinks I'm crazy, thought Newton, and he's dead right. Reaching for his flask had been automatic: a reflex action, one that had become all too swift in the past year.

Newton pondered on the impulse that had made him give away his flask to that Aussie soldier. The flask had not been a cheap one. He had paid seventy-five dollars for it in Delhi. Was it guilt that had made him give the flask away?

No, it wasn't guilt. He didn't feel guilty about quitting this doomed city. Why the hell should he? What he had felt for that soldier back there was pity – a gift for a condemned man who was innocent of any crime. That was how he felt about the ordinary soldiers. They were the victims, sacrificed on the altar of High Command stupidity and incompetence. And he bled for them.

It was ironic, wasn't it? He had found a cause to write about after all his months in the journalistic wilderness of the Orient, but look what had happened. As soon as he had written with all the passion and verbal skill at his command on a subject the world wanted to know about, he had been silenced as ruthlessly as if the tongue had been removed from his head. Newton had no doubt that his massive 10,000-word dispatch from beleaguered Singapore had been the best and most striking piece of journalism that he had ever written. Purple in places perhaps, but the drama of the situation demanded violent colouring.

He had started:

I write to you from a doomed city. The walls of the room in which I sit shake with the sound of falling bombs. Soon the sun will set over

Singapore and the dark of night will descend. It will be a night of interminable darkness . . .

The dispatch had ended with sonorous gloom:

. . . And so an Empire dies, stiff-necked with pride and blind to its shame. With it will die a dream of greatness that could have been grasped if the vision of the founder of Singapore had been equalled by the vision of the men trusted with the island's defence. The founder built a great city from a swamp and what he built will remain. But the generals built the city walls on sand and they will fall. Now the generals call for courage from the soldiers they command and the civilians they were pledged to defend. They will probably get it in abundant measure. But the heart cries out at such injustice. Must it always be so: that the crimes of the guilty must be paid for in the blood and the suffering of the innocent?

It is bad enough that the innocent are doomed. The real abomination is in the hypocrisy of those who made that doom inevitable but still deny its causes or its imminence. The people of Singapore have been deceived. The people of Malaya were deceived. The world has been deceived. History will not be deceived.

Since war came to Singapore, there have been no shortages. Except for that one commodity beyond price. Truth.

Tomorrow, the day after, or perhaps next week, Singapore will have to face the truth. It will be harsh. It will be painful. Much more painful than the truths the military leaders now find unacceptable. That their incompetence, their neglect and their sheer bungling ineptitude have hastened the end of Empire's golden day. The sun now sets on Singapore. The twilight fades and the long dark night begins.

In spite of its moralising tone, Newton had packed his article for a syndicated news agency in New York with hard facts which amply illustrated the military incompetence and colonial government complacency which had made Malaya easy prey to the Japanese war machine. One way or another it had been a scathing indictment of those in high places. He had expected that he would have some difficulty with the censors.

What he had not expected was to be called to the Cathay Building to be railed at by members of the censorship committee and told that not one word of his dispatch would be transmitted. He had the indignity of having the offending article torn up into little pieces before his eyes and thrown into a wastepaper basket. One censor had told him that his story was no better than enemy propaganda, and that a more fitting destination for it than New York would have been Tokyo.

The next day, his press permit was withdrawn and he was advised to make immediate arrangements to leave the country. Four days had passed before he was sufficiently sober to do so. Other correspondents shook their heads sadly. Newton was a first-class newspaperman when he got his teeth into a story, but he had allowed himself to get bogged down during a spell in Delhi because of a succession of boring assignments. He had begun to take refuge in the bottle. And the more solace he found in booze, the more the quality of the work he was doing suffered. Until Singapore.

A British engineer officer had told him that fortified defence works planned for Malaya and Singapore since 1938 had never been built. Newton had tried to find out why. The deeper he dug the more he was obstructed by authority from getting at the truth. And with every fresh obstruction, the stronger the smell of scandal became.

Newton had not expected his story to win him any friends in Singapore. Its destruction by the censors had been a shock, a body blow to his own morale. His pessimistic assessment of the military situation had been built on careful and reasoned analyses. His failure to get that assessment transmitted, he all too readily attributed to his Delhi syndrome: an inner fear that he didn't have the luck or the special flair to be anything better than a second team player. Whisky restored his belief that somewhere in him, waiting for an opportunity that heaven would send, was the talent to win him a Pulitzer prize – but whisky robbed him of the drive to follow his dream.

It was a strange kind of hell he had built for himself. Sober, he had the drive but not the belief in his ability. Drunk, he had the self-belief but not the dynamic. In whisky, he was happy. Cold reality made his soul weep.

Something in his soul wept now as the taxi bore him towards the docks. It had been at the heart of his gift to an unknown Australian soldier. It was as if the waiting liner offered him escape in the way that whisky offered him escape. It was no escape at all. For where he went, all that troubled him went too. Part of him wanted to leave like part of him wanted a drink. Part of him wanted to stay in the doomed city because part of him wanted to suffer – and, in suffering, find the true Paul Newton.

The taxi driver dropped him nearly a mile from the ship. It was impossible to get nearer. The roads were blocked by the crowds, either trying to reach the ship or there to say their last farewells to loved ones. Cars were abandoned by owners leaving with the single suitcase permitted. But leaving a car was nothing when already leave had been taken of fine houses and a way of life that would never return.

Carrying his suitcase, Newton joined the queue filing towards the main gate. He found himself milling along with two elderly couples. As journalists do, he listened to their conversation unashamedly. He wept some more in his soul.

The two women did not want to leave without their husbands. But the two men kept insisting, calmly, persuasively, that they must. The men, it seemed, had managed to obtain exit visas but not the liner tickets which would have allowed them to accompany their wives. So, they would stay. And whatever life was left to them would be happy only in the knowledge that their wives were safe.

"But, John," one of the women sobbed, "I don't want a life without you. Being with you is the only happiness I have." She was sixty and, in normal circumstances, a woman of some reserve – but no star-stricken Juliet could have matched the light of love shining in her eyes. Newton remained silent no longer.

"Excuse me, ma'am . . . sir. I've just changed my mind about leaving. Your husband would be doing me an obligement if he would take my passage ticket."

If Newton's impulsive intervention was for the good of his soul, it received instant reward in the hope that blazed in the woman's face. But the hope died quickly again when the husband, overwhelmed by a total stranger's generosity, declined the offer. He could not go and leave the other man, his closest friend, entirely alone.

It was then that a silent spectator to all that had taken place interrupted. Newton and the two couples turned to face a tallish woman with short blonde hair, whose attractive figure was not totally hidden by the squareness and poor cut of the navy-coloured dress she wore.

"Please take my ticket for the ship," she blurted out embarrassedly to the second husband. Her accent was American, mid-West. "Take it, please, with the blessing of God."

There were tears, emotional arguments and counter-arguments, hugs and handclasps, but nothing would shake the two Americans from relinquishing their passage tickets so that two husbands and two wives could remain together.

"But what will you do?" cried the now happy wives.

"There's an American ship due in tomorrow," lied Newton. "It'll take us straight States-side. Not just to Colombo."

Newton did not walk away from the two couples and his steamer ticket empty-handed. One of the husbands had pressed car keys into his hand and said, "At least take my car." He had also insisted on writing an IOU for the price of the liner fare.

Newton and the girl found the car after an hour's search. She tagged along with the journalist without any discussion of the subject. He assumed that their only course now was to return to the city and she seemed to have the same idea.

Newton couldn't make her out. There was something terribly unsophisticated about her. Yet she had the same nerviness and tenseness of a girl hitch-hiker he had once picked up near Bay City, Michigan, and who had turned out to be an escapee from a reform school. This girl, though, didn't have the city sparrow sharpness of the escapee. If she had escaped from anything, as likely as not it was a convent school. But she was too old for that. Twenty-six to twenty-eight, even if she had the innocent air of a fourteen-year-old. Her name was Ruth Gamage.

She sat silently beside him as he drove east along the road to the city.

"You're crazy, you know," he said to her. "You've just passed up the last ship out of Singapore."

"I had no right to leave," she said quietly. "My work is here in Malaya."

"You a nurse?"

"I've had nursing training." She glanced at him questioningly. "You told these people there was another ship tomorrow – an American ship?"

"I was lying," said Newton.

"I think I guessed."

"What were you running away from?"

She looked at him sharply, as if he had discovered a secret that only she knew.

"You were running away from something and you've changed your mind," said Newton. "Tell me about it. What were you running from?"

"God," she replied in a strangled kind of voice. "I was running away from God."

Newton almost swerved the car off the road.

61

"Did you say you were running away from God?" His face was a study. He added, more to cover his perplexity than anything else, "I thought God was supposed to be everywhere."

"He is!" sobbed the girl, and burst into tears. "That's why I had to stay. Oh, help me, please. I'm so frightened!"

Newton stopped the car and put an arm round her, trying to console her.

"Don't cry," he said. "I'll look after you. I'll see you're all right. I promise. You'll be OK with me." Over her head, he gave a despairing look towards heaven and the God that the girl was running away from. He did not voice the questions on his mind: "What, dear Lord, am I saying? What am I letting myself in for?"

"Let's just walk away from it," said Big Rich. It was dark and, somewhere beyond the road, a fire started by the bombing still flared. Four hours had passed since the British provost major had taken over their "incident". The officer had thought it was an Australian idea of a joke when Woody had told him that the crate in the upturned van probably contained more than a hundred thousand dollars. Discovery that Woody was telling the truth had an electrifying effect on him. He behaved as if the crown jewels had been left lying in the street and constituted an open invitation to gangs of murderous villains, apparently at large in the city.

No one was evincing the slightest interest in the van or its contents as far as Woody was aware, but the major started throwing his rank around in the manner of one handling the biggest security operation of the decade.

The crate of money was loaded into his car on his instructions. He, personally, would ensure its safe arrival at Empress Place. Woody and Rich, meantime, were to guard the upturned van and the bodies of the government official and his driver. The major promised to arrange for the removal of the bodies and, if the two Australians remained where they were, he would see that fresh instructions were relayed to them regarding their own movements. And, with that, he and the military policeman had driven off with the money. They had not seen him since, nor had they received any fresh orders. A civil defence party had arrived, removed Parker and his Chinese driver, and righted the truck — but the two Australians, it appeared, had been forgotten. Their hunger and their irritation had increased with every hour that passed.

Finally, it had started to rain. The van offered some protection.

It was then that the two Australians had found Parker's attaché case and, out of curiosity, opened it. It was packed tight with crisp new American hundred-dollar bills.

"Let's just walk away from it," Big Rich repeated.

Woody shook his head.

"We can't just leave this here. There's a bloody fortune."

"Well, at least let's get out of that bloody rain. We shouldn't have paid any attention to that Pommie major. The silly drongo's probably knocking back his sixth nip of grog down at Raffles right this minute." Rich looked at Woody doubtfully. "You ain't thinking of back-pocketing all that loot, Woody?"

"Why not? They'd just burn it if we handed it over. Stone the crows, Rich, we could coast for twenty years on this lot."

"Or draw twenty years' hard labour."

"Does it scare you, Rich?"

"You bet your sweet life it scares me."

"Scares me, too. But I ain't never seen this amount of money before. Never owned a penny I didn't have to sweat myself sore for. It's kinda tempting."

"It wouldn't be the same as stealing, I suppose," said Rich. "I mean, it's just paper for burning, like you said."

They made no calculated decision to steal the money. They decided only to consider the possibility while other priorities were settled. Items like food, a hot bath, and where to spend the night. So they put distance between themselves and the wrecked van.

It was only reasonable, they argued, that the British provost major could not expect them to spend the night in the gutter watching over a wrecked van.

Few people were moving in the city streets. Outside an apartment block, some British soldiers ran out of the front entrance and almost knocked Rich on his back. Rich, being the size he was, remained on his feet. It was the man who ran into him who fell, dropping the haversack he had been clutching. Rich picked up the haversack and helped the man to his feet. The haversack clanked. The man looked at Rich fearfully.

"You won't shop us, willya, mate?"

"Been doing a little thieving, have you?" asked Rich, catching on.

"Them flats is deserted. Everybody's scarpered," said the soldier. "Nobody's goin' to miss what we took. Ask me mates." His three companions, who were eyeing Rich's size with respect, made confirmatory remarks regarding the modest nature of their looting expedition.

Rich handed over the haversack and the four soldiers made off at a run.

"This town's full of bloody thieves," he commented to Woody. But Woody was looking up at the dark apartment block. The Australians' accommodation problem was solved.

They chose an apartment on the top floor. The door had already been broken open so there was no problem about entry. Big Rich made straight for the kitchen. The fridge was empty but a cupboard contained a variety of canned foods.

"See if you can fix up some grub," Woody said to Rich. "I'll see if there's any water. I want a bath."

Woody went into the bathroom. There was both a bath and a shower. He turned the tap of the shower. A flow of tepid water trickled out of the rose. It was enough. He stripped off his clothes. That was when he heard a noise. A scuffling sound and then a knock. He heard it again. It came from the bedroom next door. He picked up his service revolver and went to investigate.

He threw open the bedroom door. It was dark in the room but it appeared to be empty. Then Woody heard another sound. A choked-off sob. He crossed and threw open the slatted door of the ceiling-high wardrobe.

It was only when the sobbing figure emerged, pleading, "Please don't hurt me," that Woody realised that the occupant of the wardrobe was a young woman and that *he* was stark naked. He grabbed a sheet from the bed and held it over his body.

"Who the bloody hell are you?" he asked. The girl was too terrified to answer. Paul Newton, whom she hadn't known before that afternoon, had promised her that he wouldn't be gone from the flat for more than an hour. She had hidden in the wardrobe when intruders had broken down the door. She had thought they had gone and was emerging to make sure when she had heard somebody in the bathroom. Now, this naked man was shouting at her. It was too much for Ruth Gamage.

She fell in a dead faint on the floor.

Four

Escape

Kima, the tall Papuan able seaman who had been leading hand on the *Machiko* for three years, steadied the motorboat as Ross climbed into it from the Jacob's ladder.

"OK, Kima, we go shoreside," Ross said.

The Papuan's answering grin was like a sunrise breaking in his black expanse of face. He cast off and kicked the engine into gear. Ross took a perch beside him on the sternsheet. For the second time in twenty-four hours, Ross turned his eyes towards the Singapore skyline. This, he fervently hoped, would be the last time he would have to make the journey to the war-torn city.

The Papuan waved a huge hand in the direction of the city.

"Plenty banga-banga, Cap'n. Plenty Japoni fellas come."

"Yes, Kima, plenty Japoni fellas come," agreed Ross. They had guessed from the intense rumbling of artillery fire just after midnight that the long-awaited Japanese assault had begun. The radio had confirmed it at eight in the morning. Japanese troops had been pouring ashore in the north-west corner of the island throughout the night.

The events of the day before still loomed large in Ross' mind. The only consolation was that, although the day had started out like a mixture of pantomime and bad dream, some kind of sense had been restored and there were definite signs that the red tape and bloody-mindedness which had delayed the *Machiko*'s departure were being overridden

Much of the trouble had stemmed from the question of legal ownership of the *Machiko* following the death of Matsumishi and his daughter. By the terms of Matsumishi's will, all his property would have reverted to a nephew in Kobe, Japan, but the American Government had, not surprisingly, invalidated such a move. They had sought and won a court order to seize all Matsumishi properties, including the *Machiko*. They were not, however, in a position to implement seizure of the ship. They had passed that buck to the British colonial authorities in Singapore who, in turn – in their lumbering and ponderous way – had almost driven Ross crazy with their bureaucratic heavy-handedness.

Ross had finally found an ally in the legal department of the Hong Kong and Shanghai Banking Corporation. They had backed his move to stake a personal claim for ownership of the *Machiko* on the strength of his marriage relationship with the dead owner. The bank had told Ross that, at the end of the day, he might still lose the ship but that the trading profits accrued under his managership would be recoverable after the war. They were prepared to underwrite his managership of the vessel so that it could continue trading.

The colonial government mandarins had been impressed that a corporation of the Hong Kong and Shanghai's influence was prepared to gamble on Ross. They had shuffled their feet and hummed and hawed – but the *Machiko*'s vanished cargo was miraculously found and loaded. And all the other doors that had been barred in Ross' face gradually began to edge open for him.

It still irritated Ross that, for several days now, the *Machiko* had been battened down and ready to sail but had been prevented from doing so by recalcitrant authority. Things, however, had started to improve after the ludicrous and time-wasting episode with Randolph Moorhouse. Rawlings – an intelligence officer who had been ferreting out Japanese spies in Malaya since as long ago as 1936, and who had had his own bellyful of frustrations with colonial bureaucracy – had seen to that. He despised Moorhouse and resented being given the job of his watchdog adviser.

Rawlings had warned Moorhouse that Ross was "clean" and simply the victim of spiteful tittle-tattle stemming from the fact that the sea captain had a Japanese-American wife. But Moorhouse had refused to listen. He had a genius for pursuing the inconsequential while the important issues died of neglect. Moorhouse's security appointment had been a political sop to soothe local civilians screaming blue murder about fifth columnists – but Moorhouse, with his colossal vanity, had not seen it for what it was: a public relations exercise. He *believed* he was the new broom who would sweep up Singapore and make it safe.

Rawlings had not only given Ross a clean bill of health as far as Civilian Security was concerned, he had advised him whom he should see in the Port Authority office about geeing up clearance for the *Machiko*. His advice had proved sound.

Ross had sought out the lowly ranked official Rawlings had named and found a man who believed in deeds not talk. He was coping almost singlehanded in handing over the entire running of the port's affairs to the Royal Navy. As Jock Webster had hinted, the senior port officials had all baled out and were already on their way to India.

At the end of the day, Ross had found himself once again in the company of Hamill, the RNR officer who had breakfasted on the *Machiko* on the day the ship arrived in Singapore. If Hamill retained any misgivings still about Ross' Japanese attachments he had kept them to himself on this occasion. He had been co-operative and helpful. The formalities of outward clearance for the *Machiko* were cleared up and a provisional departure time scheduled for 1830 hours on 13 February.

As he sat beside the Papuan seaman in the *Machiko*'s motorboat, Ross reflected on the day's date. Friday the thirteenth! He wondered if it was ominous. It was not the day a sailor would have chosen to put to sea. Just as well he wasn't superstitious, he told himself, and knocked on the wood of the sternsheet as an insurance against any thought-reading gremlins lurking in the vicinity.

Hamill's office was on Collyer Quay, less than a block away from the office where Ross had been interviewed by Moorhouse and Rawlings the previous day. The place was in an uproar with naval ratings running here and there with folders full of papers.

"We're starting to burn some of the secret stuff," Hamill confessed to Ross when he was ushered in. "I take it that you've heard that the Japs have landed on the north of the island?"

"I heard it on the radio. They said the situation was under control. There was something about mopping up the Jap units that had actually got ashore."

Hamill gave Ross a look that, in American idiom, would have qualified as "old-fashioned". His snort was derisive.

"The last estimate I heard was that the Japs have more than ten thousand troops ashore. They've penetrated up to five miles and it's bloody chaos up there. We've got two whole divisions sitting on their arses up round Seletar waiting for the Japs to cross the Straits! But they've hit us from the west, where all we've got is one under-strength Aussie brigade stretched out thinner than ice-cream kiosks on the road to Jericho!"

"You don't sound too hopeful about things."

"I'm not," said Hamill. "Next week at this time, the Japs'll be

67

sitting in this office. I can't say the idea enchants me." He smiled ruefully. "You're lucky. You'll be to hell and gone out of it."

"You've got my sailing orders?"

Hamill opened a desk drawer and withdrew a large yellow envelope.

"Your orders are all in here. You're clear to Batavia, that's all. When you get there, you'll come under Java Operations Command, who will route you to Moresby. Or somewhere further along the line. It all depends on the situation in their sector."

"And our passengers?" asked Ross. But for the fact that the *Machiko* had been earmarked for the evacuation of key government personnel, she would have been allowed to sail the previous night.

"You'll have four special passengers," said Hamill. "That is, you'll have four official evacuees – people whose lives would be at risk if they were to fall into the hands of the Japanese. The four have been notified and been instructed to embark at eighteen hundred hours tonight."

"We can take more than four passengers," said Ross.

"That's up to you, and your agent fellow, Singh. Ordinary passengers had to be cleared through channels, the place out at Cluny – and that's not my province. My only brief was priority for the four government bods. You had better check with Singh while you're ashore that there isn't a busload of pregnant mums sitting on the docks waiting for you to take them to Batavia."

Hamill shook hands with Ross and wished him bon voyage. He didn't let go Ross' hand immediately but looked at him with a faint air of embarrassment.

"I . . . I heard about your wife . . . The fire . . . I want you to know I'm sorry."

Ross took his leave of Hamill and set off on foot for Singh's office. The walk would take him twenty minutes. He did not envy Hamill, nor any of the others who had no choice but to wait here in Singapore while the Japanese Army completed its conquest of Malaya. The constant thunder of guns continued to roll across the city from the north of the island. Some of the shell-bursts sounded quite near. The drone of aircraft coming nearer made Ross quicken his step. He knew they would not be British aircraft.

Woody wakened with a start from deep sleep as glass from the window imploded into the room. The whole of Singapore seemed to be blowing up just beyond the apartment block. Cowering on

68

the floor he could see clouds of smoke and flame belching upwards as bombs exploded less than half a mile away. Crouching by the window, he looked out to see a tall building collapse before his eyes. About a mile away a red patch of crowded rooftops broken here and there by the green foliage of trees erupted in clouds of smoke and dust as a blanket of bombs engulfed it. He gazed in horror as this shantytown, the homes of untold thousands of Chinese, was laid waste in seconds.

He heard the drone of aircraft receding. He heard, too, the sound of steady gunfire – artillery. It seemed to be coming from the north.

He picked his way through broken glass into the centre of the room. Big Rich was still sound asleep on the floor, comfortably stretched on the mattress which the Yank newspaperman had provided. Woody prodded Rich awake.

"I dunno," he said in wonder. "You'd sleep through the last bloody trump, Rich!"

The big man gazed in surprise at the shattered window.

"What happened?" he asked.

"A bloody air raid is what happened," said Woody. "It nearly took the roof off!"

Rich fiddled with the dressing on his ear. It had come loose as he slept.

"Can't hear anything with this," he complained. "I've been deaf since the Nips plastered us with their damned mortars up at the bridge. Where's the Yank and the sheila?"

"Next door, I suppose. I dunno. I just woke up myself when the window blew in."

"It was funny running into the Yank again," said Rich. "There must be hundreds of empty houses in Singapore and out of all of them, we pick his place to get our heads down!"

"At least he didn't kick us out. D'ye know, he seemed tickled to see us. Like we were long-lost brothers or something." Woody shook his head in puzzlement. "What did ye make of the sheila, Rich?"

"She's a funny one. The Yank said something about her being a missionary from up near Ipoh. It seems she wants to go back there. She's off her bloody head."

"Conscience," said Woody sagely. "She abandoned her flock. Ran out on them at the first sign of Nip. Now, she's got it on her conscience so bad, it's making her crook."

The Australians made their way through to the kitchen. Ruth

Gamage was sitting in a cane chair and Paul Newton was trying to persuade her to drink some coffee laced with whisky. She could smell the alcohol and was refusing it.

"Come on, honey," the American coaxed, "it's medicine. It'll steady your nerves. Those bombs scared the wits out of me, too. Come on, honey. You're shaking like a leaf."

The girl took a gulp of the coffee.

"That's better, honey." Newton looked over his shoulder. "Hi, guys. The bombs wake you up? They gave Ruth here quite a shake."

It transpired that the American had been up at 5 a.m. and had gone shopping at the Chinese market, which had been open for business as usual. He had returned with two dozen eggs but very little else. Woody offered to convert the eggs into omelettes and began frying operations.

"What are you fellas gonna do?" Newton asked him. "You know it's only a matter of time before Yamashita's tanks are rolling along that street out there."

"I don't know what we're going to do," Woody said honestly. "There's a hell of a lot of noise coming from the north of the island."

Newton straightened up from a low cupboard with four dinner plates in his hand. He leaned across to whisper in Woody's ear.

"The Japs landed during the night. I spoke to some of your guys when I was out. They said the position was hopeless. There are dozens of them, all heading for the docks, looking for boats to take them to Sumatra . . . anywhere. If I were you, I'd get out, too, while the going's good."

"What about you and you-know-who?" Woody nodded in the direction of Ruth Gamage, who was engaged in solemn conversation with Big Rich.

"I'm getting her out," whispered Newton. "Whether she likes it or not." He bent even closer. "When I was out last night, I didn't tell her but I tried a few contacts of mine about getting a boat outa here. It's all set up if I can raise enough dough."

"How much do you need?" asked Woody.

"Ten thousand Straits dollars."

"Will American dollars do?"

"With American dollars, they'd charter me a luxury yacht."

Woody told him to go to the room where the two Australians had slept. He would find an attaché case on the floor. He was to open it and help himself to enough money to get four places on

70

the boat to Sumatra, or wherever it was going. With an expression that was one large question-mark, the American did as he was told. He returned inside the space of a minute looking as if he had seen Emperor Hirohito in the hallway.

"Where the hell did you get *that*?" he hissed in Woody's ear.

"It was for burning," Woody said, with baffling simplicity. "It fell off a van."

The sampan nosed out from the creek, threading a way through the labyrinth of small boats congesting the mouth of the inlet. All afternoon, flights of Japanese planes had been attacking the bridge at the inlet's throat and the traffic using it. Fires burned all round the bridge and among the terraces of shack-like dwellings clustered along the banks of the muddy, turgid stream. The fires cast dancing orange reflections on the surface of the water with the coming of dark. The air seemed laden with eerie menace: the dancing flames and Stygian river combining to project a Dantean vision of some forbidding infernal orifice. Like the cries of the tormented came the shrieks and wailing of the living as they mourned over their dead or wept before the ashes of the hovels that had once been homes.

Ruth Gamage held her hands over her ears to keep out the sounds of suffering humanity. They rebuked her more than the silent voice of God. She was huddled in the sampan's arched rattan canopy. Beside her, Newton and the two Australians squatted, their faces grim. They were appalled at the flimsiness of the craft that was to take them to Sumatra. It did not look stout enough to withstand a gusty crossing of Sydney Harbour, far less a voyage on the open sea. When they had first climbed aboard, they had foolishly believed that the sampan was to take them to a bigger vessel out in the Roads. Now they knew differently and, on top of the travail and excitements of getting only this far on what had already been a desperate journey, none was in the mood for idle chatter.

The Chinese owner of the boat – a tiny, thin man with a narrow jutting jaw – sat like a statue in the stern, while his fifteen-year-old son – the only crewman – crouched at the bow as lookout. The latter fended off other craft as the sampan proceeded slowly past the floating homes of the boat people. He gave a guttural shout and imperious wave of the arm as they reached clear water. His father opened the throttle of the engine until it settled to a rhythmic chug-chug-chug, reminiscent of an ancient but ever-faithful lawnmower.

Steering the tiller with his feet, the sampan owner fished in a pocket for a clay pipe, which he fixed firmly between his teeth but made no attempt to light. Hands free again, he grasped the tiller and set the sampan's gently lifting bow towards the dark shapes studding the southern horizon: the islands which lay around the throat of Singapore like an emerald necklace.

Behind them the sky was red with the glow of many fires, and the tall tower of the Cathay building stood like a shadowy finger against the night sky.

Dawn was lighting the sky to the east when excited chatter between the boatman and his son roused the others. Woody and Newton clambered forward to get a better view of what was causing the boy's animated chatter and gesticulations. To the south, sitting like a candle in a saucer, was a shallow dark shape from which rose a flickering orange and yellow glare. It was another small craft and she was on fire. She drifted, slightly to starboard of the sampan's course: a beacon on their path.

As the sampan neared, its occupants could see the trim lines of the other vessel. She was a sleek motor yacht of nearly fifty feet with a long, sharp bow that would cut through the water like a kukri blade. Four people were huddled in a group near the bow while three others fought the fire raging at the after end of the long, low cabin. The cabin area was blazing fiercely, cutting off the firefighters in the cockpit from the group isolated in the bows.

"Save us! Save us!" The shout came in English and it was a woman's voice. It came from one of the figures on the foredeck and was accompanied by a frantic waving of arms. The Chinese sampan owner issued a string of orders in his high-pitched sing-song voice and swung the tiller to bring the sampan closer to the stricken yacht. The boy in the bows was galvanised into action. He came nimbly aft and throttled back the engine before putting it into neutral. As the sampan glided towards the burning yacht, he seized a long oar and prepared to conduct fending operations.

One of the firefighters – a stocky man wearing only shorts and a blue RAF cap, his glistening body streaked black – turned only momentarily from his task of hauling sea water in a roped bucket and passing it to a companion.

"Save the women!" he shouted. "Never mind us."

The sampan's four passengers were on their feet, willing to assist but without much certainty in how to direct their efforts. It

72

was Woody who took the initiative and indicated to the Chinese boy that he would hold the two craft together if the midships section of the sampan could be poled nearer to the yacht's bows. The manoeuvre succeeded and, briefly, the two vessels bumped – just long enough for a woman on the yacht to thrust a bundle into Woody's outstretched arms. It was a baby.

The vessels drifted apart again. As they did so, the sampan's skipper began shouting unintelligibly in great agitation and waving his matchstick arms. The reason was quickly apparent. Showers of sparks from the burning yacht were erupting from the cabin area and cascading over the sampan, where they continued to flicker and spurt. The sampan skipper was telling the people on the yacht to jump into the water, that he was endangering his boat by coming close. Nevertheless, he re-engaged the engine and slowly brought the sampan round again to drift close on the beam of the burning yacht.

Woody, meantime, had stood paralysed with surprise, unsure what to do with the awkwardly wriggling scrap of humanity in his arms. The baby, uncomfortable in his new and thoroughly strange cradled support, began to bawl. Woody made no protest when two slim arms insinuated themselves against his chest and relieved him of his burden. Ruth Gamage cooed softly to the child and let the blanketed bundle rest easily against her firm young breasts. The ravaged, tormented look had gone from her face. Her look was positively beatific.

The shock of the explosion was totally unexpected. The cabin area of the yacht simply disintegrated upwards in a great fiery blast. Fountains of blazing fuel flew high on the air and spilled down on the sampan. The wiry figure of the skipper was engulfed and became a blazing torch from head to toe. He staggered blindly before pitching into the sea, which was already ablaze. A curtain of fire rolled over the spot where he disappeared. The others were more fortunate. None escaped the globules of raining flame as they landed on hair and clothing, but none was under a direct torrent as the sampan skipper had been. The sampan was alight in dozens of places from stem to stern as the five remaining occupants fought to smother the acid drops of fire eating at their bodies and clothes.

Ruth Gamage was the first to realise the futility of beating with hands and arms at the burning specks. Still clutching the baby and with only one hand free to slap at clothes and hair, she struggled to the sampan's side and threw herself into the sea away from the

73

conflagration. The others followed suit, Newton surfacing near the girl and spluttering to her side. She was almost drowning in her efforts to keep the baby clear of the water.

Newton took the child from her and disentangled the mite from the encumbering blanket. The baby was coughing and choking from the sudden immersion, but was very much alive and kicking.

Woody and Rich trod water on either side of the Chinese boy and spoke encouragingly to him. He was shocked almost into trance and sobbing what the Australians took to mean, "Father, father." But his father was dead. And the sampan which had been home to the boy was settling lower in the water, ablaze from one end to the other.

Ross had stayed on the bridge the whole night. An instinct of terrible uneasiness had nagged at his mind like a toothache. The windows of the tiny bridge-house were wide open, allowing all the breeze there was to send wafts of cooling air into every corner of the shack-like erection and the cubicle of chartroom beyond. Ross had expected to be buoyed up at finally leaving behind the misery that was Singapore.

But the throb of a moving ship under his feet again had not produced the refreshing miracle balm to raise his spirits. His temper had not been improved by the frustrating delay in sailing, waiting for four VIP passengers. Sailing time had been put back until 2300, but it had been midnight before the anchor had been weighed and the *Machiko*'s venerable engines had been given "full ahead".

Ross had been handed a few shocks in Singapore. None had quite taken his breath away with its weight of overwhelming irony as the one dealt him when the passengers embarked. Leading the foursome was Randolph Moorhouse, God's gift to the British Empire and the man whose overbearing stupidity had wasted a morning, not only for Ross but for a number of hard-working government servants. Moorhouse had maintained a cold and aloof attitude, acting as if Ross were a total stranger and leaving all discussion of the accommodation arrangements to Rawlings, the second of the four government evacuees. The two other members of the party were police officers who had figured prominently in the arrest of Japanese agents in Kuala Lumpur before the outbreak of war.

Rawlings had enjoyed Moorhouse's discomfiture at coming

74

face to face with Ross and had winked broadly at the sea captain as the four had gone off to their cabins. Ross had gone straight to the bridge, consoling himself that the journey to Batavia was a short one and that Moorhouse's stay on the *Machiko* would be of short duration.

But it was not wholly Moorhouse's presence on board that caused Ross' disquiet through the watches of the night. It related in an indefinable way to his sailing orders from the Navy to proceed towards the island of Bangka and thence through the Straits of the same name along the Sumatran coast. As dawn came, no explanation for his unease had offered itself to his mind and he resolved to put it from his thoughts. The events of the next hour conspired to make this possible.

He was already reaching for his binoculars when the fo'c'sle lookout sang out his warning of a sighting dead ahead. He focused the heavy glasses on the horizon and the leaping flames which marked a ship burning like a pyre on the ocean. He slowed the *Machiko* as they approached the scene of the sampan's end, and stopped engines while they were still a quarter of a mile away.

Kima had answered Ross' summons of a hand to the bridge. Now, the captain ordered the Papuan to stand by to lower the motorboat. Seconds later, Haraldsen, the *Machiko*'s First Mate, stuck a tousled blond head round the bridge-house door to find out why the ship had stopped. Ross drew his attention to the sinking sampan, now in plain detail in the first light of day. Ross raised his glasses once more.

"There are people in the water!" he exclaimed. "Get off in the boat with Kima, Mr Haraldsen. You may not have much time. They look in a bad way."

The rescue operation took only twenty minutes. Haraldsen was back on the bridge to report the moment it was complete. Ross was continuing to sweep the sea with his binoculars, searching across every inch of ocean for a movement, a sign that a living person was still in the sea. There was none. The sampan, or what was left of it, sank from sight in a dying hiss of steam. The sea nearby was dotted with floating debris.

"There were two boats," said Haraldsen, "a motor yacht as well as that sampan. I'm not too sure what happened. A collision . . . I don't know. But we've got seven survivors: three men, a woman, a Chinese boy and a baby from the sampan, and one man from the yacht. An RAF flight-lieutenant, he says. In pretty bad shape. His back and legs are all burned. He wants to talk to you, Captain.

Says it's urgent. Something about the Jap Navy blockading the Bangka Straits."

Ross handed over the bridge to Haraldsen and hurried below. The survivors were sitting on the hatch of the after hold with blankets thrown round their shoulders. Ross' steward was handing them mugs of steaming coffee.

The exception was one survivor laid out on his stomach on a blanket with a seaman bending gingerly over him. The man was wincing as the seaman dabbed gently at his back with antiseptic ointment.

In spite of his pain, Flight-Lieutenant Mick Sharkey wanted to talk to the Captain. The Bangka Straits, he said, were full of Jap warships. The *Felicity* – the motor yacht that had been taking him to Java – had turned and run at the sight of three Jap destroyers. The destroyers had sunk at least half a dozen ships in the space of half an hour. The *Felicity* had got away only because the Japs had concentrated on bigger ships, but then a Jap Zero had strafed the yacht and started a fire in the engine compartment. They had been fighting the fire all night, and then the sampan had come along . . . The whole bloody lot had gone up with a bang. Flight-Lieutenant Sharkey didn't know why he wasn't dead.

When Ross returned to the bridge, he was deep in thought. He now had an answer for the unease that had plagued him throughout the night. Some sixth sense had warned him that there was danger in the Bangka Straits. All right, so it was only instinct, no solid evidence. But he had learned to trust his instincts. It was like smelling a storm the day before it brewed up. The senses tuned into something, he didn't know what. But all the messages of experience seemed to channel along this instinctive communication line, and it paid to listen to them.

Ross reasoned that there was more than instinct warning him to keep away from the Bangka Straits. For the past umpteen days the Jap propaganda beamed at Singapore had said that there would be no Dunkirk this time, that the British wouldn't get away. That could mean that they had moved their Navy to seal off the escape holes. The Malacca Straits were already effectively sealed. It stood to reason that the Bangka Straits and the Sunda Straits – between Sumatra and Java – would be sealed off too, in order to complete the bottling-up process.

Ross pored over the chart in the chartroom. Dare he disregard the very definite instructions of the Royal Navy about making for Batavia and following the prescribed route through the Bangka

Straits? It was an awesome responsibility. And yet every instinct told him that if he *did* follow orders, the *Machiko* would never see Batavia nor anywhere else. She would suffer the same fate as the *Felicity* and all those other ships that the Japanese had blasted out of the water. So, he made his decision – one that he knew would be irreversible and quite possibly tragic. He was gambling with the lives of everyone on board. But he knew the islands to the east. If he was going to take long-odds chances, he would take them on familiar territory.

He laid off a course on the chart, away from the Bangka Straits and towards Borneo. Then he went into the wheel-house and gave the helmsman a new course to steer. The *Machiko* heeled slightly to port as the rudder took effect and the ship's nose turned towards the rising sun.

The Filipino steward began to serve lunch when Ross took his seat at the long table. The passengers were already seated, with the exception of Moorhouse. He had not appeared. Nor had the girl, Ruth Gamage. Newton and the two Australians sat together, rigged out in borrowed clothes. No one had enquired why two soldiers had happened to be out at sea in a sampan while thousands of their compatriots were engaged in a life-or-death struggle with the Japanese for possession of Singapore, but Newton had warned them what to say if that eventuality arose.

"Say an officer told you to make for the docks and get away any way you could," he advised. "And stick to that story. Nobody's going to throw the book at you if you insist all along the line that you were obeying orders."

"The worst they can do is shoot us," Woody had observed philosophically. He was prepared to take life as it came, whether it was rough or whether it was smooth. For the moment, it was smooth. The *Machiko*, although an old ship and by ocean-going standards a very small one, was positively luxurious compared with the ill-fated sampan. Both Woody and Rich handled the silver cutlery of the lunch-table with respectful awe and lovingly fingered the texture of the dazzling white linen of the table cloth as if to make sure it was real. Neither could remember when they had last sat down to a meal in such civilised splendour.

"Will the young lady be joining us?" the captain was asking.

"She's seeing to the baby," said Newton. "She hoped it would be OK for her to eat later."

"Of course," said Ross. "And if she needs anything, all she's got

77

to do is ask. I want everyone to make themselves at home on the ship, as far as that's possible. We're going to be a bit cramped for accommodation and we'll have to do some doubling up . . . But, with a little give-and-take all round, we'll all manage along fine . . ."

He broke off as Moorhouse entered the saloon. He stood just inside the doorway and surveyed the gathering round the table with a petulant frown.

"Do I take it that we all have to eat together like monkeys in a zoo?" he demanded loudly.

Ross looked at him calmly.

"Only if that is how you normally eat, Mr Moorhouse," he replied. "But I would prefer it, if you do eat like a monkey, that you do so alone. I shall be quite happy to ask my steward to bring you some bananas out on deck."

Moorhouse reddened.

"You know perfectly well what I meant, Ross. I suppose it is expecting rather much on a tub like this to expect a little privacy with one's meals. I am not accustomed to eating in a herd."

"Well, I suggest you get used to it, Mr Moorhouse. There's a place there next to Mr Rawlings. Won't you join us?"

Moorhouse sat down next to Rawlings with anything but good grace.

"Thank God we'll be in Batavia tomorrow," he said loudly.

"No, Mr Moorhouse," Ross contradicted quietly. "I am afraid we shall not be in Batavia tomorrow."

Every eye at the table turned questioningly in his direction. Moorhouse spoke.

"Well I, for one, should like to know why."

"Because we are not going to Batavia," said Ross. "I was about to tell the others before you came in. We are all going to be together for rather longer than you all realised. And, as we shall all be living on top of one another, it's important that we all make the best of things . . ."

"I demand to know what on earth you're raving about!" Moorhouse interrupted. "What is this nonsense about not going to Batavia?"

Ross stared at him, his eyes unwavering.

"It is my decision. My responsibility. I have to do what is best for the ship. I could try to reach Batavia . . . But the likelihood is that we would never get there. We would run straight into the Japanese Navy. I'm not prepared to take that risk. Instead, I propose to take a calculated risk and make a run through the Java Sea for the Lombok Strait, and on to our original destination of Port Moresby."

"Your orders were to take me to Java. To Batavia!" Moorhouse insisted angrily.

"I may still be able to land you in Java," said Ross quietly. "But at the other end. Surabaya or one of the eastern ports. These are some of the options open if we keep well clear of Bangka and Batavia. If we head that way, we'll only run slap-bang into trouble."

Moorhouse pushed back his chair and stood up, facing Ross angrily.

"I was right about you, Ross. You're a coward."

"Possibly, Mr Moorhouse. Possibly. I am also the master of this ship. As such, I am under no obligation whatsoever to inform you of any decisions I make in regard to this ship. I have only done so today as a courtesy . . . and because the circumstances are exceptional. But let me warn you, Mr Moorhouse . . . If you contradict my authority or try to undermine it, or try to interfere with it in any way, I won't hesitate to shut you up and lock you up for as long as it takes you to get some sense in your head. Do you understand me?"

Moorhouse's bluster buckled under Ross' stare. He was defeated and he knew it. He glanced round him, looking for support. But none was evident in the looks coming up at him from the others seated around the table. Unable to advance and unable to hold his ground, he took the only course open to him: retreat. With an angry snort, he pushed his chair against the table and marched out of the saloon.

The *Machiko* continued east. During that day and that night and the day that followed, they saw no other ships and saw no aircraft, friendly or hostile. That night, they heard on the radio that Singapore had surrendered. They also heard a Japanese English-language broadcast exulting in the victory that General Yamashita had won in the name of the Emperor. Among the many battle claims made, one in particular registered with the company gathered in the *Machiko*'s saloon. This told how Japanese sea and air forces had attacked the fleets of ships and small boats trying to escape from Singapore to Sumatra and Java. It was claimed that not one boat had got through the cordon of warships patrolling near the Sunda Straits and Bangka Island. More than forty sinkings had been reported.

Woody and Rich looked over the *Machiko*'s rail at the tropical night. Rain squalls, which Ross had prayed for throughout the day to hide the ship, had come just after dark – but now the skies had cleared again and stars twinkled through the thinning cloud.

"That Captain Ross, he knows what he's doing," said Rich. "I'm kinda sorry, though, that we never saw Batavia. They say the Dutch sheilas are something special. Is that what you're thinking about, Woody?"

Woody grunted. "You got a thing about sheilas," he said. "I don't think about sheilas all the time the way you do." He was silent for a moment, and then he added, "I was thinking about all them dollars. Strewth, Rich, we could have had a bonza time in Sydney with all that dough."

"I'm kinda glad it's gone," said Rich. "It didn't do that fella Parker any good. You can't buy your way out of a coffin. And it sure as hell didn't do us much good. I reckon it was meant to be burned."

"Maybe you're right. You know, I didn't even give it a thought when I jumped into the drink. I was too worried about me going up in smoke to think of anything but keeping my skin in one piece."

"My old man used to say that if you've got a whole skin you ain't got nothing much to complain about."

"He was right," said Woody. "As long as we've got our skins, we ain't got a care in the world." The grin that had spread across his face faded. "That Chinese kid . . . That's about all he's got left in this world – his skin. Right now, a coupla million dollars wouldn't put a smile back on his face. But I know something that would."

"What's that, Woody?"

"A couple of no-good no-account digger friends."

"Us?"

"Who else? You're going to teach him how to speakee jolly proper all-the-same English. If that doesn't give him a laugh, nothing will. Unless . . . it's the other thing I suggested to him."

"And what was that?"

"Teaching you to speakee Chinee, you berk."

They went in search of the boy.

Five

The Japanese are Everywhere

The long frame bungalow with the green roof was the residence and headquarters of Major-General Tomitaro Horii of the Japanese Imperial Army. It enjoyed a splendid situation overlooking Rabaul and had been occupied by the general since New Britain had become – thanks to the all-conquering Japanese Imperial Forces – another unit in that vast territory stretching from Burma to the Philippines known as the Greater East Asia Co-Prosperity Sphere.

The boyish-faced officer standing alone on the bungalow's veranda was the commander of one of three field companies of the 73rd Engineers Regiment. Major Hitoshi Kimura was also the general's nephew. The young major was not a happy man. And it was because of his unhappiness that he had sought an interview with his uncle.

The view from the veranda momentarily took his mind off his troubles. It was a beautiful morning, the sea and sky a brilliant blue, yellowed where they met by a shimmering haze which promised a blazing hot noon. The twin harbours lay like a pair of spectacles between land and sea, the separate eyepieces of Blanche Bay and Simpson Harbour divided by the narrow strip of the Valcan Crater Peninsula. An airless calm hung over the harbours, which were dotted with ships of all sizes, but, here on the higher ground where the land rose sharply to become the hilly range ringing Rabaul, a soft breeze whispered from the heights.

A shelf of flat ground stretched out below the bungalow, one end fringed with palms. Here, two thousand men of Major-General Horii's command had been drawn up for inspection. He sat at their front astride a magnificent white horse. Now, he rode at a sedate gait to meet another officer mounted on a fine bay whose reddish-brown flanks gleamed like silk in the sun. Horii

81

saluted his chief, General Hyakutaka, and then rode a little distance behind him along the ranks of soldiers.

When the inspection was over, General Hyakutaka exchanged his bay for the comfort of a chauffeur-driven open car and departed for a staff meeting at 17th Army Headquarters. Horii, a spry and energetic man, walked up the hill to his bungalow.

Kimura greeted his uncle with military formality before bowing and, with no less formality, exchanging the traditional courtesies between a nephew and honourable uncle. Although he was impatient to speak his mind to his uncle, Kimura gave no sign of his impatience as the general ordered tea and talked vague pleasantries while it was drunk. Only when the tea utensils were taken away did the older man hint that they might now talk of other things.

"When the young seek the counsel of the old, the wise man wears a frown," he said obliquely. "He looks from his window to see if the snow falls in summer."

Kimura acknowledged the words with an inclination of the head and the briefest glimmer of a smile.

"This worthless nephew knows that the burden of his honourable uncle's important work is great," he said. "He is honoured that his revered uncle should even spare a glance of kindness for him, far less the wisdom of his counsel."

The general nodded, approving the humility in Kimura's reply. He crossed to the window and looked down at the harbour and the waiting ships.

"In this hour, both young and old must spend themselves in a divine purpose, the service of their Emperor. This humble servant of the divine will leave soon for New Guinea to bring Lae and Salamaua within the mantle of Imperial Benevolence. His time is short . . . Unless those who would use that time come not with trifling matters but with concern for prosecution of the war against Nippon's enemies, in which all – young and old, great and humble – are whole-heartedly engaged."

Kimura took a deep breath.

"This nephew seeks only to serve the Emperor where the danger to life is greatest and where he will be seen to be worthy of his illustrious uncle, whose bravery is well known."

Major-General Horii whirled round, his face a cold mask.

"What do you mean?" he snapped.

Kimura bowed his head with shame. He had been inexcusably direct. Now his uncle was being equally direct and it was his,

Kimura's, fault. He forced himself to look up and stare at his uncle in defiance.

"I am being sent with my men to a small island well behind our front troops. The shame of it is being talked about by other officers. They are saying Colonel Watanabe has ordered this on your instructions so that I shall come to no harm, so far from any fighting."

The general's face went bleak with fury.

"This is an infamous lie! You know it is a lie."

"I know it. That is why I implore you to free me from it by sending me against the enemy where my death will be a certainty."

General Horii asked the younger man to wait in the room. He, himself, went through to the room which served as his operational office. He made several telephone calls. When he returned, his face was impassive.

"There is nothing I can do," he said to Kimura. "The orders for your unit came from General Hyakutaka himself to Colonel Watanabe. The greatest strategic importance is attached to the establishment of an air base at the island called Great Tarakang. That is where you will go. The matter is ended."

But Kimura was reluctant to end the matter there.

"Did you talk to General Hyakutaka?" he pressed.

"The general told me that you had applied directly to him to be given operational duties against the enemy."

"And?"

"He has no intention of releasing you from Watanabe's force. He appreciates your anxiety for front-line action and told me I could be proud of my nephew."

"But my orders stand?"

"We must all take orders . . . whether we like them or not. I am a major-general but I must obey my commander with the same will as a private must obey his sergeant. I advise you to learn to obey your colonel as you would obey your father and not make him look a fool by going over his head. As it is, you have already made me look foolish by going direct to General Hyakutaka before coming to me. Fortunately, he assumed that your eagerness to die for Nippon was in the Samurai spirit and not occasioned by the need to escape from stupid mess-room gossip."

"But the gossip dishonours you as much as it shames me," protested Kimura.

"Close your ears to what you know is not the truth. Make

obedience your god. Only in obedience and the discipline it requires will you find true strength – the strength to endure the unendurable, to overcome the unacceptable."

The general's face softened momentarily.

"Do not be too impatient for death, Hitoshi. It will not be put off. I have waited many years for mine but it will not claim me before the appointed time. I must serve and I must obey until it comes. You must also."

Kimura felt humble before his uncle's words. He stood before him with bowed head, seized by a tremendous affection for the old warrior. His silence said all that was in his heart. Emotion welled in him. It was almost more than he could bear. He threw himself on the wooden floor, kneeling before his uncle. His continued silence spoke to the older man in a way that words never could.

It was not difficult in that moment for the general to forgive the younger man his impetuosity in seeking his help and for his failure to observe all the courtesies by direct conversation. This young relative had acted more from "human emotions" than for any other reason. And the true Japanese could excuse human frailty, no matter what form it took, perhaps more readily than any other race on earth. The general forgave it now and betrayed equally forgivable "human emotions" himself. He pulled Major Kimura to his feet and hugged him.

"Go now, nephew," he said with a hoarse gruffness. "Go now and do your duty."

Hitoshi Kimura stumbled blindly from the room and out of the bungalow. Head held high and face set in a fierce frown, he walked down the hill at a brisk pace. He was to carry a memory of his meeting with his uncle with him. He never saw him again.

For five whole weeks – while the Japanese were extending the boundaries of Empire across South-East Asia, Micronesia and the Oceanic Territories of the South Pacific – one small cargo ship was playing hide-and-seek with the Imperial Forces. So much had gone wrong with Ross' decision to give Bangka a wide berth that scarcely a day had passed without him having cause to think that he had made a major error of judgement. He had only one thing with which to console himself. For five weeks, the *Machiko* had eluded the Japanese and remained afloat.

If good luck had played any part in the *Machiko*'s avoidance of the Japanese, bad luck played a part in preventing Ross reaching

Western Java, as he intended, and in making good the little ship's escape. What he had not anticipated was the possibility that the *Machiko*'s old but normally reliable engines would break down. By then, Ross had evolved a technique of avoiding detection by the Japanese. This had involved short night passages along the south-west coast of Borneo: anchoring in remote inlets as inconspicuously as possible during daylight and then coast-hopping under cover of darkness.

It was during one of the daytime stopovers that Fraser, the Chief Engineer, had told Ross why the *Machiko* had been barely able to maintain a speed of four knots during the night. It was a trouble for which there was no miracle cure. Fraser wanted a complete shutdown of the main engine for at least forty-eight hours. Otherwise, he had forecast gloomily, "The big end's going to come sailing up through the skylight and we'll have had our bloody chips."

There had been *two* forty-eight-hour shutdowns, and still the problem had not been solved. During that time, nerves on the *Machiko* had become very frayed indeed. Ross had anchored the ship as close to the land as he dared in a jungle-flanked creek. The flat swampy terrain of the coast afforded precious little concealment but it had been chosen by necessity, not design. Three times aircraft were heard overhead, but nothing was seen through the scudding banks of raincloud. More nerve-racking was the passage to seaward of twenty or more ships, making lots of smoke and visible for the best part of an afternoon. It was possibly a Japanese taskforce or convoy, but it made no deviation from its route.

Better progress was made when the *Machiko*'s engines responded at last to Fraser's conscientious toil. But the time lost was to prove critical. While the *Machiko*'s engineroom had echoed to the ring of 28lb hammers, the Japanese had been tightening their grip on the lands to the south. Sumatra had fallen and the battle for possession of Java had begun. Ross had steamed a day and a night to the south towards Java when the broadcast was heard that was to scuttle any plans he had for continuing to Surabaya. The Dutch commander had surrendered and all resistance in Java had ceased.

Ross altered course to the east, his eyes now set on the Lombok Strait, but he was now to find the escape routes to the south were being cut off one by one. Depending almost exclusively on the intelligence he obtained from native fishing boats, he managed to keep clear of the *Japoni* warships whose movements the fishermen reported. But the result was that the *Machiko* kept edging north as she made distance to the east. Thus, instead of running clear of the Japanese forces extending the boundaries of their conquests southward, the *Machiko* kept running deeper into the areas they controlled.

The little ship was caught like a salmon trying to reach the open sea. Instead of making water to the river-mouth, she was being constantly forced to swim upstream. Ross tried not to think what the end result of it all might be but, unless he tried to force a way through the Japanese cordon, the logical conclusion to all his evasive tactics would be that the *Machiko* would eventually reach the broad waters of the Pacific and run out of fuel far from a friendly port.

A near-disaster occurred south-east of Celebes when, in the early hours of the morning, the *Machiko* had found herself amongst the tail ships of a Japanese convoy. One minute the *Machiko* had been ploughing into heavy rain squalls and, in the next, she was cutting across the wake of a Japanese tanker.

To the relief of those on the *Machiko*'s bridge, the Japanese never realised that they had a stranger in their midst. The convoy ploughed on in the direction of Timor while Ross used the banks of rain scurrying before the north-east wind to run clear of the Tukangbesi Islands. He ran into the weather, seeking the cover of the constant squalls to hide his ship. Only when he tried to turn south again did he realise how hopeless the position was becoming. Friendly fishermen revealed that there were many Japanese ships near Ambon blocking the way towards the Torres Strait. So, he kept east to the Moluccas, resigned now to the fact that he would have to go north of New Guinea and try to find a way out of the Japanese net in the wide waters of the Pacific to the north of the Admiralties, or risk running the gauntlet in the Bismarck Archipelago.

Either way, the chances were far from good. The possibly less dangerous northerly route, with plenty of sea in which to hide, had to be ruled out because of the bunker situation. So the southerly route it had to be. The only way out was through the Vitiaz Strait, which separated New Guinea from New Britain – with every likelihood that the Japanese would have that waterway sewn up more tightly than a tailor's breeches.

The ship led a charmed life. The fugitives almost became used to Japanese planes passing overhead without even suspecting that, in these waters, the ship was anything other than their own. The northern New Guinea coast was rich in one commodity: hiding-places large enough to conceal a 240-feet-long ship. There were dozens of inlets screened by forested slopes, which proved splendid daytime hidey-holes for the *Machiko*. In one, as the anchor was weighed at sunset, a group of interested spectators gathered on the shore to watch the ship's departure. Ross focused the binoculars on the group and felt a chill of fear at the realisation they were Japanese soldiers. He told no one but decided, thereafter, to keep to seaward and seek only the sanctuary of the many islands scattered between the coast and the Equator.

By the end of March, the *Machiko* had logged close on four thousand miles of sea from Singapore and was still some way short of clearing the Japanese net. Even the most pessimistic on board began to believe that Ross, like some latter-day Moses, was going to lead them in some miraculous way to a freedom beyond the wilderness. But as the hopes of others rose, so his own realisation grew that they weren't going to make it. Even making the most generous calculations, he estimated that the bunker coal would run out on the wrong side of the Vitiaz Strait – assuming they got that far. He still did not give up hope. Instead, he ordered the accommodation to be stripped of every bit of wood that could be moved: panelling, desks, bunk-boards, anything that would burn. Such coal as they had would be reserved for the final run through the Strait and around the eastern tip of New Guinea to Port Moresby. In the meantime, the wood would be fed into the furnaces.

It was perhaps this emergency measure which led to the *Machiko*'s undoing. The timber fuel did not have anything like the steam-raising qualities of coal but, quite apart from this, it caused the ship to emit belching smoke in dense grey clouds and shower fiery sparks into the atmosphere. This voluminous smokescreen undoubtedly attracted the pilot of the patrolling Japanese seaplane. He made three runs over the ship as if in some doubt that an enemy vessel could possibly be in these waters. On his fourth run, he attacked.

Only one of the four lightweight bombs dropped hit the *Machiko* but, perhaps to balance out the good fortune the ship had enjoyed for more than three and a half thousand miles, the single bomb created damage that was disproportionate to its modest size and firepower. It erupted on the foredeck, igniting drums of turpentine spirit stacked as deck cargo. Within seconds, the fore part of the accommodation housing and the ship's bridge above it were fiercely ablaze.

Ross, who had ordered everyone to stay off the decks at the first sound of aircraft engines, found he could not get from the chartroom to the wheel-house for a sea of flames. The helmsman had been killed where he stood. Forced back by the heat, Ross got out by the rear stair of the chartroom as the fire spread aft. He emerged on the boat deck level as the seaplane made another run to let its gunner pump away at the blazing ship. Then the aircraft flew off to the north. The *Machiko*, with no one to steer her and no means of telegraphing the engineroom, veered in crazy circles.

It took the concentrated efforts of everyone on board an entire night to regain some control of the ship. By then, the fire had been stopped and the emergency steering at the stern brought into use. But the damage was incalculable. The bridge, with all its charts and instruments, was gone. So, too, was the saloon and all the cabins adjacent to it. Woody and Rich, faces blackened from fighting the fire, looked at each other without speaking. This surely was the end of the line.

But Ross was not yet ready to give up. He had been making for a group of islands known as the Outer Tarakangs when the seaplane had attacked. If they could reach them, all was not yet lost.

Daylight came and, with it, confirmation of many of Ross' worst fears about the extent of the damage. With it, too, came a sight that lifted his flagging spirits. Above the eastern horizon, partially obscuring the red ball of the rising sun, was the black cone of Mount Taki, the highest point of Little Tarakang.

Major Hitoshi Kimura was studying Mount Taki through his binoculars when he heard from below his feet the harsh grating of steel on coral. The small Shohatsu supply barge tipped alarmingly to port and grounded on the reef. Kimura kept himself from falling in the sea only by making an undignified grab at the handrail which ran round the outside of the stubby steel cockpit.

When he recovered from his surprise, it was to find Lieutenant Niguchi at his elbow with a look of hangdog apprehension on his face. He was a nice kid, Niguchi, but so accident-prone that it never failed to astonish Kimura how the youngster had managed to survive officer training school. His army career had been one long chronicle of minor disasters.

88

Kimura refrained from bawling the younger man out – as Niguchi plainly expected to be bawled out – and, instead, waited for the lieutenant's explanation of the grounding. None was immediately forthcoming.

"I am most humbly sorry, Major, sir," blurted the young man. "I am most humbly sorry for this regrettable occurrence."

"Perhaps Lieutenant Niguchi overlooked something in the sea survey he made of the island yesterday," said Kimura softly. "Perhaps when he reported that there were several ways through the reef he made an error? Just as his honoured mother made a great error when she gave birth to such an incompetent."

Niguchi bowed his head.

"Far better that I should have not been born," he agreed, "than the honoured major should suffer this inconvenience."

"Inconvenience?" echoed Kimura. "We may all be drowned and you call it an inconvenience! If I may make a humble suggestion, Lieutenant Niguchi, it is that you take immediate steps to ascertain if this tin can is holed and whether or not we can get it off again. In the event that we cannot move from here, you will personally have the honour of swimming the five miles across to Great Tarakang and getting a boat to come and take us off."

Kimura watched in quiet amusement while Niguchi summoned the three bemused soldiers who were the craft's crew and, with much shouting and exhortation, organised them to cope with the emergency. Satisfied in his own mind that the barge was not badly damaged, Kimura kept out of their way and, with a chart of Little Tarakang spread out before him, resumed his study of the island through binoculars.

It took Niguchi and the crew half an hour to refloat the barge. The swell from seaward made it impossible for them to back the craft off the reef: so, instead, they used the surge from the ocean to bump the barge across the submerged barrier of coral into the lagoon beyond. Minutes later, they beached on the narrow sandy strip which was the base of Mount Taki. The cone-shaped hill rose almost vertically from the water's edge. Tangled masses of greenery grew in unruly clumps in every crevice and hollow, receding towards the summit where naked rock faces stepped back in a series of precipitous ridges.

Kimura stood on the beach, looking up. Close up, the mountain looked every bit as formidable as it had done from the sea. It was as he thought. Getting materials through that reef, on to this tiny beach and then up the face of the mountain would be the next

89

best thing to impossible. Far better to locate a landing place on the lower stretch of island beyond the mountain and find a way up that side.

"We'll leave the men here with the boat," he told Niguchi. "You and I are going to the top."

As mountains go, Mount Taki was only a modest 994 feet high – but, in the heat of the equatorial morning, it was no picnic climb. Sweat was running off the two Japanese officers in rivers when they reached the half-mile-wide crater plateau that was the summit. The climb had taken them two and a half hours and had served to reinforce Kimura's belief that trying to get heavy supplies up that side of the mountain would be a labour of madness. Colonel Watanabe wanted him to build a radio and meteorology station on the top and prepare sites for a battery of 150mm guns to command the strip of water between Little Tarakang and its more important neighbour, the twenty-mile-long island of Great Tarakang. For that exercise to be accomplished, they were going to have to create a more serviceable harbour than the narrow lagoon below and find an easier access to the summit than the east face of Mount Taki.

The two officers paused only briefly at the east end of the summit, looking back to feast their eyes on the magnificent view it afforded of Great Tarakang on the other side of the straits. The golden reef-protected beach that ran like a ribbon along the western end of the other island for five miles was fringed with swaying palms to landward and a translucent green lagoon to seaward. Just inland of the beach was the airfield and, as the two men watched, a flight of Zero fighters took off and circled into azure sky before flying off in company into the glare of the sun.

The crater was easy going after the brush-choked hollows and sheer walls of the east face. Kimura and Niguchi traversed it quickly, eager to see the panorama which lay beyond the western lip. The view did not disappoint.

Taki's western side had none of the precipitous drops of the eastern. Here, the land dropped in undulating slopes of lush green forest from about fifty feet below the crater's rim. The forest extended for fully five miles to the far end of the island and, as well as sloping down from east to west, the land dropped in a north-south direction so that it sheltered a great landlocked basin in its south-western corner. From this basin, fingers of water reached to the heart of the island, but how far they penetrated could not be judged from the crater because of the screening of forest along their edges.

Running parallel with the forested spit of land which circled the basin along its southern shore was a wide lagoon and a plainly visible coral reef. Part of the reef was above water, part of it washed by breakers, and part was totally submerged. What took Kimura's eye, however, was a narrow gap in the reef, flanked by two sentinel-like pillars around which the sea swirled white. The narrow ninety-foot gap in the grinning coral jaw was like a socket from which a tooth had been removed.

It was towards this gap that a ship was moving.

Kimura fumbled for his binoculars and wiped sweat away from the bridge of his nose before focusing on the ship. It was a freighter of about 1200 tons and it looked as if it had had an argument with a battleship. It had no bridge left worth talking about and its midships superstructure was a charred-black mess of twisted steel.

The sight of the ship provoked Lieutenant Niguchi to a state of great excitement. Kimura wondered what his junior would have done if it had been an enemy battle cruiser down there instead of a small beaten-up freighter that was ready for the scrapyard.

"Stop chattering like a monkey, Lieutenant Niguchi, and watch," Kimura ordered. "You told me that the reef south of the island was impenetrable, yet I can see a channel through it from here. Did you survey it or not?"

"We surveyed only the east side of the island, honourable Kimura-sir. I, too, can see a gap in the reef down there but the charts we have show no such opening. But ·chart is very old. British Admiralty chart of fifty years ago."

Kimura grunted. Perhaps if Little Tarakang had been inhabited, a more up-to-date chart would have been available. He studied the two pillars at either side of the gap in the reef and concluded that they were not a natural phenomenon. The coral had been built up by human hands so that the two points acted as markers for the gap in the reef. It was possible that the gap in the reef had been manmade, too. Some South Seas' pioneer had probably been as impressed as he was by the possibilities of that landlocked basin as a harbour and had dynamited a gap in the reef. But from the rim of the crater there was no other sign visible below of human settlement.

Kimura, intrigued by the fact that the ship trying to negotiate the gap had no bridge from which the operation could be conducted, concentrated his attention on the vessel. He smiled to

91

himself as he carefully studied the ship through his glasses and it all suddenly became clear. The ship was being commanded from the crow's nest high on the vessel's foremast.

There was an officer perched in the crow's nest – a figure in a battered cap and with gold braid on the epaulettes of his white shirt – and Kimura had no doubt that it was the captain. Other figures, to whom the captain was passing orders, were stationed at various vantage-points on the ship. One was amid the tangled wreckage of the bridge; another was standing by the open skylight of the engineroom and another on the housing above the poop. Obviously, orders were being relayed verbally to the engineroom and also to the emergency steering compartment at the ship's stern.

Kimura felt a strange bond of sympathy for the captain, isolated in his masthead eyrie. He sucked in his breath as it seemed likely that the stern of the ship would swing into the marker on her port side and come to grief on the reef. But the starboard turn which the ship was executing as she entered the gap was timed to a nicety. The stern swung round, missing the marker rock by what seemed inches.

Now the ship had to run the length of the lagoon before turning in a "U" to enter the landlocked basin. The deepest water was very close to the outer reef and Kimura watched with admiration as the captain conned his vessel slowly eastward, avoiding underwater outcrops of reef as he observed them from his high vantage-point. Then the ship was coming to port, bumping without difficulty over a sandbar before gliding into the flat, placid water of the basin. Kimura saw the splash of the anchor and heard the rattle of chain cable as it tumbled through the hawsepipe.

Still, Kimura did not move. He kept watching through the glasses as the captain of the ship climbed slowly down the ladder from the foremast and stood for a moment on the deck, looking up at Mount Taki. It seemed that he was looking directly into the eyes of Kimura.

The Japanese could see the Westerner's face in detail; the steady eyes, the emotionless features, the firm jaw. It was a calm face, a face without fear. Kimura sucked in his breath again at a sudden realisation. He was looking at the face of an enemy.

The thought gave him a strange pleasure. If he were to die in the Emperor's service, for the glory of Nippon, it would be good to die at the hands of an enemy whose face was so godlike in its strength. Kimura allowed a private smile to light his eyes. He reflected on what he considered a strange flaw in his character: his attitude to killing and dying, to the whole art of soldiery. It was a weakness, he knew, that from the first day he had worn uniform he had devoted more thought to the art of dying than the art of killing. He had even joined the Rentai of Engineers because of the suicidal nature of their military function in the Japanese Army. The modern military tradition was that the engineer companies were disposable, always given the most dangerous tasks in assaults as the expendable commodity. This had possibly influenced Kimura into a preoccupation with the beauty of his own death rather than the provision of a glorious end to the Emperor's enemies.

He thought about the latter now – and wondered if that sea captain with the strong face would welcome him, Hitoshi Kimura, as his personal executioner. Possibly not. There were brave Westerners, he knew, but as a whole they tended to be quite blind to the beauty of a good death.

Six

Captivity

Dawn was only minutes away. Creamy streaks of light were appearing like cracks in the black overcast to the east. Kimura stood impassively on the forward gun platform of the long, narrow landing barge. A Taisho 3 machine-gun was mounted on the platform and Kimura was standing immediately behind its squatting gunner.

The ribbed well of the barge held thirty men in battle kit, all from Kimura's engineer company. The barge was driven by a big aero-engine mounted on the stern. The noise from it was shattering. There was no throttling back as the barge approached the coral pillars which marked the gate in the reef. Lifted by the swell, the long barge seemed to race through the gap like a Hawaiian surfer. Its sharp turn to starboard sent large rippling waves across the water of the lagoon to go sighing up the beach.

The craft slowed to make the U-turn into Little Tarakang's inner basin. The first light of day was now breaking over the island as the sun rose somewhere beyond the shadow of Mount Taki. Kimura could not believe his eyes. The ship which had anchored in the basin at just a little after noon the previous day was nowhere to be seen. The basin was empty.

His first reaction was one of mortification. On his return to Great Tarakang the day before, he had personally reported the ship's dramatic arrival to Colonel Watanabe and had suggested capturing the ship intact. Watanabe's first thought had been to send an aircraft over and sink the ship at anchor. He had, however, come round to Kimura's way of thinking that the ship possibly carried valuable supplies and could even be useful for the engineering work planned for the neighbouring island.

Kimura had been gratified to be given the task of capturing the ship. The vessel was unarmed and resistance was unlikely – but it

94

offered action of a sort. The last thing he expected was that the ship would disappear overnight. To report back to Watanabe that the prize had vanished would be to invite the greatest humiliation of his life. He would much rather die than face such an eventuality.

One thing puzzled Kimura. Skilful as that captain had been, he did not believe that he was so foolhardy as to have risked taking his ship through the reef under cover of darkness. Especially a damaged ship, as the one he had seen undoubtedly was. There had to be another reason for the ship's disappearance.

And only one was possible.

If the ship hadn't escaped to sea during the night, then it must still be somewhere in the reaches of this landlocked natural harbour. Kimura recalled the fingers of water extending into the heart of the island which he had glimpsed from Mount Taki. It followed that the ship's captain, perhaps intent on concealment, had taken his vessel into one of these narrow inlets.

Kimura directed the barge's NCO commander to explore the first inlet. It seemed scarcely wide enough to take a ship and was too serpentine in shape. It eventually petered out in mangrove swamp. Kimura ordered an about-turn.

The second inlet was wider, its water surprisingly deep – but it, too, was empty. The third inlet was the one Kimura was looking for. It also had deep water and there, parked like an ox in a stall, lay the ship.

Kimura's first view of it was of the duck-like counter squatting right in midstream, with mooring ropes stretched out to either bank. A Jacob's ladder dangled conveniently at the stern, where a small boat was moored. A figure in a boiler suit appeared briefly at the ship's stern, took one horrified look at the barge packed with soldiers, and vanished again.

The barge's noisy aero-motor fell silent as crewmen threw lines round the *Machiko*'s mooring ropes. Kimura ordered two soldiers up the rope ladder, then swung on to it himself to be third to board the ship. Lieutenant Niguchi was close at his heels, sword dramatically unsheathed. He struggled manfully after Kimura in spite of quickly discovering the impracticality of climbing a rope ladder with a sword in one hand. The only unfortunate consequence was that the soldier immediately below Niguchi on the swaying ladder came close to being impaled from above when the lieutenant transferred the sword to a dagger grip to avoid injuring his major above.

95

Ross had known from the moment the barge's noisy aero-engine had been heard that both flight and resistance were futile. He had ordered everyone on the ship to assemble on the foredeck. He awaited the boarding party alone on the afterdeck.

Now that the chase was over, he outwardly appeared the personification of calmness as the two soldiers advanced towards him. But his throat dried with fear at the sight of the two unsmiling Japanese with their menacingly held rifles and wicked-looking bayonets. What might happen next was totally unpredictable, and Ross knew that the probability of being unceremoniously skewered on the deck of his ship was high rather than low. He braced himself to the expectation that the last minutes of his life was already ticking away.

The two soldiers did little to dispel that expectation. Two bayonets pricked into Ross' chest and he found himself forced back against the midships housing. There, he was held pinned and waiting for the final thrust which would end it all. He looked unwaveringly into the eyes of the two soldiers, but saw nothing there. Neither pity nor hate nor exultation nor sorrow. Nothing.

It was a sharp snarl of command from Kimura that caused the two soldiers to jerk their bayonets away from Ross' chest. Two small patches of red appeared on the once-white shirt front where the bayonets had pierced just deep enough to draw blood.

Kimura's eyes had a strange sparkle. All his attention seemed to be focused on those two blobs of red, as indeed it was, having transferred there from Ross' face. He had been tempted to let the soldiers finish their work and allow the sea captain the gift of a briefly painful and glorious death. His expectation of that death and his calm readiness for it had been written in his eyes and Kimura had experienced a feeling of overwhelming benevolence which had tempted him to grant the captain final escape from the sorrows of the world.

Had the other man been Japanese, he would have had no hesitation. The deed would have been done. But he was a Westerner and Kimura understood something of the Westerner's different code. No European would have interpreted his sanction of the captain's death as an act of benevolence. Western values were at times inexplicable, as he knew only too well from having lived amongst them. So, he had ordered his men off.

There had been something more staying Kimura's hand. By killing this man, he would be robbing himself of the chance of ever knowing him. And he was intensely curious about the sea captain. The curiosity had been aroused by watching him yesterday through binoculars. He had glimpsed a human spirit that fascinated him and allowed him to build a kind of fantasy picture. The captain's behaviour with two bayonets against his chest had simply confirmed all his instinctive impressions about the man. Now, his curiosity was greater. There was more he wanted to discover and know.

The process of discovery began immediately and took Kimura by surprise.

"Dom' arigato gozaimas'," said Ross, with a stiff little bow. His Japanese was quaintly accented but it did not escape Kimura that he expressed thanks for calling off his soldiers in the more formal rather than the colloquial manner. The courtesy could not be allowed to go unreturned and in the language that Kimura guessed to be the captain's own. He saluted Ross with military preciseness and said, "Major Kimura of the Imperial Forces of Nippon has the honour of annexing this ship in the name of His Imperial Highness. Captain and men of ship must now show obedience to officers of Nippon at all times and treat with courtesy. Soldiers of Nippon will do no harm to captain and men if orders are obeyed."

Kimura's English was good in spite of a traditional Japanese difficulty in getting his tongue round "l" sounds and a tendency to drop the letter "r" from some words. Ross congratulated him on his English and thanked him for his assurance of good treatment. He added that there was a woman and child on the ship and expressed the hope that their well-being would be especially considered.

He received the reply from Kimura that the Japanese did not make war on women and children and that they had nothing to fear.

Already soldiers from the barge were swarming over the ship. When Ross went forward with Kimura so that the Japanese major could inspect the assembled crew and passengers, it was to meet a grinning Lieutenant Niguchi coming towards them, holding the baby from the *Felicity* in his arms. Behind him, a distraught Ruth Gamage was struggling in the restraining grip of two grinning soldiers. Kimura barked a single command and the soldiers let the woman go as if they had been electrocuted. Even her struggles stopped abruptly, stilled by the same penetrating command. She stared at Kimura, startled and afraid. He ignored her. All his attention was on the baby, who was bawling lustily.

Kimura took the infant from Niguchi's awkward grasp. A smile

97

wreathed his face as he offered the baby a stubby finger to play
with. The baby quietened immediately and took a profound
interest in the finger, gurgling at it happily.

Kimura looked over his charge to Ruth Gamage.

"You are Mama?"

The girl nodded, then shook her head fiercely.

"Yes . . . No . . ."

Her answer mystified Kimura. Ross came to the rescue.

"The baby's mother was drowned. We rescued the child from
the sea. Miss Gamage has been taking care of him."

Kimura inspected Ruth Gamage critically.

"Mama-san has no sons of her own?"

Ruth shook her head, blushing furiously.

Kimura grunted, obviously none too impressed that a woman
who had all the bodily attributes of the functions of motherhood
had been deprived of that status. He returned the baby to her
arms and looked at Ruth Gamage with a somewhat aggrieved
expression at the way she snatched at the child. The hostility in
her face angered him.

He turned away and, speaking rapidly in Japanese, gave
Niguchi a long list of instructions. Then he marched off, his face
set in a frown, to inspect the ship and its holds.

Niguchi, whose English appeared to have been acquired
largely from American gangster movies, addressed the prisoners.
He repeated what Kimura had said to Ross about being well
treated if orders were obeyed. Also, there were courtesies which
would have to be obeyed, such as bowing to their captors and
showing respect to the soldiers of Nippon at all times. It was not
yet known what would happen to the prisoners but they would
probably be shipped off to a suitable camp when the arrangements had been made. They were, in the meantime, to remain on
the foredeck under guard.

They were still there waiting at midday. Ross sought and
obtained Kimura's permission to rig a hatch-cover over the cradled derricks to act as an awning from the sun and a shelter from
the rain showers.

They were still waiting on the foredeck at sunset, while their
guards prepared to spend the night on the ship. Niguchi could
tell them nothing. They must be patient. They would know their
fate when Major Kimura returned from Great Tarakang.

When he had suggested seizing the *Machiko*, it had not crossed

Kimura's mind that the responsibility for the ship's passengers and crew would be hung round his neck like an albatross. Colonel Watanabe made it only too plain to him that the question of prisoners would not have arisen if the ship had been bombed and machine-gunned, as he had first envisaged it would be when Kimura had reported the ship's presence. Colonel Watanabe had, however, acceded to Kimura's request to take the ship and make use of it and it was now up to Kimura to get on with whatever he had in mind. The prisoners did not really interest the colonel. In the first instance, he could not comprehend the mentality of people who surrendered to their enemy in expectation of mercy when the only honourable course was to have fought, with their bare hands if need be, to the death. He could have respected the Europeans on the ship if they had even tried to resist. But to give up without even a struggle not only robbed Kimura of any honour in seizing the ship, it revealed the ship's custodians as totally unworthy of the least consideration on his part.

In deference to Major Kimura's wishes, Watanabe did promise one thing. He would signal General Headquarters in Rabaul and ask that the prisoners be transported to a suitable internment centre at the earliest possible opportunity. In the meantime, he advised Kimura to establish a camp for them on Little Tarakang and put them to work. He was going to need labour, lots of it, for his engineering work on the island. He should perhaps thank the benevolence of Fate for this unexpected bounty of labourers. As Kimura knew only too well, the conscriptive recruitment of labour among the islanders of Great Tarakang had produced a workforce that fell far short of expectations.

Kimura retired from his session with Colonel Watanabe with his cheeks burning with shame. His exploit in capturing the *Machiko* had required no great acts of heroism but it had been accomplished with speed and efficiency and without mishap. Yet the colonel treated it as a kind of military joke; not the sort of enterprise any self-respecting officer could look on with pride. Kimura's shame deepened when other HQ officers congratulated him on his capture of the unarmed ship. On the surface, their congratulations seemed sincere enough, but beneath it all he felt they were laughing at him. This made his immediate transfer to Little Tarakang and away from the uncongenial atmosphere of Battalion HQ no hardship. At least he would be away from the gossip. That would help him to endure the inglorious road Fate seemed to have selected for him. On the smaller island, too, he could run things his way. In effect, he would be monarch of all he surveyed.

It was on the first day of April 1942 that Major Kimura took a last look at the roomy timber bungalow that had been his home on Great Tarakang since his arrival from Rabaul. It had originally been occupied by a German Lutheran missionary and, in many respects, Kimura was sorry to be vacating it. It enjoyed a splendid situation just above the beach – where the major had swum most mornings – and it boasted much more in the way of home comforts than he would find on Little Tarakang. In spite of this, Kimura looked forward to a more Spartan existence on the island across the straits as more fitting to the warrior's way. It was instilled into every officer trainee that an austerity of lifestyle was implicit in service to the Emperor – and a comfortable billet made Kimura feel guilty. True spiritual discipline could only be attained by daily hardship and a rejection of the things that made life easier.

One friend was to make the journey to the other island with him. Heiho was much too well-trained a dog to be just another of Great Tarakang's strays. Kimura suspected that he had once been the property of the German missionary and had been left behind when the island had been evacuated. The dog had been in sole residence when Kimura had taken over the bungalow and had happily adopted the Japanese officer, following him everywhere.

In shape and size, Heiho looked like a fox: his coat was the same reddishy-brown but his face lacked the sharp snoutiness. The nose was more snub and, consequently, the face had an altogether friendlier appearance. It had not pleased Heiho at all to be left behind when Kimura had made his forays to Little Tarakang or his visits to Colonel Watanabe's headquarters – but, on Kimura's return, the welcome had always been ecstatic. It had been Lieutenant Niguchi who had suggested that the dog's attachment to Kimura entitled it to honorary induction to the 73rd Engineers, an idea that had amused Kimura, and inspired him to accord the dog the rank and name of Heiho, army auxiliary.

Heiho had seemed to sense for about a week before the day that Kimura was on the move and had dogged his new master's footsteps in a most plaintive way. The animal's devotion had been so insistent and its demeanour so pathetic that Kimura had resolved to take Heiho with him.

So it was that when Kimura set off for the harbour, preceded by two soldiers pushing a handcart containing his equipment, Heiho trailed anxiously at the major's heels. This time the dog did not have to be restrained from following his master on to the waiting supply barge. He leapt nimbly aboard and ran sure-footedly to the bows, where he sat casting repeated glances back over his shoulder as if to ask why the ropes were not being cast off.

The dog's presence was the first hint Ross received that Major Kimura had returned to Little Tarakang to take up residence. He was working with the other prisoners, hauling and stripping trees which the Japanese soldiers had felled, when the fox-like dog appeared from nowhere and nuzzled his bare leg playfully. At first, he thought the animal was wild but the furiously wagging tail belied the supposition. He knelt and rubbed the dog's ear, much to Heiho's delight. Ross did not realise that the dog was accompanied until the voice spoke behind him.

"The silly brute is not yet a good soldier of Nippon," said Kimura. "He does not bite the enemies of Nippon. He tries to overpower them with friendship."

Ross rose and turned to face Kimura. He bowed to the Japanese officer with deliberation.

"Perhaps dogs are wiser than men," he said. "Good soldiers can be made. Good friends have to be earned."

Ross' answer pleased Kimura. It was strange how the dog had sought out the sea captain as a friend as it had sought him out for a friend.

"The captain is philosopher?" said Kimura with the glimmer of a smile. He made the word sound like "phirrossafah".

"The captain is a hauler of trees," Ross replied with an ironic smile.

Kimura stiffened.

"The captain thinks it is ignoble to work with his hands for Nippon?"

"Only philosophers think," said Ross. "Haulers of trees who work from sunrise to sunset have few thoughts other than the pain in their backs. If a hauler of trees were allowed to think, he might ask himself, 'Is my master a wise man or a fool?'"

Kimura's eyes narrowed in puzzlement.

"The captain speaks in riddles."

Ross gave a little bow.

"The honoured major must forgive this unworthy hauler of trees for thinking like the captain of a ship." He spread his hands in a gesture of apology. "He thinks like a captain because once he had a ship and men called him 'Master'. It was his great concern that his men worked well for the ship and respected him at all times . . ."

Kimura's puzzlement was still as great as ever. He made an impatient gesture with his hand, urging Ross to continue.

"As master of a ship, this one who is now a hauler of trees found that by driving his men too hard less work was done and master did not have respect of his men. But honoured major knows how master solved problem . . .?"

Kimura was not sure that he did know, but he nodded intelligently, anxious not to appear slow on the uptake. Ross helped him out.

"Honoured major is right. Master said to men: 'I will allow you more rest. I will see that when you are hungry, you get sufficient food, and when you are thirsty, you are allowed to drink. For this, the men respected the master and they worked harder than ever before . . .'"

Ross stopped, his instinct telling him that he was in danger of overplaying his hand, if he had not already done so. Kimura was no fool and it was plain that the penny had at last dropped. He now saw the reason for Ross' careful obliquity. The captain was not coming straight out and saying that the prisoners were being overworked and underfed. Nor was he even complaining that this was the case. All he was doing was paralleling his present activity with his previous position and inviting Kimura to come to his own conclusions. The captain was a cunning devil. He knew how most Japanese – and Kimura was no exception – hated criticism of Nippon or the Nipponese way of doing things, but he had been careful not to criticise either. Kimura was torn two ways. He was annoyed at what he felt was an attempt to con him and yet he felt grudging admiration for the subtlety of the attempt. His response was to assert his position.

All work had come to a standstill as the two men had conversed. Both Japanese soldiers and prisoners had stopped what they were doing and were watching the pair with curious eyes. Kimura now looked fiercely about him and spoke angrily to a sergeant, who went snarling into groups of soldiers and prisoners alike with exhortations to get on with their work.

"If it pleases me, we will talk again," Kimura said abruptly to Ross. "Now, captain must work hard like other peoples."

He turned and marched off with Heiho at his heels.

He spent most of the afternoon in earnest discussion with Lieutenant Niguchi. That evening, the prisoners were paraded to

102

pay their respects to the Rising Sun flag as it was lowered from the pole that had been erected at the encampment established near the inlet where the *Machiko* lay. When the ceremony was over, Lieutenant Niguchi read from a sheaf of prepared documents.

To the tired prisoners, the statement seemed endless. There was a long preamble about command of the island being taken over officially that day by Major Kimura, and there were a hundred and one rules which had to be observed. For all of them, the punishments listed for default appeared to be either ten years' imprisonment or death.

Then the prisoners were told that, on some unspecified future date, a ship would call and take them to an internment camp elsewhere in the Greater East Asia Co-Prosperity Sphere. Until that date, they would continue to make themselves useful with work that was essential for the Greater East Asia Co-Prosperity Sphere and its benevolent architects, the people of Nippon. Then Niguchi read out revised working hours: from eight in the morning until five at night with a thirty-minute break at midday. These were an improvement on the hours previously laid down by Niguchi and came as a pleasant surprise. There then followed a homily which attributed the new hours to the wisdom and benevolence of Major Kimura, who hoped that the prisoners would repay his kindness by increased efforts and harmonious co-operation.

As Niguchi laboured through this part of the statement, Ross' eyes caught those of Kimura, who was standing a little way behind his lieutenant. Kimura stared back at Ross without the slightest glimmer of expression on his face. His eyes betrayed only the merest gleam when Ross inclined his head in a barely perceptible movement. It was acknowledgement that the tree-hauler appreciated the wisdom of the concession and made no claim on its authorship.

As the ruler of Little Tarakang, Major Kimura ordered as the first base for his projected operations the establishment of quarters for both his troops and his prisoners which were more adequate than the makeshift shelters first erected. He chose carefully the sites for both and planned their layout.

The prisoners were to be housed on flat ground that required little clearing to the east of the first of the basin's inlets he had searched for the *Machiko*. His soldiers were to occupy slightly higher ground, adjacent to the prisoners' quarters and overlooking them. This "village" took shape in a very few days and owed something of its architecture to the style favoured by the native islanders of the Tarakang group. Base walls were constructed from the abundant coral and into these walls timber uprights were embedded to support the roof frames. Creepers were used as binding and the upper walls and roofing were finished by weaving palm leaves between bamboo slats.

The Japanese quarters were given more permanence and a rather better finish by greater use of timber framing than in the captives' buildings. The prisoners' area was staked out and a perimeter marked but not enclosed with barbed wire. They were simply advised that they would be shot on sight if seen outside the perimeter unescorted during the hours of darkness.

By the standards being set in other prison camps within the Greater East Asia Co-Prosperity Sphere, life for Kimura's captives was not too harsh during the early months on Little Tarakang. Their food, while being monotonous and well below their customary dietary standards, was adequate. Their work was arduous enough, especially to those unaccustomed to physical labour in the hot tropical sun, but it was kept within tolerable limits. Just how tolerable these limits were, they were to discover later. Their Japanese guards, while doing little to improve their comfort or wellbeing, displayed little cruelty towards them. The isolated cases of physical violence arose largely from Japanese army custom and were not unduly severe. It was quite customary for the Japanese squad leaders to discipline the soldiers under them by face-slapping or making them run round and round their parade area with full packs, and some of the Japanese employed similar "corrective measures" with the prisoners they supervised. These occasional incidents were not part of a concerted effort to be tough with the prisoners and were the acts of individuals with a bullying streak or private soldiers elevated to the unusual position of being able to dish out a little violence for a change from being on the receiving end.

The comparative mildness of the conditions stemmed directly from the relationship which sprang up between Ross and Kimura. The Japanese admired the European's calm authority as the prisoners' leader. With his own, Ross was always in command – and yet he never vaunted himself, never bullied. He led by example. He never asked others to do anything which he was not prepared to do himself, no matter how menial or humbling it appeared to be. He was always first to show the way, demonstrating time and again that true authority stemmed from an absence of self-pride. It came from a self-effacing humility.

In his dealings with Kimura, it was Ross' capacity to be humble without ever appearing servile that intrigued the Japanese major more than anything else. It was not, in Kimura's experience, characteristic of the Anglo-Saxon races. They tended to be arrogant in their superiority, especially in their relations with nationalities whose skins were not white. Memory of incidents that had made him burn with shame had helped ease the many misgivings Kimura had had about Japan making war on the British and the Americans. They had to be taught that the Nipponese people, at least, were not their inferior.

Although Kimura had been in the army since 1937, he had never had much time for the *Sakura-Kai*, the Cherry Society, nor the Black Dragon movement, whose activities of political assassination and double-dealing had paved the way for the militarist extremists to take over government of the country from the democrats. At the same time, he had had considerable sympathy for the twin philosophies on which the militarists had based the most potent of their propaganda. These were the principles of *Hakko Ichiu* and *Kodo*, on which the Japanese Empire had been founded some six centuries before the Roman Empire had come into being.

Hakko Ichiu was the admirable moral goal of making the world into one big happy family. *Kodo* was the way in which it could be achieved: the noble or kingly way, through devoted service to the Emperor-God. A younger Hitoshi Kimura had thought it strange that in order to take the first steps along the road to making the world a happy family, factions in the army had found it necessary to murder members of the Japanese Government who disagreed with them. But, then, politics had never interested him greatly. He found himself drawn in too many directions at once. He would find himself agreeing with one political argument on one day of the week and then, on the next day, being in total agreement with the well-constructed counter-argument.

Spending three years away from Japan in the mid-thirties had not so much broadened young Hitoshi Kimura's outlook as confused it. He had felt no strong vocational pull to be a doctor. It was more a case of his father persuading him that this was what he should be. Consequently, he had spent a year at Berlin University and then two more at the University of Edinburgh. It had all ended in disaster. The pain of his homecoming in disgrace, with no degree or qualification to show for all his hard work, lived with him to this day. His escape to become an officer-cadet in the army and his subsequent advances in rank had restored some family honour, but Kimura felt destined never to come face-to-face with glory. Few could have craved death on the battlefield quite as much as he wished it for himself – but the army seemed intent on posting him to areas where no enemy was ever glimpsed.

Until the day he saw Ross. Why, now, did this one man have the effect on him that he did? He was an enemy, over whom he held the power of life and death, yet he was unlike other Europeans he had known. He had a sensitivity to what was proper. His respect for Kimura was not forced or born in fear. It was sincerely offered, as between equals.

The eagerness with which Kimura wanted to respond to Ross' company frightened him as he gradually realised where their enforced relationship was taking him. The more he saw Ross and the more they talked, the more Kimura knew what he wanted of his enemy. He wanted his friendship.

Seven

The God of Hitoshi Kimura

It was Major Kimura's hour of contemplation. He had bathed leisurely in his personal bath-house with no qualm of conscience that its plumbing and fitments had been salvaged from the engineers' bathroom on the *Machiko*. A shower-head and pipes had been plumbed into the small timber bath-house in such a way that the major's orderly could stand outside and pump water by hand from buckets which he replenished from a large metal storage drum.

Toilet complete, Kimura had eaten his evening meal alone. Then, after rinsing hands and mouth, he had retired to kneel at the tiny alcove in his hut that served as his personal shrine. This *tokonama*, or alcove, contained only one object: a Buddha-type statue carved from wood, This Bodhisattva was sitting, legs crossed, with a lion reclining at his side. He held a sword in one hand and a book in the other. He represented a god for whom Hitoshi Kimura had held a particular affection since he was six years of age and had read about him in a favourite illustrated story book.

It was this god that had helped Hitoshi Kimura, at eighteen, come to terms with his father's wish that he become a surgeon. Kimura, at the time, had not known what career he had wanted to follow. But his father had pointed at this statue of Monju Bosatsu and talked about the book representing learning and the well-known fact that Monju Bosatsu was the personification of compassion. If young Hitoshi became a doctor, he would be entering a profession for which much book learning was required and for which compassion for the sick and suffering was a prerequisite. In becoming a doctor, Hitoshi would not only be pleasing the gods as a whole but Monju Bosatsu in particular. To say nothing of the pride it would bring his father and the other members of the family.

107

Looking back now, Hitoshi Kimura allowed an unkind thought to cross his mind. His father had been clever in getting him to do as he wanted by getting at him through Monju Bosatsu, his favourite god. He knew that spirituality had little to do with his father's ambitions for him. He wanted the enormous prestige of having a surgeon in the family. Surgeons in Japan were treated almost like deities and the family's standing would have been tremendously enhanced if Hitoshi could have aspired to become the chief of a hospital.

Kimura bowed his head with remorse at allowing such an unkind thought of his father to have entered his mind. He prayed silently for forgiveness, cleansing from his head and heart all filial unworthiness. He tried to change the train of his thoughts, instantly suppressing more disloyal memory at the recall of how, when he had joined the army, his father had pointed again at his Bodhisattva in approval and drawn his attention to Monju Bosatsu's drawn sword.

But Kimura's contemplative flight from one disloyalty only took him to another – his friendship for the British sea captain, Ross. A prisoner was to be spat on, to be despised: the lowest form of life. Why then, oh why did he feel for this foreigner the emotions that should be reserved only for a brother?

Was it because he saw beauty in the idea of *Hakko Ichiu* and the goal of world brotherhood? Was it because war and death saddened him when the only death that he would truly welcome was his own? Was it because he was not involved enough in this worldwide war in which so many, but not he, had found the path to glory? Did others recognise in him a terrible weakness that made him unworthy of his soldier's uniform? Was that why he saw no battles? Had the army already earmarked him as lacking in the Samurai spirit, a coward to be kept in the rear?

Kimura agonised on the possibility that he had always been an outsider in a land where individualism was a crime on a footing with blasphemy. Square pegs were not tolerated in Japan because society had only round holes to accommodate them. Kimura knew that the three years he had spent in Europe had gone some way to "de-Japanising" him. He had found so much to admire there as well as to astound him that he had not known at the time what was happening to him. It had made him an apologist for Western ways; so much so that his family and his army friends had constantly reproached him for it.

Friends? He had made precious few in the army. Part of the

108

trouble was that he was a major-general's nephew. He had rejected as friends those officers who had deliberately cultivated him in the hope of preferment because of his uncle. And others who might have become friends had stood back from him, fearing that their overtures of friendship might be misinterpreted as toadying to a general's nephew. This had all made him a man apart.

He had been glad to get away from the officer fraternity on Great Tarakang because of his feelings of isolation. But was Little Tarakang an improvement? Niguchi could be amusing but he was such a fool, and so childlike. A little of Niguchi's company went a long way.

That left the British sea captain. It astonished Kimura how much he had come to look forward to his conversations with Ross. At first, he had ordered Ross to be brought to his quarters on two evenings a week to discuss things like complaints about the sanitary arrangements, food rations, interpretations of the rules for prisoners . . . a hundred and one topics arising from the day-to-day problems of running the camp and getting the work done satisfactorily. Kimura knew that he could easily have delegated all liaison to Niguchi – but he had preferred to do it himself. He had not expected to enjoy it as much as he had.

From two evenings a week, these sessions had developed to three, until eventually they had become daily and had not been confined to talk about digging latrines and issuing quinine tablets. The talk had ranged from religion and sport to families and past adventures. Kimura had invited the sea captain to play him at checkers – and now they played nearly every night.

Kimura had had to prise from Ross the revelation that he had been married to a Japanese-American. And he had grieved for him when Ross had eventually told him of her death. No wonder the Britisher was so sympathetic to Japanese custom and manner. It was because of Ross' Japanese marriage that Kimura justified to himself again and again the friendliness he felt for the foreigner.

Kimura knew what it was to have love for a foreigner. Had that not been the reason for his own disgrace? As he knelt before the figure of Monju Bosatsu, Kimura thought often about his youthful folly, his agony-filled love affair with fellow medical student, Rita Donovan. How innocent and correct it had all been, originating in the serious – almost obsessed – way they had approached their medicine studies. It had lasted a whole year, long enough for them to reach the conclusion that they wanted to share the rest of their lives together.

Then the explosion had come. Rita's parents, fervent Roman Catholics, had been shocked that she had even contemplated marriage to a pagan Japanese. Kimura's own family had been no less horrified. He had been ordered home at once. Rita, for all he knew, had continued at Edinburgh University and qualified as a doctor. He had been forbidden to re-enter the establishment wherein he might be further exposed to the corrupting influences of romance with a foreign woman. He had returned home to Japan dutifully but miserably. His shame at causing so much parental anger was intense, and he had only escaped that anger by joining the army and hoping for a quick death in China. But much of his shame had gone with him – and the army did not send him to China.

As he knelt in deep contemplation before the small effigy of Monju Bosatsu in the quiet of his quarters on Little Tarakang, Hitoshi Kimura thought seriously – not for the first time in his life – of repaying all his worldly debts by taking his own life. He recalled conversations he had had with Rita Donovan on the subject of suicide. Her attitude to it was almost incomprehensible. According to the Westerners' strange Christian god, suicide was a monstrous sin. It had amazed him that people could be so blind that they could not see the beauty of self-administered death. Perhaps, after all, his father had been right: that marriage to anyone brought up in such spiritual darkness could only have been disastrous for all concerned.

Kimura wondered what the English sea captain thought of suicide. He decided that he must talk to him about it at the earliest opportunity. The decision chased from his mind further thoughts of making an early end to his own life. Instead, he thought about checkers. The English captain had won their last three encounters in a row. It was time for a Japanese victory.

While Kimura knelt before his shrine, Ross was parrying questions as deftly and as reasonably as he could at what constituted an informal meeting of the Little Tarakang prisoners. They were sitting on the ground under the open-sided palm-thatched shelter which was euphemistically called the eating-hall. The meetings were held frequently for the exchange of ideas and to formulate positive policies in coping with their captivity and forced labour.

Ross had evolved to the leadership of the group by common

consent. He had never been elected. It had just happened as a natural consequence of his having been in command of the ship when the net had closed around them. Until now no one had contested his right as natural leader, but a growing agitation by one person had prompted Ross to have the matter brought out into the open instead of whispered about.

The person who had been doing most of the whispering behind Ross' back was Randolph Moorhouse. In the first months of their captivity, Moorhouse had kept a very low profile, as had Rawlings and the two up-country police officers. All of them were believed to be on a Japanese "wanted" list and had gone in fear of their identities being discovered.

Long before they had reached Little Tarakang, Ross had discussed with them the eventuality that the ship might not escape the Japanese net. They had agreed to assume fictitious identities while they were on the ship and to stick with these identities in the event of capture. Lieutenant Niguchi had listed the names of all the prisoners, including the fictitious ones, without question. The Japanese, it seemed, were not interested in names, only numbers. Particularly the numbers fit for work each day. The matter of handing over papers of identification had not been pursued by the Japanese when they were told only some had survived the fire which had destroyed the *Machiko*'s bridge and most of the midships accommodation. The proof of the devastation was there for them to see.

As time had passed and the Japanese had shown not the slightest interest in the names or past activities of the prisoners, Moorhouse had day by day felt more secure. But it pleased him not at all that Ross was the spokesman for all while he was relegated to the background with no more say than a black Papuan seaman. So, his mutterings about the "Number One" – as the Japanese styled Ross – grew in volume.

Now, after discussing at the informal meeting what Moorhouse considered trivialities, Ross had thrown the ball right into his court. For openers, Ross had said, "I would have to be deaf and blind not to realise that not all of you have approved of the way I have handled things. I have made mistakes and I'll probably make a lot more. But I do want you to know that while I have been your spokesman on this island, I have been guided by only one thing – what I honestly believed was the best for all of us. Now, it's possible that you feel someone else could do a better job. If you do, I want you to say so right out in the open. Here and now."

111

Ross stared firmly at Moorhouse.

"I believe you have some thoughts on the matter?" he said.

Moorhouse avoided Ross' eyes. He shrugged.

"I won't deny that I have had reservations about your assumption that because you are qualified to run a ship that's not much bigger than a Hull trawler you also have some God-given right to represent our interests to the Japanese Imperial Army. There are others of us who have had years of experience in government, dealing with Asiatics, and it's just possible that we might be better at it than you."

"The boss still gets my vote," said a voice from the outside of the circle. It was Ross' quietly spoken Filipino steward. "One of them Nip soldiers wanted to use me for bayonet practice and the boss stopped him. I'm not sure you would have bothered. But then, I'm just one of them Asiatics you know so much about."

Moorhouse threw an I-told-you-so look at Ross.

"I suppose that reasonable discussion is hopeless if it means that the only conclusions that can be reached are those forced by your crew members on the rest of us. We are in the minority – and I'm sure your people know better than go against anything you say."

"That's hardly fair," put in Paul Newton. "Captain Ross hasn't had to call for votes or a count of heads up to now to get the backing he's needed. He has spelled out the way things have been and what the options were. I think he's done a pretty good job. Better than anyone else could have done."

"I haven't suggested that any other arrangement be made," defended Moorhouse. "All I said was that I had some reservations. I still have reservations. I think he might have been firmer with the Japanese about the work we are forced to do. It is quite in contradiction to the Geneva Convention. They have no right to use us on what is military work. We are being made to aid their war effort."

"You know that the captain raised that with Major Kimura," Newton came back angrily. "You know damned well what the Japanese think of the Geneva Convention. They don't give ten cents for it. They never ratified it and they don't feel bound by it. Work or no food is what they told the captain and you'd better believe that they mean it."

"All right," said Moorhouse, "but there are other things. Why is it that when the Japs are harassing us into working like coolies, Ross is the one that gets leave to go off hob-nobbing with that ass,

112

Niguchi, or to tell that ape of a sergeant how the derricks on the ship should be rigged. I don't see him breaking his back . . ."

"Now we're getting near the truth," interrupted Newton. "You're just goddamned jealous!"

Moorhouse denied that jealousy had anything to do with it.

"None of us know what happens when he and that Kimura get their heads together," he went on heatedly. "Playing checkers now, they are! How cosy! Well, I've got a name for that and it's consorting with the enemy."

Ross tried to take the heat out of the discussion.

"There's something that everybody had better understand," he said, after he had intervened in placatory fashion. "I think I enjoy the respect of Major Kimura because I have been able to talk to him in language he understands. And I'm convinced that our well-being here hangs on my ability to retain his goodwill. It may go against the grain of some of you here – but I actually like him. Believe me, he is a very mild character indeed compared with some of the Japanese army officers I encountered up in China a few years back and I, for one, am glad that it isn't one of these toughies who is running this island. You may not like having to work like a coolie and bowing your head to every Japanese soldier whose shadow crosses your path but I do want you to realise that things could be a hundred times worse. Major Kimura has made us many concessions and he has kept his men in order but I have absolutely no guarantee that things will just go on as they are. The situation could change overnight – *but it's not going to change for the better no matter how badly you may think you're being treated now.* One stupid or tactless act on the part of any one of us could trigger off that change. That's one of the reasons why I don't mind playing Major Kimura at checkers when I'd just as soon be getting some rest. I want to do nothing to rock the boat. I advise all of you to take care that you don't rock the boat – because it won't be just one person who suffers. It will be all of us."

It was Woody, one of the two Australians, who broke the lingering silence that followed Ross' quiet but impassioned little speech.

"The skipper's right, folks," he said. "He knows the Nips better than any of us and he's a hundred per cent right that things could be a lot worse than they are. Rich and me, we've had a nodding acquaintance with the Nips and we know that them swords that the officers trail around are not just there for ornament. They think different from us and if something gets up their back, they

113

wouldn't care two pins about wheeling some of us out for an off-lolly session. Me? I want to keep my head right where it is at this moment — on top of my shoulders. I'm all for the skipper carrying on just like he's doing."

He gave a thumbs-up signal to Ross, who said nothing but gave him a brief nod of thanks. Woody had spelt out more graphically than he would have dared just what their situation was. It quickly became evident that Moorhouse was in a minority of one as far as a vote of confidence in Ross was concerned. Not that any vote was made. When Rawlings and the two police officers endorsed Woody's sentiments, Moorhouse slipped away quietly. With him went all opposition to the status quo.

Soon afterwards, Kimura's orderly arrived to escort Ross up to the major's quarters. On an empty ammunition box, the board and checkers had been set out. There were no cushions but two small tatami mats had been laid on the wooden floor. Kimura was already squatting on one. Ross bowed and, without rising, Kimura inclined his own head in reply. He indicated the vacant mat to Ross and nodded to his orderly, a signal that he should bring tea.

Kimura, resplendent in a kimono on which were emblazoned colourful chrysanthemums, looked a different man out of uniform. Gazing at him quietly as he sipped tea, Ross felt an almost unbearable pang of sadness grip him. There was something right in the strange atmosphere of companionship which hung over these constant meetings he had with Kimura and it all but obliterated what was wrong about them. But it was that small insinuation of "wrongness" that prevented either of them truly and whole-heartedly relaxing and enjoying them.

Reality was the intruder. Or, rather, an awareness of reality that could never be totally suspended. In peace, the two could have met, could have played checkers, could have conversed intelligently and with interest on a wide range of subjects. They could have built bridges between East and West. Because both, by nature, were builders rather than destroyers. Both were made uncomfortable by war because of its wholly negative qualities. The great irony was that, inasmuch as Kimura was the man in control of the situation and was governed by the stronger need of friendship, he could not reach out too far. Ross, because he was totally within Kimura's power, could never take the initiative. His part in the friendship had to be responsive, regulated always by the leeway Kimura was prepared to allow him. The restraining factor was not a reluctance on Kimura's part to declare friendship openly – as the knowledge in his heart impelled him to do – but a reluctance to step across the boundaries dictated by war. Kimura wanted to declare Ross "friend", but he never could and never did – because he, every bit as much as Ross, was a prisoner of war.

Thus, their frequent meetings, while cordial and often stimulating, lacked that final iota of harmony that would have signified total trust. Both knew that the reality of war intruded and always would, no matter how far it was temporarily relegated to the background. And both knew how fragile was the bond that joined them. Their final loyalties lay elsewhere. Neither had any illusion in how the other would declare himself if it came to the test. And both sensed that a test there would be. Its inevitability hung over the harmonious moments like a dark cloud.

On this particular evening, Kimura came closest to a full expression of the goodwill he bore towards Ross. It did not stem altogether from the fact that he managed to beat Ross at checkers, nor from the cups of *sake* with which he insisted they should celebrate this minor Japanese victory. He reminisced about his days in Edinburgh with considerable humour and then got on to the subject of the many similarities – both good and bad – between the peoples who inhabited the islands of Japan and the British Isles.

Then he got on to the subject of contemplation and how he found that sailors – who spent much of their lives contemplating empty oceans – and farmers, who lived from the land, had a spiritual sagacity that could not be found in urban dwellers who were protected from the worst havocs of Nature. From this subject, it was an easy step to the religions of the world and his arguments with Rita Donovan about suicide.

Christians held this strange concept that suicide was ugly and sinful and yet their god virtually committed suicide by submitting himself to execution like a common criminal. Kimura could see great beauty in such a painful and lingering death and could understand why people became Christians because of it. What he could not understand was why, ever since, Christians took such a censorious view of people who tried to achieve martyrdom by their own hand.

"Because life is a gift," suggested Ross, "the most precious gift. Is a gift not to be savoured and enjoyed to the full rather than thrown away?"

Kimura smiled.

"If life is the most precious gift we can receive," he countered, "surely it is also then the most precious gift that we can give away?"

Ross bowed to Kimura's logic.

"There must be a good answer to that. But, right now, I can't think of it. Tell me about your god, Major Kimura. You probably know a lot more about yours than I know about mine."

Kimura glanced towards the *tokonama* and the carving of the Bodhisattva.

"Ah, you mean my favourite god. That is Monju Bosatsu. He was very popular in Japan many hundreds of years ago but, now, he is largely forgotten. Do you know what he represents?"

Ross confessed he did not.

"He represents intelligence, compassion and contemplation," said Kimura. "Always you see him with a lion by his side. And look, he holds a sword and a book."

"How does the sword fit in with compassion?" asked Ross.

Kimura's smile was broad.

"It is a sword which you have used," he said. "And which I might be forgiven for holding before your eyes now."

"It's my ignorance you'll have to forgive," replied Ross. "I'm afraid I don't follow you."

"Of course – ignorance!" said Kimura triumphantly, seizing upon the word. "The sword is the sword of Intelligence. It cuts the darkness of Ignorance!"

"Touché," said Ross.

Kimura did not understand the term. When Ross had explained the meaning of the term as used in sword-fighting and further explained that, in argument, it signified a meaningful strike on target, Kimura made a polite bow.

"Touché," he acknowledged. He had learned something, too.

The dog, Heiho, broke up their tête-à-tête. He had been out foraging on the hillside above the camp. He barked his return and leapt between the two men with fiercely wagging tail, greeting both with equal affection and upsetting the checker board. When it was time for Ross to go, Kimura did him the unusual honour of escorting him personally down through the Japanese camp instead of sending for his orderly to do so. It was a glorious moonlit night with the lightest of breezes ruffling the palms in sighing praise. The dog gambolled playfully across their path, turning every so often to make sure that he was still accompanied.

Near one of the huts in the Japanese camp, a group of soldiers were clustered round one of their number who was singing a plaintive song to his own accompaniment on a harp-like instrument. It was a sad song about two young lovers who had to say

116

goodbye and would not meet again until the trees were again heavy with cherry blossom.

Ross could not follow the words. Like many Japanese songs, the words had a variety of interpretations.

"It sounds a very sad song," he commented to Kimura.

"It is a very old one," Kimura replied. "It speaks of the fleeting nature of the pleasures of life. How quickly they come and how quickly they are over."

"Yes," Ross agreed absently, his head cocked to one side listening to the singer and trying to make out the words. "Fleeting . . ." he repeated. "That's a good word. Not a word that's used often . . . except in poems."

"Perhaps a better translation of what the soldier is singing is fugitive," said Kimura. "*Hai* . . . fugitive. Like a criminal who runs swiftly to escape capture. Listen . . . he sings it now . . . 'The experience of pleasure is *fugitive* – as short is the time of the cherry blossom.' " He shook his head. "Yes, it is sad. But it is very beautiful."

They paused for a moment above the prisoners' camp, which was in total darkness and quiet as the grave. Behind them loomed the dark height of Mount Taki, with a light swatch on its lower slopes where soldiers and prisoners had cleared away hundreds of trees to drive a road to the summit. To the west, the masts and funnel of the *Machiko* were silhouetted against the sky. She lay silent, having been unloaded and stripped at deck level to act as a floating wharf where Kimura's materials and equipment were landed from barges ferrying from Great Tarakang. The cargo from the holds was piled at the forest's edge covered in tarpaulins. It awaited Kimura's careful scrutiny and selection. He had already earmarked some mining engineering equipment for use by his soldiers. It would never see its assigned destination in New Guinea now. What Kimura did not want from the cargo would await an order of disposal from General Headquarters in Rabaul, once he had compiled an inventory. It would probably be shipped back to Japan.

The two men bowed their goodnights and Ross hurried on alone across the open ground of the prisoners' camp. Even as he crossed the short distance, the tropical night changed. There was a stirring of wind and a big black storm cloud dropped low over Mount Taki and blanketed the brilliant moon. Ross shivered in the sudden cold. He felt a chill of omen, as if more than the weather was about to change.

117

It was late the following afternoon, when Ross was toiling with a work party on the track that was being carved through the forest to the top of Mount Taki, that he was withdrawn and taken back to the Japanese camp. There, Niguchi was waiting for him. The young lieutenant was strutting around like a peacock, full of himself because Major Kimura had been recalled to Area Command and he had been left in charge of Little Tarakang.

"Honourable major has important business at headquarters," Niguchi informed Ross. "He say one thing before he go. Captain prisoner look after dog. Dog like you and not try bite. You clean dog every day. Honourable major say you look after dog, you not have to work. You just tell other people work. OK?"

It transpired that Heiho had taken unkindly to Kimura's departure for Great Tarakang and had tried repeatedly to follow him on to the barge. The dog had resisted attempts to remove him and had bitten at least one Japanese soldier on the hand. Niguchi found this vastly amusing.

"Dog not like Japanese too much – except Major Kimura. You bring him cookhouse every day. Get food for dog. Him Nippon soldier now, get rations like all Nippon soldiers. But must learn be good like Nippon soldier. You see, eh?"

Heiho had been tied up, appropriately perhaps, in the guard-house for his breach of discipline. He was pathetically grateful when he was released into Ross' custody and, from that moment, the pair became inseparable.

Ross told no one that he had been appointed a fulltime dog attendant and, as such, had been excused labouring duties. He knew that Kimura had rendered him a considerable personal favour – but it was not one of which he wished to take full advantage. The dog's attachment to him made that easy. He went out to work with the others as usual and the dog went with him. The actual care he required was minimal and so, too, were the so-called rations from the Japanese cookhouse. Heiho was adept at hunting for himself in the forest around the camp and, on those days when hunting was poor, he much preferred what could be stolen from around the cookhouse to what he was given.

A week after Kimura had gone, the prisoners were not marched up the hill to continue the road up Mount Taki. Instead, they were organised to help the erection of more long huts adjacent to their quarters.

No reason was given for this intense new activity, but none was needed when three barges arrived from Great Tarakang, packed

118

with Tarakangese islanders. There were a hundred islanders in each barge – men, women and children – and they were herded under guard to the new quarters, which proved scarcely adequate.

Ross tried to elicit the meaning of this influx from Niguchi but the lieutenant either did not know or he was not telling. He did, however, drop one snippet of information which set the *Machiko* prisoners speculating wildly. All he had said to Ross was, "Perhaps soon now ship come from Lae. Take you to Macassar."

For some reason, the prospect of moving from Little Tarakang induced an optimism that was almost euphoric. Ross did not share it. In fact, as each day passed and there was no sign of Kimura's return, his foreboding grew. It crystallised into genuine dread on the day that Major Tachibana arrived on Little Tarakang. With him came a weasel-faced lieutenant with a Hitler moustache who acted as personal henchman and interpreter. His name was Yoshimura.

On the day of Tachibana's arrival, the prisoners were assembled in one large group as the various working parties returned. When all had been accounted for, Tachibana arrived with Yoshimura and Niguchi in tow. The major then addressed the prisoners at some length in Japanese. When he had finished, Yoshimura stepped forward to translate.

"His excellency, Major Tachibana, compliments you on how healthy and well-fed you look and is pleased that conducting labours on behalf of His Imperial Highness has agreed with you so much. His Excellency has honour to be appointed by his Divisional Commander to redouble efforts of work on this island and thus make sure that it does not become bad example to other islands in Greater East Asia Co-Prosperity Sphere who have come under rule of Imperial Benevolence."

There then followed the details of a decree by Major Tachibana. Work was to commence at six-thirty in the morning and continue until the sun had set. The present generous rations of food for prisoners would cease forthwith because they greatly exceeded the amounts stipulated by regulations. Henceforth, they would receive two cups of rice per day and one dish of vegetables or soup. Fresh water would be restricted to one pint per person per day.

Discipline would be improved. The prisoners must school themselves in instant obedience to every command they were given or punishment would be severe. Any discourtesy to Japan-

119

ese personnel would also be punished severely.

It was when Yoshimura had finished his discourse that Major Tachibana spoke to Niguchi and pointed at the dog sprawled lazily at Ross' feet. Ross did not make out the soft-voiced question, but he followed Niguchi's answer.

The lieutenant explained in his ingenuous way that the dog was Heiho, an auxiliary of the 73rd Engineers Rentai and that the prisoner had been delegated to look after it and keep it clean.

Tachibana cut short Niguchi's elaborate explanation.

"Order the dog to come here," he commanded.

Perplexed, Niguchi shouted at the dog.

"Heiho . . . Kurra! Kurra!"

The dog lurched on to all fours on hearing his name but showed no inclination to leave Ross.

Major Tachibana became very agitated, directing a flood of invective at the unfortunate Niguchi. If the dog was an auxiliary of the 73rd Engineers, why did it not instantly obey the command of a Japanese officer?

Niguchi continued to call the dog. But Heiho took no notice.

"Go to him, boy. Go to him," Ross urged the dog, sensing danger in the situation. Heiho looked up at him, bewildered, and still made no move.

Major Tachibana turned away from Niguchi, his face cold with anger. He uttered a low-voiced command to the interpreter, Yoshimura. The weasel-faced interpreter drew his sword and charged towards Ross, who retreated a step, thinking the attack was coming against him. It was not. Yoshimura brought the sword down, cutting deep into the dog's shoulder. Then, with a deft thrust, he brought the weapon down a second time and skewered the unfortunate animal to the ground.

Ross moved to restrain the interpreter but at a word from Major Tachibana, two Japanese soldiers leapt at Ross and clubbed him to the ground with the butts of their rifles. Meanwhile, the dog squirmed helplessly on the impaling sword, squealing piteously all the time. Its struggles died as, an arm's length away, Ross struggled on to his hands and knees, half-blinded by blood gushing from a head wound into his eyes.

The taste of his own blood running down his nose and over his lips filled him with an anger such as he had never known. For the first time in his life, he tasted a desire to kill.

Eight

The Savage Time

The aircraft banked to the east of Mount Taki before dropping almost to sea level for the run-in towards the airfield on Great Tarakang. Major Hitoshi Kimura felt something akin to a glow of homecoming as he saw the familiar cone-shaped peak. It would be good to get back to Little Tarakang. He could not understand the strange hunger he had for its isolation and remoteness. It drew him like the wilderness draws back desert-dwellers after an enforced stay in a big city.

The pleasures of Rabaul had palled on him after only a few days, although the special training course for senior officers had been interesting enough. There had been plenty of passionate discussion on some of the ideas now filtering down from Supreme Command in Tokyo, particularly on the revolutionary concept of Pacification Detachments. These new units represented a style of fighting that was totally foreign to the Japanese traditions of warfare. Something of a cross between what the British called "Commando Units" and the Filipinos called "guerrillas". There was no Japanese word for the new style of fighting, so alien was it. The staff people called it *yukegi-sen*. On the whole, the idea was dismissed contemptuously by most of the officers to whom Kimura had spoken. Engaging in military operations in which the prime object was staying alive and striking only where the enemy was weakest went right against the grain of men who had been schooled to hurl themselves at the enemy where he was strongest.

Kimura blamed his "occidentalism" for seeing a certain logic in the formation of Pacification Detachments. Why waste that most precious commodity, manpower, to achieve an objective that – with some forethought and ingenuity – could be won with as little loss of life as possible? Kimura knew, however, that another factor had entered his thinking. He had been stunned with sad-

121

ness to learn that his uncle, Major-General Tomitaro Horii, had suffered a crushing defeat from the Australians in New Guinea and was himself dead. For the first time, Kimura had suffered treasonable inner doubts about the invincibility of the Japanese Imperial Army. This inner defeatism shamed him – but it would not go away. Facts simply forced him to face the truth that the mood in Rabaul had undergone a change since his last visit there.

Then, the talk had been all about how the flag of Nippon would be flying over Port Moresby by midsummer and how 1943 would be the year of the conquest of Australia. But the Japanese extension of the Greater East Asia Co-Prosperity Sphere had suffered its first major setback when the advance had been halted only a few miles from Port Moresby. In possibly the most appalling battleground in the world – the disease-ridden forests and precipitous roadless mountains of New Guinea – the resolute and unforgiving Australians had pushed the Japanese back. They had recaptured Kokoda and forced General Horii's supplies-starved troops back over the Owen-Stanley range.

It was some consolation to Kimura that his uncle had not voluntarily retreated from the high mountain ridges. The order to withdraw had come from Rabaul, where the Theatre Command had realised that they could not provide General Horii with the men and the food and the ammunition that he needed.

Fierce battles in which no mercy was sought or given were fought over nameless mountain ridges in a wild, trackless land. The Japanese were broken at a virtually unknown geographical location called Eora Creek and their retreating columns had found their way back across the Kumusi River gorge made almost impossible by the destruction from the air of the Wairopi suspension bridge. Tomitaro Horii, astride his magnificent white horse, had tried to lead his men across the white tumult of Kumusi waters and had been swept away and drowned.

Kimura remembered his uncle's words: "Do not be too impatient for death." He found a comfort in them now that he had not at the time of their utterance. Why had he been so eager to reach for that final embrace that all men know anyway? What has begun, must end. Kimura sighed. He was beginning to think like the British sea captain, Ross. He wondered what Ross would think of the Japanese reverse in New Guinea. That was something Kimura would never ask him, for reasons of pride. And, perhaps, because he felt the answer might reveal unwelcome truths. There was nothing craven about Ross in defeat and Kimura suspected it was because he was inwardly fortified by visionary powers which saw far beyond immediate conflicts and considerations.

Kimura did not feel inferior to Ross. There had been times, however, when he had felt less wise. Yes, that was what Kimura respected most about the sea captain – his knowledge of men and the wisdom he had derived from that knowledge. Kimura could have destroyed Ross but his intuitive respect for wisdom in another had stopped him, and always would. Monju Bosatsu would never have destroyed a book from which he could learn.

He recalled a conversation he had had with Ross about wisdom. Kimura had remarked that most Sino-Japanese philosophers had taught that meditation was the noblest way to wisdom. Ross had been amused and had confessed wrily that he had acquired little wisdom in his lifetime but such as he had managed to acquire had come from bitter experience.

"I've always learned my lessons the hard way," he had said. "The more they hurt, the better they stuck. I'm afraid, Major Kimura, that I am always a little suspicious of wise people who have come by their wisdom painlessly. I always feel that their day of enlightenment is yet to come."

As the aircraft on which Kimura was a passenger taxied to a halt on Great Tarakang airfield, he was lost in his thoughts, trying to analyse why the gulf between him and his fellow-officers seemed to have widened in Rabaul. Was it because of Ross? Was it because of his uncle's death? Was it a combination of many things?

Everybody in Rabaul looked on the defeat in New Guinea as an unfortunate setback. Kimura – perhaps because he had always looked on his uncle as indestructible – sensed something more than just a setback. His instincts told him, although he did not want to believe it, that the high tide of Japanese expansion had been reached. That there was only one way for the tide to go now – and that was the other way. Kimura had felt apart from the exultation with which so many of his colleagues in Rabaul had been gripped: an elated certainty that their tiny nation could humiliate and destroy the Anglo-Americans. He had seen a band of ragged Australian prisoners herded through the streets so that the native population could gawk and jeer at the humbled whites. Kimura had turned away from the spectacle with distaste. His interpretation of the code of Bushido was that the vanquished be treated with honour, not paraded like cattle.

The super-confidence of his comrades had brought to mind a saying of his Scots landlady when he was a student in Edinburgh.

He had arrived at the breakfast table one morning in high spirits, humming a melody that was all the rage in all the local dance-halls. The landlady had frowned at such early-morning happiness.

"Sing before your breakfast and you'll cry before your tea," she had admonished. It had struck him as an odd aphorism and he had been puzzled by it. In Rabaul, it had become crystal clear. The euphoria of Japan's Pacific conquests was still high enough among his countrymen to discount the New Guinea disaster as just a minor and temporary reverse to be taken in their stride. Kimura hoped it was, too, but he feared otherwise. It was tempting fate to be so arrogant in the first flush of victory. The shoguns of the War Ministry had warned the nation that the war to establish and defend the New Order in Asia could last for a hundred years, so it behoved the officers of the Imperial Forces not to be carried away by early successes, magnificent as they were. The struggle had only begun. Kimura detected in the attitudes of his compatriots an element of "singing before breakfast" and he had stood aside from it. Like the British sea captain, Ross – whose capacity for self-detachment from short-term expediency he admired – he tried to fix his eyes on more distant horizons. And his uncle's death was an omen of weeping in the evening.

Kimura was roused from his introspection by the bowing figure of the aircraft's pilot. Did the major not wish to leave the plane now that they were safely at Great Tarakang?

Kimura rose, embarrassed by his absence in reverie, and thanked the pilot more effusively than was necessary for their safe journey. Thirty minutes later, he was at Colonel Watanabe's Area Headquarters giving the colonel a detailed report of his expedition to Rabaul.

Watanabe expressed admiration and envy for the military achievements of General Horii and for the liberation of his soldier's spirit by death. His divine status among the spirits of his ancestors was assured. Watanabe also had some good news to impart for Kimura's personal benefit.

The major would be pleased to know that the tiresome business of the prisoners on Little Tarakang had been happily resolved in his absence. No less a personage than the Divisional Commander had placed one of his ablest officers, a Major Tachibana, in charge of all civilian and prisoner labour in the area. This would free Major Kimura from the degrading task of supervising the health and welfare of these worthless people and allow him to concentrate his energies on soldier's work. There was much of the latter to be done.

Colonel Watanabe enjoyed drawing attention to his own importance by lecturing his officers on the importance of Great Tarakang, his personal bailiwick, to the supply routes and lifelines on which the armies in the Bismarck Archipelago depended. He treated Kimura now to a lengthy discourse on the air base's vital strategic location, both for defence of the sea routes and for aerial attack on the enemy's land forces.

Watanabe regretted that he could not give Kimura an offensive function against the enemy. But, on Little Tarakang, with only a modest force at his command, Kimura was being entrusted with a key role in preserving and defending the vital air base. Once the whole of Papua and New Guinea had fallen to the Imperial forces, the importance of the Tarakang base would diminish. But until it did, he was not to consider that he was being isolated in a backwater. Nothing could be further from the truth. The utmost priority had to be given to the completion of the artillery locations and suitable defence bunkers, also the radio and meteorology stations. These had to be concealed from the air in such a way that enemy air reconnaissance would be unable to detect their presence. There were signs that enemy air and sea strength was growing since the masterstroke against Pearl Harbor a year ago, and it was possible that Great Tarakang's air base could come under attack from the sea as well as the air in the near future. In that eventuality, Major Kimura's versatile Engineers company would come into their own because, not only would they have to supply the personnel to man the 150mm batteries, but they would have to be trained to defend their island in both static and mobile roles.

In view of the reorganisation, Kimura's force was to be redesignated the 93rd Independent Coastal Group and, Watanabe emphasised, when he said "independent", that he meant precisely that. He said much more besides: of the need to provision for possible siege conditions in the event of supply lines being severed; of the advantages of new warfare training, such as the formation of small boat squads to repel landing ships by sailing into them with explosives; of husbanding the land of its natural resources. Kimura's head was reeling by the time the Area Commander had not only briefed him fully but had also managed to air most of his pet military theories, too. Much of it, Kimura realised, was aimed at boosting Kimura's own self-esteem – a kind of consolation for not getting the battle posting he had requested some months earlier. A lot of it, too, was connected with Watanabe's self-esteem. He saw himself as the greatest military genius since Masashige and always saw his own command as the one on which the fate of the Japanese Empire hinged. He was interested in Kimura's news from Rabaul about the New Guinea campaign – but not so much for such facts as Kimura was able to supply as to be able to air his own views on how it should success-fully be conducted.

"Your honoured uncle's death will be avenged," he assured Kimura loftily. "It is regretted now in Rabaul no doubt that his courage was not matched in diligence by those whose duty it was to maintain his supplies. There are heads bowed in shame that General Horii was ordered so far ahead of his base at Buna that any cadet in training school would have been shocked at what was expected of him. One does not lower a man over a thousand-foot precipice on a rope that is only two hundred feet long and expect him to reach the bottom with the lifeline still round his waist."

Kimura refrained from any comment that was in any way critical of Rabaul Command. On the day of his uncle's death, six hundred Japanese had died fighting on the rocky banks of the Kumusi River or been swept away in its turbulent waters. Only a few short months ago, he would have marvelled at the glory of it. Now, he saw it only as an appalling waste. For, militarily, it had achieved nothing.

He escaped eventually from the colonel's heavy presence with feelings of relief. His eagerness to be back on Little Tarakang was now acute. It astonished him that he could even admit to himself that all he longed for was the island's peace. Even more astonish-ing was the absence of shame in making the admission. The fact was that his character was flawed and he was beginning to accept the fact. He was sick of the army and its ways. He was sick of this war which had passed him by and was always being waged some-where over the horizon.

It occurred to Kimura that, perhaps, if he had married, he wouldn't have turned out to be such a lonely individual. Perhaps he would have found it easier to conform and accept things if there had been someone to whom he could have poured out his heart in a shared bed or intimate letter. But there was no one.

When he reached Little Tarakang, the Japanese camp had a deserted air. The working parties had not yet returned. Kimura summoned his orderly and told him to prepare the bath. Refreshed from it, he donned a white working shirt, a pair of fatigue breeches and slipped his sockless feet into an old and favoured pair of soft-leather knee boots. He walked down through the camp to the long hut which had been divided by three flimsy partitions to serve as company office, radio room, and quartermaster's store. A pile of signals and ordinances, all neatly numbered, had accumulated in Kimura's absence. He settled down to study them.

He had scarcely started when he heard the scream. It came from some distance off – from lower ground, where the prisoners were quartered. Kimura strode outside. More screams pierced the air, punctuated by a high-pitched wailing. Kimura strode briskly towards the sound of human pain.

The prisoners' space was deserted, as it normally was in late afternoon. There was no sign even of the guard who permanently manned at least one of the two guard-huts strategically sited at the two inland corners of the staked perimeter. Kimura realised that the screams were coming from just beyond the further guard-hut. He hurried towards it. His steps slowed as he recognised one of his own men, First-class Private Yoshida, standing over a figure cowering on the ground. Yoshida was wielding a stout bamboo stick and, even as Kimura approached, he brought it down hard on the exposed fleshy thigh of Ruth Gamage. She was scrambling on hands and knees and her tattered denim skirt was bunched round her waist, revealing a white triangle of panties and a pale expanse of buttock.

She screamed as the bamboo raised a fierce weal in her flesh. It had struck her with a sharp slapping sound. Yoshida stared down mesmerised at the mark, eyes bulging. He had not heard Kimura's approach and almost fell over from surprise when he heard his name snarled at him from a few feet away.

He leapt to attention and, in his haste, let the bamboo rod fall from his hands. Kimura picked it up and, in a sudden fit of anger, brought it down two-handed across his subordinate's shoulders. The blow knocked Yoshida sideways. Tears blinking in his eyes, he picked himself up and snapped rigidly to attention again. Kimura hurled the bamboo from him. It came to rest twenty yards away.

"Is this what a soldier of Nippon does when there are no American armies to fight?" Kimura stormed. "She is a holy woman who nurses the sick. Is she the best you can get to attack?"

127

"Major Tachibana's orders, sir. He said no one was to go near the disgraced Number One. The Jesus woman tried to take him water."

Kimura did not know what the man was talking about. It was not until he half-turned that, from the corner of his eye, he saw Ross. Thirty yards away, towards the forest's edge, a timber crossbar had been lashed between two palm trees at a height of about eight feet above the ground. Dangling from the crossbar so that his toes touched the ground and no more was a man whom Kimura slowly recognised as Ross. He was roped by the wrists and his swollen and bloodcaked face made recognition difficult. His feet and upper body were bare. His sole protection from the burning sun was a torn and mud-streaked pair of trousers that had once been white.

Kimura paled with shock.

"Cut him down!" he ordered.

Yoshida made one glance at Kimura, as if he was about to say something. The look on Kimura's face made him think better of it. He hurried across and untied the rope by which Ross had been hoisted. Then he unfastened the rope around the sea captain's wrists. Ross lay where he had been lowered, unable to move. Kimura ignored Ruth Gamage – who kneeled with her head in her hands, weeping softly – and strode over to look at Ross.

"Give him water," Kimura ordered Yoshida.

The soldier had to fetch a waterbottle from the guard-hut. He cradled Ross' head and trickled water over his dried and swollen lips. He gazed up at Kimura and his eyes lit briefly with gratitude. Kimura looked down at him, saying nothing. Finally, he turned away.

"Take him to his quarters," he said to Yoshida. "And tell the woman to go to hers."

He turned and walked swiftly across the open compound area, a fierce glower on his face. Yoshida watched him go. The soldier could still feel a sharp bite of pain across the shoulders where Kimura had struck him. He consoled himself that, considering the temper that was boiling in Kimura, he had got off lightly. But someone was going to catch it. There was murder in Kimura's eyes. Maybe that new major was for it – but old Kimura had better beware of that one. A real tiger he was! Not like that creep of a lieutenant, Yoshimura. He was more snake than tiger. Somebody would stamp on him good and proper one of these days. Well, let the officers fight it out.

128

Yoshida hoisted Ross round one shoulder and began to drag him towards his hut. From the corner of his eye, he saw Ruth Gamage watching him.

"Kurra! Kurra!" he shouted at her.

She approached fearfully. The soldier indicated that she should assist him. She took some of Ross' weight. Yoshida nodded approvingly.

"Yoroshii. Yoroshii." He beamed and, inasmuch as his human burden would allow him, he made a bowing movement. "Shitsurei itashimas," he said. He was saying he was sorry. She did not understand, but she gathered that he was in some way trying to be conciliatory. In spite of the pain from her beating, she managed a smile. Tears welled in her eyes.

"OK now. OK," she said, and felt impelled to embellish it with one scrap of Japanese she had gleaned from the soldiers. They seemed to use it as a greeting. "Buta no ko," she said tentatively, and then repeated it for good measure. "Buta no ko."

First-class Private Yoshida frowned deeply. Then he threw back his head and laughed uproariously. She could not understand the reason for his hilarity. She had merely done what the Bible had said she should do. She had shown willing to forgive those who persecuted her for the Lord's sake.

She had also called Private Yoshida the son of a pig.

Major Tachibana's smile was cold as he saluted and bowed to Major Kimura. There was no smile on Kimura's face as he returned the courtesies. His expression was as bleak as the Arctic. It did not change as Tachibana introduced the interpreter, Lieutenant Yoshimura.

"Lieutenant Niguchi said there were matters to be discussed," said Tachibana.

"Much has happened in my absence from the island," replied Kimura. "The honourable Tachibana has been most industrious."

Tachibana bowed slightly.

"A fighting man does not take kindly to being given the task of slavemaster, but His Excellency, the Divisional Commander, gave me direct orders on what must be accomplished. I obey my sacred duty without question."

"Without question?" commented Kimura airily, and then added with all the thrust of a barbed spear, "And without much exercise of the thought processes?"

129

Anger flashed in Tachibana's eyes.

"Perhaps honourable Kimura will explain that remark?"

It was Kimura's turn to give a perfunctory bow. A few strides took him behind one of the tables in the company office, where the confrontation was taking place. He picked up a sheaf of papers and then let them fall on the table again.

"Many ordinances . . . Dozens of new regulations . . . Orders on every subject from the issue of cartridges to the number of grains of rice in a daily ration. If we were fighting a war with paper, Major Tachibana, we could capture the whole of North America in a week."

Tachibana remained silent.

"I am an engineer," Kimura went on. "I build bridges and barracks and harbours. But I do not build with paper. I build with wood and iron and mortar and even atap leaves. And, for that, I need people: engineer soldiers, strong working peasant soldiers, civilian labour, prisoner labour."

"It is to intensify the labour efforts that I was sent to this island," snapped Tachibana. "I cannot properly express my amazement at the slackness and indiscipline that I found. I was tempted to make special reports to the Area Commander and to Division."

"What a great pity you didn't," said Kimura softly. "Because I am most interested in the results you have achieved." He paused briefly to let his words sink in. "Before you arrived, honourable Tachibana, the work here was a little behind schedule but it was going not too badly. We had only a small labour-force in addition to my own men but results were being achieved. There were no incidents. No epidemic or health problems. No reason to believe that, with the importation of more labour, the work could not be completed in record time. But what do I find after less than a month?"

Tachibana pursed his lips together tightly. He made no reply.

"I find that tree clearance alone, with an augmented labour-force of one hundred, is less than what we formerly achieved in one week," said Kimura. "I also find that your native labour-force has dwindled by twenty per cent through deaths in the period – a rate which, if it continues, will wipe them out and leave us without labour in a matter of months. And what do I find among the ship prisoners? Two deaths from natural causes and six unfit for work through sickness and broken limbs. You must be proud of what you have achieved so quickly, Major Tachibana. I find that even my own men have been affected by the epidemics and accidents and that nearly a quarter of them are confined to sick quarters. It appears that the wooden clubs you issued to all personnel for controlling prisoners were not limited to that particular activity and they started taking it out on each other. In the pursuit of your sacred duty, Major Tachibana, you have inflicted more casualties on my company than the British and the Americans together."

Tachibana stood, breathing heavily with suppressed rage. One hand was on his sheathed sword and the fingers clenched round the double hilt were a bloodless white.

"You go too far with your insults," he hissed at Kimura. "It does you ill to speak of casualties who have seen no battle. You speak to an officer who has been wounded eleven times with his face to the enemy and whose record is not to be examined by a so-called engineer whose bayonet has been kept for breaking open coconuts. I would remind you, Kimura, that you are not my superior officer and that although you may be technically in charge of this island you have no jurisdiction over me. I answer only to the Divisional Commander and, through him, to Tenno Heika – the divine person of His Imperial Majesty."

Kimura gave a slight bow of acknowledgement. It was so. The chain of command in the Japanese army was such that orders could only be issued by a direct superior and interpreted as coming from the Emperor himself. Thus, a mere lieutenant – given orders direct by a regimental commander – could ignore indefinitely any counter-instructions issued by a company commander, even although the latter shouted until he was blue in the face.

"I shall not exceed my orders, which are precise," Kimura told Tachibana coldly. "I shall also make it my business to see that, in the future, you do not exceed yours. Your job is to control and care for the labour-force. My job is to direct where and how it should be used."

"That is understood," snapped Tachibana.

"Good," said Kimura. "I should also like you to understand that from now on, no personnel of the Ninety-third Independent Coastal Group – which is under my command – will be available for guard duties. In different circumstances, it would have been normal to release men to supplement what you may consider is an inadequate guard-force of your own – but my men will be fully occupied in a rigorous training programme in addition to all the construction work that has to be done."

"This is outrageous," protested Tachibana. "You know that I

have less than a dozen men. My company was all but wiped out in New Guinea and this duty was given to them as a rest from battle. How can they possibly keep a watch on a hundred and fifty conscripts and prisoners for twenty-four hours a day?"

"That is your problem," said Kimura with a shrug. "Not mine."

"I shall go to the Divisional Commander about this. He said that I could count on every co-operation from the field companies of engineers for whom we supplied labour. Every conscript I raised would free a soldier for other duty. I have brought you a hundred Tarakang islanders, enough to liberate your entire company for other work. You can surely spare twenty men to help me keep the labourers at their work."

Kimura's smile was as icy as before.

"If you put the requisition for men to me in writing, I shall consider it. At the same time, you may wish to put yourself and your entire strength under the command of the Ninety-third Independent Coastal Group so that the duties of all personnel on the island can be dovetailed and organised in an efficient manner."

"I shall never submit to such blackmail," Tachibana snarled. "I would remind you that I command an infantry company. And no infantry company – not even one that has been reduced to the size of a squad – is going to play second fiddle to a bunch of road-makers!"

Again, Kimura shrugged.

"Then we must exist together side by side as best as we are able. You understand that it would be quite impossible for me to place my Independent Coastal Group under your command. It is a question of balance and proportion . . . Like asking the tail to wag the dog." Kimura's eyes narrowed. "And talking of dogs, Major Tachibana, was your company as proficient in New Guinea at killing Australians as your multilingual lieutenant is at killing dogs?"

The question punctured Tachibana's bluster just as he was blowing himself up for the next attack. He sagged visibly and he averted his eyes from Kimura's.

"I did not know that the stupid animal was yours. It did not have the sense to obey a simple command. I told Yoshimura to kill it."

"So I was told," said Kimura quietly.

"The prisoner whose job it was to look after the dog has been severely punished for failing to carry out your orders," said

132

Tachibana defensively.

"Of course," agreed Kimura. "Obviously the prisoner should have impaled himself on Yoshimura's bayonet rather than let the dog come to harm."

His irony was lost on Tachibana. Kimura had merely expressed with admirable lucidity exactly what the prisoner's duty was in the circumstances. Indeed, Kimura's attitude was becoming clear to Tachibana. The death of the dog was obviously at the root of his insolence and his non-co-operation. What a pity it was that a soldier as experienced as Kimura was allowing his entire military judgement to be clouded by a matter so trifling as the death of a pet. By morning, Kimura would probably be filled with regret at having behaved so insultingly to an infantry officer. Perhaps he, Tachibana, should make allowances. The last thing he wanted was a row which went all the way up to the Divisional Commander. Tachibana had not been exactly frank about the Divisional Commander's reason for relegating him to prisoner duties. It was no reward for having been so long in the thick of fierce fighting – more of a punishment for that trouble back in New Guinea. But Kimura didn't need to know about that.

Tachibana put forward his olive branch.

"Honourable Kimura, I humbly apologise for the death of your dog. I ask your pardon for the error." He stood penitently with head bowed.

"I understand that it was an error," said Kimura. "The matter is forgotten. But . . ."

Tachibana looked at him expectantly, wondering what pronouncement had yet to come. Kimura did not keep him long in suspense. He fished in the pocket of his breeches and withdrew what appeared to be a short studded strap. It was a dog collar.

"I bought this in Rabaul for my dog. I have no need of it now. Perhaps Lieutenant Yoshimura would like to have it? As a souvenir."

Tachibana held his breath as Kimura crossed the room to stand looking impassively into the weasel face of the interpreter. Yoshimura had listened in respectful silence to all that had taken place. Now he waited apprehensively, globules of sweat on his narrow forehead, wondering what could be coming next.

"Stand straight, Lieutenant Yoshimura," ordered Kimura. As the lieutenant strained upright, Kimura fastened the dog collar around the little man's neck. Then he stood back and admired the ornament.

133

"It suits him, don't you think?" he said over his shoulder to Tachibana. Then, putting his face close to Yoshimura's, he hissed: "Inpu no ko!" Son of a bitch!

Kimura turned away from Yoshimura and the smile he directed at Tachibana was disarming.

"What is good for one dog is good for another," he said. "Mine was house-trained when I got him. Was yours?"

Without another word, he turned and walked out into the night. Yoshimura was trembling with shame. Tachibana's face was a study of puzzlement.

"I think Major Kimura has been too long in the sun," he said. "It has turned his brain."

Yoshimura jerked the leather collar from his neck and hurled it from him. He was almost weeping.

"I have never been more humiliated," he said bitterly.

Tachibana laughed. A short snorting sound. He stared hard at Yoshimura.

"You should have kept the collar," he said. "He was right. It does suit you."

The cluster of store huts was less than fifty yards from the nearest long-house occupied by Japanese soldiers. The huts were guarded by two sentries. While the squad leader was prowling around during the evening, these two guards patrolled opposite sides of the storage area and maintained a semblance of alertness. After the squad leader's final round around midnight, however, the diligence of the two sentries declined. They would linger at the point where their beats met, they would take the weight off their legs and they would talk. Cigarettes would be produced.

From a forested bank only thirty yards away, Big Rich had a perfect view of the sentries' meeting-place. In the quiet of the hour after midnight, the Australian could hear the low murmur of the Japanese voices and see the varying glow on their cigarettes as they inhaled at irregular intervals. The conversation of the two men was desultory and Rich wondered what they talked about. The sheilas they'd left back in Tokyo or wherever they came from?

There was a rustle of foliage and Woody, bellying along like a snake, appeared at Rich's side.

"All quiet?" breathed Woody.

"All quiet," Rich confirmed. "You were quick."

"I got two tins of condensed milk. I could have taken two crates

134

of the stuff. Let's get out of here."

Silently, the two Australians stole deeper into the forest and made a wide circle of the Japanese camp. They continued the detour of the prisoners' camp, emerging from cover close to the shore on the eastern side of the perimeter. Then they belly-crawled to an atap-screened pit, referred to as the *benjo*. Its function was unmistakable and indicated clearly by the appalling odour of human excrement which hung permanently around its vicinity. From the *benjo*, the two men made no attempt at concealment and strolled nonchalantly over to the line of sleeping huts. They made for the smallest of three: the hut reserved as a sick bay.

At one time Ruth Gamage and the baby had had the hut to themselves but, because of an increase of illness and injury among the prisoners, the sleeping platforms in the hut had been increasingly occupied by prisoners who were unfit for work. Ruth and the baby had been relegated to a roughly screened-off section at one end. It had been Kimura who had appointed the American girl as the prisoners' sick bay orderly: a comparative sinecure which had allowed her ample time to care for her tiny charge. Tachibana's arrival had dramatically increased her workload.

Ruth stirred at the sound of a scratching noise on her screen. Pausing only to confirm that the baby was still asleep, she peered round the screen.

"Who's there?" she whispered.

"It's the Australian Expeditionary Force, Miss Gamage," Woody replied softly. "We got something for you."

She emerged from behind the screen and Woody thrust two tins of condensed milk into her hands.

"It's for the little one," he said. "You got a safe place to hide it?"

"I'll find one. What is it?"

"Tinned milk. And there's plenty more where it came from. How's the skipper?"

"Very weak. But he's been sleeping."

"How about yourself, Miss? You took quite a beating."

"The Lord endured a far worse scourging than I. Mine has cleansed the fear from my heart. I know now that it was God's will that I come to this place. So that I could atone for my sins and carry out the work of His Kingdom here."

"Well, just as long as you're OK," said Woody uncomfortably.

"Who's there?" whispered a voice from the far end of the hut. "Is that you, Miss Gamage?"

"It's the skipper," said Rich softly. "We must have wakened him."

"I'll have a word with him," said Woody. He turned to Ruth Gamage. "You hide that milk and get back to bed, Miss. We'll see that the skipper's OK and be on our way. Goodnight now."

"There may be something I can do for him . . .?"

Woody gently assured her that he would let her know if there was and persuaded the girl to retire behind the screen. He tiptoed past the other sleeping casualties to where Ross was lying at the far end of the sleeping platform.

"It's Woodhouse and Richardson, Skipper. We were just handing in some extra rations for the bambino. How are you feeling?"

"Like a piece of fried meat," said Ross. "My arms feel like they've been pulled out of my shoulders."

"You were strung up for two whole days," said Woody. "You wouldn't have lasted another. You were babbling when they took you down the first night."

"I've lost all track of time. I don't remember being cut down either day. Two days, you say? I keep dreaming that I saw Kimura."

"You did see him," said Woody. "It was him that had you taken down."

"Has Tachibana gone?" asked Ross.

"No such luck, Skipper. He was up to his tricks this afternoon. Made that black seaman of yours, Kima, run up and down the hill carrying a whacking great rock. But that Kima's tough as an old boot. He only fell twice and got a couple of kickings. He swears he's going to have a few Jap heads on a pole one of these days. He will, too, if he gets half a chance."

Ross stared up at the shadowy shape which was Woody.

"You said something about getting extra rations. For the baby? In the middle of the night?"

Woody grinned in the darkness.

"The Nips don't have locks on their store huts. They're not going to miss a couple of cans of milk. If they do, they're going to think it was their own lot that pinched them."

"Tachibana would have you cut up in little pieces if you got caught," warned Ross.

"He has to catch us first," said Woody lightly.

When, finally, the Australians slipped away, Ross lay in the darkness staring up at the roofing of the palm-thatched hut. His flesh seemed to be bathed in fire and every muscle and joint in his

136

body was torn with pain. He tried to concentrate his mind away from his body, as he had tried to do when suspended out there in the blazing sun of day. It worked partially, this detachment of mind from body as if he dwelled outside it. He compelled the image of Machiko to come to him and, miraculously, she was there: soothing his body with soft caressing hands and whispering endearments and encouragement until she was the reality and the pains of the flesh were the dream.

But distant words kept intruding and brought him back to the conscious world of pain. He writhed on the wooden platform in discomfort as the words came to him with clarity from beyond the screen at the far end of the hut. Ruth Gamage was praying aloud to the God from whom she had fled.

". . . And I beseech thee, Lord Jesus, to forgive those who persecute us, as You forgave those who persecuted You. Turn Thou their minds from the darkness of ignorance and evil and help this Thy servant to shine as a light before them. Make me, O Lord, an instrument of Thy will, that I may find a place among Thy saints . . ."

Her praying did not fall on deaf ears. The baby at her side wakened and began to cry fitfully. He was hungry. Ruth abandoned praying to knock two holes in one of the tins of milk that the Australians had brought. Then, squeezing the milk out on to a finger, she let the child suck the finger.

Nine

Sons of Bushido

The strained relationship between the two Japanese majors, Kimura and Tachibana – which was to fluctuate between veiled truce and downright hostility – had little immediate effect on the day-to-day lives of the prisoners on Little Tarakang. Their days were endured, like lashes delivered with measured monotony: numbered strokes in a flogging without end. They worked, they slept. They worked, they slept. Each day differed little from the one that had preceded it, except that it was another day survived.

On a diet that was alien to them and quite inadequate, the prisoners quickly became prone to deficiency diseases which wasted their bodies and sapped away their strength. Unprotected at night from the ravaging mosquitoes, they collapsed and were racked by tropical fevers. Inevitably, death claimed its harvest and the small patch of hillside near the camp began to sprout with rough wooden crosses as week followed week.

Some diversions did occur. Three times in the space of three months, the survivors of the *Machiko* were mustered with their few belongings. They were told that a ship was coming from Lae to transport them to a new camp. Surabaya was the rumoured destination the first time. But no ship came. On the second occasion, they were to be taken to Haroekoe. On the third, Celebes.

But no ship came and no explanation was given. There was speculation on each occasion that the ship from Lae had sailed past the island in the night without stopping. Some argued that no ship existed, that the Japanese had no intention of moving them. Others said – and this was probably the closest to the truth – that the Japanese had got their communications all fouled up again.

After each excitement and its anti-climactic ending, life

returned to the same monotonous misery as before. The prisoners had only one consolation. Bad as their conditions were, they could have been worse. The evidence was right next door to them in the Tarakangese camp, where the death-rate from disease and brutal treatment was three times as great as their own. It was always easy to tell when the Japanese soldiers had been given an issue of *sake* because of the screams and sometimes shots which could be heard coming from the direction of the Tarakangese camp. It was always towards there that the soldiers gravitated after nightfall in their drunkenness. The attraction was the Tarakangese women.

Not all the women lured or forced into the forest or along the beach were prepared to accommodate a posse of lust-crazy soldiers and some paid with their lives. Frequently, too, their menfolk were enraged out of passivity by what was going on and made brave but futile attempts to intervene. If Major Tachibana objected to the periodic bouts of rape, murder and mayhem that occurred, he seemed to be more concerned about the disturbance of the peace than the brutalities which caused it. He issued an order to his men insisting that the favours of the Tarakangese women should be rewarded, even when offered freely.

Certainly, it was Tachibana's infantrymen who were usually the instigators of these nocturnal forays to the Tarakangese camp, although Kimura's engineers were by no means blameless. The latter were only too happy to accept the "hospitality" of the Tarakangese women which Tachibana's guards offered with proprietorial generosity.

Kimura did not approve of what was happening but was reluctant to cross the strict demarcation line of command which he had drawn. The prisoners and the forced Tarakangese labour were Tachibana's responsibility. Indeed, Kimura was acutely aware that Tachibana had used the Tarakangese to win first blood off him in their undeclared status war.

Tachibana had found a way round Kimura's refusal to release men for guard duties by enrolling a couple of dozen Tarakangese as auxiliaries. By equipping these men with fatigue tunics, armbands and truncheons, and giving them extra food, he had purchased a ready-made police force who were only too ready to break the heads of their fellow-islanders at a nod from Tachibana.

In the *Machiko* camp, Tachibana – with the same brand of psychological cunning – had detailed Randolph Moorhouse as chief spokesman for the prisoners and a guarantor of their docility. The zeal with which Moorhouse consequently ensured that the prisoners complied faithfully with all Tachibana's demands made his previous accusations against Ross of "consorting with the enemy" appear highly hypocritical. But he saw his new role only as an overdue acknowledgement by the Japanese that he was a natural leader of men.

Thus it was that while most of the prisoners and most of the Japanese soldiers were aware only of animosities and what appeared to be occasional personality clashes on their own sides of the fence, a much subtler conflict was beginning – with Tachibana and Moorhouse on one side and Kimura and Ross on the other.

Kimura's role – in trying to improve the lot of the prisoners – was especially subtle inasmuch that not only were his methods indirect and unseen, but his motivation was not straightforward sympathy. It was much more diffuse than that.

He was guided primarily by his own interpretation of the same Bushido code which Tachibana used to justify his most brutal excesses. Both Kimura and Tachibana held to the honest belief that the way of Bushido was central to their lives and that each was truly serving the Emperor-God. The difference between them lay in the capacity each man had for self-examination.

Kimura read the small type of his personal philosophy, measuring his every thought and action against what he believed was the ideal. He continually judged himself to be imperfect. Tachibana, on the other hand, was unaware of any small type in his contract with Bushido. The terms were simple and spelled out in large capital letters. The issues in his life were black or white, with no middle tones. He was, as a soldier, the killing sword of the Emperor. He had been programmed from an early age to scythe a path in blood, giving no mercy and seeking none: one who prepares a way. He was an instrument of the New Order, a servant of a high morality which had to be established. Tachibana no more questioned the rightness of that morality than he questioned the dispassionate cruelty of the function that it had allotted him. A sword's function is unequivocal and without sentiment. It simply obeys its master.

Tachibana had served his blood apprenticeship in China, where his military masters had impressed on him that the Chinese people had to be punished for their refusal to co-operate with the New Order and for their refusal to acknowledge the superiority and leadership of the Japanese race. In 1937, Tachibana had been part of the Japanese army sweeping towards Nanking. Thirty thousand Chinese troops had surrendered to the advancing Japanese and Tachibana's unit had played a part in punishing the prisoners. His unit alone had executed more than 1300 of them. Tachibana had become very good at decapitating with a single blow of the sword but, for the most part, the prisoners had been lined up on the river bank and machine-gunned. Executing prisoners one at a time was something of a luxury to an army in a hurry.

He had been able to kill at a more leisurely pace after the city of Nanking had surrendered. There had been much work for his sword there. He had lost count of the number of his victims, recalling only that the muscles of his arms and shoulders had ached so much for three days that he had resorted to using his pistol during that time. The killing had gone on for fully five weeks and even the army had no idea of the final tally. The lowest estimate was a hundred thousand. Some reckoned that over two hundred thousand was nearer the truth, if women and children were included in the total.

Tachibana lost no sleep over his bloody deeds. A rodent exterminator does not have qualms of conscience over the pests he removes from society. And, in Tachibana's eyes, anyone opposing the Imperial Way was a self-classified rodent. The world could only be purified by their extinction. Tachibana would not have dreamed of questioning the purity of his military masters' interpretation of the philosophical ideal they had married to nationalism. His obedience was blind and untroubled by doubts.

Kimura, however, wanted to respect his enemies, because he wanted to respect himself. If what he conquered was devoid of nobility, his own purpose was robbed of nobility and meaning. The sweetness of victory's taste was like ashes in the mouth.

Kimura missed his conversations with Ross but made no attempt to interfere with Tachibana's sway over the prisoners. He concentrated on his twofold task of training his engineers as gunners and foot soldiers and completing the installations which they would defend as an independent fighting force.

The completion of the cleared track to the crater summit of Mount Taki was followed by the speedy construction of the ingeniously concealed communications centre which Colonel Watanabe had deemed so vital to operational control of the entire region. It was when building work in the crater was in process, however, that the incident occurred which prompted Kimura to emerge from his self-imposed isolation from the prisoners and step across the demarcation line into Tachibana's zone of responsibility.

For the bases of the radio building and gun emplacements on Mount Taki, large quantities of stone and rock coral were required. These had to be carried by hand from the shore or dragged up on wooden sleds. The work was reserved for the slave labour-force – and Tachibana's guards drove the prisoners mercilessly to perform it.

Kimura usually timed his movements about the island to avoid having to watch the degrading spectacle of Tachibana's men herding the once-proud Europeans in coolie labour. In particular, he dreaded seeing Ross, whom he had tried to treat honourably but whom – with the others – he had abandoned to Tachibana's tender mercies.

This day, there was no way of avoiding the prisoners as he walked to Taki's summit to inspect the building work. He felt a surge of shame as he saw how the prisoners were engaged and wished now that he had not left it all to Niguchi to deploy the labour. Certainly, some better way of transporting the stone up the hillside could have been found than the primitive method he saw.

The distress of the prisoners carrying rocks up the hill was evident. One man in particular was in a very bad way. Rawlings, the most elderly of all the prisoners, was staggering under the weight of a rock slab weighing about sixty pounds. He had carried it uphill for nearly two miles, falling frequently but prodded to resume by the bayonet of one of Tachibana's men.

Kimura was not the only one aware of Rawlings' distress. Ahead of him on the narrow track, Ross and the American journalist, Newton, were harnessed to a wooden sled loaded with coral. Ross and the American were deliberately jamming the sled against every bump in the track, blocking progress and holding up the line behind them.

Their tactics served two purposes. The constant blocking of the track diverted the guard's attention away from Rawlings and on to them. It also allowed Rawlings short respites when he could lower his burden.

The guard was screaming at Ross and Newton as the two men hauled on their ropes to get the sled moving, when Ross suddenly looked up and he saw Kimura. There was a burning ferocity in

142

Ross' stare which disturbed Kimura. The blue eyes pierced his with challenge, and more. Was it hate? The thought startled Kimura. He did not expect hate from Ross any more than he expected cringing fear. He expected only the unemotional respect due to an honourable adversary; a respect which over-rode personal feelings.

The naked emotion in Ross' eyes wounded Kimura: partly because he felt it was undeserved, partly because Ross had no right to exhibit it, and partly because it eroded Kimura's esteem for the sea captain.

The Japanese guard broke off his screaming when he, too, saw Kimura.

"Rei! Rei!" he shouted at Ross and Newton.

The two prisoners dutifully bowed to Kimura. The wounded look on Kimura's face gave way to impassivity. But behind the impassivity was anger: at Ross for that look of hate, and at himself for the confusion he felt.

Kimura walked briskly on. He had gone only a short distance when the renewed shouting of the guard made him look back. The target of the guard's ire was again Rawlings, who was struggl-ing to pick up his load but was unable to do so. Kimura saw the scrawny, emaciated prisoner pitch forward with the faintest of cries and lie still. The Japanese guard aimed a number of kicks at the sprawled body – but there was no flicker of response from Rawlings that he had even felt them.

Ross dropped his rope and went quickly down the track to where Rawlings lay. He turned the elderly man over on his back. He looked up as the Japanese guard rounded on him and, simul-taneously, Kimura arrived back on the scene.

"He's dead," he said numbly in reply to Kimura's question.

"It is to be regretted," said Kimura gravely.

"Your regret is wasted, Major Kimura," Ross replied bitterly. "I thought you would be happy. It's one more mouth you won't have to feed. Just think of it – you'll be able to save one cupful of rice a day."

Kimura winced. The guard, not understanding Ross' words but alert to the disrespect in his tone, struck at him with the butt of his rifle. The blow glanced off Ross but toppled him sideways. He got up slowly, his eyes still blazing fire at Kimura. Kimura made a restraining signal with his hand as the guard prepared to lunge again at Ross.

"There will be no more work today," Kimura ordered, as if he

143

had not even heard Ross. "Have the dead prisoner taken down the hill." He turned to the guard and repeated what he had said in Japanese. He added, "Find Lieutenant Niguchi and tell him to report to me at once. And ask Major Tachibana to come to see me, too."

"What of the prisoners, sir?" the soldier asked.

"Tell them to return to their camp. They will not disobey."

A cheer went down the line as the word was passed that work was over for the day. The cheers died as Ross and Newton came down carrying the body of Rawlings between them.

That evening, the prisoners received – much to their surprise – extra rations of rice-cakes and some fish, also some watery yam soup. The only explanation they were given for this unexpected bounty came from the interpreter, Yoshimura, who said that it was in celebration of Singapore's first year under its new name of Syonan and its rebirth as a city of *Dai Toa Kyoeiken*, the Greater East Asia Co-Prosperity Sphere. The extra food, he said, was a token of Japanese generosity inspired by the Benevolence and the Blessings of the Imperial Magnanimity.

None of the prisoners questioned this explanation. It was typical, they believed, of the unpredictability and strange inconsistency of their Japanese masters. The truth, in fact, was that Kimura had done a deal with Tachibana. And no one was more astonished than Kimura at the lengths he had gone to recompense for the look of accusing hate he had seen on Ross' face. It had haunted him, making him waver between wanting to give Ross something that would really justify his hate and doing something that would increase Ross' unknowing indebtedness to him.

It required a great deal of face-saving all round, because Kimura had no wish to show to anyone that he nurtured any sympathy for the prisoners.

So, he disguised his sympathy. It had been an inspiration to link a more benevolent attitude to the anniversary of Singapore's "liberation", of which much had been made in broadcasts relayed from Tokyo. His declaration to end the working day in early afternoon had been impulsive and Tachibana, for one, would be sure to question it and ask why he had not even been warned or consulted beforehand. The Singapore anniversary provided the perfect excuse. He had ended work early so that the Japanese could celebrate the event. And, on a day when much was being made of Imperial Magnanimity, it was only fitting that the prisoners should not be excluded from Japanese goodwill.

144

Once embarked on his course, Kimura sensed an opportunity to keep the initiative and run the island in a more enlightened and humane manner. The stumbling block was Tachibana. His co-operation was essential. Co-existence on opposite sides of a strict demarcation line had not worked. The alternative was to seduce Tachibana with goodwill and place him in a position of such obligation to Kimura that he could not resist the engineer officer's wishes without great loss of face.

So, it was not to make demands on him that Kimura confronted Tachibana on the day of Rawlings' death, but to shower him with goodwill. Kimura used the Singapore anniversary and official pronouncements on Imperial Magnanimity as the reasons for seeking greater harmony on Little Tarakang.

He invited Tachibana to have dinner with him in the evening to celebrate the rebirth of Singapore as Syonan. He had hoarded special delicacies for just such an occasion, which he wanted to mark the start of a new spirit of harmony and co-operation among the Japanese Imperial forces of Little Tarakang.

At the dinner, he presented Tachibana with six bottles of White Horse whisky which had been "confiscated" from the *Machiko*'s bond nearly a year before. He also handed over, as a souvenir, the ship's bell of the *Machiko* – which one of Kimura's men had salvaged from the mangled ruins of the bridge and lovingly restored for him. He hated parting with the bell but it had the desired effect. Tachibana was overwhelmed by the engineer officer's generosity and greatly put out by the fact that he had no gifts to offer in return.

Nor was Kimura finished. He reminded Tachibana that he had been engaged for some weeks in training his engineers as all-rounders, in a fighting sense; capable of use as gun crews, as shock troops, as boat marauders, as snipers – every aspect of soldiering. It had occurred to him that, in all this, it was a pity that a man of Tachibana's great experience of war was on the sidelines and not passing on the invaluable knowledge he must have acquired. Would he not like to take part in the training and help lick the 93rd Independent Coastal Group into shape as one of the finest fighting outfits in the Imperial Army?

Tachibana's eyes glowed. Now he saw why Kimura was falling over himself to get on good terms with him. He needed his help to make real fighting men of his bone-headed road-makers. Tachibana was pleased. Kimura could have paid him no greater compliment. It said a lot for Kimura that he had been able to swallow his pride and even ask. Well, if magnanimity was the order of the day, he could be magnanimous, too. He could forget the engineer's bloody-mindedness and make allowances for the fact that he had never seen any real action.

"There's only one condition," said Tachibana, "apart from the fact that you will have to give me an absolutely free hand with the men you want me to train. You will have to help out playing sheepdog to those damned prisoners."

Kimura bowed his head.

"If you wish. Niguchi is not getting the best out of them. I should like to see the work organised for greater efficiency."

"If I had my way, I'd shoot the lot and throw them to the sharks," said Tachibana. "Half of them are always sick and we are keeping them alive for nothing. Just mouths to feed."

"The only snag is that we cannot replace them," said Kimura blandly. "One of the Europeans dropped dead at my feet today trying to lift a rock. His heart just gave out."

"Ah, the old one? I was there when they brought the body in. I'm surprised he lasted so long. I hope you don't feel sorry for them, Kimura. The trouble is that they're soft. They just can't stand up to hard work."

"It's not the prisoners that concern me, it's the work. The radio people are arriving with their equipment next week and we're not ready for them."

"What's the point of it all, anyway?" grunted Tachibana. "The esteemed Watanabe seems to want you to turn Mount Taki into a fortress like the Rock of Gibraltar. It's a waste of time, if you ask me. We should be concentrating every man we've got on New Guinea and leaving these islands to the seabirds. Things are not going well there, you know. The Australians have taken Buna back from us."

Kimura nodded gravely.

"The American, McArthur, has boasted that he will drive us out of New Guinea and that he will keep his promise to return to the Philippines. Perhaps the honourable Colonel Watanabe takes the threat seriously. The Tarakang Islands stand between McArthur and the Philippines."

"McArthur is a bag of wind," said Tachibana with a snort of derision. "If he had a million men, he wouldn't take New Guinea back from us in twenty years. I know the country and what it's like to fight there. That place is a hell."

Tachibana, who was more than a little drunk from the amount

146

of *sake* he had consumed, slumped back on his haunches in thought at the awakening of his personal memories of New Guinea. They so engrossed him that he did not catch the question Kimura asked him.

"What did you say, Kimura?" he asked blankly.

"I merely wanted to know if it was not a rather unusual step . . . Replacing your outfit with all its experience? I mean, you've said yourself that this is a backwater. Why pull you out of a fighting zone when you were probably just the stiffening that the fresh lot needed?"

Tachibana smiled mysteriously.

"You didn't hear about us, then?" he asked slyly. He drained his cup of *sake* and stared hard at Kimura in a strangely disconcerting way. He appeared to reach a decision.

"You know, Kimura, you've shown me tonight that you're not such a bad sort. I don't mind admitting that I thought you were just a bit priggish – but I don't think that any more. You're all right. And if Tachibana says you're all right, you really *are* all right. Well, I'll let you into a little secret . . ."

"Secret?" echoed Kimura.

"Yes, secret. You want to know why they pulled my outfit out of New Guinea? Why they really did it? They thought we'd developed bad habits."

Kimura was mystified.

"Bad habits?" he repeated.

"Yeah, bad habits. Would you credit it? Bad eating habits."

He laughed at Kimura's continued mystification.

"Don't you understand Kimura? We went six weeks without any proper food. Only what could be scratched off the land, and that was nothing. The only thing we weren't short of was dead men."

Kimura was unable to hide the horror on his face.

"Don't look so shocked," Tachibana reproached him. "Believe me, if you're hungry enough, you'll eat anything. *Anything*!"

Kimura felt sick. Death by starvation was a thousand times more preferable than recourse to the obscenity that Tachibana was defending.

"You ate the enemy dead?" Kimura's voice was no more than a whisper.

"The enemy weren't always available," said Tachibana, enjoying the shock his words were causing. "And don't go taking on a holy attitude unless you've ever been so desperate with hunger that you've thought about chopping off your own finger and eating it."

Tachibana shrugged his shoulders.

"You're like the others," he said resignedly. "You don't understand. Well, at least you know now why I grudge every cupful of rice we give those damned prisoners. For every cupful they get, there's a Japanese soldier in the New Guinea jungle going without and who would crawl ten miles on his belly for it."

Kimura was at a loss for words. He knew that he would never again be able to look at Tachibana without the deepest revulsion. Tachibana, already regretting his indiscretion in confiding in Kimura, tried to make light of it.

"We civilised people try to make jokes about cannibalism," he said, "but it's no joke in New Guinea. It's a national pastime. They've been practising it for hundreds of years. It's not unknown amongst these islands. Ask the Tarakangese."

"They are a very simple and backward people," said Kimura, not wanting even to discuss the subject.

"They were once a very fierce warrior people," said Tachibana. "That was before the white missionaries came and made them stop eating each other. Do you know that it was a great compliment to be eaten by them? They ate only the bravest warriors they slew. They believed that by eating a brave enemy's heart they would acquire his courage and his strength."

"And is that what you believe, Tachibana?"

Tachibana rose to his feet and swayed unsteadily.

"If I were killed in battle, my comrades would be welcome to feast on my body," he declared proudly. He seemed to fill with emotion at the thought. His eyes moistened with tears, a phenomenon which occurred only when he was very drunk. "We are both sons of Bushido, Kimura," he went on. "I would gladly offer you my body after death if it meant that you would be able to sustain yourself from it and continue the fight to the last drop of your own blood."

Kimura got to his feet. His head swam a little from the *sake* he had drunk. Revolting as he found Tachibana, he was strangely moved by the other's unexpected emotion and undoubted sincerity.

"You honour me, Tachibana," he said, without elaboration.

"As you have honoured me tonight," Tachibana replied gravely. "I promise you, Kimura, I will train your men to be the best fighting unit in the Imperial Army. I will make real soldiers of them. They will worship you to be given the privilege of dying bravely for Tenno Heika."

Some time later, Tachibana staggered from side to side of the path down the hill to his own quarters, clutching the six bottles of whisky and the polished ship's bell. His curses, when he dropped and smashed one of the precious bottles, brought one of the duty guard running to investigate. With many apologies for his clumsy help, the guard escorted the major to his hut, where he fell asleep fully-clad on the floor without even unrolling his bedding.

Kimura had watched him go, before staggering into the forest behind his quarters. He leaned his arms against a tree and stood, bowed, his head against his wrists. And was violently sick.

Ten

Orders from Tokyo

They called it "Kimura's Cabbage Patch". In fact, it was a carefully selected stretch of land about forty feet wide and a hundred feet long. It had been cleared of half a dozen tall trees, a profusion of tropical ferns, and several clumps of tough kuni grass. Kimura's engineers had drilled small explosive charges under the tree stumps and blasted them out. Then the ground had been painstakingly dug over until every root and lump of rock had been removed. The reddish earth had been trenched and liberally fertilised with human excrement, removed daily with almost religious ceremony from the Japanese soldiers' *benjos* – a rite that was characteristic of their heritage of too many people and too little land.

Kimura himself had supervised the elaborate planting of a variety of vegetables, so that not a square inch was wasted. About a quarter of the area was given over to a local tuber which grew to an astonishingly large size and was a feature of the Tarakangese islanders' regular diet. Elsewhere, neat rows of green shoots were soon appearing, promising a harvest of soya and other beans, lentils, gourd and tapioca. Pineapple and banana plants began to flourish in a section they shared with egg plant.

Presiding almost permanently for Kimura in this exercise towards self-sufficiency was Private Sota, a round-faced Okinawan whose head was cropped to a grey spiky stubble. He was the oldest man in the Company and a happy-natured son of the soil. He nursed every plant in the vegetable garden with loving care. And it was into his care that Ross and Newton were delivered on the day following Rawlings' death. For reasons unknown to them, they had been appointed as Private Sota's gardener apprentices. The work consisted mainly of hoeing with crudely made wooden implements. Sota watched them like a hawk

150

until he felt the two Europeans could be trusted to work on their own and not remove his precious plants with the unwanted growths.

Compared with hauling rocks up the mountain, the work was pleasant and Sota was a benign supervisor after their experience of Tachibana's guards, who kicked and clubbed their charges out of sheer boredom. The changing winds of oppression which blew over the prisoners' life on Little Tarakang was a frequent topic of conversation between Ross and Newton.

"I haven't seen Old Tigerface for weeks," Newton commented one day. The two men were staking bean plants while Private Sota sat in the shade smoking his pipe.

"He's still on the island," said Ross. "I saw him setting off along the beach at the head of a dozen men with full pack. It looks like he's found more to do than read the riot act to us."

"Funny, isn't it – the way things have been a hell of a lot easier since old Rawlings kicked the bucket? D'you think it's because of this Imperial Benevolence nonsense the Nips keep preaching at us? Or did Rawlings snuffing it put a scare into them?"

"I don't know," said Ross. "Maybe there has been some directive from higher up – but I'm not banking on it lasting. Look how nasty they got after that air raid on Tokyo. It only needs something like that to make the mood change the other way and they could take us all out and shoot us."

"Thanks for that cheerful thought," said Newton.

Ross grinned.

"Sorry. But it doesn't pay to set your hopes too high any more than to let them sink the other way and get it in your head that you'll never come out of this alive. Better to take the rough with the smooth and not get too excited about either!"

"Like my two Aussie pals, Woody and Rich?" suggested Newton with a smile.

"Like Woody and Rich precisely," agreed Ross. "I'm sorry that one or two others I could name can't take a leaf out of their book. These two boys are the most resilient characters I've ever come across in my life. They take everything in their stride and it doesn't matter how often they get slapped down, they still come up smiling."

"That Woody makes me laugh," admitted Newton. "He carried more rocks up that mountain than you and I together and yet you never hear him moan. 'Wotyagot to winge abaht, cobber?' he said to me . . ." Newton gave a passable imitation of Woody's

Australian twang. " 'Me great grand-daddy was sent aht from the owld country with chains on both his legs and broke rocks in Van Diemen's Land for fifteen years before they took the irons off.' "

"They certainly breed 'em tough in Aussie," said Ross. "A lot of them don't care to be reminded too often about all that convict ancestry but I reckon it may have been the making of Australia. The first generations had to be mighty tough to survive at all and their successors haven't had it too easy carving a country out of a wilderness. Survival comes more naturally to Woody and Rich because they've got it in their blood. They're closer to the basics of life. You and I are from softer stock. We have to learn how to survive."

"Speak for yourself," said Newton jauntily. "You forget I'm from pioneering stock. My own great grand-daddy rode all the way from St Louis to the Platte River in a covered wagon."

Ross looked across at him sceptically.

"You keep the pioneering streak pretty well hidden. I'm afraid I had you measured as a bar-room cowboy who'd never got nearer to a covered wagon than the front row of the stalls at a Tom Mix movie."

"It shows that bad, eh?" said Newton. He shrugged good-naturedly. "Come to think of it, I have saddled a few bar stools in my time. Maybe too many." He frowned.

"I was only kidding," said Ross, seeing the frown. He grinned at Newton. "Just wait till this is all over. There's a bar I know in Honolulu where they serve the beer off the ice just the way you Americans like it and a pretty girl comes round and puts garlands round all the customers' necks. We'll drink a toast to that great novel you're going to write."

Newton laughed.

"Aloha! I'll drink to that. You can help me think of a title. Something dramatic – like *My Life as an Imperial Slave*, or *The Unabridged Memoirs of a Benjo Sitter*."

"How about *The Unsavoury Secret of Private Sota's Bean Garden*?"

"Aw, shit," said Newton, and they both laughed. Their merriment made Private Sota abandon his seat in the shade and come hurrying to investigate. He inspected their staking work and nodded approvingly.

"Yoroshii, yoroshii!" he said, and returned to the shade.

"He's really quite a nice little guy," commented Newton.

"Gardening's more fun than soldiering," said Ross. "He's happy here. He doesn't give a damn about *Dai Toa Kyoeiken*."

152

"That makes two of us," said Newton. He had reached the end of a row and, squatting on the ground, began to knot together strands of thick paper-like grass from a pile of the stuff. They were using it in place of string and, presently, Ross joined him at the work to augment his own supply.

"You know Moorhouse is not happy about us getting this assignment?" the American mentioned casually as he worked.

"I know it," said Ross. "He thinks we're on a cushy number."

"He also thinks it's Kimura's doing and that he's playing favourites. You know the way he used to go on about you and Kimura being buddy-buddy?"

"I thought that all that had died the death."

"So did I – but you know Moorhouse. He was threatening to take the matter up with Old Tigerface. He thinks everyone should get a turn at working in the garden."

"That's fair enough," said Ross. "I don't mind doing a stint making camouflage canopies out of palm leaves. That's what everyone else has been on since the day Rawlings died and it's not a killer like getting those rocks up the hill."

"I wonder why they took us off the rocks?"

"Because they've got a couple of tractor buggies to haul the stuff up," said Ross. "They're shifting more rock in a day than we did in a month."

"Yeah, I've seen them. But to get back to Moorhouse. If he goes sounding off to Tachibana, it could rock the boat. He's liable to cut the rations back again and have us all running up and down Mount Taki with tree trunks on our backs."

"That wouldn't surprise me at all. But there's not a hell of a lot I can do about it."

"You could talk to Kimura." He saw the way Ross' brows knitted together and added, "If you get half a chance, that is."

"I don't want to ask any favours of Kimura," said Ross. "For one thing, he would despise me for it. It would free him from any need to show kindness, because any favour or kindness he shows to us has to come from his own sense of duty or his own sense of what is right. Kimura's a high-minded man. He understands our way of thinking in a way that Tigerface Tachibana couldn't in a million years, but – at the same time – Kimura's got a deep-seated sense of good old-fashioned Japanese values. He knows that I have always respected his sense of what is proper and that was the reason why we always got on well together. I observed his rules all the time."

153

"You make it sound like a minefield of manners," said Newton.

"That's exactly what it is," said Ross. "I built up a good relationship with Kimura, largely I think because I never tried to offend against his sense of correct manners. I played by his rules as if they were my rules and he seemed to respect me for it. It's a funny thing, Paul, but when two people start respecting each other, they're half way to becoming lifelong friends. I could never make my mind up what it was that Kimura wanted of me – a good friend or a good enemy."

"Maybe both," suggested Newton.

Ross nodded thoughtfully.

"And there you have the problem, because we have to play by Japanese rules. The Japanese ask no favours from their enemies. They expect neither the benevolence nor the mercy of their enemies. And the same goes for their friends. They would never dream of asking a favour from a friend because it would take away from that friend the opportunity to give his favours voluntarily."

"Now I know why I don't have any Japanese friends," Newton said wrily. "Where I come from, a friend is a guy you don't have to put on an act for. If you need a hundred bucks, you just say to him, 'Joe, I need a hundred bucks.' And he just sticks his hand in his pocket and gives you it."

Ross smiled.

"A Japanese friend would give you the hundred bucks, too, Paul. But he'd hate your guts for having asked."

"Why, for God's sake?"

"Because you would be telling him to his face that he was a lousy friend. Someone that was so insensitive to your needs that he didn't realise you needed the money and hadn't offered you a couple of hundred of his own accord."

"OK, OK," surrendered Newton, "so, maybe it wasn't such a bright idea that you have a chat with Kimura. It's just that since we've been working on this cabbage patch I've seen him once or twice in the distance, sort of eyeing us like he wanted to come across and say something."

"If he makes the first move, fair enough," said Ross. "But it's up to him. Maybe he has more of a conscience than I've given him credit for. But he's left things a little late. He steered well clear of us while Tachibana was doing his impersonation of Genghis Khan."

"Well, Tachibana hasn't been much in evidence lately. Maybe

that's Kimura's doing. Wouldn't you say it's quite a coincidence that things didn't start looking up for us until you lipped Kimura that day on the hill when Rawlings keeled over?"

Ross thought about this.

"I hadn't thought about it," he admitted. "Maybe you're right, Paul. I just didn't see the death of one prisoner mattering all that much, even to Kimura. Because, let's face it, prisoners just don't count with them."

"I don't think Kimura gave a damn about Rawlings," said Newton, his eyes on Ross. "It was the way he looked at you. You're the one that's special. He really likes you. And you upset him the way you spoke to him. He seemed . . . hurt."

Ross stared up towards Mount Taki, reliving the scene on the hill.

"I broke the rules," he said quietly, almost to himself. "I let him down. I could have killed him when I realised Rawlings was dead and he knew it. He said he regretted Rawlings' death and he probably did regret it. But he knew I held him personally responsible . . ."

"Friend or enemy?" Newton breathed the question.

"Maybe just friendly enemy," said Ross. "It could explain the improvement in the amount of food we're getting . . . the easier work. And the last thing he would want us to think, or me to think, was that he was responsible. He doesn't want me to feel obliged to him. He doesn't even want me to think that he's trying to make amends for Tachibana's misdeeds or his own neglect . . . because that would mean admitting that the Imperial Army is capable of shameful and dishonourable conduct."

"And that, of course, is unthinkable," commented Newton. "Even though we've all got the scars to prove it. Oh, oh, speak of angels . . ."

Ross turned to see what had caught the American's attention. Both men scrambled to their feet as Kimura and Tachibana strolled slowly towards them like promenaders taking the air. Ross and Newton bowed.

Kimura was all smiles.

"Please, gentlemen, continue with your work. I am just letting Major Tachibana see how, with our modest efforts, we have transformed the jungle and made the good earth work for us."

Tachibana was eyeing Ross sternly.

"Ah, is this not the devil whose neglect caused the death of your dog?"

Kimura's eyes gleamed. For a moment they betrayed an impishness so marked that Ross would not have been surprised if he had winked at him. The gleam vanished as quickly as it had appeared.

His face stonily immobile, Kimura said, "If you say so, Major Tachibana, it must be the same one. But these Europeans look all the same to me. I cannot tell one from the other."

The two Japanese walked on. Ross was containing himself with difficulty. He all but burst out laughing but succeeded in containing his merriment until the two Japanese were well out of earshot. A snort of amusement erupted from him, much to Newton's consternation.

"What the hell was all that about?" whispered Newton. The conversation had been in Japanese and he had not understood a single word.

"Major Kimura told a very funny joke at my expense," said Ross.

"A joke? I didn't hear Tachibana laughing. Didn't he get it?"

"He wasn't meant to get it. It was meant for me and me alone. You know the old cliché, Paul, that we patronising Westerners always come out with about these inscrutable orientals all looking alike?"

"I know the one."

"Well, so does Kimura. And he just got his own back!"

For all that the gardening work was easier than moving rocks, it came near to costing Ross his life. He returned one evening badly bitten by insects. They had gone in particular for an open sore on his leg. The leg had swollen to almost twice its usual size by the end of the working day and Newton had had to half-carry him down the hill to their camp.

By ten that night, Ross was in the grip of a burning fever. The two Australians, Woody and Rich, carried him over to Ruth Gamage's hospital hut but there was little she could do for him. All her requests for medicines to Tachibana had been met with blunt refusal. The Japanese were short of medical supplies themselves and what little they had was not going to be wasted on prisoners.

A gloom descended on the camp. For all that he was no longer "Number One" with the Japanese, most of the prisoners looked to Ross for leadership. He was the barometer of their hopes and there wasn't one of them who hadn't marvelled at the way he had shaken off the ill effects of Tachibana's brutal treatment of him after the dog incident. He had kept his spirit intact and continued to lead by example. The others, consequently, had come to look on him as indestructible.

Now, it looked as though one small insect-bite would change all that and accomplish what Tachibana's torture could not. No one was more agitated than Paul Newton. Since they had been paired together to work in the vegetable allotment, a strong bond of friendship had grown up between them.

As Ross' condition worsened, so Newton's frustration grew. They could not just let the skipper die. Something had to be done. But Moorhouse refused pointblank to make immediate representations to the Japanese. His weekly parley with Tachibana was scheduled for the following morning but he had no intention of disturbing the Japanese major before then. He would try to raise the subject of medical supplies if the opportunity presented itself.

"That bastard Moorhouse is not going to lift a finger to save the skipper," Newton confided in Woody and Rich after Moorhouse had made it plain to him what his attitude was.

Woody looked questioningly at Rich.

"Feel game for a prowl, sport?"

"Sure. The exercise'll keep me from running to fat." Rich's response was delivered with a grin. He had lost three and a half stones in captivity and was a shadow of his former self.

"Let me come with you," said Newton. The audacity with which the two Australians had continued to make their nocturnal stealing raids on the Japanese filled Newton with awe, although he never felt any temptation to join them. He still had no great desire to face the appalling risk but, this time, he felt obliged to offer to go because his concern for Ross had triggered the idea.

"Sorry, sport," said Woody firmly. "Two's company, three's a crowd. You leave it to Rich and me. What you want us to look for?"

"Quinine, aspirin, anything. Maybe it's too late for any of them. Look, maybe this isn't such a bright idea."

"Nothing'll go wrong, Mr Newton," said Woody. "Like Rich said, we need the exercise."

But doubts were flooding through Newton.

"There's always a first time for things to go wrong," he said. "Sooner or later the Japs are going to miss something and they're going to realise what you two have been up to."

"We're always very careful," said Woody. "We never take too

much of anything and they haven't twigged us yet."

"But medicines . . . Have you any idea where they keep them?"

"Sure we do. There's a cabinet in that place that Ferret-face uses as an office. You know, the interpreter guy. I've seen him doling out stuff to the Nips who report to him on sick parade."

"You can't break into his office," protested Newton.

Woody grinned.

"You want to bet?"

Woody and Rich weren't to be talked out of their proposed venture. They persuaded Newton that the best thing he could do was turn in for the night and forget they had even conversed on the subject. But Newton was lying awake on the wooden sleeping platform of the main long-house some hours later when he heard stealthy movements at the far end. First, Woody rose and disappeared in the direction of the *benjo*. Two or three minutes later, Rich followed him out.

Newton waited, fully awake. The minutes dragged by, his anxiety increasing with every spaced-out second. The night seemed interminable. One hour, two, three . . . Still no sign of the Australians. He lay lathered in sweat, convinced that something had gone wrong.

He had all but given up hope when he heard a sound at the doorway. He pushed himself off the platform and moved to investigate.

"That you, Mr Newton?"

It was Rich's voice. The big man was breathing heavily.

"Where's Woody?"

"Right behind me. He'll be here in a minute. Strewth, that was a bit close tonight!"

Before he could elaborate, Woody slipped in through the doorway.

"You OK, Big Fella?" he murmured.

"Nothing wrong with me that a schooner of iced lager wouldn't put right. How about yourself?"

"A drop of stiff grog's what I could do with, sport. Christ, I thought we'd had it tonight."

"What went wrong?" asked Newton. He was on tenterhooks and impatient with the Australians for fantasising about drinks they wouldn't be tasting in a twelve-month, if ever.

"We had to come away empty-handed, Mr Newton," said Woody. "I'm sorry."

"At least you weren't caught," said Newton. "What happened?"

Woody quietly rid his system of a string of curses. He heaped them around the head of the Japanese interpreter, Yoshimura.

"What possessed the slant-eyed devil to go strolling in the middle of the night?" he lamented. "I had the bloody cabinet opened."

"What happened?" Newton repeated, trying to keep his voice down but his nerves raising it to an almost falsetto squeak.

"We heard Ferret-face coming and had to made a tactical withdrawal," Woody went on. "We learned all about tactical withdrawals in Malaya but I didn't really believe in them until tonight. I'm afraid we knocked a hole in the back of Ferret-face's office. Rich went through it like a tank."

Newton let his breath out in an expressive sigh.

"Ye gods! There'll be hell to pay! Didn't the Ferret raise the alarm?"

Rich shook his head.

"Nope. That's the funny thing. What do you make of it, Woody? I went through that wood up there like a bat out of hell, expecting bullets and shouts and whistles and general pandemonium – but Ferret-face didn't even give chase."

Woody was as puzzled as Rich.

"Could be he was out on some dirty business of his own and didn't want to have to do any explaining to the Tiger. They say there aren't enough black women in the camp next door to keep up with his appetite for getting his end away. Maybe that's where he had been."

The mystery remained unexplained but, next morning, it became obvious that the night's happenings were to have repercussions.

Moorhouse was summoned to Tachibana's presence early and emerged looking somewhat shaken. The fit prisoners – who had been assembled for the morning head count – were kept standing in a double line until Moorhouse was brought out to join them. Then Tachibana appeared with Yoshimura at his heels.

Tachibana spoke at length. Yoshimura translated at intervals. The frills and embellishments to the speech were familiar to the prisoners. Some of the main message was unexpected.

The commandant of prisoners and internees on Little Tarakang had, as a result of his interpretation of the Imperial Benevolence, instructed an improvement in the living and working conditions for them. He had done so because he was a humane and kind person. He had hoped that the prisoners and internees would respond to this initiative of humane consideration by working harder for the New Order and showing themselves willing to make greater sacrifices for Nippon, in the same way that all the peoples of Nippon were working and sacrificing themselves for the new prosperity.

The prisoners and internees, however, had not convinced the commandant that they were wholehearted in their endeavours and truly deserving of the benevolence which had been shown to them. The need for discipline among them was greater than ever and the commandant intended to enforce it vigorously.

Only that morning, the commandant had discovered an outrage for which the punishment of death would not be unfitting. An attempt had been made to break into a cabinet in the military premises of the camp, where prisoners were forbidden to go. Fortunately, no precious medicines – invaluable to the health and efficiency of the Nipponese forces on Little Tarakang – had been stolen. But damage had been inflicted on the property of the Imperial Forces and every effort would be made to apprehend the criminals responsible.

Because the commandant was a fairminded man, he was making no direct accusation against any of the prisoners. He did not believe that any of them would be so foolish or so disrespectful to the rules of the camp to venture near the area reserved for the Nipponese forces and – for that reason – he did not believe that they were shielding the likely culprit. It was just possible that the damage had been accidentally caused by a soldier of Nippon, who had forgotten to report the matter.

It was possible, too, that the incident was not unrelated to another crime. The body of a badly beaten Tarakangese woman had been found on the shore. She had been attacked and killed during the night, probably by one of her own menfolk who might have, in later regret, tried to steal medicines for her. No one, however – prisoner, Tarakangese or soldier of Nippon – had come forward to confess to the outrages or to say that they had witnessed what had taken place.

This showed a serious lack of discipline in all concerned. And it was not the commandant's intention to spare any section under his command from his wrath. His own soldiers, the prisoners, and the Tarakangese, would all be punished. As a result, all would see that Japanese justice was quite impartial.

Yoshimura ended his relay of Tachibana's discourse by saying that the spokesman for the prisoners had already been briefed on how their share of the punishment was to be allocated. That would be implemented when they reassembled for work parties in thirty minutes' time. They were dismissed until then.

Tachibana and his small entourage of guards, plus Yoshimura, moved off towards the Tarakangese camp to read the riot act there. The dismissed prisoners surrounded Moorhouse, demanding details of his conversation with Tachibana. Hot and flustered, he told them.

"I have to give them one name, the name of any one of us. That's the one who has to take whatever punishment Major Tachibana decrees."

"You mean you accepted that?" someone said. "That one man carries the can for the rest of us?"

"I was given no choice. And I wasn't given the opportunity of discussing it," said Moorhouse angrily. "So, it's up to one of you to volunteer."

"How about yourself?" Fraser, the engineer, suggested acidly.

Moorhouse faced him, flushing furiously.

"Naturally, I volunteered my own name immediately. But Tachibana refused."

"Naturally," said Fraser, plainly disbelieving.

"Let's not go along with it," put in Haraldsen, the Mate of the *Machiko*. "We tell Tachibana straight that we're all in this together. If he wants to punish one of us, he has to punish us all."

"That's fair enough to me," said Fraser.

"Tachibana would never accept that," said Moorhouse. "And neither would I. Why should we all suffer when just one person with a little guts could save us a lot of misery?"

"What we need is someone with a little guts to speak for us," Fraser commented.

"Let's not argue like a lot of old women," said a voice. "I'll volunteer. I'll be your patsy."

In the silence that followed, every eye turned to look at the speaker. Paul Newton stared at them defiantly.

"Do I take it that I'm elected?" he asked softly.

"Sorry, sport," Woody spoke up for the first time. "I reckon if anybody's got to take a bashing for being out after dark, the Nips ought to get the right man . . ."

"And that's me!" interrupted Big Rich. "And I'll flatten any man who disagrees with me."

"Keep out of this, Rich," said Woody gruffly. "Ain't you ever going to get any sense? I've told you a hundred times that you never never volunteer for anything. You wait until you get asked."

The big man rounded on his friend, his normally kindly features twisted with real anger.

"I've been taking orders from you for just about as long as I can remember and I ain't taking no more. So, just pipe down, Woody, or you'll have me to reckon with as well as the Nips." Rich glared at the faces all round him. "That goes for you, too, Yank," he snarled at Newton. "And anybody else that wants to argue."

Moorhouse beamed his approval.

"Our Australian friend is right," he said. "Let's have no more argument. We owe him our thanks."

"He's not going to do it," insisted Woody.

"I warned you," muttered Rich and, standing back, delivered a straight-armed punch to the point of Woody's jaw. He went sprawling in the dust and lay there, half senseless.

Woody was still groggy when, a short time later, the prisoners were reassembled and Moorhouse indicated to Yoshimura that the big Australian was the one chosen to represent them. Yoshimura grinned. He disliked big men and enjoyed opportunities to humiliate them. He barked an order to two guards, who hustled Rich over to a mound of heaped broken coral. Rich was ordered to pick up a hardwood log nearly five feet in length. It weighed upwards of fifty pounds. He was made to carry it on his neck and shoulders, his hands raised to support it on either side. He had to hunch his head well forward to support the heavy log.

The guards ordered him to climb to the top of the mound of coral. He did so, feet slipping on the uneven surfaces.

"Kugate!" screamed one of the guards. Big Rich did as he was told. He kneeled.

He was kneeling there on the biting coral when the other prisoners moved out of the camp to their work areas. He was still kneeling there when they returned in the evening. He was allowed to stumble and crawl back to the sleeping hut at sunset. But the kneeling treatment was continued for three successive days. During the entire time, he never uttered a sound nor uttered any expression of the intense agony he endured. He did not even speak a single word to Woody when his friend brought him food in the sleeping house and gently rendered first aid to his torn and numb knee-caps.

It was not until the fourth day, when it was realised that the punishment was over, that he spoke. By then, he was so crippled

162

that he could not walk without assistance. He smiled at Woody, who had constantly begged him to break his self-imposed silence and say something to him, even if it was only to curse him.

"I beat the bastards," he said triumphantly. "I knew I could." He patted Woody's hand. "I had to do it, Woody. The way I did, I mean. Without a squeak, not even to you. I knew that if I made one little squawk . . . just one . . . I was finished. You see, don't you? I had to show them."

There were tears in Woody's eyes.

"You bloody great boulder-headed ox," he murmured. "You didn't need to do it. You should have let me."

"Sorry, old sport," said Rich. "You know I was the only one. Anybody else would have cracked. I was the only one who could beat them."

He never spoke about his three-day ordeal again. He had said all he intended to say on the matter. It was over.

On the day the big Australian's ordeal started, however, another incident of note occurred. At its centre was Paul Newton, who had to report to Private Sota as usual for work in the vegetable allotment.

Newton's spirits were at a low ebb. He was still greatly concerned at Ross' condition and his impotence to be of any real help to the fever-racked Briton, who was getting weaker and weaker. He was also riddled with a mixture of guilt and relief that, despite his own noble intentions, it was Big Rich who was undergoing the kneeling torture down in the camp and not him.

Private Sota – interested only in the growing vegetables – was blissfully unconcerned with the other excitements on Little Tarakang, although he seemed exceptionally well informed on them. And, on this day, he was disposed to talk about them.

He told Newton that Tachibana had arrested the husband of the murdered Tarakangese woman that morning and that it had caused much excitement among the Japanese soldiers. The unfortunate man was going to have his head lopped off for sure and the soldiers were wondering if they would be allowed to witness the event.

Newton was horrified and – communicating with Sota in a mixture of sign language, mangled Japanese and pidgin English – tried to ascertain more details. Had the Tarakangese man murdered his own wife?

Sota was amused at Newton's naivety in thinking that the Tarakangese had anything to do with his woman's death. No, the real culprit was probably one of Tachibana's own men. Most likely that ratfaced lieutenant who spoke the Tarakangese language. He was never away from the Tarakangese camp and it was well known that the ratfaced one was prepared to mount anything living and female between the ages of nine and ninety.

Would Tachibana have an innocent man killed? It took Newton some time to convey understanding of his question to Sota. The Okinawan looked at the American pityingly. It had nothing to do with guilt or innocence. It was for discipline – to set an example as a warning. That was how things were always done in the Imperial Army. You didn't have to commit a crime to be punished, you just had to be available when the commander or the squad leader wanted to show who was boss. That was life, of course. The one on top always took his anger out on the one underneath.

Sota said Major Kimura was different. Some officers were like that. They preferred to treat their men in a fatherly way and love them as if they were his children. As far as Sota was concerned, Kimura was OK. Not like Major Tachibana. He liked to make his men fear him. That was why he was taking it out of the poor Tarakangese savage and punishing the big Australian with the kneeling-on-stones torture. He was even punishing the two Nipponese soldiers who were on guard the night before for neglecting their duty. They had been ordered to drill with full packs for seven days. Their punishment, the Okinawan observed, will keep the others on their toes when they go on guard. Tonight, they would be shooting at every shadow that moved.

It was late afternoon when Major Kimura came to the vegetable plot and spoke to Private Sota. Newton was ordered to go with the major to his quarters. He had a job for the American prisoner.

Kimura's orderly was waiting at the doorway. Beside him was a bucket of water and he held a scrubbing brush in his hand. He handed the scrubbing brush to Newton and, speaking in his own tongue and with a variety of miming actions, indicated that Newton was to scrub the wooden floor.

Even by Japanese standards, the room was spartan. The slight recess with the carved Monju Bosatsu buddha offered the only concession to decor. The planking of the floor had been made from a good redwood, native to Little Tarakang. In normal practice, the timber would have been seasoned on the stump for upwards of three years before being used in construction, but such refinements as seasoning the timber had been forgone in the need to put the Japanese camp up quickly.

The bare floor was spotlessly clean but was blemished in one corner, where a broken bottle lay with its creamy glutinous contents oozing away from the fragments of glass. Beside it, a small cabinet was open. On the single shelf of the cabinet, there were other bottles and what appeared to be ointment jars.

The orderly disappeared but Kimura remained, hovering around, as Newton cleared away the mess from the broken bottle and began scrubbing operations. He had scarcely started when Kimura ordered him to stop. He drew attention to some angry marks on the American's forearms.

"Have you a disease?" Kimura enquired.

"No, Major, they're just insect bites. It's from working amongst the vegetables and with the earth."

"I am told that Captain Ross had such bites and is now very sick with fever."

Newton stared at Kimura boldly.

"He may die if he does not get medicines."

"Major Tachibana has medicines."

"But Major Tachibana will not give medicines for prisoners. He says they are for Nippon soldiers only."

Kimura nodded.

"That is so. There was an order from headquarters. Major Tachibana is strict about obeying orders. Major Tachibana tells me that, last night, someone tried to steal medicines from Nipponese camp. Very bad. Punishment for prisoners who steal is death or ten years' confinement."

Kimura crossed the room to the open cabinet close to Newton and took a jar from the shelf. He looked down at Newton, who was still on his hands and knees, and frowned deeply.

"It is not good for prisoners who may have disease to be working in room where Nipponese officer must sleep. To protect Nipponese officer, prisoner must cleanse himself."

He handed the jar to Newton.

"Prisoner will put on arms where insect bites. Will kill poison which insect leaves in blood. Will make impossible for poison on prisoner to pass to Nipponese officer."

Newton removed the top of the jar and stared at the white ointment inside. Then he did as he had been told. He rubbed some of the salve on his arms. Its soothing effect on the angry red marks was instant. The ointment had a pleasant antiseptic smell.

Kimura then took a bottle from the cabinet. It contained a yellowish liquid.

"Prisoner will take also, in case of fever. One measure." He indicated the screwtop of the bottle as holding the amount required. "Prisoner will return now to camp. Will not work in room of Nipponese officer for three days. Prisoner will take medicine, make certain that disease does not pass to officer of Nippon army."

With that, Newton found himself dismissed from the task of scrubbing the floor. He was returned to the prisoners' camp under the aegis of Kimura's orderly, who had instructions that Newton was to be confined to the sick quarters for three days under quarantine.

On his way, Newton passed the mound of coral where Big Rich was kneeling with the big log held on his bowed neck and shoulders. He could do no more than shout an encouragement to the Australian, an act which earned him a threatening rebuke from the soldier guarding the big man.

In Ruth Gamage's sick quarters, Newton delightedly displayed to her the ointment and the medicine he had received from Kimura. He had no intention of wasting any of the precious substances on himself. They were for Ross.

He stood by as Ruth forced a measure of the yellow liquid between Ross' lips. She then treated the sore on his swollen leg with a liberal application of the white ointment.

That night, Ross' fever began to subside and his slow recovery began.

Unknown to the prisoners, there was a sequel to the incident of the medicines in the Japanese camp. Tachibana had got to hear of the American being quarantined by Kimura and that he had been given medicines by Kimura. He put two and two together and came to the conclusion the Kimura had cunningly found a way to improve the life chances of the prisoner who had been Kimura's choice as spokesman for the small band of Europeans. Tachibana chatted with Lieutenant Niguchi and uncovered a little more about Kimura's relationship with Ross: the games of checkers, the discussions. There was, too, Kimura's blatant insistence on having Ross as one of the helpers in his vegetable project – a far from arduous job.

Tachibana decided it was time that he had a word with Kimura about any kind of friendship with prisoners. Tokyo had given precise instructions on just that eventuality. He went to see Kimura one evening.

166

After the customary preliminaries, in which Tachibana had effusively complimented Kimura on his contribution to the new harmony with which they were fulfilling their functions on Little Tarakang, he gently reminded Kimura that too kind a heart could be a serious handicap to an officer of the Imperial Army.

"Working every day with prisoners," said Tachibana smoothly, "I have to guard against my own good nature. One can so easily become too fond of certain prisoners in the way that one becomes attached to a stray dog."

The particular metaphor was tactless, Kimura thought with a start of anger, but he smiled at Tachibana.

"By the same token," he replied softly, "one must guard against a constant association with prisoners so brutalising the senses that one forgets they are human beings and treats them like dogs."

His own metaphor turned on him, Tachibana acknowledged the barb with a smile as gracious as Kimura's.

"I do not criticise your humanity, honoured Kimura. I thought merely to warn against an excess of it. Was it not an excess of kindness to give medicines to a prisoner when we are so short of them for ourselves?"

"But that was a calculated kindness, Tachibana. You perhaps did not know that I had training as a doctor. Disease makes no distinction between Japanese soldiers and foreigners; it attacks both with impartiality and equal virulence. In giving medicine to a prisoner who was working in my quarters, I was protecting myself and my men from contamination by him."

Tachibana continued to smile but there was a coldness about it.

"In China, when we fought plague, we exterminated the rats who carried it."

"Do you suggest we exterminate our prisoners?"

"Their work here is virtually over. I was reminded of this today when I heard the test salvoes being fired from the Taisho Fours on Mount Taki. Soon there will be no more work for the prisoners to do – and we are under no obligation to feed any who do not work. The merciful thing might be to kill them and be done with them."

"You may be right," said Kimura. "But until I receive orders . . ."

"Ah, yes, orders," said Tachibana. He fished in the pocket of his tunic and withdrew a piece of paper. He unfolded it and handed it to Kimura. "This order is relevant to what we have been discussing. It comes from the War Office in Tokyo and has been signed by His Excellency himself, General Tojo."

Kimura studied the piece of paper. It was addressed to all commandants of prisoner-of-war and civilian internee camps. He read:

> Prisoners of war must be placed under rigorous discipline inasmuch as it does not contravene the law of humanity. It is directed that care must be exercised not to become obsessed with the mistaken idea of humanitarianism or influenced by personal feelings towards those prisoners of war which may grow in the long time of their imprisonment.

The document was marked as signed by Hideki Tojo, Minister of War.

"Interesting," commented Kimura. "What do you make of it, Tachibana?"

"It is a warning that we must not let ourselves be carried away by humanitarian feelings for our prisoners of war. Talk has come to my ears of the respectful way you have treated the English ship captain. It has even been said that when you heard he was sick, you found a way to get medicines to him through this American who was working in your quarters." Tachibana shrugged and gave a wave of the arms that suggested he deprecated the idea. "It is just stupid camp gossip, of course, but I admit it disturbs me. It concerns me that what may be ordinary kindness on your part is not interpreted by higher authority as a contravention of an order coming direct from His Excellency, the First Minister of the Imperial Government."

"Your concern for me is greatly appreciated, honoured Tachibana. If there is gossip, as you say, then I must be careful in future not to be swayed by my more humanitarian instincts."

Tachibana bowed.

"I would have said nothing. But we are more than comrades-in-arms. I like to think I am also your respected friend."

Tachibana's unctuous delivery of that final statement made Kimura's gorge rise. He felt a sudden and overwhelming despair at the irony of things that governed all human relationships, and his own in particular. What dreadful compagination of circumstances had decreed that, while he must suspend all compassion for one set of human beings, he had to acknowledge this self-confessed cannibal monster as *friend*.

Eleven

The Withering Vine

The fighting war was coming nearer and nearer. It rolled like a tide from the south and west, leaving little sandbanks of resistance isolated here and there behind the rippling surge of its frontal waves. As McArthur's campaign of reconquest gathered momentum, island after island was bloodily conceded by the Japanese Imperial Forces, while on the mainland of New Guinea the Australian Army fought firmly along the northern coast, prising the stubborn Japanese from every maritime toehold.

One by one the outposts of the Greater East Asia Co-Prosperity Sphere were falling. American and Australian warplanes ruled the waters round the Vitiaz Strait and, after the momentous Battle of the Bismarck Sea in March 1943, the Japanese had to give up supplying New Guinea by sea convoys. Supplies were ferried by submarine and barge from their bases in New Britain.

Early in the year, the Russell Islands were reoccupied but they were empty. The Japanese had already left. In mid-summer, the Trobriands fell, uncontested. The Americans landed in New Georgia, the Australians in New Guinea's Huon Gulf. In August, the bitter battle for Guadalcanal began.

The port of Lae was wrested from the Japanese in September, while defeat stared them in the face in New Georgia. The islands of Kolombangara and Vella Lavella would soon be entirely in American hands.

All these events were but a distant thunder to the occupants of Little Tarakang and only occasional echoes reached them. That the war was not now going well for the Japanese was apparent in the drastic tightening of supplies to the island. To Major Tachibana, it was an affront that some of the dwindling supply of rice had to be diverted to the prisoners and troublesome Tarakangese. It was a further affront to him that he was kept on

169

the island as a glorified jailer while his services to the Empire could have been usefully employed on any one of a dozen not-too-distant battlefronts. But his former Divisional Commander had been killed in an air crash and it seemed that Tachibana had been filed away and forgotten.

The completion of the various installations on Little Tarakang had not, in the event, signalled the redundancy of the prisoner labour-force. Its usefulness to the Greater East Asia Co-Prosperity Sphere was saved by the alarming deterioration of Japanese shipping strength and the long overdue realisation by someone in Rabaul that nothing had been done to ship most of the *Machiko*'s cargo back to Japan and that no survey had been furnished by the Navy to assess the ship's possible restoration to seaworthiness.

A naval officer had been flown to Great Tarakang and thence to the smaller island to carry out the survey. He and Major Kimura had spent three days examining every part of the ship. His consequent report had been full of ifs and buts.

The *Machiko*'s bottom was covered in marine growth and, *if* she could be dry-docked, there was every hope that she could be restored, etc. There was, however *no* chance of the ship being towed to a dry-dock.

If, however, some of the marine growth could be removed where she lay, other options were opened. These options were discussed at length and all the pros and cons carefully considered.

In short, the ship could be returned to seaworthiness by reconstruction of the navigation platform and bridge. The ship needed some form of control centre. It was not imperative that the living accommodation be rebuilt but, on the other hand, something would have to be done about the living space if the hold space was going to be required for cargo. The engines of the ship could be made operative without much difficulty but there was very little fuel left in the bunkers to drive the vessel. She had arrived at the island burning timber and could, presumably, leave it using the same fuel. This, however, was an inefficient method of firing the boilers and was not to be recommended for several reasons.

The long report ended with an account of the general unsuitability of Little Tarakang to carry out the repair work required and the inadequacy of existing plant on the island to undertake the task. It carried, however, the optimistic footnote that nothing was impossible and that restoration to seaworthiness could be achieved with much improvisation, some ingenuity, and a great deal of work.

To headquarters staff in Rabaul – already occupied by more urgent pressures, constant air raids, and the imminent threat of American landings in New Britain – the document must have seemed like so much gobbledegook. It passed through the hands of a number of senior officers faster than a live grenade and was dispatched to Major Kimura on Little Tarakang with the recommendation that he "implement those aspects of the report which were feasible within the current circumstances obtaining in the area and with a view to bringing the damaged cargo-carrier to an optimum state of serviceability in the Imperial Cause".

Kimura read the report a dozen times and, each time he read it, he was conscious of the personal challenge leaping at him from the document. Here, it seemed, was a task of such proportion that it was the perfect answer to the inactivity and boredom facing the occupants of Little Tarakang in the months, possibly years, ahead.

Vague as his orders were, he took them as a mandate to rebuild the *Machiko* as a ship that would proudly fly the emblem of the Rising Sun. He was seized with an enthusiasm which excited and astonished him.

Kimura had Ross brought up to the Japanese camp for consultation and bombarded him with questions about the *Machiko*. How would he go about repairing the fire-ravaged ship? What materials would be required? Could the damaged hydraulic steering system be replaced by improvising a rod and chain system? If the *Machiko* was stripped to deck level where the fire damage was worst, could the midships section be rebuilt, not with metal but with unseasoned timber from the lush abundant forest of Little Tarakang? Could the same forest supply logs for the *Machiko's* bunkers that would prove a workable if not ideal substitute for coal? How did one go about scraping the barnacles and other marine growth off the bottom of a ship when there wasn't a dry-dock within a thousand miles?

Ross, still weak from fever, reeled under Kimura's questions. At the same time, the idea of transforming the sorry hulk that had been his command to something of her former glory lit a fire in him that started from a flicker and grew in intensity. The tired frame of skin and bones that he had become sparked with a new vitality. In defiance of his physical condition, new energy flowed in him. For the first time in months, he could dare to look into the future and not be dismayed by what he saw.

Rusting and immobile, the *Machiko* had represented no hope

171

in the future for him, only the bitter past. A *Machiko* restored was something else again. Kimura's soldiers could not sail the ship. They could bring in a crew, of course – but there was no indication that this had even entered their thinking. Why were they not bringing in a Navy Salvage team right from the start? No, the restoration of the *Machiko* was a Japanese army exercise – for which they *needed* Ross and for which they *needed* his crew.

Ross dared not consider what possibilities beckoned on that day when the *Machiko* might be able to venture out beyond the imprisoning reef to the open sea. But the seeds of hope for freedom were planted in his consciousness on the day of that first consultation with Kimura. Freedom . . . With the *Machiko*, it was possible. How might it be achieved and when? These were imponderables . . . But it was the existence of the possibility that mattered. It was something to hold in the heart when the spirit was weary and the body shivered with pain and fatigue. It was something to nurse in the secret labyrinths of the mind. Something to hide and preserve for the day when it could be unfolded and brought to the light and translated into more than a thought, more than a secret dream, more than a possibility . . . into a reality.

So it was that the prisoners and the Tarakangese labour-force did not become redundant and an embarrassment to their captors when the cleverly camouflaged radio installations and artillery emplacements on Mount Taki became fully operational. Instead, the entire force was diverted towards a new end – the re-creation of a ship.

And, if the task kindled new and unspoken hopes in the hearts of the *Machiko*'s men – as it did in her master – it also sparked an unexpected enthusiasm in the soldiers of Kimura's 93rd Independent Coastal Group. Working on the *Machiko* was infinitely more interesting to them than the endless programme of training which Kimura had mapped out for them and on which there were never less than fifty men engaged at any one time. Kimura had something like 130 men on his strength, who were broken down into squads of ten. Ten squads were kept continually in rotation through field work, artillery watches, infiltration patrol training, assault training, static defence, mobile defence, amphibious defence, and so on. There was no shortage of weaponry and Kimura was not going to be satisfied until every man in his unit was proficient with every one, from the standard issue rifle to the drilled team work of manning the 150mm field guns on Mount

Taki's summit. He was determined that his "Road-makers", as Tachibana so contemptuously called them, would be able to adapt to any situation. The officer shortage – he and Niguchi were the only commissioned officers – did not dismay him because he believed that the strength of a good army lay in the quality of its NCO's, and he was well-staffed in this department. In any case, Colonel Watanabe was sending him two young apprentice officers.

With between twenty and thirty men permanently engaged on communications, administration, stores and catering, and with five squads on rotation training, Kimura was left with about fifty men available for the kind of work in which they had originally been trained – field engineering. And, in this respect, the task of restoring the *Machiko* was a godsend. The great enemy in garrisoning an otherwise uninhabited island devoid of any social distractions was boredom, so that work of any kind was welcome for its absorption of time and thought. But the *Machiko* was more than work. Kimura felt this right from the start and his men felt it, too. It was a challenge quite out of the ordinary and it excited them. They would turn this blackened hulk into a ship that would sail the ocean as proud as any queen. It suddenly became the most important thing in all their lives.

One of the strangest aspects was the effect on the relations between the prisoners and Kimura's soldiers. For quite different reasons, the challenge of the *Machiko* uplifted them. For the prisoners, the ship represented their salvation. It had brought them to their captivity and surely now it would take them out of captivity. Like Ross, they did not formulate their thoughts immediately into plans of escape. It was enough to think only that here, in full view, was the vehicle which would take them away from this hated place. For the first time, therefore, the soldiers and the prisoners became engaged on a common purpose with a shared will. Master-and-slave attitudes were forgotten, deep enmities and bitter grudges were laid aside as first one problem and then another was encountered and mutually overcome.

The first job to be tackled was the scraping of the *Machiko*'s bottom. It was Ross who suggested to Kimura how this might be accomplished. He recalled watching a Greek tramp ship captain get round the expense of a dry-docking operation by conducting a Heath-Robinson bottom-scrape by running scrapers attached to wires underneath his ship and then keel-hauling the scrapers. Surely it would be possible to try something similar.

A prior requirement was steam on the deckline. Fraser, the Chief Engineer – like a small boy in the toy department of a large store – roamed round his beloved engineroom, checking everything. The main engines and boiler-room had escaped the deck fire and only needed a clean-up. Fraser's headache was in checking every inch of cable and piping which fed energy from the engineroom to the other parts of the ship. Much of the electric circuitry had been destroyed, so Fraser delegated Millarship, the Third Engineer, to recheck every line and draw a plan showing all the break points. The steam and water lines running the length of the deck were still in reasonably good order and Fraser promised to have both available for use as soon as he could get the donkey boiler into action.

Ross and Kimura, meantime, had gone in search of suitable pieces of metal which might be pressed into service as scrapers. They found none. Either the shape was wrong or the piece of metal was too light or far too cumbersome. This time, it was Kimura who came up with the solution. He made a sketch in the notebook he carried and showed it to Ross.

"There are plenty of hardwood trees on the island," he said. "Why should we not make an instrument of our own design?"

His idea was quite simple and Ross saw its possibilities immediately. Kimura was suggesting that they select a tree and cut a four-foot section of trunk which was about twelve inches in diameter. They would spike two lengths of chain to each end of the trunk. Kimura's sketch showed a diamond shape, with the heavy log running across the centre between the east and west points of the diamond. The top two legs of the diamond represented one chain and the bottom two legs represented the other. Each chain would be attached to wire rope on port and starboard sides of the ship and the log lowered under the keel, so that when it was hauled to port or starboard with tension on it, the rubbing motion scraped the ship's bottom.

"It'll work," said Ross, "but we'll need something more abrasive than timber to shift the barnacles we've collected down there. Why don't we bind the heavy log with chain or even barbed wire, so that it really bites into them?"

They decided to make two log scrapers, one for the forward end and one for the after end. They could be worked at the same time.

Work also began on the mangled bridge and midships area: dismantling twisted framework and setting to one side any salvageable item that could be put to future use. Niguchi, who had once worked as an architect's assistant, was brought in by Kimura to draw plans for the new deck housing and bridge which would replace the old. Working from sketches Ross made of the original layout, the young lieutenant showed a considerable aptitude for the task and a surprising understanding of what was required. Before leaving Japan on military service, he had not previously set foot on a ship.

Kimura was delighted. Quite by chance he had discovered that there was at least one thing in which Niguchi excelled. Everyone, but everyone, wanted to see Niguchi's beautifully drawn plans. All expressed their admiration and said that when the job was finished, the *Machiko* would be the finest-looking ship afloat.

There were more than a hundred different varieties of tree in the forest of Little Tarakang. There were many palms – sago palm, sugar palm, oil palm, betel palm, coconut – and there was scarcely any part of them that could not be put to some use or other as food or in the service of man. There were half a dozen species of tall, slender camphor trees with sweet-smelling wood that blunted axes and saws but made tough and durable pillars. There were shorter ramin trees, favouring peaty swamps, and mighty teaks that towered to over a hundred feet. The Japanese soldiers seemed to know, without being told, which tree out of many to select for felling and to what use its timber might be put. So, while work started on cleaning up the *Machiko*, parties explored the nearby woodland selecting and felling trees for her renovation.

It would be a gross overstatement to say that the prisoners were happy and contented in their work during this period. Their food was still inadequate. Fever and dysentery still took their toll. Tachibana and Yoshimura still made life miserable for them. And Moorhouse continued to irritate everyone.

But, if the prisoners were not happy and contented, at least a change had taken place. They were less unhappy, less dispirited. As the end of their second year on Little Tarakang approached, they had reached that stage of having become so used to the hardships that were their daily parcel that they had become inured to them. What had overwhelmed them as abnormal in the first six months was, in the fourth six months, so commonplace that it was accepted without comment. They had changed, without being fully aware of just how much they had changed.

A change was taking place, too, in Tachibana. Kimura was

aware of this more than anyone. Tachibana still took squads of his engineers to all parts of the island, making them climb cliffs and run through swamps as part of the general training programme, but training for war soon began to pall on Tachibana as a substitute for the real thing. He took to drinking heavily during long sessions which the Europeans referred to as "sulking in his tent". He scoffed at Kimura's enthusiasm for the *Machiko* operation and yet seemed jealous of the occupation it gave Kimura.

The trouble with Tachibana was that he was bored. It was boredom that led him to drinking heavily. It was boredom and a drunken moment which provided him with the sudden ambition to learn English.

He decided at first that Yoshimura should teach him English. But Yoshimura, who went in abject fear of his senior officer and was intent on pleasing him at all times, proved a very bad teacher. He was afraid to correct Tachibana, with the result that when Tachibana went to show off a word or a phrase before one of the European prisoners, he encountered dazed incomprehension instead of instant understanding. Furious, he would return to Yoshimura to vent his displeasure and tell him what an incompetent teacher he was.

He looked around for a better teacher. And he found one in Ruth Gamage. Her role as nurse to the sick meant that she was permanently confined to the camp area, so she was always available whenever the mood for an English lesson took Tachibana.

A third person was always present at the English lessons. The baby who had been rescued from the sea was never far away from Ruth, night or day. He was a robust child and was the one person in the camp who never went short of food. Even Tachibana, who had a heart as hard as Aberdeen granite, doted on the child in a way that the other prisoners found grotesque. They could not reconcile their knowledge of the man with the simpering caricature of an adult who gurgled and cooed at baby Luke. Tachibana even allowed the little boy – who toddled here, there and everywhere – to play with his sword.

Ruth Gamage had no hesitation in correcting Tachibana's grammar or pronunciation. She was a born schoolmarm and went about teaching Tachibana the rudiments of English with a seriousness and prim air that quelled the occasional lustful glances Tachibana cast at her slender neck or carelessly spread legs. Unaware herself of any ability to arouse sexual attraction in men, Ruth was innocently ignorant of the reason or the cause of

176

these stares, which she sometimes intercepted. She was equally unaware of the side of her personality that damped down any ardour that her anatomy provoked. But her "backs-straight-and-pay-attention" tone of voice, delivered in a rather high pitch, acted like a cold shower. It completely de-sexed her and Casanova himself would have taken to the hills at the sound of it.

The textbook she used to teach Tachibana English was the only book in the camp. It was the Bible which Fraser, the Chief Engineer, had brought with him from the *Machiko*. The choice of lesson book was to make Ruth get entirely the wrong impression of Tachibana.

As his English slowly improved, so Tachibana's interest grew in some of the stories Ruth used for her lessons. He quickly became dissatisfied with getting only a glimmer of a story. He wanted to hear the rest. But Ruth's Japanese was inadequate and his own English was not nearly far enough advanced. Communications kept breaking down.

One consequence was that Tachibana took to borrowing the Bible and getting Yoshimura to translate passages to him. It would have given Ruth no comfort to know that Tachibana was most captivated by the gory stories of slaughter and treachery which abound in the Old Testament. Not that he confined his interest to the Old Testament. The Gospel versions of the crucifixion fascinated him, as did certain passages in the gospel of John, which he made Yoshimura translate to him time and again.

Seeking to enlarge his understanding of the stories even more, he talked frequently about them to Ruth. He asked many questions. After a particularly searching session, Ruth returned to her quarters with sparkling eyes and her breast heaving with excitement.

She retired behind the privacy of her woven palm-leaf screen and went down on her knees. Tears streaming down her face, she gave thanks to the God from whose face she had once turned away.

"Thank you, dear Lord, for sending me to this desolate place," she cried. "Thank you for giving me the gift of tongues, that I can speak with the heathen and bring him to your holy light."

Ruth Gamage was convinced that she was about to make her first conversion to the Christian religion. And what a convert God had provided. Not since Saul had been blinded on the road to Damascus had there been a conversion of comparable magnitude. God had sent Major Tachibana to her. And she would lead him to the light.

It did not matter that they said he was a butcher and a murderer. She had seen his cruelty for herself often enough. What mattered was that he had come to the Word. And, with her to guide him and take him by the hand, he would repent of his sins and seek forgiveness before the throne.

The new year was less than a month old. For the Japanese on Little Tarakang, the year 2604 on their calendar was to bring little comfort for them. For their prisoners, the year 1944 began without any special recognition. Early January brought a bigger than usual share of tropical downpours which turned the camp area into a sea of mud. The rainstorms were followed by a period of clear weather with a refreshing breeze cooling the island by day and fanning it gently by night.

It was on a splendidly balmy evening with a tip of orange moon climbing from behind Mount Taki that Lieutenant Yoshimura entered the prisoners' compound and made his way to the "sick" hut. He told Ruth Gamage that she was to follow him. Major Tachibana wanted to speak English with her.

Ruth followed obediently, puzzled that Yoshimura led her in the opposite direction from the one to the Japanese camp. They passed the Tarakangese quarters along a long stretch of palm-fringed beach that was silver in the moonlight. Ruth hoped that little Luke would not wake up and fret because she had gone. Despite this nagging worry, she walked with a light step. She was convinced that the time was near when Major Tachibana would take the momentous step of embracing the Christian faith. She felt sure that it was only a strange shyness which prevented him asking her. She wanted more than anything to be the one who baptised him. She had hinted at it in a roundabout way but he had either not understood or pretended not to understand what she was talking about. Now her heart beat a little more quickly. This night-time summons could only mean that he had been thinking about what she had said and had reached a decision.

Her first doubts occurred when she and Yoshimura came upon Major Tachibana. He was sitting cross-legged in the sand, a bottle within hand's reach. Ruth Gamage blinked in disappointment. Major Tachibana looked drunk. Furthermore, he was almost naked. His only garment was a white loincloth. She had seen plenty of ordinary soldiers going around the island in this garb, but never Major Tachibana.

Tachibana beamed when he saw her and made a long garbled speech in Japanese. Ruth turned desperately to Yoshimura.

"What is he saying?"

Yoshimura smiled.

"Major Tachibana says he feels very benevolent towards you. That is why he sends for you. He says that perhaps tonight he will permit you to join him in water-bathing ceremony you tell him about."

"You mean Major Tachibana wants me to baptise him as a Christian?"

Yoshimura conveyed this to Tachibana. Then they exchanged words. Tachibana seemed quite angry with Yoshimura. The latter turned to Ruth.

"Major Tachibana does not understand the meaning of word you used – 'baptise'. There is not good word for this in Nippongo. I cannot explain to him. He says that you talked of bathing in water. Prisoners not allowed to bathe in water. But Major Tachibana says for you OK. He give permission."

"You must tell him that there's been some misunderstanding. I want to baptise him in the name of the Lord, as the Lord Himself was baptised in the River Jordan. If I baptise him with water, the Holy Spirit will come to him and his sins will be forgiven. Does he want to be baptised in the lagoon?"

Yoshimura looked at her doubtfully.

"I do not understand what you say."

Tachibana angrily demanded to know what all the talk was about. Yoshimura tried to explain, but he plainly had been baffled by what Ruth had said. Finally, he turned again to Ruth.

"Major Tachibana says that you talked with him of bathing together in water. Honoured Japanese custom to bathe in water. He give permission for you. Now you bathe in water or he get very angry."

Tachibana got to his feet. He lurched drunkenly and then, with sedate steps, waded into the water. His ankles covered, he stood there, waiting. He stared impatiently at Ruth. She made no move. She was terrified.

Tachibana barked impatiently at Yoshimura.

"What is he saying now?" whispered Ruth.

"He says you better get clothes off pretty damn quick. He is getting angry."

"I can't possibly take my clothes off," she protested, almost in tears.

Yoshimura translated once more. There was no mistaking Tachibana's anger now.

"Major Tachibana wants to know if you are deformed or stupid," Yoshimura said to Ruth. "How can you bathe with clothes on? He has never heard anything of such silliness. He says all clothes must come off pretty damn quick or he will order me to get hard stick and beat you into water."

Crying softly to herself, Ruth slipped off her tattered frock. Then, seeing Yoshimura nodding encouragement to complete the process, she lowered the long-legged bloomers she wore. Tachibana stared in astonishment at the contrast between the pale white skin of her body and the red-brown colour of her legs and arms. No wonder she kept her body hidden, he thought drunkenly. It was as if she were painted in stripes. The body held no attraction for him. He wondered how European men ever got round to breeding with women if they were all as ugly as Ruth Gamage.

Lieutenant Yoshimura was not quite so disinterested in Ruth's natural endowments. He remained quite impassive, but a trickle of saliva wet his lips and he curled his tongue inside his mouth. The woman would make an exciting change from the big-hipped Tarakangese women.

Ruth entered the water and waded out to a depth that covered most of her embarrassment. Tachibana followed. For a time, he splashed water on himself. Then he spoke to Ruth in Japanese. She had to call out for Yoshimura to translate.

"Major Tachibana is waiting for you to perform ceremony," the interpreter called back. Ruth felt a glow of hope. He *does* want to be baptised, she thought.

She bowed her head and began to pray aloud. Tachibana watched her, mystified. His mystification turned to alarm as she advanced on him with a look of determination and, before he could work out her intentions, she seized him by the back of his head and pushed him under the water.

Only Yoshimura heard her cry: "In the name of the Father, the Son and the Holy Spirit . . ." Tachibana, totally surprised, swallowed a large quantity of sea water. The water stung his eyes and filled his nostrils. The madwoman was trying to drown him!

He spluttered to the surface, shaking himself free of the claw-like hand gripping the hair at the back of his neck. Seizing Ruth by an arm he threw her from him. She went under and came up spluttering. She staggered into shallow water. She was almost on

180

the beach when he caught her and struck a savage blow at her. It struck her on the back, just below the left shoulder. She went face-down in the sand.

Tachibana stood over her for a moment, eyes glaring and breath coming in spluttering gasps. Then he aimed a kick at the sprawling, weeping woman and walked away.

Yoshimura threw a question after him. He turned momentarily.

"Teach her to have some respect for a Japanese officer!" he said brusquely, and continued along the beach.

Ruth struggled to her hands and knees. She had sand in her mouth, her nose, her hair. Tears and sea water coursed in rivulets, making little tracks through the sand caked on her face. She sobbed in despair, her senses scattered to the wind. Time and place had lost meaning. A fog of bewilderment had taken over her mind.

She was dragged back to reality by a hand seizing her hair. She let out a cry of pain as the skin of her scalp lifted and she was bodily lifted round and thrown so that she fell on her back in the sand. She turned terror-filled eyes upwards to stare into the grinning weasel face of Lieutenant Yoshimura. He stood astride her body unfastening the belt of his trousers. At first, she did not comprehend. Then the look on his face, the deliberate unbuttoning of his trousers, made his intentions all too plain. She screamed.

The scream was silenced as he fell on her with such vehemence that the breath was knocked from her body. By the time she managed once again to gasp air into her lungs, she could feel the first tearing pain of impatient violation. She writhed and struck out with her hands. A stinging blow on the end of his nose momentarily reduced Yoshimura's ardour. Snarling at the sudden pain, he struck angrily at Ruth's face with his clenched fist. Her head was dashed back against the sand of the beach and blood welled from a three-inch break in her skin just below her left eye. Yoshimura seized both her wrists and pinioned them on the sand. She continued to writhe in an effort to free her body from underneath him. He struck her another savage blow. Her struggles weakened. He forced her thighs brutally apart with his knees and once again forced himself on her. Pain exploded in her as her flesh seemed to tear apart under the force of his frantic thrusting. She cried and cried as the brutal stabbing violation came again and again. She tried to turn her face away from the

181

hot foul breath of his mouth as he panted like a slavering animal inches from her own mouth. She started struggling more fiercely than ever when, with a heavy grunt, he withdrew from her body and suddenly let her go.

He remained on his knees fastening his trousers. She struggled into a crouching position, eyeing him with loathing and fear. He was buckling his belt as if he had already forgotten her presence. His sword in its scabbard lay where he had put it down on the beach a few feet away. She made a sudden dash towards it.

As soon as he realised the reason for her sudden movement, he moved, too. But she reached the sword first. Even if it had been her intention to unsheath the sword, there was no time to do so. She swung at him with the scabbarded weapon as he threw himself at her. She had struck out with all her might in a wide swinging blow. It caught him fully across the face, from nose to side of jaw, catching him off balance as his momentum carried him forward. He pitched past her to fall on the beach near her feet. Before he could move, she struck again, bringing the scabbard down on the top of his head. The blow dazed him. She backed away. He got to his knees, staring up at her with gleaming eyes, his lips curling over bared teeth. He was making a low snarling sound like an animal.

Ruth turned and ran.

He shouted to her to stop. She kept on running. With a cry of fury he took off after her. The moonlight accentuated the white gleam of her naked body as she ran. She stumbled once, striking her toe against a piece of driftwood. She cried out briefly at the pain and kept running . . . Past the Tarakangese camp . . . Past the staked perimeter line of the *Machiko* camp.

Big Rich, emerging from the *benjo*, and shaky on his feet from the onset of a dysentery attack, turned in astonishment at the sight of a naked Ruth Gamage running towards him.

"Help me, help me, please," she cried. "He's going to kill me." She collapsed into the big man's arms.

"Who's going to kill you, lass?" he murmured. She did not need to answer. Yoshimura, eyes wild, came towards them at a run. He stopped at the sight of Rich and stood, gulping for breath, staring at them.

"She die," he said. "She try to kill me. So, now, she die."

He made a sudden lunge at Ruth. The big Australian was taken by surprise at the speed with which Yoshimura moved. The interpreter yanked at Ruth's hair, getting enough of it to pull her

182

away from Rich and throw her to the ground. He aimed a vicious blow at her as she fell and then lashed a kick at her as she lay on the ground. It was his last act on this earth.

Rich fell on him with an angry cry. Two massive hands fastened themselves round Yoshimura's neck. The Japanese felt himself being slowly lifted. Briefly, he dangled in the Australian's grip, his toes just touching the ground. Then, with an angry snarl, Rich lifted Yoshimura clear of the ground. Yoshimura's eyes were popping and strange little gasping coughs were spluttering from his mouth. His legs kicked out wildly. Rich tightened his stranglehold. The kicking of Yoshimura's legs became feebler and feebler, until they stopped altogether.

Yoshimura was dead.

Twelve

Execution

What annoyed Kimura more than anything was that a whole working day on the *Machiko* was being lost as a result of the regrettable incident. He sat hunched at the long table of the camp office, his booted feet resting on the centre trestle. Some papers were spread out before him.

Tachibana had done the correct thing, of course, in confining all prisoners to their quarters for the time being. And it had been an extraordinary act of courtesy on Tachibana's part that, instead of summarily dealing with Yoshimura's murderer as he was entitled to do, he had invited Kimura to preside over an official inquiry.

"This is more than just a breach of discipline on the part of a prisoner," Tachibana had said. "An officer of the Imperial Forces has been murdered. Colonel Watanabe is going to ask questions, even Tokyo. For both our sakes, we must show that we followed a careful procedure and a correct one and that it was not a neglect of discipline on the part of either of us that led to the incident. We could have the Kempei-Tai running all over the island wanting to know what happened to Yoshimura. It could be awkward for me and it could be awkward for you. Far better if we show that we acted jointly and acted quickly."

So Tachibana's courtesy had not entirely been without self-interest. He just wanted to make damned sure that no one came snooping around asking questions and finding out that while his second-in-command was being strangled, he was a mile away snoring his head off on the beach, dead drunk.

The proceedings were relatively short. The Australian prisoner, Richardson, had been brought in and questioned. Yes, he admitted, he had killed Lieutenant Yoshimura with his bare hands. Why? Because the little rat had attacked Miss Gamage and

184

would have killed her, that's why. Did he realise that the offence of merely striking a Japanese officer was punishable by death and that, for the crime with which he was charged – that of killing an officer of the Imperial Forces – there could be no hope of mercy? Yes, he knew that. He expected no mercy.

Kimura noted the gash on the side of the Australian's head. It had taken three guards to control the prisoner after he had killed the little interpreter. These guards were now summoned and they told how they had come upon the Australian holding Yoshimura by the neck and shaking him like a rat.

Ruth Gamage, dressed in a pair of baggy shorts and a man's shirt, had been summoned at the express wish of Tachibana. With Kimura's assent, he also did the questioning. He spoke only in Japanese, which meant that Kimura had to repeat the questions to her. She looked from one man to the other in a complete daze. She seemed to be in a state of severe shock.

She stared dumbly at Kimura when he translated. "Are you aware of the severe punishments for showing disrespect or insubordination to an officer of the Imperial Forces?"

"Yes," she mumbled.

And did she agree that anyone guilty of this offence deserved to be punished with the utmost severity? Blinking back tears, she said, "I suppose so."

And had she shown disrespect to an officer of the Imperial Forces? While Kimura asked the question in English, Tachibana stared at Ruth so hard that she could not look him in the eye.

"What do you want me to say?" she cried.

"Please just answer Major Tachibana's question," said Kimura. He was not sure exactly what had happened between Tachibana and the woman the previous night. Nor did he understand why Tachibana was asking the question.

"Major Tachibana thinks I showed him disrespect," she sobbed tearfully. "But I didn't . . . I didn't mean to . . ."

Tachibana spoke rapidly to Kimura, who said:

"Major Tachibana wants to know if it is not a fact that he went out of his way to show you special kindness? He also wants to know why, as a result of his benevolence, you insulted him in front of Lieutenant Yoshimura?"

Ruth turned pleading eyes in Tachibana's direction.

"I didn't mean to insult you," she cried out in a beseeching wail. "Don't you understand? I only wanted to win your heart for Jesus Christ . . ."

Tachibana continued to stare at her in a stony-faced way that completely unnerved her. Kimura translated what she had said and looked at Tachibana in puzzlement. Why should she want Tachibana's heart for her god? Had she attacked him with a knife? Tachibana, boring at Ruth with his eyes, fired a question at her.

"I don't know what you're asking me," Ruth screamed at him.

"Please do not shout at an officer of Nippon," Kimura rebuked her sternly. "Major Tachibana asks if you feel no shame for what has happened. Lieutenant Yoshimura is dead and the Australian will certainly die. Do you not deserve to die, too?"

A shudder ran through her. Eyes gleaming with a strange light, she cried out, "Yes, yes, yes. Let me die . . . Not the other man . . . I want to die . . . I don't want to live . . . It is me you must kill for it was me who sinned . . ."

She sank to her knees, hands clasped in front of her.

"Grant me death," she murmured softly. "Grant me death that the Lord and father of us all might grant me eternal life."

Tachibana and Kimura exchanged looks. Kimura was convinced the woman was completely deranged. She talked in riddles, one minute protesting her innocence and the next declaring her guilt. It was a strange facet of Western religions that their priests and holy people tended to rant and rave rather than aspire to holiness through the disciplines of meditation and silence. Tachibana, however, seemed to appreciate the woman's desire for death. He was looking at her with grudging admiration.

"Ask her if she saw the Australian strangle Yoshimura," he said to Kimura.

Ruth remained on her knees and looked at Kimura with startled eyes when he put Tachibana's question to her. He repeated it when she did not answer.

"Yes," she whispered, and the memory of it brought back all the horror of the night before. Another shudder racked her and her face seemed to dissolve. She let her head fall forward on to her hands on the floor and she lay there, letting the sobs convulse through her.

Tachibana signalled to a guard, who carried her out none too gently.

"Do you really want to punish her?" Kimura asked.

"No," said Tachibana. "If she wants to die, let her do it with her own hand. Let us get this business finished. The Englishman who speaks for the prisoners wanted to be heard. We shall hear the wretch if you have no objections. I shall write the order of execution for the Australian while you question him. He does not understand Nippon-go."

Moorhouse was brought in. He looked extremely nervous.

"You wished to speak to the officers of this inquiry?" said Kimura. "You have been granted the opportunity."

"I . . . I . . ." Moorhouse licked his lips. He suddenly remembered that he had not performed the compulsory courtesy of bowing. He did so belatedly. Kimura sighed with impatience.

"Major Kimura, Major Tachibana," Moorhouse bowed again as he began, "let me first of all express my deep regret at the unfortunate death of Lieutenant Yoshimura . . ." Liar, thought Kimura. No one with the possible exception of the sow who mothered him was going to mourn the passing of Yoshimura.' Moorhouse was continuing, "All of us have been shocked by the tragedy . . ." He took a deep breath. "However, on behalf of His Majesty King George's subjects incarcerated on this island, I wish to make the most earnest request to you, the representatives of His Imperial Majesty of Japan, to take no action against Private Richardson or any other prisoner without a fair and proper trial before a constituted court and with legal representatives present."

Tachibana looked up from writing and pushed a document in front of Kimura. Kimura acknowledged receipt of it with a flicker of an eye and Tachibana resumed writing. Kimura picked up the document he had been passed and eyed Moorhouse solemnly.

"This order," he said, "is a direct instruction to the commanders of all prisoner-of-war and civilian internee camps from General Hideki Tojo, First Minister of Nippon and Minister of War. I shall translate for you. It says: 'In the event that prisoner is guilty of act of insubordination, he shall be subject to imprisonment or arrest . . .'" Here Kimura paused before continuing with emphasis on the final words of the order. "'. . . *and any other measures deemed necessary for the purpose of discipline may be added*.'"

Kimura let the words sink in. Then he went on, "An officer of the Imperial Forces has been murdered by a prisoner. It is within the power of Japanese commander to have prisoner shot for far less serious crime than murder. Do you accuse Japanese commander of acting in improper way? Do you challenge authority of Japanese officers to act with justice? This is military area, and law here is military law."

Moorhouse bowed nervously.

"I acknowledge your authority, Major Kimura, and Major Tachibana's, too. I do not accuse you of anything. If this is a properly constituted military court, I would merely make the humble petition that it takes into account all the factors surrounding the death of Lieutenant Yoshimura and, in its wisdom, seeks to dispense mercy as well as justice."

"These are fine words," Kimura said, with a slight inclination of the head to accord his appreciation, "but, noble as they are, they cannot deflect justice from the course it must follow. Circumstances may demand mercy, but facts demand justice. It is fact that Lieutenant Yoshimura is dead. It is fact that Private Richardson killed him with his own hands. It is fact that the killer has openly confessed his crime before this inquiry. It is fact that he has asked for no mercy to be shown to him. It is also fact that the woman, Gamage, witnessed the crime and has testified to the guilt of Private Richardson. Can you present us with more facts?"

"No," murmured Moorhouse.

"Then you are dismissed."

When Moorhouse had gone, Tachibana pushed across the piece of paper on which he had been writing. It was dated and headed with the Area Command location. A sub-heading said simply, "Death Punishment Order". There followed:

1 To be carried out on Private Richardson, prisoner.
2 To be witnessed by Lieutenant Niguchi, 93rd Independent Coastal Group.
3 Executing officer, Major Ito Tachibana, 76th Div. Special Guard Section.
4 Issuing officer and officer to whom confirmation of execution is to be presented – Major Hitoshi Kimura, Commander, 93rd Independent Coastal Group.

"All you have to do is sign it," said Tachibana. "You can leave the rest to me."

Kimura signed his name and returned the form to Tachibana. He was thankful it was all over. Now, he could get back to work.

Two of the *Machiko*'s crew had to hold Woody back from breaking out of the long-house when the small procession from the Japanese camp came in sight. Tachibana was at the front in full uniform. He was followed by Rich, who was flanked on either side by two guards with rifles and fixed bayonets. Lieutenant Niguchi brought up the rear. They had to pass close to the prisoners' long-house, where four of Tachibana's men had been posted with orders to shoot any prisoner venturing outside.

Woody didn't give a damn about the guards. The moment that he saw Big Rich and his escort, he knew exactly what the Japanese were up to and he knew he couldn't allow it to happen. Anything was preferable. Better to die fighting. He made a sudden charge for the door, shouting Rich's name at the top of his voice.

Two of Ross' men cut him off when they realised the Australian intended to charge right out of the long-house. But it took four men, eventually, to hold him down. He was fighting mad and screaming all the time to Rich to break and fight for it.

Rich heard his friend shouting and felt a glow of comfort. Woody's words were unclear, as if somebody was trying to shut him up, but Rich guessed exactly what he was trying when he saw the guards round the long-house raise their rifles and cover the doorway. Tears glittered in Rich's eyes. Oh, Woody – he thought – you dear stupid lovable bastard. Rich looked around him. The temptation to throw himself on the nearest guard and grab his rifle was considerable. The Japs would get him and Woody in the end, of course, but they would take a Jap or two with them.

Rich put the temptation away. He didn't want Woody to die just to prove to him that they were cobbers right to the end. Rich knew that. Woody didn't have to prove it. In any case, Woody hadn't got used to the idea of dying as *he* had in the last twenty hours or so. Since early morning, he had become quite reconciled to the fact that the Japs would never let him off for wringing Yoshimura's neck. Well, he intended to show them that they weren't the only ones who knew how to die. He would look them straight in the face and let them see the stuff Australians were made of. The next one they saw, he hoped, would be coming at them with a bayonet.

Tachibana had halted the procession as a result of the distur-bance coming from the prisoners' sleeping-house. He ordered one of the guards covering the door to investigate. The guard kicked open the flimsy frame of woven palm-leaf. The men who were holding Woody down scattered before his bayonet. He placed a foot on Woody's chest and held the bayonet at the Australian's throat.

"All right, you bastard, kill me!" Woody screamed. The guard shouted something to Tachibana. It was a request to comply with the Australian's wishes. Tachibana refused the request. Instead, he let Rich know that he could advance to within five yards of the long-house and say farewell to his friends there. He should also advise them to stay quiet. Rich amazed himself with the jollity he managed to get into his voice.

"Hey, Woody, old sport. Keep the lid on that old steam kettle of yours," he called. "Save your steam until you got a Lewis or something to even out the odds. Like that day up on the Kerbau."

Woody pressed against the restraining bayonet.

"What are they going to do to you, Rich?"

"They're takin' me for a walk on the beach," said Rich. "It's nothing to get all excited about."

"They're going to have to take me, too!" yelled Woody.

"Like hell, they are! Look, Woody, I'd like to have you along — but you've been wipin' my nose all my life. I'll take care of this myself. I showed them before, didn't I? When they tried the rock treatment. Well, I'll show 'em again. It's my party, Woody. You ain't invited."

"Oh, God, Rich! Rich!" Woody's voice was strangled with passion.

"So long, old sport."

Rich turned and walked back to where Tachibana was waiting. The guards fell in around him.

As the small party moved off towards the beach, the soldier with his bayonet at Woody's neck stepped back and motioned the Australian into the long-house. Woody was calm now. He went and sat against the wall. He rocked gently back and forward, his arms clasped around his knees. He stared straight ahead of him at nothing, and saying nothing.

The others left him alone but, after a few moments, Ross went over and sat down beside him.

"Talking doesn't help much," Ross said softly. "And I wouldn't blame you if you told me to go to hell. But Rich was right, Woody. Your committing suicide wouldn't have helped."

Woody remained silent, so Ross went on, "I'm going to need you, Woody. We're all going to need you. We've been cooped up in this hell-hole too long and we've all wondered about whether it's worth going on living or not. But just giving the Japs an excuse to shoot us and finish it isn't the way. Better if we have an objective, some kind of prize. Better if we find a reason that's worth dying for."

A spark of interest showed in Woody's eyes. He glanced sideways at Ross.

190

"A friend is worth dying for, Captain. Can you give me a better reason?"

"Yes, Woody . . . freedom. Your freedom and mine. The freedom of all of us here who are prepared to risk dying for it."

Woody's interest was now more than a flicker.

"What makes you think we have a hope in hell of getting away from this godforsaken island?" he asked.

Ross smiled.

"I'd say the odds against us getting away with it are about a thousand to one. That's why I haven't sounded anybody out yet. You're the first. I just want you to think about it and let me know what your position's going to be when I start taking names . . . Whether you want in or out."

Woody's eyes gleamed.

"I made up my mind a long time ago, Skipper. I've been thinking about it ever since they put us to work on that broken-down old ship of yours. Rich and I talked about it. We were going to . . . Well, what the hell does it matter what we were going to do? Rich . . . Rich . . ." He broke off. It was more than he could do to talk about Rich at that moment. He turned his face away from Ross so that the captain would not see that he was crying.

The small party, in which Rich was the central figure, had halted on the beach about half a mile past the Tarakangese camp. The big Australian glanced only for a moment at the shallow trench which had already been dug. It seemed scarcely big enough to accommodate the body of a man. Rich looked back towards the low end of the island, in the direction of the camps and the forest beyond. The setting sun was dipping below the distant green rim.

Rich turned as a finger gently tapped his shoulder. Lieutenant Niguchi stood there, holding a strip of grey-coloured cloth.

"When the sun sets, it will be time," said Niguchi. "You have three minutes. Major Tachibana asks if there is anything you wish to say before he kills you?"

"How will it be done?" Rich asked hoarsely.

"According to Japanese Bushido custom," replied Niguchi. "With the sword."

Tachibana had taken his sword from its scabbard and was holding it two-handed. He was staring grimly at Rich.

"Off-lolly?" Rich asked Tachibana, returning his stare.

"Off-lolly," said Tachibana.

"You'd better make it good, old Tigerface," said Rich, his eyes

191

never wavering from Tachibana's face. He held up a hand and showed Tachibana the index finger. "One chop, you frozen-faced bastard. That's your ration."

Tachibana understood without Niguchi having to translate. He bowed and held up one finger to signify that he understood.

"Let's get on with it then," said Rich and, with a final triumphant stare at Tachibana, turned to see the last red tip of sun disappear below the far horizon. He nodded to Niguchi, who fastened the strip of cloth round his eyes with trembling fingers. Rich dropped to his knees and bowed his head.

Tachibana's sword flashed in the fading light. From the watchers, a long sighing sound was emitted – as if they had all held their breath and let it out simultaneously. Tachibana carefully wiped the blood from his sword with a cloth he had taken from a pocket. Then he stood over the headless body of the Australian and drew a long knife from a sheath below his tunic.

Niguchi turned away, sick with horror, as Tachibana plunged the knife into the corpse and mutilated it further. The young lieutenant could watch no more. He turned away and stumbled off along the beach, retching audibly.

It was some hours later that Ross was taken, under an escort of two guards, to Tachibana's quarters. Tachibana was dressed in an all-white kimono and sitting on the floor. In front of him were two bowls of *sake*. Sitting on the floor opposite him was Ruth Gamage. She seemed to be in trance or shock. She was making a low wailing sound, her eyes tightly shut. She was rocking back and forward on her heels and seemed oblivious, not only of Tachibana and of Ross but of all outward reality.

All communication had certainly broken down again between Tachibana and Ruth. It was because of this that Ross had been sent for. Somewhat impatiently, Tachibana explained to Ross that out of respect for the Christian woman's god he had not once, but twice, tried to express great benevolence to her only to encounter a wall of incomprehension, due to the woman's stupidity or madness.

It was not until Tachibana pointed angrily to the book at one side of Ruth that Ross noticed the Bible for the first time. Tachibana roundly cursed the book as the product of devils and said it was the cause of Ruth's madness. First, there was the nonsense about the bathing ceremony and, now – when he had gone out of his way to get her on good terms with her god through the feast ceremony – she just sat babbling like one who was insane.

"What feast ceremony do you mean?" asked Ross, mystified by Tachibana's remarks and the man's bizarre relationship with Ruth. "And what has it to do with the Christian god of the woman?"

"I learn the English language from the woman," said Tachibana. "And she tells me many things about her gods – the one who sits in heaven like the Buddha, the one who comes to the earth to die, and the one who lives in the wind like a spirit. She speaks of three gods that are one god." Tachibana let out a grunt of anger and smacked a hand against his knee to emphasise his disgust. "I tell her of Japanese gods," he went on. "I tell her that when soldier of Nippon die, soldier becomes god to people of Nippon." He snorted expressively. "Woman tells me that when Christian soldier die, he too becomes a god and lives forever in the home of the Father god."

"Yes, I can see roughly what she meant." Ross nodded doubtfully. "You do not believe this?"

"I believe woman," replied Tachibana. "I believe woman when she tells me that bathing ceremony is very important to people of her god. I also believe her when she tells me that divine feast is important way to talk to her god. It is very strange to Japanese but I ask woman to show me how person can talk with god and get strength from god by eating god."

"Eating god?" Ross stared at Tachibana, taken aback. Then, understanding suddenly dawned. "She told you about Communion? Holy Communion? Where bread is eaten and wine is drunk?"

Tachibana was nodding enthusiastically.

"Yes, yes. Exactly so. But she say bread is not bread but flesh of her god."

Ross felt progress was being made. He waited now for Tachibana to elaborate and explain where understanding had broken down.

Tachibana, however, was perplexed that Ross did not apparently understand all without further elaboration. When Ross did not speak, the Japanese rose and went to the small recess that represented his own personal shrine or *tokonama*. From the central shelf, he took a small dish which he showed to Ross. The action seemed to bring Ruth Gamage back to reality. She stopped her low-pitched wailing and screamed, "Take it away, you beast! Take it away!"

Tachibana exchanged a look with Ross, as if to say, "You see. She is completely irrational."

Ross stared at the contents of the dish and felt his stomach turn. "What is it?" he asked.

"It is the heart of the brave Australian soldier," said Tachibana.

Ross thought he was going to be sick. The whole of his insides were heaving as he turned his head away. He did not know what he had expected – but it had certainly not been this.

"Please take it away," he asked Tachibana, his voice a whisper. At that moment, he wondered how it could be that a race that had given him his sweet and beloved Machiko could also have spawned the evil monster standing before him with a look of growing anger darkening his face.

"Does this sight offend you, Colonial pig?" he shouted at Ross. "Have you no more stomach than woman to look on something that should be sacred to all who call themselves Christian? This is not bread that you can use to pretend to be flesh of your god. This is real thing, the flesh of one of your own kind who died a brave and memorable death and became a god only today. I spit on you and your gods!"

He was shaking with anger. He called in his guards and told them to return the two prisoners to their camp.

"Beat them back to their kennels like dogs," he shouted. The guards made a show of driving the pair before them. Ross staggered under a blow from a rifle butt which struck him in the kidney area. But he still managed to put an arm round Ruth Gamage and protect her. Out of Tachibana's sight, the guards relented. The execution on the beach had satisfied any hunger they'd had that day for violence. More than one had been sickened by talk that Tachibana had not only executed the Australian but had mutilated the body afterwards.

Ruth huddled against Ross, weeping uncontrollably. She could scarcely stand up. Later, he carried her into the section of hut where little Luke was sleeping peacefully, unaware of the horror and violence of Little Tarakang.

Ross laid Ruth down on the wooden platform that served as her bed. He stayed with her, sending away those who came to ask if there was anything they could do. He allowed her to cling to him in her grief and bewilderment. He tried to find words that would comfort her. He found himself lying about what Tachibana had done.

"He was only trying to frighten us. It wasn't what he said it was," he murmured. "It was a nasty and cruel joke. Try to forget it ever happened."

Calmer, she clutched at his words like a lifeline in a whirling sea. Ross was right. It was a cruel and evil trick on Tachibana's part. No human being would do what Tachibana had said he'd done. It was what she wanted to believe, so she believed it.

"We'll not even talk about it again," Ross soothed. "To anyone." At the back of Ross' mind was the unpredictability of what Woody might do if he were ever to learn of Tachibana's ultimate outrage. The strange thing was that the Japanese officer seemed to have got the idea stuck in his head that he was honouring both the man he had killed and this poor confused woman. How innocent she really was: so bravely trying to inspire godliness and provide answers for the world, before she had even learned all the questions.

Ross wondered what brutality she had suffered at Yoshimura's hands before running naked into the camp the night before. They had got little from her: only that the interpreter had attacked her. Had he raped her as well as beaten her? They would never know the whole story in all probability. Poor kid. In the short space of twenty-four hours she had been subjected to more horror than lots of people encounter in the whole of their lives. On top of two years of sheer hell, it was possible that her mind had buckled completely.

"Try to sleep," he coaxed her gently. "Try to sleep. Little Luke is going to need you in the morning. You're the only mother he's got."

"I'm going to need him," she replied, her eyes suddenly clear. "It's not Luke that needs me, Captain. It's the other way round. I can see that now. He's all I've got to hold on to . . . Now that even God has forsaken me."

"God hasn't forsaken you, Ruth," Ross said softly. "It's just that He's got an awful lot on his plate right at this moment. We always expect Him to be right where we want Him all of the time, because people like us take Him as a very personal God. But He's like the wind when we need a breeze to fill our sail . . . Sometimes He's there just when you need Him, but sometimes there just isn't enough breath in heaven to keep you going along. That's when you think He isn't there at all. Like now. But, come tomorrow, He could whistle up a hurricane and maybe that would be more than we bargained for. What do we say then? That there's too much God? No, Ruth. We don't control the force of the wind any more

195

than we control the force of God. We go where the wind takes us, through rough seas and smooth, through the calm and through the storm, through familiar shallows and through angry seas that there never was any human chart for. We never see the wind, Ruth – but it's always there, never sleeping, never stopping, always moving with a will of its own . . ."

Ross kept speaking soothingly, comfortingly, conscious that he was putting into his own sailor's choice of words those of a gentle grandmother who had held him close and comforted him as a small child. It was language Ruth seemed to understand as she hung by a thread from the precipice of her sanity. She responded to it, pulling herself back to reason.

She was sleeping peacefully when, finally, he stole away. Outside, in the moonlit splendour of the tropical night, he leaned for a moment with his back against the wall of the "hospital". He felt drained, exhausted. He was not a formally religious man. The ceremony and ritual bored him, whether they were High Church or Hindu Festival. His open mind had, however, been interested – often stimulated·– by the translation of religious ethic into human habit as he had observed it in the way men of many races and differing beliefs lived their lives.

Ross wondered if he had been right to whisper platitudes in Ruth Gamage's ear in order to help her cling to the wearing shreds of her faith. He had fed her with answers and certainties as if they were rooted in his mind. But could he have shared the doubts which multiplied there with the passing of his days and gave birth to a thousand questions and a myriad of riddles?

"Oh God," Ross breathed aloud, "I believe. But what is it that I believe in?" It was almost a cry of agony. He was crushed by the thought that man was supposedly made in the image of God. But when he looked at the works of man, why was it that in so many places he could only see the works of the devil?

196

Thirteen

Seppuku

Of the twenty-three islands that made up the group known as the Outer Tarakangs, seven had been occupied by the Japanese. By far the greatest concentration of men was on the principal island, Great Tarakang, where the airfield was situated and Colonel Watanabe had his Area Command headquarters. There were more than three thousand Japanese on the island, including the Navy pilots and backup personnel who operated the airfield. Watanabe's area was one of three which came under Divisional Command, located in New Britain. The other areas were one in northern New Guinea and one centred on a small group of islands a hundred miles east of the Tarakangs.

As the war progressed, each of the areas was encouraged to become more and more independent of Division and become separate entities, responsible for their own fortunes as McArthur's Allied Forces advanced, cutting communication lines and isolating pockets of Japanese in their wake.

Some of these pockets of Japanese garrisons were mopped up as men and ships became available. These operations were considered sideshows to the main event: the thrust towards the Philippines. Other pockets of resistance were left "to wither on the vine". Cut off from their own forces and starved of all supplies, these island garrisons were left to die or to fight to the death in the event that the Allies ever got round to winkling them out.

In addition to the three thousand men Colonel Watanabe had on Great Tarakang, he had another thousand scattered among the half-dozen other occupied islands of the group. These – in the same way that the Divisional control had been broken down – were fully independent, but all were subservient to one basic purpose: the defence and continued operation of the airfield on Great Tarakang. It was because of the airfield that Colonel

197

Watanabe believed that the Allies would never leave Great Tarakang "to wither on the vine". This was less because the airfield posed a major threat to the Allied advance than because it represented a major prize for their own air forces. From Great Tarakang, the Allies could greatly increase the range of their targets further west in the Philippines and Borneo.

Watanabe had always believed, however, that the airfield itself – or rather the aircraft operating from it – would play a vital part in the defence of Great Tarakang against any attack. So, it was with a heavy heart that he summoned the commanders from the other islands in his area to a special emergency meeting at his headquarters in the spring of 1944. These commanders included Major Hitoshi Kimura from nearby Little Tarakang.

Watanabe faced them solemnly down the length of the long teak table in the operations room.

"Gentlemen, I shall not dwell on the unhappy circumstances which have forced me to bring you all together, perhaps for the last time. You know, as I do, that in the near future this island will come under attack from the American beasts and their allies. If they succeed, it will be because not one of us is left alive. In the event of this island falling – and it is certain to bear the brunt of any attack – you will carry on the fight from your own bases. You will make the enemy pay a high cost for every inch of ground you cede to him. There will be no surrender."

The officers round the table nodded gravely as Watanabe spoke. He imparted now the news which was the underlying reason for their summons.

"Yesterday, I received orders which greatly impair our chances of successfully holding these islands against the overwhelming odds we are likely to face. At dawn tomorrow morning, the hundred and fifty operational aircraft stationed on Great Tarakang will begin taking off to join a naval taskforce six hundred miles away at sea. They will not be returning to the island. As you know, we have had great difficulty maintaining fuel supplies for the aircraft. Tankers destined to supply the island have failed to reach us, with the result that for every bomber we put in the air, three have had to remain idle on the ground through lack of fuel. It is essential that these aircraft be moved to bases closer to their source of supply. The onus on our land forces to defend with great resolution becomes, therefore, that much heavier."

When the conference was over, Watanabe drew Kimura to one

198

side to congratulate him on the concealment of the artillery positions and communications post on Mount Taki.

"They are quite invisible from the air," said Watanabe. "We had some aerial photographs taken of the entire area, so that we could draw maps showing all the defence locations – but we couldn't find any of the Mount Taki installations. You have done your camouflage work extremely well, Kimura."

Kimura basked in the senior officer's praise. Watanabe was notorious for his parsimony with compliments and to be singled out for any was a rare honour indeed. Kimura's pleasure did not last. He reported with some pride on his efforts to make the *Machiko* a worthy new addition to the Japanese fleet, but his enthusiasm was greeted by Watanabe with an indifference that was painful.

"Your enterprise is commendable, Kimura," said Watanabe, "but in the present position it is a complete waste of men and resources. We have more or less been abandoned here by the Navy, so what use is that ship going to be? The Navy certainly won't try to fetch it and we are going to have our hands full with the Americans any day. All your work has been for nothing."

"But, sir," protested Kimura, "in a week or two, the ship will be ready for sea. We are already beginning to reload its cargo of machinery, which will be invaluable to the war effort at home. Surely, some effort must be made to get the ship to Japan – or at least to Manila or some other area where it will be of use. You yourself have often spoken of how desperate we are for ships."

Watanabe did not like the rebellious tone of Kimura's voice but, for the moment, he was prepared to overlook it.

"That was before the Navy decided to evacuate Great Tarakang," he replied. "They won't be sending ships to evacuate us. We shall fight here, Kimura, and we shall probably die here. Under the circumstances, I do not propose to lose any sleep over what happens to a burnt-out old freighter that has been rotting in your lagoon for over two years."

"But what's to be done with it?" asked Kimura.

"Get rid of it," said Watanabe. "Or, at least, get it seaworthy enough to bring it across the Straits to Great Tarakang. The Navy can then come and collect it or we shall sink it as a blockship in the harbour and deny the Americans the use of the port if they ever drive us out."

That was that. Kimura knew better than to argue. But there was one other matter he had to raise with Watanabe. In the event of

199

an American attack on the islands, what were his orders regarding the prisoners and civilian labour-force? Were they to be evacuated to another island before the Americans attacked, or what?

Watanabe's indifference to the fate of the prisoners was even more pronounced than his indifference to the fate of the *Machiko*.

"They are superfluous to the defence of the islands," said Watanabe, "and the longer you have to feed them, the greater the embarrassment they will become. The moment that they are no longer of use to you, Kimura, you will dispose of them."

"Dispose of them, sir?"

"Dispose of them," repeated Watanabe. "Do I make myself clear?"

Kimura felt the blood rise to his cheeks.

"I would prefer it, honoured Colonel Watanabe, if you would put my precise instructions in writing."

"Very well, Kimura," said Watanabe coldly, "I shall put your orders in writing. That way, there will be no possible excuse you can make for their misinterpretation."

Kimura returned to Little Tarakang, hating Watanabe for the position in which his superior had placed him. The order, to kill his prisoners in cold blood as soon as their usefulness had come to an end, was contrary to all the laws of warfare and civilised conduct. Watanabe knew this but it didn't trouble his conscience in the least because he believed that, in the very near future, every Japanese in the Tarakangs would be wiped out and would be beyond any reproach or retribution. The prisoners were the means by which Watanabe could take revenge for his death and the destruction of his forces *before* these eventualities occurred. It offended all Kimura's sense of Bushido proprieties and the chivalry on which they were based.

It was still two hours from sunset when the barge that had ferried him from Great Tarakang put him ashore on the smaller island. He stood for a moment on the pontoon jetty and watched as the barge turned in its own length and roared out past the *Machiko* to make its homeward journey before dark. His sour mood lifted a little as he gazed up at the *Machiko*. Maybe she wasn't all that much of a ship but what a transformation had been made in her appearance in the last few weeks. They had cut holes through from the main deck to the tween-deck to house the massive hardwood timbers which had been used as the framework for the new bridge. It had looked strange at first: all ribs and starkly grotesque. The construction had retained a kind of giant matchstick ugliness as the decking and weather-front had been added, but the many different hues of raw timber had been clad with heavy canvas which Ross had had cut in strips from an old hatch tarpaulin and bound by long thin bamboo battens to the weather-front. The canvas had then been tarred with a thin mix of pitch and linseed oil, which gave a sombre appearance. But it bound the whole together and contrived to make the makeshift bridge-house look part of the ship instead of an unsightly addition.

Kimura went aboard the ship. It was a hive of activity, with both Japanese soldiers and prisoners hard at work side by side. He found Ross at work with Fraser and a Japanese NCO in the steering flat. The idea of steering the ship from the newly constructed bridge had been abandoned as beyond their ingenuity but Fraser had come up with a plan to overcome the impracticality of protracted use of the emergency steering gear, which was cumbersome and difficult.

The *Machiko* had a steam-operated steering engine geared direct to the rudder quadrant. As the steam line to the engineroom was intact, Fraser had devised a means of linking the emergency steering wheel to the steering engine, so that when the emergency wheel was turned it opened a valve to operate the steering engine. It involved a greatly simplified system of rod and chain than that required to link the steering flat with the bridge. Fraser had simply contained the system within the poop area.

The Japanese NCO, almost ecstatic with the success of their efforts, explained the working of the apparatus to Kimura. His compatriot's enthusiasm merely stirred up the bitterness in Kimura at the burden Watanabe had laid upon him.

He wanted to tell the soldier – and Ross and Fraser, too – that their labours were just a waste of time. The whole project was meaningless. He studied Ross, whose naked back was running with sweat as he tightened a gland-nut with a heavy monkey-wrench. The sea captain had been very quiet and uncommunicative of late: a cold hardness about him that had not been there before.

Had Kimura's preoccupation with the *Machiko* project been less intense, he might have been able to pinpoint a distinct steeliness in Ross' attitude to the time of the Australian soldier's execution. It had, in fact, soured the reasonably harmonious relations that captors and captives had enjoyed since the start of the *Machiko* operation. Kimura had noticed a new spirit amongst the prisoners. It had manifested itself in a willingness to put new vigour into their work and outdo the efforts of his own soldiers. He had mistakenly attributed this new dignity they brought to their labour as pride provoked by the challenge of his project. It had awakened a competitive spirit in them as if they were grimly determined to prove to the Japanese that, man for man, they could match them in anything.

This new spirit among the prisoners had pleased Kimura when, perhaps, he should have been warned by it. He would have been surprised to discover how different from his own attitude to the matter was the attitude of Ross and the other prisoners to the death of Private Richardson. In his own view, the entire incident was a regrettable, timewasting distraction from the job in hand – but justice had been done and both Japanese and prisoners alike could take heart from the brave way in which, from all accounts, the man had paid for his crime. His death squared the account with some nobility. And that was that – the matter closed.

But that was not the way the prisoners looked on it. In their eyes, Richardson had killed a man making a murderous attack on a defenceless woman. He had been tried and condemned without any attempt to adhere to the basic concepts of justice. And he had been executed in a manner that was medieval in its barbarity.

Kimura hoped that the man's brave death would have suitably inspired the prisoners. It had – but not in any way he would have wanted. It reminded them – if any reminder was needed – that they and the Japanese were irreconcilably opposed on sides that were engaged in a war to the death. From the moment of the Australian's death, the prisoners had ceased to accept the role which had been thrust upon them two years before: that of passive victims of war who had been eliminated from the game.

In no one was this attitude more pronounced than in Ross, in whom the instincts of peacemaker throbbed much more strongly than warmaker. He had taken his sea captain's sense of responsibility with him into captivity, keying his own actions and behaviour not to the dictates of self-interest but to the interests of ship and crew. He had led the way in showing that what he was powerless to change had to be endured with quiet courage.

But the death of Big Rich and the bestiality of Tachibana had brought Ross to the realisation that enduring was not enough. Each death that had occurred in the *Machiko* camp had sparked in Ross a desire to strike back at the Japanese and keep striking. His capacity to be selective in the targets of his anger had started to blur in that moment on Mount Taki when he had looked up from Rawlings' body and seen Kimura standing there. He had not really seen the man – only the uniform. And he had felt living hate. Subsequent events had made him step back from his hatred but, since the day Tachibana had beheaded Big Rich and savaged his corpse – all seemingly without any protest from Kimura – Ross had with cold deliberation subdued the instinct to respond to human warmth in any shape or form from a Japanese.

He looked up from tightening the gland-nut on the steering engine to see Kimura staring at him with a sadness that was naked on his face. As their eyes met, there rose in Ross a compulsion to respond; to offer a smile, words, anything that would lift that expression of naked unhappiness. Ross squashed the compulsion as it was born. He let hate ooze in his mind with the thought that, if the need arose, he would kill this strangely likeable man with as much mercy as his chum, Tachibana, had shown to Big Rich.

Kimura blinked, almost recoiled, from the burning hostility in Ross' eyes. It was almost as if the Englishman was reading into his mind. The Japanese turned away stricken with an upsurge of guilt. He had been thinking that by far the worst part of the burden that Watanabe had placed on him was going to be ordering this man's death without any just cause. Indeed, he was wondering if there was any way that – for the first time in his life as a soldier – he could possibly disobey a direct order from a superior officer. His heart had told him there was not.

He climbed out of the steering flat and left the ship as fast as his legs would take him. Why was he seized with this agony of shame that was greater than any man should have to bear? He spent three hours before his tiny personal shrine that evening, bowed in the silence of meditation. But the questions only kept repeating themselves. No answers came to him.

While Kimura agonised in silence, Ross, Newton and Woody had found a quiet corner of the prison encampment where they could confer undisturbed.

"We are going to have to make our move sometime within the next ten days," Ross told them. "The problem is: do we wait until the *Machiko*'s at sea or do we do it when she's still tied up here and landlocked?"

"I think we've got to take the ship while she's still tied to the land," said Newton. "We all know how slapdash the Nips are at guarding us. They don't seem to give a damn. We could take them completely by surprise. If we wait until the ship gets out in the ocean, things could be different. For starters, there's absolutely no guarantee that they'll take us with them if they move the ship out. And, if they do, they might lock us in the holds. They might make damned sure that there's no funny business out of sight of dry land." He turned to Woody. "What do you think, Woody? You're the military expert."

Woody shrugged.

"When we make our move is important," he acknowledged. "What is more important to me is how we do it. Once we've worked that out, it's just a case of waiting for the right moment to go into action. Whatever we do, we're going to need weapons. That might not be so easy at sea."

"Any bright ideas?" asked Ross.

"They have quite an arsenal up there in their camp," said Woody. "And, like Mr Newton says, the guards are slapdash. Especially at night. They've been doing the same old routine for two years and nothing has ever happened. They've got to the stage where they think nothing ever will. They're island-happy – bored out of their minds. You could steal every gun in the place and they probably wouldn't find out about it until morning. I think we should take the guards out, help ourselves to the guns we need and take the ship while the Nips are still snoring their heads off. We could be out in the lagoon before they twig what's happening."

"They're not just going to let us sail away," said Ross.

"Agreed," said Woody, "but they don't have anything heavy enough to sink the ship. Their guns up on Mount Taki are facing the wrong way. They could make things hell of a dangerous on deck with all the machine-guns they've got, but with water between us there's no way they're going to storm aboard and turn us round."

Ross nodded.

"A hundred and one things could go wrong, but we've all known that from the start. The thing is that, with one notable and perhaps inevitable exception, everybody in the camp is in favour of action. Everybody knows what will happen if things go wrong but they're all ready to run the risk. Even Moorhouse has said that although he thinks the whole idea crazy, he doesn't want to be left out. I agree with both of you that we try to take the ship where she lies – because there's no way of knowing in advance what plans the

204

Japs have for us. They might sail the ship out of here tomorrow and leave us here for another two years. And that's the one thing that we've all decided isn't going to happen."

"So, let's get down to brass tacks," said Newton. "This is one ball game that can't be played off the cuff. We hit a home run off our first strike of the ball or we all end up dead. There ain't gonna be any second chances. So, we plan our play right down to the last little detail with every guy on the team knowing exactly what he has to do. You, Woody, have said that the first priority is that we get ourselves some hardware from the gun store. OK, plan number one. How do we hit the gun store?"

Woody grinned at the look of expectancy on Newton's and Ross' faces.

"We do like they do in the detective novels," said Woody. "First, we case the joint."

"When?" asked Newton.

"What's wrong with tonight?" came the reply.

It was Newton's turn to grin.

"Well, I was going to manicure my toenails – but I can put that off to another night. You mean all three of us should go?"

Woody eyed Ross apologetically.

"If you don't mind, Skipper, there wouldn't be any need for you to come along. You're the one who's going to be needed to get the ship away from this island and there's no point in running unnecessary risks."

"I'd go with you like a shot," said Ross, "but you're right, Woody. I might be more of a liability than a help, trying to keep up with you in the jungle."

"That's not what I said," insisted Woody. "For all I know, you could be better in the bush than Mr Newton here."

"Well, thank you very much for that vote of confidence!" protested Newton.

"Think nothing of it," said Woody. "The truth is that it's not going to bother me any to keep a Yank in his place. I'd feel kind of funny though, having to order a captain about."

Woody looked up at the moonless sky. There was a lot of low cloud about. The chances were that a rainstorm wasn't far away. It could be wet and unpleasant in the forest tonight – but the Nips, he reckoned, would be staying under cover.

Lightning had been forking around the heavens for several hours before the rainstorm finally broke over Little Tarakang just after

205

midnight. Major Tachibana, stretched out on the beach some distance beyond the Tarakangese camp, woke as huge drops of water splattered across his face. He sat up with a start, still extremely befuddled by the amount of *sake* he had consumed earlier in the evening. His first reaction was to reach out for the bottle stuck upright in the sand, only an arm's length from where he lay. He drank straight from the bottle until the volume of spirit in his mouth made him choke. Spluttering and coughing, he set the bottle in the sand again and looked about him.

The depression that had gripped him all day had lifted in direct proportion to the liquor he had put inside him. Now, he wondered what had caused it. Had it all been due to his hatred for this wretched island and his imprisonment on it? He realised that the rain was soaking him through. He threw off his tunic and exulted in the feel of the rain on his bare arms. He threw off all his clothes until he was naked but for his short white underpants. The rain on his body was wonderful. He ran a few paces, bellowing with pleasure at the joy of the pure clean water on his skin.

He returned to where his clothes had been cast off. His belt and sword lay on the sand. He took the sword from its scabbard and made cutting movements in the air with it. He moved further along the beach, like a grotesque ballet dancer: leaping and whirling the sword at imaginary enemies, lost in the world of his own mime.

Tachibana was not alone on the beach.

Less than five hundred yards away, within the shelter of the forest that fringed the beach, two figures were huddled. One lay on the ground, moaning softly and cursing, while the other bent over him.

I think your leg's broken, sir," said the kneeling figure, Seaman Mark H. Tillerton of the US Navy.

"I know my goddamned leg's broken, you fool. I've been saying so for the past fifteen minutes. Oh, God – what a goddamned mess!" The man on the ground writhed when a slight movement sent a spasm of fiery pain coursing through his leg. "I need splints, Tillerton. Look around and see if you can find a couple of pieces of wood."

"We'll need something to tie them on with," said Tillerton

The injured man cursed impatiently.

"There's plenty of jungle creeper. Use that."

Tillerton foraged in the scrub. He returned with two stout pieces of wood that were reasonably straight. A second expedition yielded several lengths of creeper. He had set the splints in place and was binding them to the injured man's leg when his patient suddenly seized him by the wrist.

"Tillerton, listen. Did you hear something?"

Tillerton cocked an ear. The only sounds he heard were the soft wash of the surf and the steady splatter of rain on the tree canopy overhead. Then there was another sound – a human sound? No, more an animal sound – a strange banshee-like cry.

"What the hell was that, sir?" he whispered.

Lieutenant Lemuel Bennett, USN, had not the faintest idea what the sound was – but he didn't like it.

"It came from the beach," he said. "You'd better go and take a look. Take the carbine – but, for Christ's sake, don't fire unless it's absolutely life or death!"

Tillerton rose and took the carbine. He had strapped it to the side of the compact radio pack. He checked the magazine. Cautiously, he moved to where the line of trees met the beach. The beach seemed empty. He ventured out of the trees on to the beach.

He had gone only half a dozen paces when there was a blood-curdling cry from less than ten yards away. The terrifying shock of it made him jump, literally. He jerked round to face the sound, his feet leaving the ground. Surprise at what he saw paralysed him in the seconds following. A half-naked man, hair streaming and apelike, came bouncing towards him with a two-handed sword held high above his head.

Tillerton had no time to raise the carbine. He saw the sword coming in an arc at his head and ducked, taking a step forward to get below the whirling blade. The surprise of seeing his victim step towards him instead of shrinking away from the intended blow completely threw Tachibana. Worse still, the American sailor ducked, so that his shoulder took the full momentum of Tachibana's charge. The point of collision was Tachibana's solar plexus. He stopped in his tracks, the sword flew out of his hands, and he collapsed as if he had been sandbagged. Finding the Japanese at his feet, Seaman Tillerton brought the butt of his carbine down on his attacker's skull. The crack sounded like a pistol shot in the night. A grunt exploded from Tachibana as he slumped from the sitting position to lie prostrate on his back, out to the wide.

Tillerton stared in disbelief at the first Japanese he had ever seen in his life. His hands were trembling. It was reaction. Fear, triumph and relief had shaken his emotions in quick succession and he couldn't quite believe that his first encounter with the enemy had ended so quickly, and so emphatically, in his favour.

He admitted to himself – although he was never going to admit it to Lieutenant Bennett – that only the slowness of his reactions had prevented him firing the carbine. Thank heaven he hadn't. The beach would probably have been swarming with Japs by now.

He dragged Tachibana up the beach and sprawled him against the trunk of a palm. Using some of the creeper intended for Bennett's splints, he lashed the Japanese in a sitting position, his wrists jerked back behind the tree. Satisfied that Houdini would not have got out of the bonds, he returned to answer Bennett's questions about what the hell was going on and where was he going with the ties for his splints.

"I bagged me a Jap," said Tillerton proudly. "He came at me with this."

Bennett goggled at the two-handed sword which Tillerton plunged upright into the soft ground in view of the officer.

"Christ!" murmured the officer. He looked with new respect at the seaman, who was barely nineteen years old and, in Bennett's experience, one of the greenest specimens he had ever been saddled with. Not that the lad didn't have guts. He had been one of three volunteers for this mission. Bennett had only taken him because the other two were married men with families.

The two Americans had been on Little Tarakang for twenty-four hours. They had landed the night before and had hidden up on the south slope of Mount Taki to observe the port and airfield across the Straits. Unaccountably, they had been told to abort the mission when they had made their midnight radio report. Bennett had broken his leg on the way down the mountain, when they were in sight of the beach.

Now, he was not looking forward to the hazardous journey back over the reef to where the submarine would be already waiting for them.

"We'd better get the hell out of here," he told Tillerton. "There could be more Japs about."

"The beach was clear," said Tillerton. "I don't know where my guy came from. Must have been sleeping on the beach. He was only wearing short underpants. Maybe he thinks he's some kind of Tarzan."

Tillerton had retrieved the rubber dinghy from its hiding place and had helped Bennett down to the water's edge, when Bennett had a sudden thought.

"You're sure that Jap's dead now?" he asked Tillerton.

Tillerton looked at him in amazement.

"Dead? Hell no, sir. He ain't dead. I got him roped to a tree. Do we take him with us?"

It was Bennett's turn to be astonished.

"You didn't kill him?" It had not occurred to him that Tillerton had not finished off his attacker. The notion to take a prisoner back with them had a lot of appeal. A real bonus for the Intelligence boys. But the thought of getting the dinghy over the reef with a prisoner, and himself with a broken leg . . . No. It was going to be tricky enough without having to watch a Jap.

"Get up there and make sure that Jap's dead," Bennett said to Tillerton.

The seaman stared at him.

"What if he ain't, sir?"

"Then kill the bastard."

"How, sir?"

"You've got a knife, don't you? Just make sure it's quiet."

Tillerton stumbled up the beach, his mind a turmoil. Killing a guy in a fight was one thing. Killing one when he was trussed up like a turkey was another. Did the lieutenant expect him to cut the guy's throat? Tillerton's stomach turned over at the thought. He couldn't do it, not even to a Jap.

Tachibana was exactly as he had left him. Out cold. Tillerton wondered if the man was already dead. He was just lying there. Didn't seem to be breathing. He took out his knife and bent over the trussed Japanese. There was no sign of life that Tillerton could see – and he wasn't all that eager to look too close.

He sheathed the knife and walked back down the beach.

"He dead?" asked Bennett.

"Reckon so," said Tillerton. "Musta hit him a lot harder'n I realised."

Bennett breathed a sigh of relief. He looked at his watch.

"They'll be waiting for us. Let's get going."

Two of Tachibana's own guards found him in the morning. He was fully conscious but volunteered no information on how he had come to be tied to a tree. They found his clothes for him, and his sword scabbard. But no sword. When the men asked the major where his sword might be, he did not even answer. He just scowled at them. So, they asked no more questions.

He stumbled up through the Japanese camp alone, looking neither to left nor right. When he reached his quarters, he summoned his most trusted sergeant. Sergeant Asato had served with him in China. Tachibana gave the sergeant a string of orders. Asato bowed and left, saying that all would be done.

The major then spent thirty minutes composing a letter to Major Kimura. He bathed, taking a long time. Then he dressed in his kimono and ate the meal of rice and pork which Sergeant Asato brought to him.

When he had finished, he summoned Asato once more.

"In one hour, it will be time," he told Asato gravely. "You know what is to be done?"

"Honoured Major Tachibana confers great honour on humble Sergeant Asato. I weep with pride at great honour. All will be as Major orders."

Alone, Tachibana kneeled on a mat before his *tokonama*. His meal had quelled the hunger of his body. Now he concentrated his mind on the ritual act of *seppuku*. It was the only course, he believed, which would atone for the great shame he had suffered for failing to kill the American he had found on the beach and allowing himself to become his prisoner. Why had the man not killed him? Why had he rubbed in the shame by taking his sword and leaving him tied to a tree? The humiliation of being cut free by his own men still burned in Tachibana. He felt degraded as he had never felt in his life. Only by *seppuku* could he cleanse himself of the degradation.

His final pains, suffered in silence and dignity, would be the payment of all wordly debts. Honour would be restored to his spirit and memory of his earthly existence would be respected.

As he meditated, a great calm came on him. The time came nearer but he stilled a stirring impatience for the moment of liberation. As if from a long way away, he heard the footsteps of Sergeant Asato outside. Now, it was time.

The curved knife lay on the mat beside him. He picked it up briefly, feeling with approval the razor sharpness of its blade. He pulled away the folds of his kimono, baring his stomach. Now.

He took a two-handed grip on the knife and moved his body towards it as he thrust the blade into his lower abdomen. Then, deliberately, he pulled upward – making a deep vertical cut – and bowed so that the knife sank deeper into his body. Blood gushed out over his wrists and ran warm over his thighs.

Sergeant Asato entered. He had changed into his best uniform and was wearing his sword. He strode over to the kneeling figure and unsheathed his sword. He spoke only two words.

"Honoured Excellency?"

Tachibana leaned even further forward, the knife embedded in his innards and his hands still clutched round the handle. He made a barely perceptible nodding motion of the head. Sergeant Asato, with a little cry of grief-filled ecstasy, brought the sword down across the bared neck before him. Tachibana's head rolled on the floor.

Fourteen

Invitation to Die

It was just after noon when Sergeant Asato presented himself to Major Kimura. The sight of the sergeant, dressed as if for a ceremonial parade, astonished Kimura, although not as much as a twitch of a facial muscle displayed his surprise. He accepted the letter Asato handed to him, wondering as he did so what the reason was for the sergeant's expression. The man had a look of such glowing sublimity that Kimura wondered if he was either drunk or drugged.

Then Kimura read Tachibana's letter, with growing shock and incredulity.

"You carried out your orders?" he asked the sergeant.

"Yes, Shosa."

Kimura reined in any emotions he felt.

"Shosa Tachibana instructs me in his letter of farewell to thank you for your great loyalty and friendship. He wants his body to be burned. Have your men make the preparations."

When Asato had gone, Kimura summoned Lieutenant Niguchi and ordered the return of all prisoners to their quarters. He also ordered a full alert and gave instructions for patrols to search the shoreline. Then he went to Tachibana's quarters.

The odour of death in the hut was so strong that he had to cover his mouth and nostrils. He stared at the appalling scene only long enough to satisfy himself that Asato had carried out his late commander's orders to the letter. Then Kimura sought the fresh air.

His dislike for Tachibana had died with the other's final act of atonement. Mixed, however, with the new admiration and respect he now felt for the dead major was the feeling that Tachibana's sacrifice had been tinged with stupidity. He had done a glorious thing, certainly – but he had been so wrapped up in the payment of his personal shame that he had let his military responsibilities go right down the drain. It shocked Kimura to learn that armed enemy forces were at large on Little Tarakang. Were they still here? Or had it been a small reconnaissance party who had departed as swiftly and silently as they had arrived?

Neither alternative offered any comfort. Both pointed directly to one very strong likelihood: that an attack in force was imminent. Kimura felt shock at the way he had allowed all his own military priorities to become mixed up. *He* had been so wrapped up with his beloved *Machiko* project that he had almost forgotten the real purpose of his presence on the island. Instead of immediately raising the alarm as he should have done, Tachibana had become so obsessed with his personal honour that all sense of wider duty had been obscured from his mind – but he, Kimura, was just as guilty in his order of priorities. That ship had taken over his mind. In the same way, close contact over a long period with the prisoners had made him soft and forgetful of his real obligations. Perhaps Colonel Watanabe's attitude was right. He did not treat his own death as a matter of consequence, so why be troubled over the deaths of a few prisoners?

Kimura reasoned to himself that he did not personally have to involve himself in the "disposal" of the prisoners. All he had to do was summon Niguchi and the lieutenant would carry out his orders without question. It was easy . . . Except for Ross.

Why was it that the blood of this one man was the one thing that he did not want on his conscience? Was it because he sensed in him all his own ideals? Was that the stumbling-block? He could destroy this man but not his spirit. The only spirit destroyed would be Kimura's own. By killing Ross, Kimura would be committing a kind of spiritual suicide. He would be murdering himself – and that would be a negation of honourable suicide. One committed suicide in order to redeem one's spirit, not to destroy it.

Kimura sent for Niguchi to tell him about Tachibana's death and what had provoked it. The news seemed to take the young lieutenant's breath away. The younger man had entertained little admiration for Tachibana while he was alive and was not now regretful of his death. He seemed much more affected by Kimura's news that the war – which for so long had been remote and distant from them – was about to strike Little Tarakang. Ingenuously, he said to Kimura, "I was afraid that the peace we have had here would not last forever."

Kimura looked at him sharply.

"Did you think that you could escape the war, Niguchi?"

The lieutenant could not hide his confusion.

"You will think me foolish, Major Kimura . . . But we have been here so long and we have worked so hard . . . I thought that life here would just go on and on as it has been – without change."

Kimura stared at him.

"Do you mean to say that you have been happy here, Niguchi?"

The young man's embarrassment increased at the directness of the question. He wanted to make excuses for himself but could not do so when the major stared at him in that way.

"I was homesick at first, sir," he mumbled. "But after a time I became . . . well, not unhappy. There was so much to do, and the work interested me and made me feel important." He flashed a look of utter misery at Kimura. "I had never felt important before, sir."

Kimura felt a warm glow of sympathy for the young officer. It was as if he was seeing the young man as a human being for the very first time. Before, he had always looked on him as a happy-go-lucky and rather accident-prone youth who had still a lot of growing up to do. Now, he saw a living person with fears and hopes and sensitivity. There was something basically happy and innocent about Niguchi. He had not volunteered to die for his country; he had been conscripted. Killing and dying were not things that Niguchi had any particular talent for. They were just things that he had been told were expected of him. And he had been taught to do what was expected of him.

"Do you want to die, Niguchi?"

Again, the directness of the question startled the younger man. He pulled himself to attention and tried not to appear as flustered as he undoubtedly was.

"It is my duty, sir," he said fiercely.

Kimura had to restrain a smile.

"That is not what I asked, Niguchi. I asked you if you wanted to die. And tell me the truth. Forget, if you can, that I am your commander. Think of me as an older brother. Your answer is important to me."

Niguchi still hesitated. It was not easy to think of Kimura as an older brother.

"Tell me," said Kimura.

Niguchi swallowed.

"I do not want to die, sir," he said.

214

"And how do you feel about killing, Niguchi? Do you want to kill?"

The lieutenant looked around him in agonised appeal, as if praying to the atap walls of the command hut to come to his assistance.

"I would rather build ships than kill," he blurted out.

Kimura nodded sadly. He reached into the breast pocket of his tunic and withdrew a folded sheet of paper.

"Read that," he ordered the lieutenant.

Niguchi read, and then stared at Kimura with soul-filled eyes.

"This is the order of Colonel Watanabe?" he asked.

"Yes, Niguchi. How do you propose it should be done?"

Niguchi bowed his head.

"Do not ask me, sir. I beg you."

"Are you suggesting that Colonel Watanabe's orders should be disobeyed?"

Niguchi did not answer. He remained with head bowed, silent.

Kimura tried a different approach.

"I will not compel you to answer, Niguchi. Your silence tells me what I want to know. So, I shall ask you something else. Do you hate the enemy more now than when you came to this island with me?"

Niguchi looked up. He had expected Kimura's rage – but there was no trace of anger in the major's face. The fact emboldened him.

"It is my shame, honoured Major Kimura, that there is no strong hate in me for others. Beat me without mercy and I shall still not hate you. Because I know you and respect you, I could not hate you. Because of my own unworthiness I would accept your blows as deserved . . ."

"But the enemy, Niguchi? I am not the enemy."

Niguchi made an apologetic little shrug of the shoulders.

"Before I came to this island, I had not seen the enemy. It was easy to hate people I had not seen. Now . . . the men from the *Machiko* . . . I have no fear of them . . . They are still the enemy – but I have no hate for them."

"Why? Do you not think they would rejoice at the destruction of Nippon?"

"Perhaps. But they seem to long only for their own homes where their wives and children live – as I have longed to see my home and look on the faces of my brothers and sisters."

Kimura sighed. He took a metal cigarette box from his pocket and flicked open the lid.

"Have a cigarette, Niguchi, and relax. You are not on parade and this little chat we are having is quite informal. So don't look so worried."

"Thank you, sir," said Niguchi, accepting a cigarette.

Kimura lit a cigarette for himself. He blew a cloud of smoke.

"It shames me, Niguchi, that I have never taken you into my confidence. I am afraid I have always looked upon you as a rather incompetent officer."

Niguchi smiled; the frank smile of one who knows his limitations.

"I regret my great incompetence, sir. I have been a great disappointment to the honoured Major. I do not deserve his kindness."

"Don't be misled by it," said Kimura. "It betrays only my own incompetence. To be kind, I should have been harder on you. If I had, perhaps you would be more ready to welcome the death that awaits us both very soon."

"I am not afraid to die, sir," Niguchi protested. "I said only that I did not want to . . . yet."

"I know, I know," Kimura smiled. "You are ready to die, but you would prefer to live. Our problem – because it is as much your problem as it is mine – is one of living with honour, rather than one of dying with honour. I find little honour in the prospect of having to murder the captain and crew of the British ship. Yet that is what I have been told I must do. Honour demands that I must do my duty but my duty demands that I act with dishonour. My dilemma, Niguchi, is how to satisfy both my honour and my sense of duty."

The younger man's brow creased in a frown.

"The old Taisha at our officer training school used to say that honour is a duty and duty is an honour."

"And that is what I have always believed," said Kimura. "That duty and honour were indivisible. Now, it seems that if I do my duty, I forfeit my honour. And if I fail in my duty, I forfeit my honour. And no matter what I do, I must still forfeit my life."

"Shosa, you are not contemplating . . .?" Niguchi, eyes wide with alarm, did not complete the question.

"No, Niguchi, I have no intention of emulating Tachibana. That would not be fulfilling my duty . . . It would be simply passing it on to you. Nor would *seppuku* satisfy my honour. It would only prove that I have a greater fear of life than I have of

216

death. It would signify my moral weakness, not my strength. A young Englishwoman tried to tell me about this a long, long time ago and I thought she was crazy, but now I think I'm beginning to understand what she meant."

"An Englishwoman, Shosa?"

"Yes, does that surprise you? I wanted to make her my wife. *Seppuku* was one of the greatest of sins in her eyes. We used to argue about it. I remember her saying that dying by one's own hand was to take the coward's way out. It made your death a defeat. But if you kept the inner spirit pure and lived what you believed to the last agony man could inflict on you, your death would be a victory. Your spirit would live forever."

Niguchi made a face.

"I did not like Shosa Tachibana but, whatever he was, he was not a coward. Do you think he was a coward, Shosa?"

"No, Shogi, I do not think Tachibana was a coward. He was brave as any tiger. But is bravery alone enough? Is it more worthy to be brave than wise. Can a man be both? Would you say that Tachibana was a worthy man?"

"When he was alive, I did not like him much," confessed Niguchi. "I did not think of him as worthy or unworthy."

"What about the ship captain, the man called Ross. Would you say that he was a worthy or unworthy man?"

Niguchi frowned thoughtfully.

"I have not considered it," he said. "He has a proud eye. He smiles sometimes to conceal anger. I feel I would like him if he would allow it. He makes me feel . . ." Niguchi groped around for the right word ". . . respectful," he finished.

"Ha!" snorted Kimura. "Then he must be a worthy man. I, too, feel a respect for him. I have felt it from the first day, when we watched him bring his ship into the lagoon. Do you remember that day on the mountain, Shogi?"

"It seems a lifetime has passed since then," said Niguchi. "Why should it be important to you, Shosa, whether I think the English *shoko* is worthy or unworthy?"

"It was talking about Tachibana," said Kimura. "I always thought of him as an unworthy man and I was reminded of something in the writings of Confucius about unworthy men."

"It is my shame that philosophy has never been a strong point with me," Niguchi apologised. "I would likely qualify as unworthy in the eyes of Confucius."

"Most of us would," said Kimura. "But it was what in our sight

217

constituted unworthiness that inspired the philosopher to make the comment I had in mind. He said that when we see an unworthy person, we should examine our inner selves."

"So that we might discover our own unworthiness?" suggested Niguchi. "But what if we saw a worthy person?"

"He had something to say about that, too," said Kimura with a smile. "He said that we should endeavour to emulate him."

It took Niguchi a moment to connect Kimura's reply to his question with the previously voiced thought that the English sea captain was "a worthy man". When he did, the dilemma which faced Kimura seemed to slide into a new and revealing perspective. How could Kimura, with honour, kill a "worthy man" – a man whom one should endeavour to emulate? A fresh thought occurred to him.

"Shosa," he said, a tentative edge of inquiry to his voice, "if the positions of you and the English *shoko* were reversed . . . If he had to choose between ordering your death and the death of all of us and between what he believed was honourable, what would *he* do?"

"I do not know," said Kimura, but his eyes gleamed with a sudden thought. "But it would be interesting to find out. Perhaps it would all hinge on what *he* thinks of me? Whether he sees me as a worthy or an unworthy man?"

The drone of aircraft overhead prompted Kimura to leave the command hut and go out into the bright dazzle of the sunlight. Niguchi followed him. They looked up to see a line of nine fighter-bombers curve in from the sea to cross the island on a northerly course.

"That's the tenth formation I've seen," Kimura said to Niguchi, shielding his eyes from the sun and squinting into the heavens. "By nightfall, they'll all have gone."

The same flight of aircraft had been watched by the prisoners, confined in their camp only a short distance away. They sat around in knots of three and four. They had plenty to discuss. The intense air activity – much more than they had seen for weeks – would on its own have provided a topic for endless speculation. Added to it, however, was the sensational matter of Tachibana's mysterious suicide and the sight of several squads of Japanese in battle kit hurrying off in different directions.

The tension, which had slowly been building up in the prisoners' camp since the day of Big Rich's death and had increased as

218

the work on the *Machiko* neared completion, quivered to a new intensity with the events of the day. And among none of the groups discussing these events was it more evident than among the three men of the "escape committee": Ross, Newton and Woody.

Strain showed on Ross' face as he all but accused the other two of holding out on him over their previous night's reconnaissance sortie.

"You swear it wasn't you who jumped Tachibana?" he asked, his eyes trying to read their faces. Woody's patience was wearing thin at Ross' persistence.

"How often do we have to tell you, Skipper? Mr Newton and I ain't liars. We never saw hide nor hair of Tachibana. If we had, I wouldn't have left him trussed to a tree. I would have cut the bastard's throat!"

"All right, all right," said Ross. "I'm sorry if I've harped on about it. It's just that it doesn't make sense. If you two didn't tie Tachibana to a tree, then who the hell did? It must have been some of the islanders from the other camp or it must have been some of the Nip soldiers."

"That doesn't make sense either. If it had been any of the islanders, Tachibana would have been in amongst them with a machine-gun the minute he was set free. If it had been any of the Nip soldiers, he would have been raising hell and shouting bloody murder until he found the ones who did it. He wouldn't have crept back to his camp and committed hara-kiri." Newton paused after he had made his point and looked squarely at Ross. "You're the expert on the Japs, Captain. Just what would it take to make a tough cookie like old Tigerface creep off and slit his belly open?"

Ross shook his head.

"I just don't know. Something must have happened to cause him a terrible loss of face. Something so big that he just couldn't live with the shame."

"Maybe the Nip army has suffered some terrible defeat," said Woody. "Maybe they're going to surrender the islands. Where have all them planes been goin' off to today? They've all been flying north and I haven't seen any coming back."

"Maybe old Hirohito's kicked the bucket," said Newton, "but that's a hell of a lot of maybes. And it doesn't explain how Tachibana got himself roped to a tree. The question we should be asking ourselves is: does any of this make a difference to our plans? We saw last night that getting our hands on some guns

219

would be a cinch. All we need is a rainy night."

"Why wait for a rainy night?" asked Woody. "I say the sooner the better. The longer we wait, the more edgy we'll get. What do you say, Skipper?"

"I don't know," said Ross. "I think that you, Woody, feel something is in the air. I know I do. And that if we hang off, we may miss our chance. At the same time, we could rush things and grab ourselves a lot of grief. Once we go, it's essential we get clean away from the island and that would depend on the harbour at Great Tarakang being nice and empty when we make our break. Whether we wait for a rainy night or go tomorrow is less important than making sure that, whenever it is, there isn't a Jap destroyer sitting across the Straits."

"But there hasn't been anything bigger than a tug over there for months," said Newton. "You've heard the Nips go on about supply boats not getting through and how it was always 'Maybe ship come tomorrow'."

"All the same," said Ross, "if we're going to make a run for it in the open sea, we'll know we have a chance if the Jap Navy has nothing bigger than a tug to send after us. All they need to blow us out of the water, you know, is a ten-knot trawler with an anti-aircraft cannon on her poop. There's no point in making a break in order to get sunk within sight of the reef."

"So, what are you proposing, Captain?" asked Newton.

"That every day from now on, we wangle things so that one man can slip away and check what ships, if any, are in the anchorage at the other side of the Straits. It would mean getting round the south side of Mount Taki and getting high enough up to get a view of the anchorage."

"Have you anyone in mind, Captain? It could be dodgy, bearing in mind it would have to be done during the day." It was Woody who had spoken.

"I've already spoken to Kima. He says he'll do it."

"The big Papuan sailor?" asked Woody.

Ross nodded.

"For some reason, the Japs let him wander all over the place and don't bother him. They think he's a bit mad. It suits him to let them think that."

All three men looked skywards as another formation of nine aircraft came in low from seaward and winged northwards.

"There's definitely something happening," said Woody. "Something big."

220

The sudden appearance of Kimura's orderly had come as a surprise to Ross. He had made the journey up the hill to the Japanese camp with the soldier, wondering what Kimura's unexpected summons meant. It had all been exactly as it was all those months before: the tea ceremony and the polite, inconsequential talk; the checker board set out; Kimura, relaxed and pleasant in his chrysanthemum-emblazoned robe.

The game of checkers had taken place. Ross, his mind partly on the hazards of the intended escape, played badly. Kimura seemed two moves ahead of him all the time. The game reached the stage where Kimura had Ross at his mercy – and Ross knew it. He was about to concede the game when Kimura made a strange move.

"Are you sure that's what you want to do?" Ross asked.

"I am sure," answered Kimura with a smile.

Ross made the move which extricated him from a seemingly impossible situation, taking three of Kimura's men in the process. The positions reversed, it was now the Japanese who was trapped. Ross took advantage of the new situation to win the game.

"You have won," said Kimura.

"No," said Ross. "You allowed me to win."

Kimura inclined his head slightly, a gesture that was neither acknowledgement nor denial.

"It was an interesting game," was Kimura's only comment.

"Do you wish another game, Major?"

"Thank you, but no," said Kimura. "All things must end. Even games."

Ross felt vaguely uneasy. He waited for Kimura to break the silence but the Japanese seemed content to sit staring at Ross with a look of quiet enjoyment on his face. At last Kimura spoke.

"Not only games must end. All that begins must end. Even our lives. Has the captain thought of how his life will end?"

Ross' uneasiness grew. He replied carefully.

"I prefer to think of how I will live and how I will go on living."

"But one day you will die. How would you like to die?"

Ross smiled.

"Peacefully – of a ripe old age."

Kimura smiled in response.

"Let me offer you a hypothesis, Ross-san. Let us suppose for the sake of argument that you could choose the manner of your death, but not the time. And the time was soon . . . How would you choose?"

Ross met the challenge of Kimura's questioning stare.

221

"I'm a man of the sea, Major – and I've fought many battles with the sea which I've been lucky to come through. If, in the end, the sea were to have me, I would not complain."

Kimura nodded, approving the sentiment.

"It is good. It is good – the ambition of a worthy man."

"Not exactly an ambition, Major. Unless one can have a hypothetical ambition."

"Let us consider another hypothesis, then," said Kimura blandly. "It is an amusing pastime, is it not? Like playing checkers."

"Possibly, yes," said Ross with a shrug, "although you know what they say about hypotheses. I seem to recall someone describing a hypothesis as an unsupported platform for the launch of the least supportable unlikelihoods."

The extravagance of Ross' definition caused Kimura's eyebrows to arch slightly but the meaning was understood. Kimura brushed it aside.

"Consider our game of checkers, Ross-san. Was it not a great unlikelihood at one stage that you should win? In one moment, I was the master. In the next, you were the master."

"Yes?" said Ross uncertainly. Kimura smiled.

"My second hypothesis is this. Suppose that it was not the Rising Sun that flew over this island but the flag of the British Empire. And suppose that you were commander and I was your captive. What would you do if your King in London ordered you to shoot this Japanese Shosa called Kimura and all his men?"

Ross felt his blood run cold. He knew that this was no idle question and he dreaded to think what it was that had inspired Kimura to ask it.

"Would you obey your King?" asked Kimura. "Answer me truthfully."

He seemed to be holding his breath, waiting for Ross to speak.

"I would not obey my King," Ross said slowly, "because such an order would convince me that he was no longer worthy to be my King."

"You would betray your King?" There was a hint of reproach in Kimura's voice.

Again Ross chose his words with care.

"Some might look at it that way. I would interpret my disobedience differently. To obey would be to betray myself and all I believe. I think I would rather die."

"You would die for your enemy?"

222

"Yes – if he had surrendered to my protection and had every reason to believe he had it."

"You would take your own life, Ross-san?"

"No, Major. You cannot defend what you believe to be right when you are dead. I would accept the responsibility of not obeying an order to murder – but I would not abandon all those other responsibilities with which I had been trusted. I would not abandon what power I had until it was taken from me. If my King truly wanted someone to murder his enemies, then he would have to hire a murderer. Not me."

It was Ross' turn to hold his breath. He could feel sweat running off the back of his scalp and down his neck. His throat and mouth were dry. It required concentrated effort not to show the agitation he felt. Kimura said nothing. He sat there, eyes half closed as if deep in thought. Ross, fearful that he might have said the wrong things, could not remain silent.

"There's one thing about your hypothesis that gives me much consolation, Major Kimura," he said, and managed to smile broadly.

"Yes, Ross-san?"

"It is some knowledge of my King in London and His Imperial Highness, the Emperor of Nippon. They are both personages of great nobility of mind. It is quite inconceivable that your Emperor or mine would ever order any of their officers to carry out cold-blooded murder. Their honour would be offended. Such an order could only be made by some totally dishonourable person deliberately abusing a position of power he did not deserve to occupy. Someone who did not deserve the respect and obedience of those under him, nor the trust of his own superiors."

It was a wild, almost desperate shot in the dark from Ross – but it did not fail to register immediately with Kimura. It was almost as if Ross had named Watanabe for him. A startled gleam flickered in Kimura's eyes, briefly, and the eyebrows gave the barest perceptible lift.

Kimura made no comment on the likelihood or otherwise of his hypothesis. Instead, he startled Ross with a most un-Japanese question, inasmuch as it was blatant fishing for a compliment.

"Ross-san," he said, "do you consider me a worthy or unworthy man?"

Ross' involuntary start of surprise made Kimura realise immediately that he was guilty of a breach of manners. Before Ross could answer, he got in first.

"Do not answer, Ross-san. Such a question is unforgivable. Politeness would force you to speak what I wish to hear and not with the knowledge of your heart."

"Perhaps you should hear the answer anyway," said Ross. "It may or may not be what you want to hear but I am not afraid to speak truthfully." He paused and Kimura looked at him as if dreading what might come next. Very deliberately, Ross said, "Major Kimura, in all the time we have known each other, you have done nothing to make me think that you are an unworthy man."

Kimura sighed. He closed his eyes and nodded his head back and forward. It was an acknowledgement that those who asked for the truth were not always rewarded with what they wanted to hear but with what they deserved. At the same time, there was an acknowledgement that what he had heard was not as disagreeable as it might have been.

Ross had taken a chance. He had warned Kimura that he occupied a position high in his esteem but the real test had still to come.

Woody and Paul Newton were waiting for Ross, curious to know why Kimura had sent for him. They knew from the look on his face that something had happened. Ross held up a hand to stop the eager flow of questions with which they greeted him.

"Kimura's had orders from somewhere . . . Tokyo . . . I don't know. But it's bad. I don't know if it changes everything or it changes nothing," he said.

"What kind of orders?" Newton's voice reflected the anxiety Ross was making no attempt to hide.

"I think he's under orders to wipe us all out."

"Holy Christ!" breathed Woody. "That kind of settles things then, doesn't it? We go for the guns tonight."

"No!" The word exploded from Ross. "It's not as straightforward as that. It's not Tachibana we're dealing with here. Kimura is a much more complex man. I think the only reason he sent for me was to sound me out on what I would do if I were in his shoes."

"You've got to be kidding," said Newton. "Hell's teeth, Captain, you know the Nips better than anyone. You know what an order is in the Imperial Army. It's a command straight from God. Even Kimura would pull his own eyeballs out if he was told that's what he had to do."

"Maybe," said Ross. "But I think he's a deeply troubled man.

He's looking for an honourable way out. There can be no other reason for bringing me into it. I think he genuinely wanted my reaction . . . my advice even."

"Holy Christ!" repeated Woody. "I hope you tried to talk him out of it, Skip."

"That's what's worrying me, Woody," Ross replied. "I don't know if anything I said would have the slightest influence on him. For all I know, our goose is already cooked. Our little chat tonight might just have been his way of letting me know that he's got his orders and he's sorry."

"That does settle it then," said Woody. "We have to chance it tonight."

"No," said Ross again.

His caution puzzled Newton.

"Why the hell not, Captain? Tomorrow, we could all be dead. I'm with Woody on this. There's just no sense in waiting around to see if Kimura's going to give us the chop. Doing something's better than doing nothing."

"I still think we should wait," said Ross. "It's a hell of a gamble, I know, but something in my bones says we should give Kimura a chance to show his hand."

"That could be too late," said Newton softly.

"I know it, damnit!" Ross spoke with a rare edge of irritation. Newton was the first to recognise that it stemmed from the burden of responsibility he felt for the lives of everyone in the camp and not just his own. He also had to admit to himself that he and Woody were reacting to the situation in a strictly personal way. Their impatience demanded action. It had nothing to do with a collective sense of responsibility.

"We've waited two years," said the American. "I reckon another twenty-four hours isn't going to make all that much difference." He grinned lop-sidedly at Ross. "Besides, I've come to respect your instincts, Captain. What do you say, Woody?"

"A hell of a lot can happen in twenty-four hours," said the Australian resignedly. "But if that's the way the skipper wants it . . ."

Rather less than four hours were to pass before something happened that was to introduce a new and quite unexpected twist to the situation. Ross, unable to sleep, was lying awake in the long hut when he became aware of a figure groping his way along the edge of the sleeping platform. A hand touched his ankle and shook it gently.

Ross peered up into the dark face of Kima, the Papuan seaman.

"Cap'n, Cap'n. You come *benjo*. No speak now. You come quick, eh?"

The Papuan was already at the door of the hut as Ross clambered down from the platform, trying not to disturb the gently snoring Fraser. Kima beckoned as he reached the doorway. He was already moving silently in the direction of the *benjo*.

Behind the atap screen of the latrine, two men were standing beside the tall figure of Kima. One, like Kima, was black and shirtless but had a bush hat perched on his head. The other man, too, wore a bush hat but was uniformed. What made Ross start with surprise, however, was the sight of the sub-machine-guns which each man carried.

Fifteen

Visitors

The man in uniform was the first to speak.

"My oath, Captain, the big fella sure picked a hell of a place for us to meet! The pong's enough to knock me flat on me back!" He stretched out a hand. "The name's Corrigan. And this here's me guide and guardian angel, Matthew. They used to call us 'Coast-watchers'. Now, we're dinkum AIB."

"Dinkum what?" asked Ross, still recovering from the surprise of finding two armed strangers in the *benjo*.

"AIB," said the other. "Allied Intelligence Bureau. Nip-watchers. We're the eyes and ears of the military johnnies. But this is a turn-up, ain't it? We didn't know the Nips had a prison camp on Little Tarakang. This island's full of surprises."

It turned out that Corrigan and Matthew – a Papuan like Kima – had been observing the camp for most of the day. The latter had made contact with Kima and the nocturnal visit to the camp had been arranged. The two visitors could not stay long. They had to return to the refuge of the forest before sun-up. But their mere presence on the island made Ross' heart soar with joy.

"How did you get here?" he asked Corrigan.

"The bloody hard way," said the Australian. "By canoe. We were on Tarakawei – that's about fifteen miles north of here – but things were getting a little hot for us there and it's a smaller island. There's enough bush on this island to lie low for years and, in any case, it gives a nice view of the place that the boys back at HQ are really interested in."

"Great Tarakang?"

"Yep. It's next for the chopping-block. Our boys should already be on the way."

"Troops, you mean?" Wild hope was soaring again in Ross. "Will they land here?"

227

"That wasn't on the schedule," said Corrigan. "Although they might get round to it if they pull off the number one objective. And that's the air base just across the water. It's the air base that interests Matthew and me. Base wants a daily report from us on all activity there, plus a bulletin on all Jap warship movements in the Straits. We're going to need your help."

"We've just been waiting the moment to get ourselves some guns. With *your* help, we could maybe take over the whole island."

"How many Nips on the island?"

"Maybe a hundred and fifty. Not more than two hundred."

"Too many," said Corrigan thoughtfully. "They could have another couple of companies over from Great Tarakang in a matter of hours – and it's going to be hard enough doing my job without fighting battles. No, it's better if the Nips don't know we're here."

"How can we help then?"

"For a start you can tell me why the top of Mount Taki's swarming with little yellow men. We thought we had nothing more to do than find a nice hidey-hole on the mountain and send in our reports – but the Nips seem to have people camped up there. We couldn't get near the top."

"They have a radio station up there and a battery of guns trained across the Straits – and they're pretty well hidden. We should know. They had us building the damned things and then covering them over with rocks and screens. The main aerial mast is sprouting out of a growing tree and the crater is surrounded with machine-gun nests. It's like the Maginot Line up there."

"Is it, by God? Base said the Nips only had a handful of men on the island. Probably just a timber-cutting operation. But you say they've got artillery pointed across the Straits?"

"And enough shells to keep them firing for a couple of months. We unloaded tons from the barges."

"Did you see anything of a couple of Yanks the night before last?"

Corrigan's sudden change of subject was unexpected. Ross peered at the Australian, puzzled.

"A couple of Yanks?"

"That's what I said. The American Navy wanted someone spotting for them here and landed two men from a sub. But they took them off again when they discovered that Matthew and I were moving here from Tarakawei. I just wondered if they had tried to contact you."

Although Ross had seen nothing of the two American navymen, he immediately grasped a possible connection with the mystery of Tachibana. He told Corrigan of the Japanese major's suicide.

"You think the Yanks left this Nip officer tied to a tree? For God's sake why?" Corrigan was astounded. "Why didn't they finish the job and hide the body? Or take him with them when they went?"

"You had better ask them," said Ross.

The two men talked for more than an hour. In that time, Ross passed over as much detail as he could about the situation on Little Tarakang, including the possibility that the Japanese might be planning a rather drastic solution to the prisoner problem.

"I can't promise to be much help," said Corrigan. "But one of us will be watching all of the time. And if anything *can* be done to save you, we'll do it. That I do promise. And, if it's any comfort, you can rest assured that before this night's over I'll have told base all that you've told me. Then, it's up to them. I'm sure they won't leave you in the lurch – but what they do about it is their decision. In the meantime, Captain, I think that the fewer who know about Matthew and me, the better. OK?"

He promised to return the following night. Ross could not ask him to do more. He shook hands with the Australian and his Papuan companion. Then he watched them slip quietly into the forest and disappear.

He nodded to Kima, and the Papuan loped silently off towards the long hut. Alone, in the dark, Ross stood for a moment trying to let the nervous tension drain from his system. He was trembling from head to foot, his body's reaction to a day of shocks and nerve-tingling moments. He looked up at Mount Taki. It stood dark against the sky, silent, unchanging.

Taki's grey cone on the horizon ahead was Major Buster Low's first ever glimpse of the Tarakang Islands. Fifty feet below him, the sun glinted on calm ocean as the Mitchell hurtled over the sea. Low was puzzled and faintly relieved. They had been warned back at the Dobodura base, to which they had moved from Moresby some months before, that they could expect a hot reception in the Tarakangs. But no enemy Hamps patrolled the skies.

Low had expected the Jap fighters to strike as soon the Mitchells of 106 Squadron had come within a hundred miles of the islands ahead but their flight had been as peaceful as a milk-run.

Well, so far, so good. Maybe the Tarakangs would prove a much easier target than G-2 had led them to expect. They had not received much attention in the past from the US Third Bomb Group for two reasons. One was the extreme range from Dobodura of the cluster of islands and the second was the enemy's estimated air strength between the New Guinea base and the Tarakangs. It was a hell of a long way to go with only a twenty-eighty chance of getting as far as the target area.

The diamond formation of Mitchells was now near enough the target area for Low to dispense with the necessity for radio silence. He made a quick check with his navigator that the conical shape was Mount Taki. The navigator consulted his co-ordinate map and confirmed the fact. And they were bang on course.

Low flicked the radio switch.

"This is Kalamazoo Leader, Kalamazoo Leader. We'll be scrambling in about two minutes from now. That ice-cream cone ahead is Mount Taki. Our target is exactly eight-point-three miles due east of the summit and just over two miles from where we cross the coast. You can't miss it. But make damn sure you miss that mountain. Keep it on your left bow. Close up, Antelope Leader. Do you read me? Do you read me?"

"We read you, Kalamazoo Leader," crackled a voice in Low's headphone. "This is Antelope Leader. We'll close up and keep it tight."

"Kalamazoo Leader to all units. Drop your bellies. Drop your bellies. Ninety seconds from target."

The Mitchells jettisoned their auxiliary fuel tanks. They splashed into the calm sea like outsize eggs. To Low in the lead Mitchell the coast seemed to be rushing to meet him.

"Scramble," he shouted into the radio.

As if controlled by a single switch, the Mitchells rearranged into flights of two, with a single aircraft bringing up the rear. They roared in low over the south-west corner of Great Tarakang in pairs.

Ahead, Low could see the flat expanse of airfield. It was deserted. Not a single plane on the runways. Down one side of the field was a straggle of atap-walled buildings, on the other a fringe of forest. Low swung his Mitchell to the right to run straight over the fringe of forest. The trees, he reasoned, hid the camouflaged bays where the Japanese planes were dispersed.

The Mitchell on his left wing tracked towards the buildings which flanked the airfield on the side near the Straits. Low was climbing at full throttle as the first of his napalm bombs erupted in sheets of orange flame along the wooded perimeter line of the airfield. A parallel bank of liquid fire unrolled along the huts to the left of the airfield as the B25 to port banked away towards Mount Taki.

Puffs of anti-aircraft fire followed the waves of attacking aircraft as they climbed away from the island to the north and regrouped at three thousand feet. They circled west of the Little Tarakang and came swooping in towards the Straits a second time. The airfield was alight with napalm on two sides, like a giant flarepath. Black smoke gushed from the blazing fringes.

This time, streams of anti-aircraft fire came rushing to meet the Mitchells as they roared in from seaward. They hurtled through it to plaster the airfield with a mixed pattern of fragmentation and delay-fused high explosive. A fury of thundering explosions erupted in their wake. One Mitchell, an engine blazing, could not make height as it banked away. It screamed away out over the waters of the Straits, one wing dipped so low that the tip was near the mirror-like surface. Out across the Strait it wheeled, wings almost vertical. The port wing-tip sheered clean off as it made brief contact with the coral reef below Mount Taki. The aircraft shuddered and crashed belly-first against the base of the mountain. It exploded in a bubble of smoke and flame.

Low regrouped his squadron north of the island then led them on a north-south run through the Straits, allowing the twin .50 calibre turret Brownings to direct their firepower at a cluster of landing barges in the harbour and an encampment just beyond. Resuming their diamond formation well to the south of the island, the Mitchells headed for New Guinea. Behind them, one end of Great Tarakang seemed to be ablaze and smoke drifted over Mount Taki, investing it with the appearance of an active volcano.

Major Low had only one message for his squadron before resuming radio silence.

"Kalamazoo Leader to all units. Kalamazoo Leader to all units. Well done. That's all. Over and out."

The attack had gone well but Major Low was puzzled. The only Japanese aircraft he had seen had been a wrecked Zeke at one end of the airfield. He had expected the runways to have been hotching with Zekes and Hamps. The Japs couldn't have hidden all their airplanes in the jungle. That airfield back there had looked dead. He shrugged his shoulders. It was a lot deader now.

The roar of the aircraft and the noise of the bombs falling just across the Straits had not cheered the prisoners on Little Tarakang in a way that, otherwise, it might have done. From early morning they had once again been confined to their camp. This in itself had not given rise to uneasiness. But the arrival of Lieutenant Niguchi with orders that they were to assemble at noon with all their belongings had triggered off a wave of nervous speculation. Were they being moved to the ship? If they were not, what was happening?

Niguchi had told them nothing. Only that Major Kimura would be making an important announcement to them later in the day. Waiting had increased a growing unease. In particular, Paul Newton and Woody were alarmed at signs of considerable activity up at the Japanese camp. Although they could only guess at what was going on, it looked very much as if the Japanese were evacuating their quarters. They were certainly moving lots of their material up Mount Taki.

"We've missed our chance," Woody told Ross, his tone accusing. Newton found himself reluctantly agreeing that what the Australian said was true. Whatever was going on, it looked like the Japanese had forestalled any chance to raid their armoury. They seemed to be moving everything that could be carried up the hill.

Ross told them about Corrigan. Not even this news reassured the other two. It was something, certainly, but what could two men do to stop Kimura lining up all the prisoners in front of a machine-gun, if that was his intention?

"You wanted us to wait until Kimura had shown his hand," Newton reminded Ross. "Well, it looks like that's just what he's going to do. And I don't like it."

Ross had to quell a deep unease of his own.

"Kimura won't kill us," he said. "If that's what he intends, why should he tell us to gather all our things together?"

So the Nips won't have the bother of collecting them all afterwards," suggested Woody grimly. "I'm sorry, Skipper, but I think you've been doing a bit of wishful thinking where Kimura's concerned."

"We'll soon know," said Ross.

The sight of the American bombers wheeling in the skies around Little Tarakang caused an excitement that was tempered by a gnawing uncertainty. No sooner had the roar of aircraft engines faded to a distant drone to the south than Niguchi was back at the *Machiko* camp. He brought a summons for Ross and Ruth Gamage. Kimura wished to see both of them immediately.

Luke, the little orphan of the *Felicity*, did not want Ruth to leave him and clung to her. Niguchi signalled to her to bring the child, too. The child immediately quietened when she carried him. She and Ross followed Niguchi up to the Japanese camp. The activity there was intense, with every hut being emptied of its contents. What Newton had guessed was true. The Japanese were indeed moving out.

Kimura's command hut had been stripped bare and the radio annexe next door was empty. Kimura was kneeling on the floor before a metal trunk which he was filling with papers from neat little piles laid out on the bare floor. He rose and turned to meet them, acknowledging the stiff little bows of Ross and the woman. Ruth set Luke down. The child ran towards Kimura and genuflected artlessly to the Japanese officer – a trick that the late but unlamented Tachibana had taught the child.

The Japanese beamed with pleasure and returned the child's compliment with exaggerated solemnity. When the boy tugged at Kimura's sword scabbard, he acquiesced by unstrapping it and handing it to the child. Possession of the "toy" seemed enough for the child. He sat down heavily with the sword across his knees and smiled contentedly at the watching adults. It seemed almost with reluctance that Kimura drew his attention away from the small boy and faced Ross.

"Ross-san remembers those things of which we talked?"

"We have talked of many things, Major Kimura. I remember them."

"It is well." Kimura paused briefly. "Talking time is now finished. Time now only for duty. Time for all prisoners to die."

Ross' heart missed a beat but he stared steadily at Kimura. Ruth Gamage gave a little cry. She made a move as if towards the child on the floor, but a slight movement of Ross' hand stilled the impulse.

"This prisoner is ready to die if Major Kimura makes the order," said Ross slowly, "but he asks Major Kimura not to dishonour the name of Japan by killing all the prisoners . . ."

Kimura waved him to silence and stared angrily at Ross.

"Kimura is not a murderer," he snapped. "Ross-san will listen!"

Ross pursed his lips and waited for Kimura to continue. The Japanese waved a hand in the direction of Ruth Gamage. "Is not the mama-san a holy woman?" Kimura demanded impatiently.

"That is so," agreed Ross.

"She is a Jesus woman?" persisted Kimura.

"In a way, yes."

"In Japan, women are not priests," Kimura stated. "It is function of women to serve men." His stare now was defiant. "But people of Nippon are very tolerant people. If European people want women as priests, people of Nippon say OK. It does not matter if such a way is not Nipponese way."

Kimura continued to stare at Ross as if expecting the sea captain to contradict him. But Ross offered no contradiction. In a slightly gentler tone Kimura said, "Ross-san knows of step young man takes when he becomes priest of Buddha? He starts new life. Former person is dead, new man is born. New man takes new name, so that bad things done by former person stay in past. New person lives only for way of perfection. Is it not same with woman *sensei* who lives for Jesus-God?"

Ross was silent, following what Kimura had said but baffled as to what point the Japanese was trying to make. It was Ruth Gamage who came to his assistance.

"What Major Kimura says is true," she said, her eyes shining with a vitality that had been absent since the awful day of Private Richardson's death. Since then she had been almost trance-like in a bleak acceptance of her day-to-day survival on Little Tarakang, reserving what little animation she showed for her devotion to the child playing happily on the floor. But now a spark of something had returned as she faced Kimura. " 'Ye cannot follow me except ye are born again!' " she exclaimed.

Kimura stared at her with surprise, shocked that she should interrupt without any invitation from him. But he forgot Ruth Gamage as his eyes searched Ross' face for the flicker of comprehension which now appeared there.

"I understand what Major Kimura says," Ross acknowledged. "It is the belief of many religions in both east and west that to enter the priesthood is a rebirth . . ."

Now Kimura was smiling.

"Time now for all prisoners to leave their former persons behind and become disciples of the woman *sensei*. They will build temple where they will live and seek only perfection. For them, no more war."

Without fully understanding what it was that Kimura was driving at, Ross caught his breath, not daring to let his mind race ahead to the wrong conclusion. Nevertheless, he could not altogether still the sudden surge of hope that flared inside him.

"Major Kimura wishes the prisoners to become like priests . . .? To build a temple . . .?"

"Just so," said Kimura, nodding eagerly. "Today at noon all prisoners die. All get new names and vow to follow way of perfection and peace. Ross-san will see that their obedience is absolute. All will live in peace with Nippon and temple land will be respected. Only if Ross-san's people leave temple land will Nippon Army be angry and soldiers shoot Ross-san's people. This is way it must be."

It took Kimura twenty minutes of patient talk to communicate fully to Ross the plan that he had formulated. Ross was staggered not only by its naïve simplicity but also by its almost Machiavellian circumvention of the blind obedience to orders that was the Japanese code. Kimura had found a way to disobey a direct order from a superior and, simultaneously, carry that order out to the letter. And if its defensibility was doubtful, there was no doubt at all about its ingenuity.

What Kimura proposed to do was to move all the prisoners and the Tarakangese labour-force to a promontory at the extreme west of the island called Java Point. They would be provided with axes, hand-saws, spades – the basic implements of survival – and a quantity of food from what little the Japanese had. Kimura had already sent a squad of men to Java Point to mark the boundary of what he called the "temple land" with a line of stakes across the neck of the 500-yards-wide promontory.

The prisoners were to remain within that boundary at all times, where they would enjoy complete immunity from interference by the Japanese. In return for that immunity, they would refrain from any acts which were harmful to the Japanese. In the event of a breach of the boundary rule, action would be swift and the Japanese soldiers would be given orders to shoot on sight anyone not complying.

From the tin chest of documents Kimura showed Ross the written order he had received from Watanabe for disposal of the prisoners. Like all the orders emanating from Area Headquarters it was numbered. Kimura translated Order No. 1753. It was titled, "Order Regarding The Disposal of Prisoners, Internees, and Surplus Labour-Force Personnel". It was itemised:

1 In the event of an enemy attack on the islands within the Area or at such time when the above personnel have ceased to be of any functional service to the Imperial Forces, they will be liquidated.

235

2 The execution of this order will be the responsibility of Major Kimura, 93rd Independent Coastal Group, who will ensure its compliance.

3 Major Kimura has been verbally instructed on the importance of executing the order without delay at the appropriate time.

4 Method of disposal: Major Kimura has been given discretion to dispose of the unwanted personnel in as humane a manner as possible.

Area Commander:	Colonel Watanabe
Date:	25 April 1944
Time:	11.45 a.m.
Place:	Area HQ, Tarakang Islands
Method of Issuing Orders:	Issued in my presence in writing to Major Kimura
Place to report after completion of Order:	Area HQ.
Also to be informed:	18th Army HQ.

Kimura returned the document to the tin chest and told Ross that it was his intention to transmit a radio signal to Area Headquarters that evening, saying that Order No. 1753 had been carried out. Ross could not resist a quiet smile. Kimura had certainly, in his discretion, devised "as humane a manner as possible" for the disposal of the prisoners – but he wondered what Colonel Watanabe's interpretation would be. Kimura was disposing of the prisoners on paper, writing them off as "dead" so that they could be "reborn" with new names as the disciples of a most unlikely holy order headed by the prisoners' woman *sensei*, Ruth Gamage.

Ruth's reaction to Kimura's astonishing proposals surprised Ross. Ever since her attack by Yoshimura and the subsequent events he had had genuine fears for her sanity. She had seemed to shut herself in a mental world of her own. And yet she had continued to go through the motions of living normally – as far as that was possible on the island – without any dramatic outward signs that her mind had actually snapped. Little Luke had been her saving grace, giving her a focus outside herself: someone on whom she could lavish care and affection and someone who loved her warmly and unreservedly in return. Now, as Kimura outlined his proposals and revealed the part that he wanted Ruth to play, her eagerness took Ross by surprise.

She seemed to come fully alive again before his eyes, as if Kimura had opened the shutters on some dark recess of her mind and the light had come flooding in. This time she did not make the mistake – as she had done with Tachibana – of believing that she had won a convert to Christianity. She knew that Kimura's strange act had not been prompted by anything that she, personally, had said or done. He had arrived at his state of enlightenment along his own heathen path and she was awed by the fact. For the very first time in her life, her mind touched on the possibility that there were perhaps more ways to God than the one she had heard declared – and had declared herself – since her earliest childhood.

Ross marvelled quietly at the sudden change in her. It was as if *she* had been "dead" and was born again. Her eyes glowed with new animation, as if some flickering source of light within her had been recharged and was now running at full power. It was an animation devoid of aggression and fanaticism. There was a serenity founded on humility, on weakness rather than strength. Ross looked at her and thought: blessed are the meek . . .

Even Kimura was affected: overlooking her Western propensity to speak before she was spoken to, but approving the thoughtful respect and humility of her remarks. He had one final act to perform. Absenting himself briefly, Kimura returned carrying two boxes. The larger of the two was of gaily coloured cardboard. He opened it first and took out a saffron kimono decorated with a pale blue flower design.

"It was present for my sister," he said. "But I shall not see well-loved sister again." He handed it to Ruth Gamage, pointing as he did so at the tattered men's shorts and shirt she wore. "*Sensei* needs suitable garment. You wear."

Ruth bowed, thanking him graciously as she accepted the kimono. Kimura turned his attention to his other box. It was wooden, with a varnished exterior and small carrying handle. He opened it and carefully withdrew the carved statue of the Bodhisattva, Monju Bosatsu. This, too, he handed to Ruth.

"Please care for my Bodhisattva in your temple," he said solemnly. "Today, I burn house to live on mountain like fox. Monju Bosatsu will remind people who enter temple that honourable war is against blindness of ignorance and that there is no honour where there is no compassion."

Ross felt a strange dryness in the throat and caught his breath as he waited for Ruth's reaction, fearing her rejection of what in her eyes was a heathen idol. She did not reject it. She accepted it reverently, her eyes moist with the misty promise of a tear.

"Your gift will be treasured, Major Kimura," she said softly.

Kimura bowed.

"Now, go."

They were dismissed. Ross wanted to say thanks but Kimura turned his head away as if to emphasise the finality of their dismissal. He bowed briefly and stooped to pick up Luke from the floor. The child still had Kimura's sword.

Ross handed the sword to Kimura and their eyes met. Kimura's face was impassive, not a trace of any emotion. Ross murmured, "Thank you, Major Kimura. Sayonara."

Kimura said nothing, but a gleam entered his eye. It acknowledged the farewell.

As Ross walked down the hill, with Luke on his shoulder and Ruth Gamage by his side, he patiently answered the barrage of questions which the young woman fired at him about the significance of the Bodhisattva in the box she carried. She wanted to know all he could tell her about the Japanese religions of Buddhism and Shinto. He was no expert but he tried his best to shed some light on oriental beliefs and customs of which Ruth's ignorance was total.

"You're not thinking of switching religions?" he asked her, with a mischievous smile.

She answered with the first smile he had ever seen on her face. It transformed her.

"No," she said. "Nothing would ever make me do that."

"Well, I'm glad I asked. It made you smile. You should do it more often. It becomes you."

She glanced at him sideways, a happy light still in her eyes.

"I think you're right, Captain Ross. I should smile more often. I've discovered a lot about myself today . . . And it's like seeing the world as it is for the very first time."

"Do you like what you see?" asked Ross.

She smiled again.

"No, not necessarily. But, before, when I saw only the bad things, I was blind to so much else that wasn't bad. The world is like me – not all good, but not all wicked. I don't think I've ever had the world or myself or God in perspective before. Now, I'm getting a perspective."

Ross looked down at the ragged-clad young woman with her unkempt hair and sun-seared face. There was respect in his look.

"You know, Miss Gamage, I think you have the makings of a very wise woman."

She smiled yet again.

"Coming from you, that's a compliment. I'm not wise yet, Captain Ross – but I think I'm learning. The hard way – from experience. You were a bit nervous back there with Major Kimura, weren't you? In case I said the wrong thing and offended him?"

"I had qualms," admitted Ross. "I know this temple idea probably sounds crazy to you . . . It may even be offensive to your own beliefs . . . But the lives of every one of us here depend on all of us taking it absolutely seriously."

"Oh, I take it seriously," said Ruth Gamage. "Major Kimura has opened a door for us, at the risk of his own life and all he stands for. I want him to have his temple, Captain Ross, and I'm going to do everything I can to see that he gets it, and one that's worthy of him."

As her ability to smile had surprised Ross, so too did her vehemence now.

"The temple idea isn't all that important," he said. "What Major Kimura has given us is something we didn't have before – time."

Her expression as she stared up at him was shocked.

"Time?" she echoed. "Is that all it means to you?"

"I'm a practical man, Miss Gamage. Kimura produced this temple idea as a device for not murdering the whole lot of us in cold blood. And, as a means of saving our skins, we've all got to go along with it. But we mustn't get too carried away. Kimura knows and I know that my crew aren't going to be turned into cloistered acolytes at the wave of a wand. At the shake of a bayonet, maybe – and it's in that context we have to see it."

Ruth Gamage bit her lip unhappily, saddened by Ross' words.

"There's a certain amount of truth in what you say," she conceded, "but as I'm not one of your crew, it doesn't apply to me. I don't intend just to pay lip-service to our side of the bargain. I intend to go along with it all the way."

There was an element of high farce in the ritual that took place in the *Machiko* camp at noon. Major Kimura appeared briefly to make a statement before the assembled prisoners. The gist of this was that, in three hours' time, the camp would be burned to the ground and all prisoners still surviving at that time would be shot. In the meantime, all prisoners who wished to abandon their lives voluntarily and embark on the way of perfection as new persons under the leadership of the *Sensei* Gamage could do so by passing through the bamboo archway erected for the purpose. When they had passed through the archway, they would leave behind their former lives and past identities forever. Once through the archway, they would give their former names to Lieutenant Niguchi, who would enter certification of their "deaths" in the records required by the Imperial Army.

An irony was that Lieutenant Niguchi entered "death by natural causes" against every name on the list, thus maintaining a practice that the Japanese had followed with every prisoner death on Little Tarakang – whether death had occurred from a brutal beating or any of the many diseases that had taken their toll.

Warned by Ross to enact their part in the farce as solemnly as they could, the prisoners filed through the archway in a sober line. For them, it was but the final absurdity of many, and they all knew that their lives depended on it.

It was Ruth Gamage who provided a totally unexpected note of drama. Leading little Luke by the hand, she emerged from the "hospital" clad in the vividly coloured kimono. But it was not the striking kimono that caused the line of waiting men to gasp. It was the sight of her head.

She had attempted to shave off her crown of unkempt blonde hair. And she had not made too good a job of it. Little tufts sprouted here and there from her otherwise bald head. Her scalp trickled blood in several places where she had cut herself with the far from razor-sharp implement that she had used.

There was reproach in Ross' eyes as she approached him, but only defiance in hers. And whatever the prisoners may have thought of the disfiguring effect, there was no mistaking the respectful awe of the Japanese soldiers, who gazed at her with hushed and respectful solemnity.

There was a wait while the Tarakangese from the other camp were herded up and ushered through the archway in rather bemused fashion. No undue ceremony of recording names here. They were simply counted like so many sheep.

The entire company of prisoners and islanders, numbering more than a hundred and thirty, then had to share the burdens of cooking pots, bags of rice, tools and personal belongings and start on the march to Java Point. There was a track of sorts in places but, for much of the way, it was virgin forest. It was late in the afternoon when the last straggler passed through the staked

240

boundary on to the half-mile-long promontory. It was not an unpleasant place: sandy beaches on either side, not too densely covered in trees and vegetation, a garden of rich flowers and many fruits. There was no natural fresh water but Niguchi pointed out a gentle waterfall and pool not far from the neck of the promontory. It was on the forbidden side of the boundary stakes but Niguchi made it clear that it could be safely considered temple land. The stakes had simply been hammered home where the ground was soft enough to take them. The rock around the waterfall had not been receptive.

The Tarakangese immediately set about the construction of palm and bamboo huts – an art in which they were outstandingly proficient and speedy, not a nail being required in any part of the construction. They were friendly people and did not hesitate to put their expertise to work to help the *Machiko* prisoners erect shelters of their own.

The day's events had, of course, come as a totally unforeseen development which demanded a complete rethink of all the talk and plans to seize the *Machiko*. These had already been given a new perspective by the appearance on the island only the night before of Corrigan and his Papuan companion. Consequently, when Ross and his two main abetters finally got together for a conference of war, late that night, the trio were bodily weary and a little punch-drunk from all that had happened.

They found a rocky plateau at the extreme end of Java Point, where they could sit away from the others and discuss a new strategy. It was a brilliant moonlit night and beyond the point the sea was a shimmering mirror. Woody was the one who summed up the way they all felt.

"I feel like Alice in bloody Wonderland!" he said. "I just can't keep up with it. I don't know what the hell is going to happen next. I think that if I as much as blink me eyes, Mount Taki will fall over or General bloody McArthur will come swimming ashore towing the Manly ferry!"

He looked up in alarm as Paul Newton gave a strangled little exclamation, even before he had finished speaking.

"Blink your eyes over there, Woody, and tell me what the hell is that!" exclaimed the American

Woody and Ross, who were both sitting with their backs to the sea, turned to follow Newton's gaze. They both scrambled round and got to their feet, spurred by surprise at the sight that met their eyes. Newton, too, got to his feet.

241

"Well, Woody, what do you make of it? Is that by any chance the Manly ferry?"

"It's a bloody aircraft carrier!" said Woody. "Christ, she's close! And there's something wrong with her."

"She's listing badly," said Ross. "Stopped a torpedo maybe."

The Australian turned wide-eyed to Ross.

"Whose is she, Captain? One of ours? Or one of theirs?"

"Hard to tell," murmured Ross. "But don't raise your hopes too high. My guess is she's Japanese."

Ross was right. They were looking at the *Yamazakura*. She had come to Little Tarakang to die.

Sixteen

The Yamazakura

Signal lamps had been flashing between the aircraft carrier and the top of Mount Taki for most of the night. As a consequence, in the first light of day, Rear-Admiral Tukijiro Ugaki was going to attempt what – in Major Kimura's eyes – was a near impossible feat of seamanship. He was going to bring the *Yamazakura* into Little Tarakang's inner basin.

The carrier had lain off the island during the night but, at the first streak of day, an armada of small boats had been launched and now preceded the big ship through the gap in the reef. The *Yamazakura* had a pronounced list and seemed much too broad to make the passage through the reef but there was, in fact, several feet clearance on either side as she glided slowly into the turquoise waters of the lagoon. By going ahead on the port engine and astern on the starboard, she made the awkward turn into the lagoon with much more ease than the *Machiko* had done more than two years previously. Then she stopped engines, making way and no more, as the small boats streamed ahead of her: the crews sounding with lead-lines and indicating to the parent ship where the water depth was safe.

Kimura stood on the beach, near the point where the Tarakangese camp had been, watching anxiously as the most difficult manoeuvre approached. The carrier had to swing to port and complete the U-turn from the lagoon into the deep inner basin. It was during this part of the operation that the *Machiko* had briefly grounded on the sand-bar.

The carrier had a marginally greater draught than the fully laden *Machiko* but her 510-foot length was double that of the merchant ship's. Where the *Yamazakura* held an advantage was in her unimpaired steering system and her twin-screwed manoeuvrability. The *Machiko* had been severely handicapped by the fact

243

that Ross had had to con the cumbersome emergency steering from the top of the foremast by verbal relay to the stern.

Rear-Admiral Ugaki had no such problem. There was no agonising delay between the issue of a vital helm order and its execution. His task was still by no means easy and, as the *Machiko* had done before, the *Yamazakura* grounded on the sand-bar across the mouth of the basin. She had almost completed the big turn by then, but a burst of the high-powered engines – which were capable of driving the ship at twenty-five knots – was sufficient to thrust the carrier forward into the deep, wide waters of the basin.

Within minutes of the anchor cable rattling out, a pinnace carrying Ugaki was on its way shorewards. Kimura greeted the naval officer formally on the landing stage near the *Machiko*. In the absence of other accommodation, the two men adjourned to the merchant ship to confer. The new saloon on the merchant ship was primitive compared with what the carrier could have offered – a fixed table and rough wooden benches – but it sufficed.

Kimura was curious to know why Ugaki had risked the dangerous entry into Little Tarakang when it would have been much easier to have gone into Great Tarakang. Ugaki told him.

"You must know that an American invasion fleet has been sighted?" said the admiral.

Kimura nodded. "It is several days away. But everything points to Great Tarakang as its likely destination."

"Precisely," said Ugaki, clasping his hands in front of him. He was a podgy little man with a benign face. "It is because Great Tarakang is the most likely destination of the invaders that I chose your island, Major Kimura. The Americans will almost certainly strike at the beaches in the Straits. Our final mission would be in vain."

"Your final mission?"

"Yes, Major Kimura. We have only fuel left for two days' steaming, perhaps less. When it became apparent that, because of damage we suffered from an American warship, we were slowing down our taskforce and placing it in danger, we asked permission to sail against the reported enemy convoy alone. That is the task with which we have been honoured – but its success depends on a number of factors. We must first make repairs to correct the listing of the ship so that our aircraft can take off. It is also essential that when we strike, we do so with maximum surprise

244

and in a manner that causes maximum damage to the enemy. We have accepted that we all must die . . . But we are determined that our deaths shall set a glorious example to the Imperial Navy by giving Tenno Heiko a victory."

Kimura made a soft moaning sound. It was an unarticulated expression of his admiration, bordering on reverence.

"You do my command a great honour with your presence, your excellency. We, too, are ready to die but must wait for the enemy to strike at us. For the moment, all that we can do on the island to assist you in your glorious mission will be done."

Ugaki made a modest little bow.

"A little time is all we need, Major Kimura. Time to cure that list on the *Yamazakura* before the Yankees make their assault. By tomorrow, it should be complete. My only concern is that the ship is vulnerable to air attack in her present position and I would be happier if she were concealed here in this inlet."

They discussed the possibility of moving the *Machiko* and Kimura told the naval commander something of the ship's history and how the plan to sail the ship away had been abandoned only forty-eight hours before, when the report of an imminent invasion had been flashed from Great Tarakang. Ugaki asked to inspect the ship and was relieved to find that there was no reason why she should not be moved out to the basin so that the *Yamazakura* could take her place. A message was promptly despatched to the aircraft carrier for an emergency crew to be mustered and sent ashore at once.

As he surveyed the scene from the deck of the *Machiko*, Ugaki had a sudden thought. He turned to Kimura.

"Do you have any camouflage netting?" he asked.

Kimura had, in some quantity. It had been used to cover the artillery positions up on Mount Taki but had largely been replaced by the specially constructed screens made by the prisoners. He offered to have it put at the admiral's disposal.

"We shall take all that you can spare," said Ugaki. "The *Yamazakura* will take a lot of covering but it can be done." He pointed along the tree-lined inlet. "This place is perfect. It is wide enough to take the ship and yet narrow enough for us to rig a canopy that will hide it from the air completely. Everything depends on the Americans never suspecting that we are here. Then, if their landing ships dare to anchor in the Straits, we shall deliver a blow that could wipe them out. We could steal out of here and have all our aircraft in the air within an hour of first light."

"And we shall support you," said Kimura. "We took great trouble to conceal our field guns on Mount Taki in the belief that any attack from the sea would be directed at the airfield and harbour. The guns command the Straits in a way that could not be accomplished from the other island. We hope that they, too, will come as an unpleasant surprise to the enemy."

"What if they land on the far side of Great Tarakang?"

"It's a possibility," said Kimura. "But, if they do, they will have to fight their way through twenty miles of jungle to reach the airfield. It could take them months."

"What if they land on this island to use a springboard for an assault on Great Tarakang?" asked Ugaki.

"That, too, is always a possibility – but the Area Commander has always believed that the airfield would be the primary target. If the enemy comes here first, then it will be my job to make him pay as dearly as possible. I do not have enough men to cover all the shoreline, so there is little chance of us stopping a landing. For that reason, we have already abandoned the low part of the island. My men and I are now living in dugouts on the mountain. Defending the artillery positions is my number one priority but I can't do that if my men are scattered all over the island. The Americans are welcome to come ashore but they won't find it easy to knock us off that mountain."

"And what about this old tub? Were you just to leave her here for the enemy?"

Kimura smiled ruefully.

"My lieutenant would be unhappy to hear you call her an 'old tub', Honourable Ugaki. He and his men worked very hard to make it fit for sea. It rather grieves them now that it was all a waste of time. Today, I planned to send some of my engineers aboard and blow the bottom out of their pride and joy."

The admiral made a face.

"I sympathise with your lieutenant, but I have to confess that she is one of the strangest ships I have ever clapped eyes on. Still, it does seem a waste. Perhaps we could use her as a fire-ship and sail her into the American ships?"

Kimura made no comment on the admiral's suggestion. He said, "A small tug was being sent over from the other island yesterday to tow the ship across the Straits to use as a block ship – but it was shot up by American planes and ran aground in the harbour."

"Well, we can forget about scuttling her for the time being," said Ugaki. "The important thing is to get her out of this inlet. She can lie at anchor with a guard-watch aboard until we decide what's best. What happened to the original crew?"

"They were captured and used as a labour-force," Kimura replied impassively.

"And?"

"They were removed by order of the Area Commander when their usefulness had ended," said Kimura.

In spite of his promise to contact Ross, Corrigan did not show during the first night at Java Point. Ross was disappointed but not surprised. The sudden removal from one end of the island to the other had been a totally unpredictable development.

The first morning at Java Point had been strange. The absence of any guards had induced a kind of euphoria which made any kind of organised effort hopeless. A holiday atmosphere had developed in which any kind of work was regarded as anathema. Both the *Machiko* prisoners and the Tarakangese were affected by the sudden release from the pressures of being a captive labour-force. Now, all they wanted to do was sit in the sun, enjoying the idyllic weather conditions prevailing over the island.

But there was work to do. The hastily erected shelters had been adequate for one night but required refinement and improvement. The meagre food supplies had to be rationed and distributed fairly. Before the morning was half gone, Ross found himself almost wishing for the heavy authority of the Japanese to restore an order and discipline to the strangely mixed community and its new freedom.

He knew it was an artificial freedom – but it was a freedom of sorts. A Tarakangese elder seemed to be the undisputed boss of the islanders and, through him, a loose kind of government was set up to organise the day-to-day living – although, by consensus, it was agreed that an earnest start would have to wait until next day.

One person was unaffected by the prevailing *mañana* atmosphere. Ruth Gamage took her mandate from Kimura seriously and spent much time trying to get the other Europeans interested in selecting a site on which to build a temple. She found that while nearly all were sympathetic and ready to listen to her ideas, none had the foggiest notion of how the construction should be tackled. The Tarakangese were much more helpful, although communication was a problem. The white woman was a curiosity to them and they treated her in a way that disconcerted her at first: touching her and examining her in a grossly familiar manner one moment and showing her the greatest deference and respect the next.

The islanders were unanimous in their approval that a temple should be built. Furthermore, they knew how it should be built. A "spirit house" they called it – and then they dismayed Ruth by showing some insistence that this "spirit house" would be the reserve of men only. It would be taboo to women. However, they did not belabour the point when Ruth tried to give them the picture of the temple she had in mind – one that was completely new and different, one which could be entered by people of different colour and belief, where all good "spirits" could be revered.

The Tarakangese sidetracked her for a time by promising to build a special house for women. It was Kima, the Papuan, who tactfully pointed out to her that the islanders were talking about a "menstruation house": a kind of monthly place of retreat for menstruating women.

Oddly enough, Ruth found an unlikely ally in her talks with the islanders in the shape of Randolph Moorhouse. He made it very plain to them that he was a big noise in the service of the British King and they took him at his word. They even coined a special name for him, which Kima loosely translated as "the white-haired one with the face of a rising storm". Moorhouse took it as a compliment to his natural authority in dealing with Asiatics.

But not even Moorhouse could persuade the islanders that an immediate start on Ruth Gamage's temple was desirable. By and by, OK – but not today. In any case, first, they had to pick out erema trees. This baffled both Moorhouse and Ruth. They were still none the wiser after two of the Tarakangese spokesmen took them on a guided tour of Java Point, pointing at various trees and making voluble but – to Ruth and Moorhouse – quite unintelligible speeches about each. They had to search for Kima once again to act as interpreter.

He explained that the islanders intended to build *lakatoi*. Ruth and Moorhouse stared at him, uncomprehending. Kima repeated the word. *Lakatoi*. Then he made undulating movements with his hands to depict the waves of the sea, and followed it up by miming paddling movements. The truth dawned on Ruth and Moorhouse.

The first priority of the Tarakangese was the building of outrigger canoes. They had no intention of staying on Little Tarakang any longer than was absolutely necessary.

Moorhouse was greatly perturbed. He went straight to Ross to tell him that the islanders would have to be watched and possibly restrained. If they were not, they could possibly endanger the lives of everyone by contravening the absurd agreement which had been reached with the Japanese.

Ross was in no mood for an argument. He promised to speak with the Tarakangese headman about it if Moorhouse insisted, but he was sure a mass exodus by sea was not an immediate likelihood. It would take weeks, if not months, to build enough canoes to accommodate all the islanders and a lot could happen in that time. He asked Moorhouse if he had read any significance into the raid on Great Tarakang the day before by American bombers.

"Only that the war's getting closer," replied Moorhouse. "And that this island could be next for the bombs."

"I think it means more than that," said Ross, refraining from making any mention of Corrigan or his conversation with him. "I think the bombers were softening up the other island for a landing. I think that help may be nearer than any of us have dared to hope, Mr Moorhouse."

Moorhouse was silent. It was in his nature to disagree with Ross and accuse him of undue optimism. But he was human enough to want to believe that the sea captain could just possibly be right. He was quite dazed. All argument went out of him, banished by the flood of hope which Ross had unwittingly released inside him.

"You know, I've almost forgotten what life in a civilised society was like," he said in a vacant kind of way. He seemed to be clawing at his memory to recall life before Little Tarakang. "None of us will ever be the same again," he said absently. "And neither will the world we knew. It'll all be changed. It's almost frightening to think of it. Being free again, I mean. Really free."

It was the only time Ross had ever seen Moorhouse betray a human face and speak without the mask of what he believed himself to be.

"We're not free yet," he cautioned.

Moorhouse glanced up quickly at Ross, rather in the manner of one who has been found naked and suddenly realised the fact. He reached desperately for his haughty mantle to cloak his embarrassment.

"There's one good thing about it if our people are as close as you seem to think," he said brusquely. "Perhaps it will put an end

249

once and for all to this insane idea of storming your ship and trying to make a run for it."

Ross acknowledged this with a smiling inclination of the head.

"It was a gamble we were prepared to take. No one's happier than I am that it has come to nothing. None of us anticipated that Major Kimura would invest us all with holy orders."

"Blighter probably got cold feet," said Moorhouse. "He probably realises that the Japs can't win the war and that there's going to be a hell of a stink anyway about the way we've been treated. Well, he hasn't bought my gratitude with this nonsense about building a temple. He must think we're off our rockers. I'm certainly not taken in by his pantomime act and mumbo-jumbo morality. The Japs have no sense of moral decency."

Ross shrugged.

"You're entitled to your opinion. I would have thought that Major Kimura needed quite a lot of moral courage to do what he did. He was under orders to kill us. But he found a way to spare our lives."

"Because he hopes it will save his own skin. I'm afraid he doesn't pull the wool over my eyes the way he has always pulled it over yours, Ross. I, for one, hold him responsible for every crime that has been committed on this island – and I hope I live to see him pay for these crimes. Hanging's too good for him."

Ross looked at Moorhouse with distaste, thinking that if he had to make any judgement on the worth of Kimura or the Englishman, it would be the latter who would be found wanting. He was saved the need of further argument by the arrival of Kima, who obviously had something to impart. Ross excused himself abuptly from Moorhouse and went to meet the big Papuan. It transpired that his compatriot, Matthew, was waiting in the bush just beyond the Java Point boundary markers and wanted to talk to Ross.

Ross walked into the forest in the direction Kima had indicated. He had taken only a few steps into the damp gloom when a hiss made him turn. Matthew materialised like a ghost at his side. He had a message from Corrigan. The Australian wanted to meet him above the waterfall near Java Point.

"When?" asked Ross.

Matthew raised two fingers.

"Sun go down. Two hours."

"Two hours after sunset?"

The Papuan nodded vigorously. Then he disappeared into the forest as swiftly and silently as he had appeared.

The USS *Crystal River* pitched and rolled as the convoy steamed steadily westwards at an even ten knots. In the troop decks, men of the American 11th Corps were passing the time as best they could – but more than one was of the opinion that combat with the Japanese was an infinitely more preferable pastime than that of subjection to the endless stomach-turning movements of the *Crystal River*.

The bad weather had come as an unpleasant surprise but it had not slowed down the convoy. It was now just a little over seven hundred miles from its destination – the island of Great Tarakang. The bad weather, however, did present problems. Areas of low pressure were piling into each other like rolling tumbleweeds along a 2000-mile-long track parallel to the Equator, closing in every airfield between Wewak and Milne Bay.

The weather was very much on the minds of the officers gathered in the Ops Room of the *Crystal River*. It worried General Darren S. Budge in particular. "Operation Stingray" was his first operational assignment since he had been given his second star and it was the first operation of any kind with which he had been trusted with overall command. He wanted nothing to go wrong.

It was no consolation that the weather report for the Tarakangs and the area to the west promised clear skies and calm seas. What did it matter if conditions were ideal over the battle area but the air support that had been promised was grounded and useless behind them and was likely to remain that way for several days?

"There's not a damned thing we can do about it, gentlemen," he told the small gathering. "We shall just have to face the fact that 'Operation Stingray' may have to proceed without any aid from the boys out of the wild blue yonder."

"We could slow things down," suggested a bald-domed major. "Put D-Day back by twenty-four hours and hope that the weather back there relents."

"I'd hate to do that," said Budge. "We've no guarantee that the weather will relent. We could postpone the evil day and be no better off."

"At least the Air Force gave the airfield a good clobbering yesterday," said the USN Commander, who was Intelligence Co-ordinator for the operation. "And the debrief at Dobodura does indicate that the Japs may have already withdrawn all their aircraft from the Tarakangs. The Mitchells that hit the airfield yesterday morning didn't encounter a single Jap fighter and didn't see any on the field itself."

"That's the one thing that gives me grounds for optimism," said Budge. "My decision, gentlemen, is that we hit the island right on schedule." He turned to the major with the bald head, who was frowning. "You don't look too happy, Major Goldman."

The major scratched his hairless dome in perplexity.

"With respect, General, you're taking a hell of a risk going in there without any air support."

"That's what we're paid for, Major," said Budge icily, "taking risks."

They were interrupted by a knock at the door. A blue-shirted navyman entered and handed a sheet of paper to the naval commander. Everyone in the room looked at the Intelligence Co-ordinator as he read the signal. When he had finished reading, he passed it to the general.

Budge swore as he read.

"This is all we goddamned need!"

The group of officers round the table waited to be enlightened. Budge nodded to the Intelligence Co-ordinator to go ahead and tell them.

"It's from AIBHQ at Moresby," he said in a flat voice. "Their man on the island across the narrows from Great Tarakang has reported more than a prison camp on his island. A Hosyo-class aircraft carrier arrived this morning. It's holed up in a creek not ten miles from the landing beaches."

"Is that one of the big ones?" asked an army officer in an awed tone.

The Intelligence Co-ordinator smiled grimly.

"As a matter of fact, no, but big enough to put three squadrons in the air – and that's enough to make a hell of a mess of this force. The Hosyo-class carriers are not much more than seven thousand tons deadweight – midgets compared with the Akagi or Kaga types and not quite so fast – but you'd better believe that one of them spells big trouble for us."

"It's unusual for a Jap carrier to be operating on its own," said Budge. "What I'd like to know is where the rest of the pack is? We've got six destroyers – and it looks like we could be running straight into the Jap fleet." He stared accusingly at the USN Commander. "Your Intelligence people said the Japs didn't have anything bigger than a trawler in the Tarakangs and that the big stuff had all pulled back to the Philippines. They said this operation would be a cakewalk!"

"With respect, sir, an enemy taskforce was reported six

hundred miles north of the Tarakangs only a few days ago. You saw the reports." The Intelligence Co-ordinator stared angrily at Budge.

"Yeah," snarled Budge. "And they weren't supposed to be there either! They appeared outa thin air!"

"There's a hell of a lot of ocean up there, General. We can't give any advance guarantee of what the Jap Navy is going to do. In any case, Admiral Donovan's taskforce caught up with the Japs and chased them off. The last we heard they were running for home as fast as they could go. This carrier in the Tarakangs could be one that didn't make it. The AIB signal said that she was listing badly and possibly damaged."

Budge's anger subsided, but he was still far from happy.

"Even if this carrier's a maverick, she still represents a major threat to 'Stingray'," he said bitterly. "She has to be neutralised!" He thumped a fist on the table. "All I want is for somebody to tell me how the hell we do that when we can't put a single plane in the air!"

Very little of the moon's light penetrated the canopy of forest. Ross had fallen several times and his breath was coming in great panting breaths as he tried to keep up with the two shadowy figures ahead of him. Two years on Little Tarakang had not been the best preparation for this kind of jungle game.

Corrigan and Matthew waited for Ross to catch up.

"Not far now, Captain," the Australian encouraged. "There's beach just up ahead. We'll see the whole length of the lake from there."

The lake he referred to was the broad inner basin where the Japanese aircraft carrier had anchored that morning. Only the aircraft carrier was no longer to be seen. When they reached the beach, Ross stared across the water and gave a gasp of surprise.

"That's the *Machiko* out there!" he exclaimed.

"Do your old heart good to see her out there?" asked Corrigan. "Here, take a look." He handed Ross a pair of binoculars and waited while Ross focused on the moonlit shape of the *Machiko*.

"They've got people on board," commented Ross. "Someone has just lit a cigarette."

"Half a dozen sailors from the carrier," filled in Corrigan. "They went aboard when they took off the crew who moved the old scow out to the anchorage. They're just guards, I reckon. They had rifles but nothing heavier."

The noise of distant hammers against metal echoed over the water from the dark edge of the basin.

"Are they working on the carrier?" asked Ross.

"They been hammering away since they got 'er tucked nice and cosy in that creek where your ship was lying. That big ship is like a hive of bees . . . all the scurryin' around that's goin' on. Lots of comin' and goin', too, between the carrier and the soldiers up on the mountain."

Ross looked quizzically at the Australian.

"So, you got me all the way here to have a look. We're here, we've had a look. What was the point?"

"The point is," said Corrigan slowly, "that you have had your look . . . You've seen where your ship is . . . And now you tell me how we handle the tricky bit."

"Tricky bit?" said Ross.

"Tricky bit," repeated Corrigan. He took a deep breath. "How do we bottle that Nip carrier in the creek and keep her there until the boys in the B-25s get here and blow her to Kingdom Come?"

Ross passed a hand over his forehead.

"The *Machiko*?" He breathed the question. "You want to use the *Machiko*?"

"It's all there is. I had an idea that we could steal the ship like you planned and kind of use 'er as a dock gate. Sink 'er, so that that Nip stays right where she is."

"You're crazy," said Ross. "It wouldn't work."

"Why not?"

"Well, assuming that we managed to take the ship, in the first place, and that we managed to get her across the entrance to the creek in the second, scuttling her there wouldn't keep the carrier inside."

"Why not?" repeated Corrigan.

"Because the water's too deep. The whole of this inland basin is like a pit – a bottomless pit. The only shallow water is at this end, where there's beach and a bit of a shelf, and at the far end where the lagoon meets the basin."

"That kinda knocks my bright idea on the head," Corrigan said sadly. "Pity."

"I'm not sure it was so bright," said Ross. "It would be suicidal. The Japanese wouldn't just sit and watch. They would make damned sure that not one of us ever got off this island alive."

"I know the odds," said Corrigan quietly. "Maybe I was asking too much in hoping that your people would go along with me. It's different for you. But Matthew and me . . . Well, we both know that people in our game don't stick around long enough to see their old-age pensions. We saw it as our lives against the alternative."

"What alternative?" asked Ross.

Corrigan made a sad kind of a smile.

"Captain. Two, maybe three nights from now, the Yanks are going to hit Great Tarakang. It won't be a big show, like Guadalcanal and some of the other islands. Just a small one, with twenty or thirty ships and maybe no more than seven or eight thousand men – part of the Eleventh Corps that they've managed to spare from a bigger and more important push. Can you imagine what's going to happen to them if that Nip carrier is out on the ocean somewhere close when those boys hit the beaches? Can you imagine what it's going to be like on those twenty or thirty ships? The Battle of Tarakang, Captain, could turn out to be one of the biggest disasters of the war. That's the alternative, Captain."

Ross was silent for a moment.

"I get your point," he said. "I apologise."

"No need to apologise, Captain. I don't want to be a hero. But Base are pretty desperate. There's bad weather from here to South America by the sound of it and we'll be lucky if we see a friendly plane in this part of the world before this time next week. That's how bad it is." He scuffed sand with the toe of his boot. "Matthew and me were a kind of forlorn hope," he went on. "They wondered if we could do something, anything, to stop that carrier. Maybe if we had a couple of limpet bombs . . . Or could even make them . . ."

Again, he kicked sand with his boot. It was an angry, despairing expression of the frustration that ate him. Ross looked out across the tranquil expanse of water. Scarcely a day had passed in the last two years when he hadn't pondered on how many new sunrises he would see. Life expectancy had been a hope calculated no further than the next setting of the sun. But the last few days had changed that. Deliverance had ceased to be a dream. It had become a real and imminent possibility, almost tangible in its nearness. It was hard to let go the firmly seized lifeline. He turned to face Corrigan.

"There's something we could do," he said.

Corrigan looked at him eagerly, alert and attentive. He smiled.

"I knew I was right about you, Captain. I knew it. My instincts's never let me down yet. I knew you would come up with something."

"It's still a hell of a long shot and there's a hell of a lot of ifs and buts," Ross cautioned, "but if the important thing is keeping that carrier where she is, then it might just work. Do you really think we could get aboard the *Machiko*?"

"Too right," replied the Australian, "but the strong-arm part is for me to worry about. It's what to do with the bloody ship if we do get aboard that flummoxes me. Just keep talking, Captain."

Ross' plan was not particularly elaborate. The *Yamazakura* could be contained in the inner basin, if not in the creek where it was moored, by simply blocking the entry to the basin. By scuttling the *Machiko* on the sandbar where the lagoon met the inner harbour, the aircraft carrier could be locked forever within Little Tarakang's great lake.

Corrigan was enthusiastic.

"I said there were ifs and buts," Ross warned him. "And they're pretty big ones. Say we do get aboard the *Machiko* and get control of the ship . . . That could be when our troubles really start. It could be hours before we can move her."

He explained to Corrigan that the chances of boarding the *Machiko* to find her boilers with steam up and ready to move under her own power were remote. Preparing her to move could take half a day. By that time, their pirate act could be discovered and the ship blasted out of the water.

There were several options, Ross declared. The worst was that the Japanese had no steam on the boilers. If that were the case, the enterprise could be doomed before it had properly begun. The most fortuitous possibility was that they found steam raised and the ship virtually ready for sea. Ross considered this most unlikely. They could rule it out.

"What does that leave, Captain?" asked Corrigan.

"They've taken the ship out to anchor," said Ross, "and my guess is that, like good sailors, they want to keep the ship in some kind of readiness. They'll have steam on the windlass, should they want to haul up the anchor. Or they may want to use the derricks if they load supplies. It all depends what they intend to do with the ship."

"So?"

"So that's the option we reckon on. It could still be very, very hairy. All hell is liable to break loose the moment that anchor chain starts to rattle in. They'll hear the noise all over the island. But there's a way we can overcome that . . . Maybe . . . And there's a way we could move the ship without turning the engines . . .

256

Although I've never actually seen it done . . . In fact, it's all one hell of a risk from start to finish . . ."

"But could it work, Captain? *Could it work?*"

"There's only one way to find out," said Ross. "We give it a try."

Seventeen

The Suicide Game

The camouflage nets which Major Kimura had provided were scarcely adequate to hide the *Yamazakura* but, in twenty-four hours, six squads of his engineers had done a fairly effective job of screening the aircraft carrier from aerial detection. The netting had been used to obscure the outlines of bow and stern and a variety of ideas had gone into making the broad expanse of flight-deck look anything other than what it actually was. Whole trees had been felled, laboriously hoisted aboard, and manhandled along the deck until the ship looked like an island across which a small tornado had swept, leaving an uprooted forest in its wake.

Rear-Admiral Ugaki and Major Kimura surveyed this battlefield with some satisfaction, undismayed by weather reports which indicated that most of the Allied air bases to the south and east were probably closed in by the exceptionally severe conditions. Ugaki was taking no chances that the *Yamazakura*'s presence in the Tarakangs might be discovered prematurely. He wanted the first hint to come when the ship's three squadrons of aircraft swept in with bombs and torpedoes to annihilate the invasion fleet which, he was sure, would soon be anchoring in the Straits beyond Mount Taki.

Before overside operations were restricted by the camouflage improvisations, Ugaki had ordered the *Yamazakura*'s one and only seaplane to be lowered into the inlet. It had been followed by four torpedo-like craft which had caused some excitement among Kimura's men. Like the seaplane, they now lay moored astern of the carrier.

"How do you like our Kaitens?" Ugaki asked Kimura. The two officers were completing their survey of the work done by Kimura's soldiers and stood in the awning shade provided by the nets across the carrier's stern.

"They look like torpedoes," said Kimura. "But what is the small shield with the mast on top?"

"They *are* torpedoes," replied Ugaki. "And that shield you see is a miniature conning tower with a periscope on top. A pilot sits inside and guides the torpedo to its target."

"And his own death?" said Kimura with awe.

"The pilots are all special volunteers," said Ugaki. "They know the risks. There is an escape hatch which can be used just by pushing a button. It allows them to leave the Kaiten when it is close enough to the target to be certain of hitting. Most pilots, however, prefer to make absolutely sure. They remain to the end."

Kimura sighed expressively.

"They must be very brave men."

"They are – and they know that even by leaving the missile at point-blank range, they have little chance of surviving the explosion they cause. The warhead contains nearly two tons of TNT. That causes quite a bang."

The admiral told Kimura how the Kaitens had been developed from the Navy's standard 93-Type torpedo and were normally operated from a parent submarine carrying four to six on her deck.

"We were simply transporting them," he said, "but we cannot deliver them now – except at the enemy. They are ideal for this situation. They have a range of nearly fifty miles at reduced speed and are good for about fourteen miles at top speed, which is thirty knots. If the enemy fleet anchors in the Straits, our Kaitens can be amongst the landing ships within minutes of clearing your lagoon."

"Are your repairs going well, Excellency?"

"By tonight, we shall be ready for sea. Then, it will be a question of waiting. Everything depends on how close the enemy are – and that I intend to find out. I must go now and brief the seaplane pilot personally for his role in that. Then I shall speak to the assembled crew and tell them of the glory that awaits us all. No doubt you, Major Kimura, will be anxious to return to your hilltop?"

It was a polite dismissal. Kimura took the hint.

They had made their farewells when Ugaki had an after-thought.

"Oh, Major Kimura, about that cargo ship which you and your

men have taken such pains to rebuild and make fit for sea . . ."

"Yes, Excellency?"

"Congratulate them on their work and tell them that I intend to ensure that its first and last voyage flying the Rising Sun will be a glorious memorial to their efforts. Alas, I do not have time to go into details, but I am sure that your men will take heart from my promise that their work was not in vain."

Kimura bowed in response, curious, but he refrained from delaying the naval commander by seeking to satisfy that curiosity. He ordered the last of his men ashore. When they were assembled, he signalled to the squad-leaders to take them back to their posts on Mount Taki. He followed, alone, taking his time through the charred remains of the former camp.

Looking down on the site formerly occupied by the prisoners, he allowed himself to wonder how Ross and his crew were faring at the far side of the island. Then, resolutely, he put all thoughts of them from his mind. As far as the Imperial Army was concerned, they were dead. They no longer existed.

The "dead" men of Java Point had listened to Ross in silence. He had gathered them together to give them the facts of the situation as it now stood. He held back nothing, knowing that he could not ask them to risk their new-found freedom and their lives without telling them frankly and fully what was involved.

Their silence was eloquent. Ross had lifted their hearts to the heights by telling them that an Allied invasion fleet was nearby. But almost in the same breath as he had promised deliverance, he had spelled out how the means of their deliverance was in jeopardy from the Japanese aircraft carrier which was moored only four miles from where they stood.

If this was bad news, it was a shock to discover that Ross had still not come to the crunch. They listened as he told them about Corrigan, a revelation not without comfort. So far, nothing had been said which suggested a direct threat to their own security. The worst that could happen would be a prolonged period of sitting things out while a decisive battle in which they were not involved was fought to a conclusion.

But then came the hammer-blow, as Ross pointed out that they could not stand by uninvolved. Their involvement could be the decisive factor in the battle – the difference between victory and defeat for the approaching Allied force. A silence continued long after Ross had finished with a request for volunteers to board the

Machiko and scuttle her at the basin's outlet to the lagoon.

Each man was weighing in his mind the appalling invitation that Ross had made. In the very moment that the cup of freedom had been tantalisingly held to their lips, they were being asked to cast it aside and embark on an enterprise which few, if any, would survive.

Ruth Gamage was the first to have her say. She pointed out that any action of the kind Ross described would mean a complete breach of the conditions laid down for their transfer to Java Point and a threat to the immunity they now enjoyed. Even to attempt it would be to invite Japanese reprisals of the most merciless kind.

"What Miss Gamage says is true," Ross replied. "The actions of a few of us could put at risk the lives even of those who want no part of what I've proposed. I hope, however, that those of you who don't want to become involved will not oppose the action because of that risk." He faced Ruth. "I can't keep you out of any discussion, Miss Gamage, and I want to make it clear that I am not asking for the active participation in the enterprise of yourself or anyone who – by age or unfitness – could not be reasonably expected to take part . . . But I do ask you to accept the lesser risk and not to stand in the way of the others."

"It's not a question of risk," Ruth Gamage came back heatedly. "It's a question of principle. You gave your word to Major Kimura."

"No, Miss Gamage. I accepted conditions which he laid down. He warned us what might happen if we disregarded these conditions . . . and that's what we now have to do. Disregard them . . . and risk the consequences."

"You're playing with words!" declared Ruth.

"No, Miss Gamage. Not words – lives. That's what this is all about. Lives! And there are thousands at stake here, not just our own. I have made a decision which wasn't easy to reach. I want my freedom just as much as you or any man here. And I want a world where principle matters and where people can argue all the day long about what is right and what is wrong. But this hasn't got anything to do with right or wrong, or what I want or what you want. We have a choice of two evils, Miss Gamage – and nearly all of the consequences are disagreeable. So, please, all I ask is that you don't make it any more difficult for us than it already is."

Passion, and the strain he felt, gave Ross' words a vehemence which would have been hard to challenge, far less oppose. Ruth Gamage did neither. She bowed her head, not in defeat but more

261

to gather herself before meeting again the passion and the pain which seemed to burn in Ross' eyes.

When she raised her head again, it was to meet Ross' stare with calm eyes and an expression that was devoid of anger or reproach. She spoke with a contrition in which there was dignity.

"I cannot bring myself to approve what you want to do – but neither can I condemn it. So, you need have no fear of me doing or saying anything that will make things more difficult for you than they already are."

"Thank you," said Ross softly, and there was gratitude in the message conveyed by his eyes from his slightly higher vantage-point. He had chosen the stump of a tree as a platform to speak to the group around him and she had been right at the front. Now, she turned to leave and men stood aside, leaving a small avenue to let her pass.

"You don't have to leave us, Miss Gamage," Ross called after her. "Whatever we decide now affects all of us . . . Those who go with me and those who stay."

Stopping, she turned and faced him.

"I think the important decision has already been made, Captain Ross. You made it for us. Now, we're going to need all the help we can get – and I'm going to ask for it."

"Ask for help?" said Ross. His face was not the only puzzled one.

"Yes, Captain Ross. There's not much I'm good at but I do know how to pray."

A smile lit her face at the sudden memory of a comforting voice in the nightmare aftermath of the darkest night of her life. She recalled the voice talking about God as being like the wind: always there, always moving, and not always responding according to the whims of man. She called out to Ross.

"I can't guarantee that my prayers will be answered, but maybe I'll whistle up a hurricane."

He remembered his words of that dark night. And a smile softened the lines of strain round his eyes.

"A breeze will do," he said.

She went off to find a place of solitude to pray, little Luke trailing at her heels. The full significance of the final exchange was lost on the watching men but the interlude provided by Ruth had given them a breathing space to consider the devil's choice before them. They responded to a man, ignoring the inner voice that asked: "Why now? Why me? Have we not endured enough?"

262

Ross found he had more volunteers than could be used. Even Moorhouse had not dissented. He spoke for more than himself when he said, "It's not as if we really have any choice this time at all. We have been asked to do something, anything that will keep that Jap carrier where it can't do any harm. We can't just say, 'Sorry, there's nothing we can do'."

But Moorhouse was not in the team chosen by Ross for his boarding party, a decision which he accepted gracefully enough when Ross asked him to take charge of the party that remained at Java Point and might have to be evacuated hurriedly into the forest to escape reprisals by the Japanese. It would surely be only a matter of time before friendly troops landed on the island but someone would have to organise things in the interval. It had to be assumed that those chosen for the boarding party would not be returning to Java Point.

The names of those who would make up the boarding party were agreed with not a little argument and not without some heart-searching on Ross' part. His own name topped the list. It was followed by Haraldsen, the Mate; Dewhurst, the Second Engineer; Thomson, the Third Mate; Millarship, the Third Engineer; Kima and O'Toole from the deckhands; Macmillan, the Carpenter; Rodriguez and Tan Ling from the stokehold gang; plus non-crew members Woody Woodhouse and Paul Newton.

Ross' Filipino steward argued strongly to go. So, too, did the young Chinese who had been rescued from the sea south of Singapore. Ross over-ruled them, emphasising that some fit and able men had to remain behind to protect the Java Point contingent.

With the addition of Corrigan and Matthew, the boarding party consisted of fourteen. Each had a role to play and it was vital that each knew the details of action planned in case casualties occurred or anything went wrong. There was also work to do before Corrigan and Matthew arrived to join them two hours after sunset – and this not only involved the boarding party but every able-bodied man, including the uninvolved Tarakangese.

The latter willingly agreed to help and soon Java Point was echoing to the ring of axes and the measured scraping cuts of two-handed saws. Kimura had provided the tools – but it was not a temple that was being built.

It was almost dusk when the seaplane found the convoy. The pilot did not go too close. Circling at a distance, he called Mount Taki, giving his position. Then he counted off the ships of the convoy, giving a description of each. The radio station on Mount Taki – with a direct RT link to the *Yamazakura* – relayed his report to Rear-Admiral Ugaki as it was being made.

Ugaki had been on tenterhooks for more than four hours, waiting for the seaplane to report. Its continued silence had made Ugaki fear that it had been lost and that, without precise details of the landing fleet's whereabouts, he would be at a severe disadvantage in the execution of his intended attack. Now he breathed happily again.

A navigating officer had plotted the convoy's position on the chart. It was 367 miles from the Tarakang Straits and on a direct course towards them. Ugaki made some quick calculations. The Americans were undoubtedly timing their assault for first light on the day after tomorrow. That meant that he could time his own sortie from Little Tarakang for the same hour – but it would be leaving things rather tight. Better to quit the island before dark the following day and to be cruising well to the west of the island when the Americans reached the Straits.

The earlier sailing time meant exposing the *Yamazakura* to bomber attack in the late part of the afternoon but, he reasoned, air attacks were likelier to come earlier in the day to allow the aircraft daylight to return to their distant bases. There was no carrier with the approaching landing fleet and no sign of a supporting taskforce anywhere near it. The scouting seaplane had been sweeping far to the eastward and, in consequence, had almost missed the convoy altogether. No wonder the pilot had been late reporting. He would be nearly out of fuel.

Ugaki sighed. He could put more aircraft in the air than the enemy had ships in their convoy. Then there were the four Kaitens, each capable of accounting for a ship on its own. With luck, that entire enemy force *could* be wiped out.

He gave an order for a signal to be sent to the scouting seaplane, authorising its recall. This had no sooner been done than Mount Taki were relaying a new message from the pilot. There was no chance of him reaching Little Tarakang before dark and, in any case, his fuel would give out long before he reached the island. He requested permission to attack the convoy.

Ugaki's aide looked questioningly at him. The admiral nodded.

"Permission granted. And tell him: 'We salute you. We are with you in spirit.' "

Out over the ocean, the gun crews on every ship in the convoy had been standing to in the hope of getting a potshot at the seaplane which had been circling for almost half an hour. Now it was getting dark. They could not quite believe their eyes when the seaplane, soaring at a thousand feet against the darkening cerise of the western sky, turned and came straight towards the convoy. It was heading straight for the *Crystal River* and showing no sign of deviating from its course.

The lead destroyer, angling across ahead of the *Crystal River*, was first into action. Tracers arced into the sky and the rapid hiccoughing voice of pom-poms echoed over the waters. The leading rank of ships joined in on a single cue and a hail of crimson fire rose to meet the darkly silhouetted seaplane as it dropped lower and lower, unwavering in its lumbering ninety-knot track straight at the *Crystal River*'s bridge. At fifty feet and only five hundred yards from certain collision, the seaplane's tail section disappeared in exploding fragments and the cabin was obscured in a sudden gush of black oily smoke. The forward movement of the aircraft seemed to go into slow motion as the nose fell and the tail-less pencil of fuselage spun in a slow half circle. The wreckage hit the sea with a forward splash and sank, leaving a faint cloud of steam and smoking oil.

An hour later, General Darren S. Budge was discussing the incident with his staff on the *Crystal River*. All realised that it meant any element of surprise had now been removed from the assault on Great Tarakang. The enemy would be waiting for them. Worse, the convoy could now expect to come under heavy attack from the air during the whole of the next day and all the way to their destination.

The Intelligence Co-ordinator tried to inject a note of optimism.

"If the Japs still have aircraft on the island, I think we would have known all about it long before now," he reasoned. "They would have hit us days ago. And yet all we've seen is one crummy seaplane. My guess is that it came from that carrier."

"I just hope to God you're right," said Budge. "Is there anything more from Moresby?" It annoyed him that instead of having a direct contact with the "coastwatcher" on Little Tarakang, messages from the island had to be filtered down the AIB network to Port Moresby and then relayed back along to the convoy via the US Naval radio links.

"They're definitely going to have a crack tonight at blocking the channel and penning the carrier inside the reef – but we were given no details."

"What can two men do?" moaned Budge. "What we need is a squadron of bombers. Is the weather report any better?"

"No, sir. But a squadron of Mitchells is standing by at Dobodura ready to take off at the first possible break in the weather. It's the same bunch who hit the Tarakang airfield the other day. So, they know the way and what to expect when they get there." The Intelligence Co-ordinator hesitated a moment. "Sir?"

"Yes, Commander?"

"We really should do something to help those men on Little Tarakang. They have asked again for some kind of support. There is a very definite likelihood of reprisals against the prisoners on the island whether the attempt to stop the carrier succeeds or fails."

"What do you suggest?"

"We could send one of the fast escorts ahead and land a small force. One of the specialist units."

Budge glowered.

"Their job is to get that damned airfield," he snapped.

"With all respect, sir, I don't think that the airfield poses any threat to this operation. It's that carrier!"

Budge realised there was some sense in what the naval officer was suggesting but he still hesitated.

"Do we know what kind of strength the Japanese have on the small island?" he asked.

"Almost to the last man," the Intelligence Co-ordinator replied triumphantly. He laid a sheet of paper on the table in front of the general. "It's all there, sir. Most of the Jap force is on Mount Taki, which overlooks the Straits. They've got a radio station there with big transmitters, and three field guns looking down on the beaches where our main force is due to land. We reckon the Japs don't have any more than two companies all told on the island. There is, of course, the carrier there now. Its crew could number between seven and eight hundred."

"Why wasn't I told about that artillery on the mountain?" asked Budge in bewilderment.

"You were, sir. You said the Air Force would have to take care of them. That was before the weather closed in."

Budge lit a cigarette to cover the confusion he felt. He wondered if he was cracking. The strain of the past few weeks had been intense. He had been getting repeated headaches and

266

hadn't been sleeping. It was all a hell of a lot for one person to take. But maybe that was what was wrong – he had been trying to do too much himself. He drew on the cigarette and recalled his days as a junior officer. Then, he had reserved a special hatred for senior officers who were one-man-bands, refusing to trust the younger men by delegating and never listening to advice.

The bald-headed major was looking at him strangely. Budge faced him.

"Well, Major, what do you think we should do?"

"I think we could spare one of the assault companies for the small island. They could be there by morning."

"A holding action – until we get there?"

"We can't risk anything more. And yet we have to make a response to the poor devils on that island. They're sticking their necks out for us."

"What if the Japs rush reinforcements from the big island to the little one?"

"They'll have to draw them from the landing area we're headed for. That would make our tactics look good. Feint with the left, they fall for it – and we sock 'em with the right."

"And maybe the destroyer could take care of any reinforcements from the big island, sir," put in the Intelligence Co-ordinator. "All our reports suggest that the Japs have only small craft in the harbour at Great Tarakang. Nothing that a destroyer couldn't take care of."

"What about the aircraft carrier?" asked Budge.

"The destroyer could take care of it, too," said the Intelligence Co-ordinator, "if it doesn't get its planes in the air."

"Maybe we should have sent a destroyer ahead in the first place," said Budge.

"We couldn't have been sure that the carrier was on its own."

"We still can't be sure," said Budge.

No. 4 Commando Group was made up of men from the 2nd/6th Cavalry Regiment and had been attached to the American 11th Corps to train for an assault on the island of Morotai. A call to action had come sooner than any of them had expected when they had been put aboard the *Crystal River* as part of the force bound for Great Tarakang.

The leader of No. 4 Commando was a rangy six-footer from Ballarat, where his parents had a prosperous farm. Lew White, himself, had gone in for law and had joined the army the day after he had graduated – straight from University Training Corps. Now, at twenty-six, he wore a major's crown on his shoulder and was in charge of one of the toughest and best-trained bodies of men in the Australian Army.

He liked Americans but it angered him the way that McArthur's headquarters seemed to minimise the Australian contribution to the successes of the South-West Pacific Forces. If the Aussies won a victory – and their successes in New Guinea had been considerable – it was announced from Allied HQ as an "Allied" victory. When the Yanks took an island, it was a "great American victory".

Now, here were he and his men taking part in a largely American show and he wondered if history would ever record No. 4 Commando's part in the reconquest of the Tarakangs. He had his doubts. If the overshadowing of the Australian effort by the Americans had a single redressing feature, it was in the effect it had on Lew's men. Conscious always of American eyes upon them, it sharpened a competitive streak which made them strive to be better than the Americans in everything they did. The big test was ahead at Great Tarakang. No. 4 Commando felt under a heavy obligation to prove to the world in general and the Americans in particular that, when it came to soldiering, the Aussie was the best in the world.

Lew White, staring out to sea over the rail of the *Crystal River*, started almost guiltily at his thoughts when there was a tap on his shoulder and he turned to look into the friendly eyes of General Budge's staff-major.

"Action stations for you, Lew," said the other major. "General Budge wants you and your men to be ready to board the USS *Maclay* in exactly thirty minutes when she comes alongside. Your men will get the message over the tannoy but the general wants to brief you himself."

"What's it all about? Any idea?"

"It's your kind of show, Lew. Somebody has to go in twenty-four hours ahead of the rest of us. Your boys have been elected."

Corrigan and Matthew had appeared right on time, two hours after sunset. The long outrigger canoe had come gliding in from the west lagoon. It was laden with their equipment and provisions.

"OK?" Ross greeted Corrigan.

"OK," the Australian confirmed. "The canoe was where we'd

hidden it and there's no sign of Jap anywhere along the north island. You got your volunteers and the rafts?"

"Twelve volunteers, all reasonably fit. Including myself. The rafts are over there on the beach."

Corrigan walked with Ross along the beach, where the volunteers were sitting on the sand beside the rafts. Corrigan inspected the rafts.

"Hey, they're pretty nifty, real professional looking."

"We got expert help. The paddles are pretty crude – but they'll do. We had a trial regatta before you came."

"We'd better get started," said Corrigan. "We've got a long hard night ahead of us. You want to say your goodbyes to the people you're leaving on the point?"

Ross looked across the dark promontory with its tallest trees silhouetted against the north sky. He could hear the faint murmur of Tarakangese voices.

"The goodbyes have been said. We're ready when you are."

They launched the rafts and tied them in a line astern of Corrigan's canoe. The twelve distributed themselves around the rafts, three to a raft. On each raft, one man took the crude steering oar roped to the stern while two manned paddles. They manoeuvred out into the lagoon.

Corrigan and Matthew dipped their paddles. They used slow easy strokes. At first, the line of rafts behind them got in some disarray, straggling in all directions. But, as the raft crews improved their balance and settled themselves, they gradually tuned their movements to the fragile equilibrium of their transport. Now, they moved ahead steadily in silent procession.

After half an hour they had reached the bend in the lagoon at Little Tarakang's most south-westerly tip. The procession turned east, parallel with the spit of land that lay between the south reef and the waters of the inner basin.

Corrigan made a signal that he was beaching and made a left turn to lead the flotilla into the shallows of the spit's south shore. They started to ground and, at another signal, the men waded in the water and dragged their craft on to dry sand. Corrigan, Matthew and Ross began to unload the canoe. The radio and other equipment were carried up the beach to be deposited at the base of a tall, waving palm.

At this point of the spit, the ground was sandy across its whole breadth. Its mane of trees was thinner. Ross and Corrigan explored it while, with the exception of Matthew and Kima, the others lay on the sand recovering from their exertions.

The spit was less than three hundred yards wide. Ross and Corrigan reached the north shore to look out at the grey shape of the *Machiko*, swinging at anchor. She was in darkness and looked utterly deserted. Corrigan studied the ship through binoculars. There was a Jacob's ladder over the side, amidships, and a boat rode at its base, painters out fore and aft.

"Not a sign of life," Corrigan muttered. "We could be in luck." He passed the binoculars to Ross. He scanned the *Machiko*.

"What's that they've got stacked on the foredeck?" Ross was unaware that he was whispering.

"I didn't see anything," said Corrigan.

"Drums of something. They weren't there before." He passed the binoculars back to Corrigan.

"They look like oil-drums. Don't mean anything to me," the Australian said. "Let's get Matthew on his way."

They returned to the south side of the spit. Matthew and Kima had stripped naked and were smearing their bodies with grease.

"You know what to do?" Corrigan asked.

Matthew nodded.

"All Japoni fellas – chop-chop." He made a gesture across his throat with his hand.

The two Papuans then strapped on belts, to which were attached long wicked-looking knives. In addition, Matthew's belt had a flashlight clipped to it. The two men clambered into the canoe and pushed off into the lagoon.

Originally, Corrigan had intended to lead the attack himself, but Matthew had persuaded him to entrust Kima and himself with the task of silently disposing of any Japanese on board the *Machiko*. As the two naked Papuans set off to take the canoe along the lagoon and into the inner basin, Corrigan felt a qualm of pity for the guard-watch on the anchored ship. Meeting that pair on a dark night would be enough to scare anyone to death.

When the Papuans had gone, the rest of the party began to haul the rafts across the sandy spit to the shore fronting the inner basin. By the time they had manhandled the four makeshift craft to places of concealment near the water's edge, Matthew and Kima had reached the inner basin. From the beach, Ross watched the low outrigger glide silently towards the *Machiko* and come to rest against its anchor cable.

For a brief moment, Matthew and Kima could be seen, silhouetted, as they climbed the anchor chain quickly and with ease. They seemed to go up as if walking on four feet, with both hands and feet outstretched. They reached the top and disappeared.

Ross waited as the minutes ticked slowly away. At any minute, he expected to hear shots and a general hue and cry from the ship. But the *Machiko* remained dark and silent. Ross could feel his heart thudding behind his ribs like a caged tom-tom.

After what seemed an æon of time, a light flashed three times from the ship. Corrigan let out a sigh that sounded as if he had held his breath since the Papuans had boarded the ship.

"They've done it!" he exulted. "All right, lads. Let's get moving."

The men moved in a startled flurry, like pigeons released from a basket. The waiting had wound their nerves to vibrating point and the relief of action made their haste clumsy and over-frantic. Composure returned as they bent their bodies against the weight of the rafts and pushed them out into the basin. The four rafts – two with four and two with three men – splashed out towards the *Machiko*.

Minutes later, Ross scrambled across the boat moored alongside the *Machiko*'s side and pulled himself up the ladder, sailor-style, favouring one side for his hands. On deck, he stumbled over something. A very dead Japanese sailor stared up at him from a pool of blood.

Eighteen

The Machiko

There had been six Japanese on the *Machiko*: two on the deck, two in the engineroom, and two asleep in the PO's quarters. They were all now dead. The stealth and efficiency with which Matthew and Kima had gone about their deadly work made the others now look at them askance. The Papuans enjoyed the awe they caused, puffing out their chests and beaming happily. Kima expressed disappointment that there had not been more Japanese to kill.

All seemed quiet in the inlet little more than a quarter of a mile away where the *Yamazakura* lay. Corrigan now surrendered the leadership to Ross. This was his bailiwick – and there was no time to lose.

Dewhurst and Millarship, the two engineers, were despatched to the engineroom. Dewhurst returned to report.

"The main boilers are stone cold but the Nips have been using the Cochran."

It was much as Ross had expected. They could forget any idea of moving the ship on the main engine. They would have to depend on the little Cochran boiler. This supplied the steam for donkey services in port, although it could be coupled with the main steam range at sea to supplement the output of the main boilers.

"The Cochran it is, then!" said Ross. "We'll need steam on the foredeck. Take Rodriguez and Tan Ling and see what you can do, Mr Dewhurst."

"Aye aye, sir," said Dewhurst, grinning at Ross' lapse into the shipboard formality of "Mister" after two years of first names only. He paused. "The Nips were burning timber . . . I was thinking of using that coal we kept. Even if it means shifting twenty tons of those Tarakang logs we put aboard."

Ross grinned back at him.

272

"This is what we saved the coal for."

Dewhurst went off with the two firemen.

Ross turned to Kima.

"We're going to need two big hatch-boards and they have to be lashed between two of the rafts. O'Toole will give you a hand. Organise it, will you, Kima? And it could make things easier if you use that whaler that the Japanese Navy left alongside. We can use it to tow the rafts."

Woody and Paul Newton were spared seamen's work. They were to take charge of the rifles and the ammunition that had been in possession of the Japanese and they were to act as watch-keepers, warning of any approach or any undue activity near the carrier.

Ross led the rest of the party forward. On the way, they stopped to examine the "oil-drums" Ross had observed from the shore. They were tar barrels, sitting in line on the hatch-tops and connected with lengths of tarred hemp.

It was Haraldsen, the Mate, who said, "What do you reckon the Nips were going to do? Make a bonfire of the old ship?"

"Or a floating bomb," called out Corrigan, who had gone right forward. "What do you make of this?"

On wooden chocks under a tarpaulin was a torpedo of the type dropped by aircraft. Nearby was a partly constructed wooden cradle which puzzled the group of men until Ross noticed that the central section was of a depth and shape roughly equal to the torpedo. The cradle, although not in place, was intended to fit over the fo'c'sle-head like a bowsprit.

"They were going to fit the torpedo over the bow like a bloody figurehead!" he exlaimed. "And have the decks running with burning tar!"

"Shades of Nelson!" said Haraldsen. "A bloody fireship!"

"For what?" asked someone.

"Our landing ships," answered Corrigan. "When they put in an appearance."

The questioner gave a snort that might have been of disbelief.

"Bloody mad!" he said. "Setting the decks afire and steaming along with a torpedo for a bow fender. Bloody suicide!"

"And that's an old Japanese custom," observed Ross. "Let's just thank our lucky stars that they weren't working a night shift on this little lot. Kima and Matthew might not have got aboard quite so easily as they did." He moved towards the timber cradle with an air of purpose. "Come on, let's clear this junk out of the way.

We're going to need deck space around here for our hawser. Chippy," he addressed the carpenter, "we'll want blocks and tackle, stoppers, heaving lines and our best manila bow rope."

"All in the forepeak. I'll need some help," said the carpenter. "There ought to be a munday hammer down there, too."

"Get something to muffle it," said Ross, although he was not optimistic that the sounds of the operation now in prospect would be less than noisy enough to awaken the dead. Already from the direction of the engineroom he could hear the donkey boiler racketing away loudly enough to be heard on the Japanese carrier.

Thomson, the Third Mate, went off to open the deck line drain-cocks to empty water from the steam line. The group on the fo'c'sle were paying out a mooring rope in lengths on the fore-deck when steam began to crackle and bang through the deck pipes to the windlass. By then, Ross had unshipped the spare bower anchor and had it slung under the bow davit, ready to be hoisted over the side. Below, Kima and O'Toole had the Japanese whaler and the two rafts ready to receive the spare anchor. The two rafts had been joined by having two heavy hatch-boards lashed to them. Two towing lines from each raft ran from them to the whaler's stern.

"We're going to need more hands to crew that whaler," Ross announced. "And better if they are armed. Just in case the carrier sends out a boat to see what's happening. They must have heard the noise by now and, sooner or later, they're going to realise that something funny's going on."

Haraldsen, Corrigan, Matthew and Paul Newton were detailed to join the two seamen in the boat under the bows. A ladder was lowered to allow them to climb down. They took all the rifles but two.

Then began the task of putting the spare anchor over the side. It weighed almost half a ton and the most difficult part of the operation was hoisting it on the davit and working it clear of the fo'c'sle bulwark. Once this was done, the anchor was lowered gently until it straddled the hatch-boards lashed to the two rafts.

"Now we'll see just how good these rafts are," said Ross, and gave the signal for the anchor to be eased down further until its weight was taken by the hatch-boards and the rafts. At first, it seemed that the anchor would sink the rafts. They all but sub-merged as the weight came down on them, but as the distribution of weight was evened out and ceased to be concentrated down through the head of the anchor the rafts settled in the water showing little freeboard.

Next, one end of the manila mooring rope was run through a fair lead and lowered to be shackled to the spare anchor. On deck, the carpenter took turns of the rope round the drum-ends of the windlass.

Ross checked to see that the rowers were ready in the whaler. They were.

"OK, take her away," he called out.

The men in the whaler bent their backs to the oars.

"Run her out to the lagoon like I told you," Ross called after Haraldsen. "You know where I want it."

"Aye aye, Captain," Haraldsen called back softly.

The whaler moved away, pulling the harnessed rafts behind it. Kima had secured the anchor to the hatch-board bridge between the rafts. It lay on the boards between its floating supports and from it the mooring rope streamed away to the bows of the *Machiko*.

Paul Newton could feel the sweat running down his back as he rowed. With the exception of Kima, none of the occupants of the Japanese whaler were expert rowers and the craft tended to zig-zag ahead of its tow: the two rafts, between which was straddled the spare bower anchor from the *Machiko*. The heavy rope attached to the anchor now trailed in the water of the basin, making the task of hauling it more arduous.

Slowly, the whaler made distance away from the *Machiko*. The whaler was now abreast the end of the spit, where the inner basin joined the lagoon. Haraldsen, manning a steering oar at the whaler's stern and occasionally sculling with it, kept the whaler on a straight course from the *Machiko* – cutting across the entry to the basin at a sharp angle, passing close to the spit on the starboard side to pass into the lagoon with the Mount Taki end of the island close on the port side.

"Ship your oars," called Haraldsen. He studied the position of the drifting boat and seemed satisfied.

"OK, Mr Corrigan, you can make the signal now," he said.

Corrigan took a flashlight from his belt and, standing, aimed at the distant shadow that was the *Machiko*. He flashed the light twice. An answering light winked twice from the *Machiko*'s bows.

Haraldsen tapped a perspiring Kima on the shoulder.

"Got that blade of yours, Kima? This is where we drop the hook."

275

Kima nodded. He slipped over the whaler's side into the water and swam to the harnessed rafts. Clambering aboard, he hacked with his long knife at the lashings which held the two hatch-boards in position. When this was done, he gingerly lowered himself into the water and swam back to the whaler.

Haraldsen now cast off the tow-line to one of the rafts.

"All right, lads. Let's have you on those oars again," he said hoarsely. "Just one short, sharp burst should be all we need."

The men in the whaler bent on their oars like a race crew waiting the starting pistol.

"All together . . . now!" signalled Haraldsen.

The whaler surged away, quickly taking up the slack on the single tow-line remaining. The raft to which it was attached dipped as the whaler took its weight with a sharp tug. There was a squeal of timber against timber as the raft squirmed free of the untethered hatch-boards and the anchor on top of them.

The forward movement of the whaler came to a sudden jerking stop while, for a moment, the full weight of the anchor rested on a few precarious inches of hatch-board. The side of the raft nearest the whaler rose high as the weight was briefly concentrated on its distant side. The raft upended and turned completely over as the hatch-boards slipped and the anchor slid with a splash to the sea-bed nearly thirty feet below.

Ross peered from the bows of the *Machiko* towards the basin entry. A light flashed for a second time. They had known from the sudden jump on the mooring rope that the anchor had been dropped but this was the signal that the operation had been successful. He felt his heart leap with excitement. The waiting had been agonising. Throughout every minute, he had expected a hail of gunfire from the shore or, at least, some indication that their mischief had been detected by the Japanese. But the island was black and silent, as if there was no one there.

He looked at his watch. In another hour it would be light. Well, now came the really noisy part. He nodded towards the carpenter, who was tending the mooring rope.

"I'll slip the cable," he said.

The *Machiko* was still moored on her port anchor. Working with an air of purpose, Ross stoppered off the chain cable running out through the port hawse-pipe and located the joining shackle just above the stopper. The joining shackle was secured by a hardwood plug passing through the pin and one lug of the shackle. Ross now set about removing the plug. He placed a metal spike against the plug and struck methodically at it with a heavy hammer that he held in a shortened grip. The plug seemed reluctant to move. Ross persevered. At last he felt a movement in the plug. The noise of the hammer echoed across the dark basin.

Suddenly the plug shot free. A single blow with the hammer was enough to remove the pin from the shackle. All that was now holding the *Machiko* to the port anchor cable was the chain stopper which Ross had attached. Now, with two quick hammer blows, he released the tension on the stopper. It was thrown off by the anchor cable. There was a screech of metal against metal as the freed end of the anchor chain parted company with the *Machiko* and rattled out of the hawse-pipe to fall with a splash into the waters of the harbour. The ship drifted until all her weight was taken by the rope streaming out past the end of the spit to the lagoon.

Ross disengaged the gear of the windlass so that only the drum-ends operated and turned on the steam. There was a great rumbling of sound as the winch rotated. The carpenter reeved more turns of the mooring rope round the drum-end as the rope tautened until it was heaving in wet rope and throwing off a shower of droplets wrung from the manila. The *Machiko* began to move, slowly hauling herself towards the spare bower anchor that was now firmly holding to the bed of the lagoon.

Twice, the *Machiko*'s stern slewed but, by directing the carpenter to let the bower rope go slack and then getting him to heave away again, Ross manoeuvred the drift of the ship towards the basin entrance so that her approach was almost broadside on. As the *Machiko*'s stern came level with the end of the spit, the ship was angled across the narrow neck of water with her bows on the lagoon side of the entry. There was a rending of metal as the bow section grounded and her momentum carried the *Machiko* stem-first into the beach facing the end of the spit. She jarred to a halt, grounding at such an angle to the contours of the beach that she was thrown into a fifteen-degree starboard list.

Ross, stationed right in the bows and braced for the impact, was still taken by surprise by its violence, and went sprawling on the foredeck. The carpenter, too, was thrown from his feet but the bow rope had gone slack in his hands. Its work, in any case, had been done. He secured the rope and closed the steam valve on the still rotating winch. Ross left the carpenter to it. He was already hurrying towards the engineroom.

There, he found Dewhurst nursing a gashed head. He, too, had been knocked off his feet as the bows had grounded and had fallen against the platform rail. Millarship was giving him first aid.

"You'll live," pronounced Ross, examining the wound, "but you'd better get up on deck. I'll help Mr Millarship take care of things down here."

"I'll be all right," insisted Dewhurst. He managed a weak grin. "Besides, you two might make a hash of it."

"OK," agreed Ross. "Let's get on with it. We're in perfect position right across the main channel."

The method of sinking the *Machiko* had been suggested by Fraser, the Chief Engineer. He had once seen a ship go down in Genoa harbour – by accident, the result of an engineer's mistake – and he reckoned it was as good a way as any of sending a ship to the bottom. Now, Dewhurst led the way across the engineroom to the port side of the ship and along a metal walk-way. They stopped before a solid-looking fixture of two clamped metal domes, mounted against the ship's side and with massive pipes jointed to its bell-like ends.

"That's where the water comes in . . . And then it goes around and around," said Dewhurst, paraphrasing the words of a popular song. "This is the main salt water injection valve, Captain. All we need to do is slacken off a few nuts and water pressure will do the rest. Once the pressure starts, there's no way of tightening these nuts back on. They'll blow like bullets. I suggest you stand well back and get ready to beat a hasty retreat."

First, the two firemen in the stoke-hold were warned to get up on deck. Millarship, working with a wrench and heavy hammer, began the process of easing off the nuts on the injection valve. A tiny seepage of water bubbled from the steel lips of the valve's outer casing.

"That's enough," ordered Ross. "I'll finish off." He would have no argument from either Millarship or Dewhurst and insisted they both get up on deck. Millarship looked up, sweat streaking his face. The first hiss of escaping water had made him go rigid with fear but he was prepared to see the job through to the end.

"Do as the captain says," said Dewhurst. "It's his ship. I reckon he has the right to finish her." He turned to Ross. "Don't wait until the last minute," he warned. "A few more turns on some of these nuts and you'll be getting a rare old shower-bath. That'll be when to get the hell out of it."

"I know what to do," Ross snapped impatiently. "Now, vamoose – the pair of you!" More softly, he added, "And thanks."

He watched them climb up the ladder, their footsteps echoing. Then, he turned all his attention to slackening the nuts further. Just as Dewhurst had predicted, water suddenly began to spray from the seams of the valve and spurt out from the bolt-holes. Then it began to jet at Ross as he continued to slacken more nuts. He stood to one side of the big valve as he worked, aware that if it did blow suddenly it could shred him all over the main engine.

The force of escaping water was now lancing at him like rods. He could scarcely stand up against it, far less operate the wrench. Suddenly one nut exploded outwards with a crack, taking with it half a bolt that had sheered in two. It flew across the engineroom, pinging and ricocheting off ladders and gratings. Then another bolt shot and one domed half of the valve casing began to creak and move as if in protest. Water jetted from the empty bolt-holes and surged from the lips of the casing, forcing them apart.

Ross stood back, water streaming from him. It was now impossible to work within arm's length of the valve and remain upright. He retreated to the ladder and climbed to a higher walk-way, where he remained, looking down on his handiwork. A weary sadness filled him. Part of him would die with this ship. They had worked so hard to keep her alive. Now, he waited to see if the simple wound he had inflicted would prove mortal.

Water was now erupting like a geyser from the valve casing. Suddenly, like shots from a machine-gun, the remaining bolts began to pop. Then the casing came apart and was carried in a tidal wave, upward and outward, mangling through a steel ladder and wresting it from its supports. Water spewed like a gravity-defying Niagara in a terrifying upward gush. Ross found himself engulfed in this leaping gusher and swirled along by it. He seized a hand-rail until the worst of the torrent had washed over him and its initial force was spent. The engineroom began to fill as the spewing river began to seek its way to every corner and opening: rushing, bubbling and frothing into the boiler-room and curling and cascading into the wells and crevices of the far side of the engineroom.

Where, before, Ross had seen the salt water injection valve, only a turbulent boiling mass of water was now visible as the sea poured in. He reached a ladder and began to climb. He was all but thrown off when the ship moved violently. She had been listing to starboard but, now, with a hideous creaking and groaning, she lurched the other way: going over ten degrees to port and then, with another great shudder, tipping over further until she listed a full thirty degrees to port. The lights of the engineroom flickered and went out with a spluttering hiss, leaving Ross in total darkness. He resumed climbing the ladder which, because of the ship's new list, was at a grotesque angle to the perpendicular. No starlight flickered above to guide Ross. The skylights above had been battened down for blackout purposes.

He reached the top walk-way and groped his way along the hand-rail to the door. The cool, sweet taste of fresh air filled his nostrils and guided him to the deck. He staggered into the supporting arms of Dewhurst.

"Thank God you're all right," the engineer said with feeling. "I was just on my way back for you. We're going to have visitors. There's a motorboat coming out from the Nip carrier."

It was Woody who had raised the alarm that a motorboat had appeared at the far side of the deep-water basin. He had passed the news to the group in the whaler, who were standing by in the lagoon, close to the *Machiko*'s starboard side. Haraldsen had immediately brought the whaler alongside so that Corrigan and Matthew could reboard the ship. They had no sooner done so than the *Machiko* had made her violent lurch and developed her steep list to port.

Dewhurst had appeared to tell Corrigan that Ross was still in the engineroom and the Australian had immediately taken charge of the situation. Ross' command was sinking under their feet and fighting the Japanese was Corrigan's province. The Australian's decisive reassumption of control provoked neither debate nor disobedience. It was taken for granted in the situation.

Corrigan's first act was to order all the seafaring personnel into the whaler. The exception was Dewhurst, who was instructed to find Ross if he could. Corrigan, Matthew and Woody prepared, in the meantime, to provide a welcome for the Japanese boat which could be heard chug-chug-chugging towards them.

"If we can lure that Nip boat alongside, we'll have the jump on them," Corrigan said to Woody, his eyes searching the deck for anything that would give him inspiration. His gaze came to rest on a rolled-up Jacob's ladder. "There's just the thing," he exulted. "Can you two hump that ladder up forward? I'll show you exactly where I want it."

Woody and Matthew manhandled the ladder to the port side of

the foredeck and streamed it over the rail.

"Don't make the damned thing fast," he cautioned Woody, who was about to do precisely that. "If any Jap does get his foot on that ladder, he'll get a nasty surprise."

The rail over which the ladder had been placed was a removable section, where a gangway could be placed. Corrigan removed the two small bolts which held it in place. He kept glancing all the time at the dark shape of the approaching boat. It was now only two hundred yards away. They heard the motor slow to a gentler beat. It was obviously going to approach with caution.

"The Nips must be absolutely baffled by us moving the ship," Corrigan whispered to Woody. "God knows what they're thinking . . . But I'm hoping they think their guard crew got stoned out of their minds on jungle juice and decided to sail her round the harbour."

"Just what do you have in mind if they come alongside the ladder?" asked Woody.

Corrigan reached into a pouch at his waist and palmed a grenade.

"This," he said. "And I want you and Matthew to push one of these over the rail. Think you could manage it?" He pointed at one of the tar barrels that the Japanese had left on the hatch.

A glint appeared in Woody's eyes.

"You bet your sweet life," he murmured.

A grinning Matthew helped him free one of the drums from its timber chocks. They manhandled it to the rail and propped it clear of the scupper.

The motorboat was still keeping a respectful distance.

"What are they waiting for?" muttered Woody softly. He looked anxiously over the side. "We'll be up to our necks in the drink if they don't hurry up. The old scow's sinking fast and I don't like the way she's tilting over."

"Just keep out of sight behind that barrel, chum," advised Corrigan. "Lie flat on your back and be ready to push it with your feet when I give the word. Matthew, you nip aft and see if that engineer and the captain are OK. Get them into the boat."

The Papuan nodded and, crouching low behind the bulwark, began to work his way aft. Suddenly a light flared from the Japanese naval launch. Its beam lit the midships area of the *Machiko*, swept slowly forward to the bows, and then back the length of the ship to the stern.

281

A voice shouted from the launch. There was no response from the *Machiko*.

The twenty-two-year-old lieutenant who had hailed the *Machiko* was bewildered. What had started out to be the most glorious day of his short life was not working out at all as it had been planned. Only the previous evening – after Admiral Ugaki had personally congratulated him on being chosen from the many volunteers – the young man had written his last letter to his parents, saying his farewell. He had not gone into detail about the mission for which he had been chosen. He had said simply that it was of great importance and that he did not expect to return.

In fact, the lieutenant had been chosen to lead a suicide crew aboard the *Machiko* and complete the preparations for sailing her like a live blazing torpedo into the expected enemy landing fleet. All his men were volunteers like himself. His orders were to commence getting up steam at dawn so that the ship could sail in late afternoon. He was to lie in the western lee of Little Tarakang, ready to launch his fireship at daybreak the following day against the enemy ships.

Activity on the *Machiko* during the night had been heard but not seen by the *Yamazakura*'s watchkeepers but it had aroused no undue suspicion. It was assumed that the men Admiral Ugaki had put aboard the freighter had been ordered to rig the forward derricks or perform some other work which had to be done. There could be no other explanation for the winches working during the night.

The lieutenant's astonishment was considerable, therefore, when he realised that the *Machiko* was not where she should have been. Worse, she seemed to be blocking the sole exit passage to the lagoon and was listing very badly.

The lieutenant's first thought was to report the phenomenon immediately to the *Yamazakura*. But he hesitated. What had *happened* to the ship? It was surely his first duty to equip himself with some facts. Had she dragged her anchor? Were the men aboard all drunk, or dead, or what? Why did they not answer him? He ordered the searchlight to sweep the ship once more – and what he saw helped him decide on the action he had to take. *The freighter was sinking. It was sinking before his very eyes!*

Caution left him. He ordered the boat coxswain to go alongside the ladder streamed from the *Machiko* just forward of her strange-looking bridge.

The lieutenant had twenty-two men in the boat. Corrigan and

Woody could hear their speculative chatter as the boat coxswain put his engines astern almost alongside the ladder. They heard the bump of the boat against the ship's side.

Corrigan pulled the pin from his grenade and counted silently.

"Now!" he shouted to Woody.

Woody, lying flat on his back with both feet braced against the tar barrel, thrust hard with his legs.

Barrel, rail, ladder . . . all went over the side together. Almost in the same instant, Corrigan rose from behind the shadow of the bulwark below the bridge. He lobbed the grenade into the boat below and hurled himself flat. There was a sequence of noises; screams of pain as the barrel and six-foot section of guard-rail flattened half a dozen men; shouts of alarm from other occupants of the boat; then the ear-shattering blast that blew the boat and its occupants to smithereens.

The two Australians waited a moment or two before peering cautiously over the *Machiko*'s side. Smouldering spars and pieces of clothing littered the dark water. Here and there, a head bobbed, an arm moved. But the owners were beyond all human help. They were incomplete: legs gone, hands missing, bellies ripped apart – the wreckage of what had been men.

The *Machiko* gave another great lurch to port. For a moment, it seemed that she would go right over but she settled with the port rail awash from stem to stern and her masts tilted at sixty degrees from the perpendicular.

Woody and Corrigan, clinging for dear life to anything solid their hands could grasp, slithered on the deck and felt the waters of the basin come splashing over their feet and ankles. They climbed and crawled across the slope that was the No. 2 hatch until they reached the high starboard side.

Looking aft, they could see two figures. Dewhurst had gone and was already in the whaler, drifting close in the lagoon, but Matthew and Ross were still aboard the *Machiko*. Woody and Corrigan struggled aft to join them.

"Why the hell aren't you in the whaler?" Corrigan reproached Ross.

"I was waiting for you. What happened to the Japanese boat?"

"It won't give us any trouble," replied Corrigan. "I suggest we abandon ship, Captain."

"After you," smiled Ross. "Captain's privilege. I've told Haraldsen to stand off in the boat . . . in case the *Machiko* plays any more games. That means we have to jump for it."

283

Woody and Matthew were the first to go, followed by Corrigan. They could walk almost upright down the starboard side of the ship, then they had to jump into the lagoon. Ross waited until they had been hauled aboard the whaler before making his descent. He stood poised for a moment, looking down at the water. Away to the east, the sky was lightening. It would soon be dawn.

"So long, old girl," he murmured, and launched himself out and into the waters of the lagoon.

The sun was now twenty degrees above the horizon and blazing the threat of century temperatures before noon. The fourteen, whose scuttling operation of the *Machiko* had succeeded beyond their wildest expectations, were dug in on the spit – waiting for the Japanese counterstroke which, they were certain, must eventually come. They had been aware for some time of considerable Japanese activity on the far shore of the basin. Officers from the *Yamazakura* had come down to the beach to study the sunken *Machiko* through binoculars. The freighter had keeled over completely on to her port side and was now lying with her masts and funnel horizontal and partly submerged. Finally, a boat had emerged from the inlet and a party of Japanese had clambered over the wreck before reboarding their boat and returning to the inlet.

Ross and his group had lain doggo in their shallow trenches on the spit, watching and waiting. They had elected to remain there, rather than try to return to Java Point, for the sole reason that they wanted any Japanese reprisal to be directed at them and not at those who had remained with Moorhouse. They realised that, with not enough weapons to go round and with very little ammunition, they had little realistic hope of lasting five minutes against the most modestly mounted attack on the spit – but they were determined to remain nevertheless. What hope they had was now pinned on the help which was known to be near. Corrigan had retrieved his radio and had assiduously tapped away at the key, letting the outside world know precisely what their predicament was.

Now, something was happening at the far inlet. Crouched next to Ross, Corrigan focused his binoculars on the opposite shore, moving aside a cluster of leaves from the branch from which they had screened their sandy trench.

"What the hell?" he said softly.

Even with his naked eye, Ross could see the cigar-shaped craft which was now making a lot of wake for its size as it turned into the wider waters of the basin.

"It looks like a torpedo," exclaimed Corrigan, "with a little saddle-hatch on top!" He passed the glasses to Ross. "What do you make of it?"

Ross could only agree that it looked like a torpedo. And it was obviously operated by a man inside the little cockpit. The device was now moving at quite a speed straight for the wreck of the *Machiko*.

Some fifty yards short of the wreck, a figure suddenly appeared and splashed into the water. The Kaiten, for that's what it was, kept speeding for the yawning tunnel-mouth of the *Machiko*'s partly submerged funnel. There was a lightning flash and then the island of Little Tarakang trembled as a cloud of smoke and flame leapt skywards for five hundred feet and began to spill in every direction. The blast was awesome. Palms near the end of the spit were blown flat and others within half a mile of the explosion had the leaves shredded from their tops to leave swaying, denuded stems. A wave of furnace-hot air whipped sand in leaping clouds and raged over the men entrenched on the spit, tattering their shirts like paper and singeing their hair. None was seriously hurt but — stunned, blinded and scorched, and with their screens of foliage swept away — they staggered around and crawled from their shallow foxholes, shocked and disoriented. Woody was the first to recover and realise how totally exposed they now were. He helped Ross and Corrigan to their feet, urging them to run for the cover further along the spit. Then he herded the others, shouting at them and bullying them to move quickly.

But even as they ran, they could hear shouting in Japanese from the far side of the basin. There was a rattle of machine-gun fire and the crack of rifles. The water close to the beach began to leap and splash with bullets. The sand of the shore began to spurt in jumping lines around the feet of the running men and, higher, the whining flight of bullets streamed past their heads and thudded into the trunks of bare, leafless palm trees.

Thomson, the young Third Mate of the *Machiko*, gave a little cry, kept running a few paces and then pitched forward on his face. Ross ran back to him and stooped to hoist him on his shoulder. Then he saw the blood on Thomson's temple. He turned him over. The bullet had exited through the younger man's left eye. He was quite dead.

They finally reached the shelter of friendly trees and threw themselves down, exhausted. Woody brought up the rear supporting a casualty. Dewhurst had taken a bullet through the knee.

"Well, now they know we're here," Corrigan said to Ross. "It won't take them long to get a hunting party together."

They bound up Dewhurst's knee as best they could. Then Ross went with Corrigan to scout the north shore of the spit. The forest was quite dense at this part of the spit, enabling them to look across the basin in some certainty that they could not be seen.

For the first time, they were able to observe the effect the Kaiten had had on the *Machiko*. The torpedo had literally blown the scuttled ship in two. Only the bows and the stern were now visible – the bow section jutting from the water on the Mount Taki side of the channel and part of the stern protruding near the now desolated end of the spit.

"Wide enough?" asked Corrigan.

The same question had been going through Ross' head. Was the gap of water between the two visible portions of the *Machiko* wide enough to allow the Japanese aircraft carrier egress to the lagoon and the sea beyond?

"I don't know," Ross admitted. "But, if I were the captain of that carrier, I'm not sure I would be over-anxious to try getting my ship through there."

"Looks like he's maybe going to try it anyway," said Corrigan. He pointed across the basin. "Look."

Like a rabbit backing out of a burrow, the great stern of the carrier was appearing from a tunnel of verdure. There was something unreal about the sight of the ship's ungainly rear end emerging from between the high trees flanking the inlet; a monster totally alien to that green environment. It whipped up white water before it and they could hear the plunging thud of the reversing propellers.

As the big ship wheeled into the basin, sailors on the foredeck were still hurling branches of trees over the side: the remains of the ship's elaborate camouflage precautions. The carrier turned slowly and nosed towards the end of the spit.

A motorboat – which Ross recognised as the same one to have taken the inspection party to the wreck of the *Machiko* – cruised in the vicinity of the carrier's quarter. It was crammed with men in steel helmets and carrying rifles. He guessed that this contingent would soon be landing on the spit – the hunting party that Corrigan had anticipated – but for the time being they seemed in no hurry.

It then became apparent that they were waiting for the carrier to attempt its passage to the lagoon and were standing by to counter interference from either side of the channel. Ross found he was holding his breath as the carrier steered slowly for the gap of water marked by the wrecked extremities of the *Machiko*. The Japanese ship was now broadside on to Ross and Corrigan. Her stem glided past the end of the spit into the lagoon.

The noise of metal grinding against metal came shrieking across the water towards them as the carrier's progress came to a sudden halt and her bow suddenly rose about twelve feet. Ross and Corrigan raced through the trees to get a better view of the end of the spit.

From the fringe of the denser forest into which they had fled only a short time before, the plight of the carrier was plainly visible. She was jammed hard and fast with her fore section in the lagoon and her mid and after sections still in the basin.

"'The *Machiko*'s done her job after all," Ross said hoarsely to Corrigan. "There must be chunks of her all over the seabed in the gap and the carrier tried to ride right over the top. The way her bows are sticking up in the air, my bet is that she's sitting high and dry on top of the *Machiko*'s main engine."

"And we're going to have company," said Corrigan, pointing.

The launch had somehow manoeuvred past her stranded parent ship and was close to the beach of the spit on the lagoon side. Helmeted figures were wading ashore on to the spit itself.

"Get the others," yelled Corrigan. "Anyone who's got a gun. Let's keep the Nips out there in the open." He was already unslinging his sub-machine-gun.

Ross was running to do as the Australian said when a totally new and unexpected sound rent the air. It sounded like an express train flying in the air at about tree-top level. It passed close and he stopped in his tracks and looked back. A loud explosion came echoing from the direction of the stranded carrier.

Suddenly the air seemed alive with what sounded like locomotives whirring by overhead. A succession of explosions came from the end of the spit. When he reached the others, it was to find them shouting and waving and cheering.

Out at sea, just beyond the reef, a sleek destroyer had all her guns blazing away at the sitting target off the end of the spit.

Nineteen

The Day Before "Stingray"

The Mitchells were flying at a thousand feet in a perfect diamond. Looking down at the millpond surface of the ocean, Major Buster Low marvelled at the difference in weather conditions they were now enjoying from those at Dobodura over the past few days. He made a silent prayer that the weather over Dobodura would be showing a dramatic improvement when 106 Squadron made the return trip to New Guinea. If there was no improvement, they'd never find the goddamned place!

He hadn't been too popular with some guys in the squadron when he had volunteered to get the 106th in the air for this mission and gamble on finding a gap in the clouds on the trip back. But the pilots who had been with him longest knew that he wasn't a glory hunter intent on adding to the row of medals he already had. They had understood his motives. They knew that if any outfit had to go to the Tarakangs and bail out General Budge's landing fleet, the job had to go to the 106th. They were easily the best qualified for the type of operation required and, what is more, they had been to the Tarakangs before. In fact, they were the only outfit that had been to the Tarakangs before.

A voice crackled in Low's earphones.

"Calling Kalamazoo Leader . . . Calling Kalamazoo Leader . . . If you can hear me, Kalamazoo Leader, come in, please. This is Grandstand, Grandstand . . . Calling Kalamazoo Leader."

"I read you loud and clear, Grandstand," said Low. "This is Kalamazoo Leader. Nice to hear a friendly voice, Grandstand. Over."

"I have a message for you, Kalamazoo Leader, from Grandstand Captain. Hurry along, Kalamazoo Leader. Hurry along. The show has started. We are engaging Bandit Queen. Do you read me? We are engaging Bandit Queen. We have her corralled. Over."

288

"This is Kalamazoo Leader, Grandstand. I read you. We should be with you in about five minutes from now. Can you give me a co-ordinate on Bandit Queen's position? Over."

The requested information came back immediately from the radio room of the USS *Maclay*, callsign "Grandstand". Low passed it to his navigator. A few moments later, the navigator pushed a map in front of Low and pointed to a pencilled cross.

"The Nip carrier is right there," he said, "the eastern end of that big lake. She must still be inside the reef."

"How far is that from the mountain?" asked Low.

The navigator tapped the map with his pencil.

"The top of the mountain's here . . . That's about two and a half miles from the carrier. If we make our run-in from the south-east on a three-one-five-degree course, we can run clear across the low end of the island without having to get much higher than treetop height. Best way, though, maybe to come in close from the end of the Straits on two-seven-five and run right down the lake."

"We'll follow the lake," said Low. "I just hope that that Japanese son-of-a-bitch is exactly where the Navy says."

The Mitchells jettisoned their belly tanks with Mount Taki in sight and sped in low towards Little Tarakang in flights of two. They had no difficulty pinpointing the *Yamazakura*. A spiral of smoke from a fire started by the shells of the *Maclay* showed exactly where the aircraft carrier was stranded like a beached whale.

The aircraft roared in at fifty feet, releasing their bombs at pointblank range and with deadly accuracy. As the squadron wheeled to a thousand feet and regrouped to the west of Little Tarakang, the success of the attack was all too evident. A curtain of smoke was ascending from what was left of the *Yamazakura*. She was still exploding as countless fires raged throughout her shell and ignited torpedoes and ammunition.

"Good shooting, you guys," Low congratulated his fliers over the radio. "We'll leave what's left to the Navy. Now, let's blow the top off that mountain!"

When they made their second run, the Mitchells saturated the crater of Mount Taki with a mixture of napalm and high explosive. They left it ablaze from end to end so that the cone seemed to burn like a roman candle – a torch thrust from the blue sea.

Unscathed, the Mitchells turned for home. Not all of them were to make it. Back at Dobodura, the base was again clouded in.

Lew White believed that the place to lead was from the front. For that reason, he was the first man of No. 4 Commando to set foot on Little Tarakang. As the outboard-driven rubber dinghies had swarmed through the opening in the reef like waterborne hornets, they had been greeted by light rifle fire from the eastern end of the spit that divided the lagoon from the inner harbour. It had been enough for the Australian major to direct the dinghies to port, so that they headed towards a stretch of beach on the spit away from the shelltorn Japanese aircraft carrier.

As Lew's dinghy had neared the beach, some men had run out from the trees above the beach and made frantic waving signals with their arms. Ignoring rifle fire from the end of the spit, these men had come down to the water's edge, shouting a welcome to the Australians.

"Get back under cover!" Lew yelled at a gaunt skeleton of man in the rags of what might once have been a ship's officer's uniform. He momentarily ignored the man as he plunged up the beach, urging his men to follow him to the cover of the trees. The gaunt, ragged man, grinning like a schoolboy, could not keep pace with Lew's athletic stride but followed him in a staggering run.

There were more men crouching among the trees, all as ragged and skinny as the first man, but Lew acknowledged their presence only with a wave of the hand and kept his attention firmly on his commandos as they streamed up the beach from the dinghies. Not until they were all safely within the cover of the trees and green bush of the sandy spit and the dinghies were buzzing back out across the lagoon, did he turn his attention to the man who had met him at the water's edge.

"Are your people all here?" Lew asked the man.

"That's what I've been trying to tell you," said the man, who was happily excited and yet agitated at the same time. "There's half a dozen of us not here. They're trying to hold off about thirty Japs who landed on the point near the carrier. You've got to help them."

Haraldsen — for it was he who had greeted Lew White as he stepped ashore — gave the Australian major a brief but lucid account of the situation on the island.

"So there are no Japs behind us?" said Lew, indicating the forest to the west. "The garrison soldiers are all still up on the mountain and the jokers who are firing along the beach came from the carrier?"

"As far as I know, yes," said Haraldsen.

Lew wasted no more time. Telling Haraldsen and the others to remain under cover and out of sight, he deployed his own men in two sections. One was ordered to advance towards the end of the spit along its north shore. He led the party skirting the south beach, where they had landed. They set off at the double, hugging the cover of the bush fringing the shore.

The Australians were guided by bursts of small-arms fire from up ahead.

Ross cursed the designer of the Arisaka rifle as he stood, the weapon aimed at the charging scuttle-helmeted figure, and tried to recock and fire. He could not get enough strength into his fingers to draw the bolt back. He dropped the rifle to waist height in order to get more leverage but, even as he did so, the Japanese marine was on top of him with a dervish shriek screaming from his lips. Ross had been firing through the lower branches of a bushing frangipani that was rich in white trumpet-shaped flowers. The Japanese marine, with bayonet gleaming at the end of his rifle, plunged straight at the bush. The thick but fragile frangipani twigs snapped like brittle candy stalks under the man's weight as he lunged at Ross. The bushing tree did not stop the Japanese nor slow his momentum but it threw him slightly to one side so that the bayonet thrust at Ross' heart struck into the soft flesh and chest muscle just below his right shoulder.

Ross felt a flame of pain as the steel seemed to hook him under the shoulder-blade and carry him backwards, impaled. For a moment, he hung, skewered on the end of the bayonet by his shoulder. His weight dragged the rifle down and the Japanese marine – progress halted and straddled thigh-deep in battered frangipani – yanked his rifle free. Ross fell backwards, his head swimming with nausea and his torn shoulder a sea of pain. He felt that his arm must have been wrenched from its socket. He looked up at his enemy through a wavering blood-red mist.

The Japanese seemed to move like someone in a slow-motion film: swaying this way and that, face contorted, as he disentangled himself from the flowering bush. Then he was free. Ross caught the flashing glint of sun mirrored on bloodied bayonet as it was held high above him. He sank back on the soft, warm earth, eyes closed against his pain. He did not care about the thrust he knew was now coming. It could only bring release.

But the thrust did not come.

Paul Newton, only a few yards away, had heard Ross' involuntary scream as the bayonet had pierced his flesh. His last bullet gone, Newton had heard the scream from beyond the frangipani and known it was Ross. A sudden and terrible anger had gripped him. It had been a death scream, he was sure; and the thought of Ross dying now, after enduring so much, was more than the American could bear. It filled him with a trembling fury such as he had never known.

Plunging through the bush, he burst on a tableau he would never forget. Ross lay sprawled on his back as if asleep, his chest and right arm covered in blood. Above him stood the Japanese marine, about to thrust viciously at the fallen sea captain. The Japanese looked up, eyes wide with alarm at the sound of Newton's sudden intrusion upon the scene. He reacted slowly and, even as he began to turn the rifle in his hands to meet the new threat, Newton was launching himself forward. Hands clasped around the barrel of his useless rifle, he swung it like a club as the Japanese half turned. The stock of the fiercely swung rifle smashed into the marine's face just below the visor of his helmet. There was a sound like the thwack of a lumberjack's axe thudding into a redwood pine. The blow knocked the marine off his feet and he collapsed backwards into the frangipani from which he had so recently disentangled himself. His rifle fell at Newton's feet. Dropping his own weapon, Newton seized it. Still driven by the blind, savage anger that had gripped him, he leapt after the fallen Japanese. The marine had made no attempt to rise and was spreadeagled across a cushion of bushing frangipani as if he had fallen out of a tree. Newton thrust the tip of the bayonet into the bloodied face under the scuttle helmet and pulled the rifle's trigger. The rifle kicked in his hands and there was a puff of smoke and the smell of scorching. Newton stared in horror at the gluey red pulp that bubbled under the helmet's rim and had once been a human face. He retreated a step, dazed with shock. Then he was aware of men gliding out of trees and across the small clearing. An Australian-sounding voice was saying, "That's one very dead Nip, mate. See if you can do anything for your chum there, willya? We'll take care of the other Nips."

It was moments later that there was a sudden roar of aircraft engines and the ground began to shake as bomb blasts reverberated from the end of the spit. Buster Low's Mitchells had arrived from Dobodura.

Major Hitoshi Kimura stumbled round the defence perimeter of his force on Mount Taki's summit. Evidence of the appalling carnage wreaked by the American Mitchell bombers was everywhere. Fires still raged across the entire crater area. The cascading napalm had burned and defoliated every living bush and tree and, in those patches where the flames had subsided, the ground was oil-blackened and smouldering with the smoking skeletons of trees thrusting upwards like charred stalagmites.

The fiercest of the fires covered the site of the communications centre. Its elaborate camouflage had concealed it from the air but afforded no protection from fire and blast. Indeed, its blanket-like cover had constituted a firetrap of frightening efficiency. The dried rattan used so extensively in its fabric had conducted the ravaging flames like a prairie fire swept by a gale through dried grass, causing end-to-end conflagration in seconds.

None of the three 150mm guns had survived the air raid. Two had disappeared under a cluster of direct hits from high explosive bombs. The third had gone in a bomb-burst avalanche and cartwheeled down the east face of Mount Taki amid tons of rock, to finish in the lagoon.

Worst of all to Kimura's shocked eyes was the toll in human life. Of the dead, nothing visible remained of at least one-third. Of the remaining two-thirds, there was evidence aplenty: bodies charred beyond recognition of identity but recognisable as human carcases. Some of the wounded were in a pitiful state and would not survive the setting of the sun. Others, less severely wounded, were traumatised into crawling, stumbling wrecks.

Those of Kimura's men in defence holes that had not been buried by collapsing earth or engulfed in flaming napalm had survived comparatively unscathed. He mustered them now to search for living among the devastation. Then he gathered the survivors in a bushy hollow fifty yards below the crater of the mountain. A sergeant reported the roll. Fifty-three men had survived the American attack. Of these, seventeen were unable to walk. Thirteen more had wounds but were not totally incapacitated.

Kimura marvelled at the sergeant's stoic acceptance of the fact that, in the space of several minutes, the force on Mount Taki had been reduced to a fragment of its original size. The man now fidgeted, uncomfortable before him, as if he had something on his mind. Kimura asked him if there was something he wished to add.

"It is a request by the badly wounded, sir."

"What about the wounded, Sergeant?"

"They have asked for grenades, sir."

"Grenades?"

"Yes, sir. It is their common wish. They know that they can only now be a burden . . . That they cannot fight . . . They seek your permission to die."

Kimura stared at the sergeant impassively but he wanted to cry aloud in grief. The whole world seemed to be crushing on his shoulders and the burden was unbearable.

"I shall speak with them," he said to the sergeant.

He walked across to the low end of the hollow where the severely wounded lay on the ground. Four of the men were unconscious. Others lay with their eyes shut, fighting the pain in their bodies but deprived of the oblivion that would free them from it. Some stared at what was going on around them with blank fatalistic calm. The eyes of the latter now seemed to bore into Kimura as he approached.

"Which of you asked the sergeant for grenades?" Kimura asked.

"It is the wish of us all," said one man, who was lying with a blanket across his middle. The blanket oozed blood from the massive abdominal wound it concealed. Sweat was running down the man's face and neck in streams and it was an effort for him to speak.

"What Aso says is true," said another. "Those of us who can, have discussed it. The others are dying anyway. They would approve."

Suddenly, one of the casualties, who was lying quite inert, moved.

"Shosa! Shosa!" The words came out in a faint cry.

Kimura walked over to the figure on the ground. He stared down at the man as he stirred. The body, partly covered by a blanket, was naked and hideously burned. A right leg and foot protruding from the blanket was charred black, as was the right shoulder and the right side of the face. The place of the right eye was a black and bloody slit. The scalp was shrivelled.

"I am Shosa Kimura," said Kimura.

"Shosa . . . Shosa . . ." The words came clearly and the mouth-hole, where the lips had been seared to nothing, moved in what seemed to be an obscene parody of a smile. "Shosa . . ." it said again.

"Who is this man?" asked Kimura, looking around him.

One of two soldiers, who had been acting as medics and trying to make the wounded more comfortable, straightened up from his task.

"It's Lieutenant Niguchi, sir. I carried him down here myself. I saw him get it. I'm afraid he won't last long."

Kimura dropped on one knee and gently touched the uninjured left shoulder.

"Niguchi," he said softly. "It is I, Shosa Kimura." Even as he knelt by the young officer, he could not reconcile the figure on the ground with the lieutenant Niguchi he had known. The mouth-hole moved again with supreme effort.

"Let . . . die . . ."

No more words came. Niguchi lapsed into unconsciousness. To Kimura, it was a great astonishment that the human frame could endure such injury as Niguchi's and retain a spark of life.

He stood up. Briefly his eyes met those of the man with the abdominal wound. He nodded to him wordlessly, then strode away.

At the far end of the hollow, he signalled to the sergeant to accompany him a little distance away from the others.

"I want every man, who is able, to be ready to move out of here in five minutes," he said quietly. "We are going back down the hill."

"And the wounded, sir?"

"Give them the grenades they ask for."

Kimura was leading the walking survivors down the hill when a series of explosions echoed from the hollow they had recently vacated. Kimura did not look back.

He halted the men at a hillock overlooking the site of the former camp. On his left the land sloped down to the open ground where the prisoners had been housed. Beyond, lay the waters of the inner harbour. He ordered his men to dig in. As they did so, he ventured on a lone reconnaissance as far as the lake shore.

Firing, which had echoed from the spit for most of the morning, had long since stopped. Smoke still spiralled from the mangled remains of the *Yamazakura*, which now resembled an untidy metal causeway littering the neck of water between the spit and the Mount Taki side of the island. Kimura wondered if there was anything he could have done to have saved the *Yamazakura* or to have repelled the enemy soldiers who had been landed on the spit from the American destroyer. He doubted it. In any case, the air raid had altered the entire situation and made such speculation a waste of time.

Before the planes had come, his main task had been to defend the installations on Mount Taki. Now, there was nothing on Mount Taki left to defend and he had only thirty-six men left. His force had all but been obliterated without firing a shot.

No help, he knew, would be coming from Great Tarakang. The 93rd Independent Coastal Group had become a meaningless entity. It had been formed to defend something which no longer existed. It existed itself now for no other reason than to die. It could accomplish nothing more militarily positive against the enemy than a fleabite. So, all that Kimura had left to ponder was the nature and the timing of that fleabite. There was a futility about it that suddenly, for Kimura, seemed to epitomise the entire wasteful futility of war. The presence of thirty-six Japanese soldiers on a formerly uninhabited island, now once again reverted to a dot on the ocean without military, political, or geographical significance, was an academic fact entirely without consequence of any kind. If they had been stranded on the moon, their chances of doing anything to effect the affairs of men and nations could not have been more negligible.

All that was left to them was the dying. For what? For Nippon? For glory? For nothing?

Kimura looked out across the silent water towards the spit. It was so quiet and peaceful now, so beautiful. His eye was attracted by a blaze of colour nearby. A bush that was a riot of orange and gold blossoms.

He went towards it, feasting his eyes on the colour. He pulled a blossom and stared at it, taking in every incredible detail of its natural beauty. A sadness rose in him. By picking the flower, he had begun the process of its withering and death.

He bowed his head in apology before the bush for the unthinking destruction of its blossom. He felt a wistful pang of envy for the flower he now held in his hand. In your life, he thought, you have blazed into glorious beauty. This, in your short time, you have achieved. I envy your fulfilment. Because it is so much greater than mine. I have achieved nothing with my life and so I am humble before you, less than you. I am nothing.

Kimura looked up at the hillock where his men were. He wondered if they were as eager as he in that moment for the welcome embrace of death and a new beginning. The chance to start afresh with the failures and bitterness of this life expunged. Only death could wipe the record clean and restore to his eternal being the purity and perfection with which he had entered the world. Only death and the beauty of welcoming it like a lover could compensate for the evil and ugliness of his life.

He walked purposefully back along the path that had once linked the prisoners' camp to the Japanese quarters. Ahead he could see the track that had been hacked through the forest to Mount Taki's summit. Only wisps of smoke now rose from the mountain's top to hint at the morning's hail of destruction from the skies. It stood green and serene against a brilliant azure sky.

The mountain will look down on my bones, thought Kimura. This place that I have known will be a fitting place to die. I will become part of its earth and the dust of my flesh will nourish the seeds that fall upon it. And the orange flowers will grow a hundredfold to repay one crushed blossom.

Major Lew White was not displeased with the day's work. He had expected much tougher opposition on Little Tarakang than he had so far encountered. It had taken his men thirty minutes to win complete control of the spit and rescue the surviving members of the party who had successfully blocked the Japanese aircraft carrier's escape from the island. The destruction of the carrier by the American bombers had been awesome, aided as it was by hits on the ship's bomb stores or torpedo racks. There had been no survivors.

The only resistance Lew's men had encountered had come from the marines which the carrier had landed to hunt the harbour-blocking party. The arrival of the Australians had been timely. Another few minutes and the Japanese would undoubtedly have overrun the six or seven men who had tried to hold them off. As it was, the Jap marines had fought fanatically even when they discovered that the odds had changed dramatically against them. Scattered and isolated into groups of two and three, they had fought to the last man. Two Australians had died and another fifteen been wounded in the process.

The casualties had been ferried out to the American destroyer by the dinghies bringing in the second wave of Lew White's commandos. Leaving a young officer in charge of the landing area, Lew had led the bulk of his force on foot round the west shore of the inner harbour to Java Point, only to find a deserted camp. However, a patrol sent out along the north shore of Little

Tarakang made contact with a party of scattered prisoners and, in no time, small groups of Europeans and dozens of Tarakangese islanders came pouring out of the forest to greet their liberators.

Lew detached some more of his men to re-camp the liberated prisoners at Java Point for the time being and to have food brought ashore for them from the destroyer. Then he pressed on through dense forest, moving east now, towards the area below Mount Taki where – he had been told – the prisoners and the Japanese had been housed in permanent camps.

Towards nightfall, a scouting party ahead of the main group came under fire from Japanese entrenched on a hillock overlooking the burnt-out remains of the former camps. Lew ordered lookouts posted and bedded his men down in the forest. It would be time enough to probe the Japanese positions at first light. In the meantime, he had no intention of being caught off guard if the Japanese chose to make any nocturnal forays.

The rising sun was still hidden behind Mount Taki as the Australians advanced in three sections through the bush that fringed the site of the former Japanese camp. Here, they were halted, while Lew White – in the centre section – studied the hillock some thousand yards away where the Japanese were entrenched. He believed that the crest concealed the first of several defence lines strung along every ridge between the old camp and the top of Mount Taki, and that getting to the top would prove a long and bloody process. They would need assistance. Frontal assault would be suicidal. The only way up the mountain – and it was one in which his men had been well trained – would be to infiltrate by way of the bush and take out the defence posts one at a time at close quarters.

"It looks mighty quiet up there," whispered McEachern, Lew's second-in-command. "You think the Nips are still behind that ridge?"

"According to that coastwatcher joker, Corrigan, they weren't this low down the mountain two days ago," said Lew. "But we're taking no chances. Has Foster made contact with that Yankee destroyer yet?"

"They were talking five minutes ago."

"Good. I'm going to ask them to lay down a softening-up barrage on that hill. When it starts, I want you take the left section up through the bush and get above that crest. But don't get too close too soon. I wouldn't like to write and tell your missus that you had your head blown off by the American Navy."

McEachern grinned.

"I'll keep my head down. You going to mark that hill?"

"Red smoke. Green for us. These Yank gunners are pretty good. You saw what they did to that carrier."

They both stared at each other in surprise as, from away to the south-east, there came a rolling thunder of gunfire. It went on without stop.

"What in the name of hell?" said McEachern.

Lew White smiled.

"Reinforcements have arrived," he said. "But don't expect the cavalry to come riding over the hill. Those boys are only interested in the other island. Let's hope they save a few Japs on Great Tarakang for us."

The first salvo of six-inch shells from the USS *Maclay* was airborne within thirty seconds of the two curling smoke signals lobbing out in separate arcs from the green of the island. The first, curling red towards Mount Taki, indicated the bushy hillock which the gunnery officer had already identified from directions radioed by the Australian troops on shore. The second, showing green smoke, located the point beyond which the Australians had halted their advance towards Mount Taki.

Five salvoes straddled the hillock before a message of thanks was relayed from the shore, with a request from the Australian commander to cease fire. Lew White could not believe that the accuracy and intensity of the short barrage was wholly responsible for what he was seeing.

The Japanese were pouring in a stream from behind the crest and were charging in a running mass straight for the fringe of forest where his centre section were crouched with arms at the ready. Conspicuous to the fore of the Japanese was an officer in a white short-sleeved shirt with a sword brandished high above his head. He did not falter in his stride as a torrent of fire from the Australians cut down at least a dozen men on either side of him. Nor did the charge falter nor the banzai cries diminish in volume. On they came. On into the cleared area where charred timbers marked the old Japanese camp.

Relentlessly, the Australians poured streams of fire from automatic guns into the rushing Japanese, swathing them down like reeds before a sickle. Great gaps appeared in the rushing ranks. The stream became a trickle. A flood of about forty men became twenty. Twenty became ten. Now, only half a dozen individual running men, many yards from each other, kept on. The Australians had to select targets instead of just raking the killing ground.

The white-shirted officer bore a charmed life. He seemed immune to the curtain of deadly fire screaming about him. He was the last to fall. The sword was still high above his head and he was less than 150 yards from the Australian line when a ground-raking burst of fire seemed to cut the feet from him and end his bounding advance in mid-stride. The sword flew from his hand and he pitched headlong on his face, his arms outstretched.

The sound of firing died and a strange silence descended on Little Tarakang. The sounds on the morning air came from a distance, from beyond Mount Taki where the low rumble of continuous gunfire rolled on undiminished. There, the battle for Great Tarakang was just beginning. It was some considerable time before Lew White and his Australians were to realise that the battle for Little Tarakang was over.

The appearance, some time after the Australian guns had fallen silent, of McEachern's men waving from the ridge where the Japanese charge had started was the first sign Lew White had that no more onslaughts were to be forthcoming. The Australians ventured out of the trees to advance warily across the battlefield which they had won without a man being scratched. They advanced slowly, awed by the carnage that they had caused and mindful of stories about wounded Japanese keeping a grenade to take an enemy with them as a last act. But only five Japanese were alive on the bloody hillside – and all were too severely wounded to commit any last-breath acts of heroism.

Amongst those still alive, but only just, was the white-shirted officer who had led the charge. Curiosity led Lew White to the outflung arms and sprawled body of his enemy. He turned Major Hitoshi Kimura on to his back and stared down at the unconscious figure, trying to understand what madness, what fanaticism, had inspired that pointless and stupidly suicidal charge at the Australian positions.

Lew shook his head in bewilderment. He called up a medic.

"This joker's still alive," he told the medic. "Better see what you can do for him."

He took a final look at the Japanese officer. The left leg and foot of the fallen Jap was a pulpy shred from below the knee. It was a gruesome sight.

Lew walked a few paces and picked up the sword that had been thrown some distance from the white-shirted officer. Then he strode up the hill to find McEachern.

Epilogue

Memories wakened in Ross as soon as he saw the necklace of islands which lay around the throat of Malaya to the south of Singapore. Peering from the window of the Dakota as it banked on to a new course at five thousand feet, he could see the islands green and lush, scattered on a carpet of blue ocean. Was it only three and a half years ago, nearly four, since the *Machiko* had made her fateful dash across these waters towards the Borneo coast? It all seemed several lifetimes away. The time on Little Tarakang had seemed an aeon all on its own.

He wondered if he would ever again see any of the people with whom he had shared those days on the island. He doubted it. He knew from old, and from much travelling, how earnest promises to keep in touch somehow hardly ever materialised. It was funny, though, how so many of the Little Tarakang survivors had all ended up in Sydney just six months or so before the end of the war.

He had been routed there from the hospital in Moresby, where the doctors had done an impressive job on that bayonet wound and fattening him up again. He had put on a stone and a half in the hospital. He had flown down to Sydney with Dewhurst, who had been in the same hospital. Then, in Sydney, they had met up again with Paul Newton and Ruth Gamage – both waiting a ship passage back to the States. Somehow or other, Woody, the perky Australian, had heard they were all in Sydney and had travelled three hundred miles from some upcountry bush station to see them. Not that Woody had much time for cities or city life. To him, they were all right for a good time every now and then but he had shed no tears when it had been time to return again to the wide open spaces of New South Wales.

In all of them, the biggest change had taken place in Ruth Gamage. Gone forever was that youthful naivety which had been so pronounced a trait in her. She had become a mature woman, quite different from the gawky school-girly person that they had fished out of the water near the Banka Straits. Her hair was growing again by then, and this, of course, changed her appearance dramatically. The short style suited her, made her seem more purposeful and in command of herself somehow. She was prettier with it, too.

And, of course, where Ruth had gone, young Luke had gone, too. A quiet, reserved small boy, but getting sturdier every day. Ruth intended to adopt him legally. Ross had said little when Ruth had confided in him that it was her intention to return some day to Little Tarakang.

"What on earth for?" he had asked.

"To keep a promise," she had replied. "I'm going to build that temple, you know."

His tolerant but unspoken disbelief had not escaped her. It seemed only to make her determination more vehement than ever when he had reminded her that Little Tarakang was an uninhabited island which would revert to jungle when the last troops had left it – if they had not already done so.

"That only makes it all the more perfect for what I have in mind," she had stated. "It will be my mission in life to make Little Tarakang a refuge for all the oppressed and persecuted of this world. It will be a haven for people of any colour and any creed who seek after peace and the brotherhood of nations. No one will be turned away."

She had gone on to outline with enthusiasm her plans to campaign from coast to coast in the States to raise the money to realise her dream. Some of Ross' doubts wavered before her unshakeable certainty.

Of those who had found their uttermost resources tested in the heat and misery of Little Tarakang, each had found something. Some discovered the true frailty of their beings. Some discovered strengths that they did not know they possessed. For Ruth Gamage, the discovery was of a faith so different from what she had believed a faith should be that the new bore no comparison to the old.

The old was founded on pictures described to her by others of a fairytale world. It was as elusive as a dream. The new was founded on pain and an empty belly and the smell of death and a true recognition of these conditions. And it was as real as a growing tree.

Ross could not share Ruth Gamage's certainties but he could admire the qualities in which they had found roots. He had wished her well and the realisation of her dreams – and with such sincerity that she had wept on parting.

Tears streaming down her face, she had thrown her arms round him and sobbed her goodbyes. With a breaking voice she had promised, "I'll pray always for fair winds for you, Captain. God bless you and keep you – and send you no more hurricanes."

Ross' farewell with Paul Newton had been merrier – a fact which owed something to the protracted dinner they enjoyed in the restaurant of Tattersall's Hotel and the three bottles of wine they consumed with it. There had been no shortage of certainty about what Paul Newton intended to do with his life. He had already taken the first steps. Since his release from captivity, Paul had already drafted an outline of a novel and airmailed it to a literary agent in New York. A cabled reply had reached Paul in Sydney. The agent had shown the outline to two Madison Avenue publishing houses and one had already offered a five-thousand dollar advance on the still unwritten novel.

The farewell dinner with Ross had also been a celebration to launch the career of Paul Newton, novelist and future candidate for a Pulitzer Prize. It had been an evening of much reminiscence and great hilarity. The two men had discovered that, in addition to all the miseries they had shared, there seemed to be equally as many absurd and delightfully funny happenings in their store of common experiences. It was not until they stood before a taxi waiting to take Paul Newton to the harbour that a moment of solemnity came.

Newton's fierce handshake and slightly slurred "So long, Skipper, old friend" suddenly seemed too casually inadequate for the moment. Impulsively, he grabbed Ross in a bearhug and found himself at a loss for words.

"Goddamn it, I don't know how to say goodbye!" he cried hoarsely. But somehow he had. And Ross' final sight of him had been of him waving from the open window of the taxi until it disappeared from sight at the end of Lower Pitt Street.

Now, as the Dakota neared Singapore, thoughts of Newton and Ruth Gamage and Woody and the days on Little Tarakang filled his mind. A memory leapt unbidden, too, of the friend who had been called an enemy. He had never found out what had happened to Kimura, although he assumed that the Japanese major

304

had died on the island. He had never been given any details about the final reoccupation of Little Tarakang by the Australian commandos who had landed from the destroyer – only that the Japanese on the island had been wiped out.

From the window of the Dakota, Ross could make out the sprawl of the city and harbour-front as the aircraft banked yet again to descend towards Seletar. Still standing like a grey obelisk was the tower of the Cathay Building, dominating the avenues leading to it. A union jack flew once more from its top. The city had been reoccupied by British and Australian forces some three months before. The roads were full of ships of many nations, still in their wartime grey.

Transport from the airfield consisted of an RAF "gharry" which ran the Dakota's passengers – mainly service officers like Ross himself – to Raffles Square. A room had been reserved for him in an officers' hostel run by a welfare organisation. He arrived in time for dinner, which was a leisurely affair. After it, he retired to a large lounge, comfortably furnished with cushioned cane chairs, to enjoy a post-prandial coffee before making his way to bed.

It was in the lounge, his coffee on the table beside him, that Ross glanced idly through the newspaper that another resident had left lying on the next chair. The paper was a morning edition published in Singapore that day.

His attention was taken by two full pages of reporting on the trials before military tribunal of Japanese war criminals. In one court, seven Japanese officers had been tried in the same dock for a variety of offences against Allied prisoners of war in Siam. Six of them had been sentenced to be hanged. The report of the closing proceedings of this trial occupied nearly one and a half pages of the newspaper. Tucked away underneath it was a shorter piece headed: APPEAL FOR MERCY REJECTED. A sub-title said: FIRING SQUAD SENTENCE FOR ISLAND ATROCITIES TO STAND.

Ross felt an icy chill run through him as he read that an appeal lodged by his defence counsel, Captain A.J.C. Sainsbury, Middlesex Regiment, on behalf of Major Hitoshi Kimura, had been turned down by the Supreme Commander, SEAC. Captain Sainsbury's plea – that an affidavit from a repatriated internee and a few captured documents were insufficient grounds for the establishment of guilt on a capital offence – had not swayed the Supreme Commander.

Kimura's conviction – the article stated – had hinged on two documents produced in court and no other evidence. Sainsbury had contended that the first – an affidavit – was not substantiated by any corroborating testimony, and that the second – while implying that a crime had been carried out – was not in itself proof that any crime had been committed.

The first of the two documents was an affidavit given to investigating officers of the War Crimes Commission in New Guinea by Randolph Moorhouse, a former Government Officer in Singapore. Moorhouse had listed crimes against British and Australian internees and against the native Tarakangese population which had taken place on the island of Little Tarakang, where Kimura had been military commandant. The crimes included the decapitation of an Australian soldier for trying to defend a female internee from a savage attack by a Japanese officer.

The second document produced was one signed by the accused, Kimura, and was a notification to his Area Commander, Colonel Watanabe, that Order No. 1753 had been fully implemented. Order No. 1753 had been described by prosecuting counsel repeatedly as "the infamous Order No. 1753". It was headed "Order Regarding the Disposal Of Prisoners, Internees and Surplus Labour-Force Personnel" and there was no ambiguity about its contents.

The prosecution had argued that the document in Kimura's hand amounted to a confession that he had ordered the deaths of more than a hundred and fifty internees and Tarakangese islanders. The tribunal's attention had been drawn to a list of names recorded by the Japanese and the blatantly false record that they had "died from natural causes" – all on the same day.

Answering this, Sainsbury had contended that surely it was incumbent upon the prosecution to have instigated some inquiries on the spot, if only to produce one scrap of physical evidence, one solitary witness to whatever it was they alleged took place. The passage of time since the crimes, plus the remoteness of the Tarakang Islands, made this impracticable – the prosecution had replied. And a member of the tribunal had commented that, if the accused had disposed of all the witnesses, it was hardly surprising that none of them was available to testify. Another had regretted the fact that the Area Commander, Colonel Watanabe, had not survived the Tarakang campaign to stand in the dock alongside the accused.

The newspaper report ended by saying that, although the

office of the Supreme Commander had issued a short statement announcing the rejection of the petition for mercy, no reasons were given. It was believed, however, that his decision not to intervene in the decision of the court had been influenced by the accused officer's refusal in court to deny any of the charges brought against him. When invited by the tribunal to repudiate the charges or to offer mitigating evidence on his own behalf, Kimura had declined to do so. The tribunal had plainly taken his silence as tantamount to an admission of guilt – a conclusion with which the Supreme Commander had been unable to disagree.

Before sentence was pronounced, Kimura had asked leave to make a short statement and this had clearly not aided his counsel's plea for mercy. The statement was quoted in full: "I, Hitoshi Kimura, offer my grateful thanks to the honoured officers of this court for their conduct in these proceedings and for the verdict they will deliver. I submit to that verdict as just and deserved."

For some reason that Ross could not glean from the newspaper report, the tribunal had refrained from a sentence of death by hanging. He had been sentenced to face a firing squad. The paper gave no indication of when the sentence was to be carried out.

Ross put the paper down. His coffee sat on the table beside him, untouched. He found that his whole body had gone cold but his face was bathed in sweat. It oozed out of him as his mind burned with the knowledge that if Kimura were to be executed a bigger crime would be committed than any that could be laid at Kimura's door.

Why had Kimura not spoken up? Why had he not told the tribunal that most of the people he was accused of killing were very much alive and, with a little effort, could be traced? The answer had to be that Kimura *wanted* to die. And, knowing Kimura, Ross could guess at the reasons. The Japanese major *felt* guilty – not for himself but for the likes of Tachibana and Yoshimura and Watanabe, for the whole Bushido-crazy gang of militarists and killers who had dishonoured Nippon with their war. He saw his own death as an apology for *them*.

Well, perhaps there was still time to stop it. Ross picked up the newspaper and checked the defending counsel's name – Captain A.J.C. Sainsbury of the Middlesex Regiment. That was it. He had to find Sainsbury. Now. Tonight. Before it was too late.

The other guests in the lounge looked up from their coffee and their reading matter in surprise as Ross elbowed blindly past

307

a group standing gossiping and barged from the room without a word of apology. Out in the street, he hailed a passing trishaw.

"Take me to police headquarters," he told the trishaw boy.

Ross found himself delivered to Collyer Quay, not at a civil police station but at the headquarters of the Provost-Marshal. It served his purpose. A suspicious but, in the end, helpful sergeant of redcaps listened to his request for help in locating a Captain Sainsbury of the Middlesex Regiment. The sergeant not only came up with the information but offered to run him to Sainsbury's billet – a bungalow out towards Jurong – on the way to his own billet.

Behind the wheel of the jeep, the sergeant seemed keen to satisfy a strong curiosity about his preoccupied passenger.

"Been in Singapore long, sir?" he asked conversationally.

"I arrived only this afternoon," replied Ross.

"Staying for a bit, are you, sir?"

"No. I'm taking over a ship in Bangkok. I'll be flying up there as soon as I can fix up a crew and arrange transport."

"Big ship, is she?"

"No, quite a small one really. One the Japanese left behind."

"Them Japs have a lot to bloody answer for," stated the MP. "Right shambles here, there was, when we first arrived. Our boys up in Changi were like bloody skeletons. But we're sorting out the bastards who done it. Hanging's too good for 'em, if you ask me."

Ross looked sideways at the redcap. He felt a slight envy for his uncomplicated view of the world. The sergeant had recently been in charge of an escort party whose job it had been to attend the executions of convicted war criminals. He now talked about the work with some enthusiasm, ending almost apologetically.

"It's all in the name of justice, sir. Justice has got to be done."

"I wonder," murmured Ross. "Some might call it judicial revenge."

The sergeant laughed.

"An eye for an eye and a tooth for a tooth? Don't you agree with giving the heathen blighters a taste of their own medicine then, sir?"

Ross didn't reply. He sat in silence, recalling a medicine that Paul Newton had brought to him by courtesy of Kimura. It had saved his life. Could he now repay Kimura with the medicine that would save his life?

Captain Sainsbury was on the point of leaving for what had promised to be a most convivial party when his unexpected visitor

308

arrived. His resentment at Ross' unannounced intrusion on his leisure time faded as Ross explained the reason for it. The army officer's face clouded.

"You're too late," he told Ross in a subdued voice.

"Too late?"

"I'm sorry," said Sainsbury. "Major Kimura was executed this morning. I was there . . . At the beach where . . . Look, you'd better come in. I want to talk about it. You knew Kimura . . .? Of course, you must have done . . ."

Sainsbury confessed that, because of Kimura, he had been in quite the wrong mood for the party. He had just intended to get very drunk. He could now do that just as well at his bungalow if Ross would join him. He insisted on sending the military policeman and his jeep away.

Ross, still numbed by Sainsbury's blunt revelation of Kimura's death, allowed himself to be ushered into the kitchen of the bungalow. There, Sainsbury took a bottle of whisky from a cabinet and filled a bucket of ice from the refrigerator. He set them on the table with two tumblers and signalled to Ross to sit opposite him. And, there, they sat and they talked.

Ross found himself telling Sainsbury about Kimura, from the very first encounter on the decks of the *Machiko* right up to that final meeting when the Japanese had outlined his bizarre plan to "kill" his prisoners on paper. The more he talked, the more sharply Kimura's good qualities seemed to etch themselves in his mind.

Sainsbury heard him out; asking only the occasional question, frequently nodding his head in sad agreement. Ross was confirming for him something that he had sensed.

"You know, I felt a genuine liking for the man," Sainsbury confessed. "I knew from my very first meeting with him that he wasn't the mass murderer that they said he was. And I'm still in a state of shock that the tribunal found him guilty. I couldn't believe my ears when it was announced. The evidence just wasn't there to convict. It shook me, I can tell you. The trouble was that Major Kimura didn't exactly help his own case. He was courteous and pleasant with me but very firmly refused to co-operate in his own defence in any way. He just smiled that polite smile of his and said, 'What is spoken cannot be unspoken. What is done cannot be undone. The arrow in flight cannot be recalled.' Then he would go all orientally inscrutable on me. He just wouldn't be budged."

"How did you find him?" asked Ross. "Happy or unhappy?"

Sainsbury squinted sharply at Ross over the top of his steel spectacles.

"Strange you should ask. Before the trial, he was unhappy. Like someone bearing the guilt of the whole world on his shoulders. Afterwards, he was like a new man. Completely serene. As if his sentence of death was an exoneration. He accepted it like other men would greet a free pardon."

"Perhaps that's exactly how he saw it," said Ross. "It's a small consolation but still a consolation of a kind to me that Kimura wanted to die. Death was probably the only thing left that made any sense to him. I'm glad that they shot him and didn't give him the indignity of hanging. Why did they?"

"Because of his leg," said Sainsbury.

Ross stared at him, mystified.

"I don't understand."

"Didn't you know, then? He only had one leg. I don't suppose he would ever have been taken prisoner otherwise. He had a leg shot off during the fighting for that blessed island you've been telling me about."

Ross buried his face momentarily in his hands.

"Oh, my God," he muttered. He stared at Sainsbury. "You mean they had to prop him up to shoot him?"

Sainsbury turned his head away. The vivid memory of what had happened on a quiet Singapore beach only that morning was all too clear in his mind.

"I'm afraid so, old chap. That's why he wasn't hanged. It gets a bit complicated stringing up a fellow on crutches."

Sainsbury splashed more whisky into their glasses and spooned ice in them.

"I feel bloody sick about it. I did the best I could for Kimura but I can't help feeling that I failed him miserably. He should have got off. There's a vindictiveness about these war crimes trials that's bloody obscene. God knows that a lot of the Japs they've had in the dock committed some barbaric acts but a lot of the surviving victims don't even want to know about the trials. They refuse to testify. They don't want vengeance. They just want to go home and forget. A lot, of course, will never forget and there are plenty who will never forgive. Maybe I would feel the same way if all my friends were buried alongside the Burma-Siam railway – and yet I hope to God that if I had survived the kind of horrors these men suffered, I would have more left than a bleak and sterile bitterness. But maybe I shouldn't say that. I didn't experi-

310

ence what they experienced, so I'm not qualified to speak."

Ross smiled ruefully.

"The Japanese have a saying that experience is a cruel tutor but the wise man distils its most bitter lessons with a joyful heart."

"But the trouble, as we both know," said Sainsbury, "is that human nature being what it is, that's much more easily said than done." He gave a despairing shake of his head. "Not being able to do anything for Major Kimura is the bitterest experience that I've ever had. I've got to confess that it has left me with no joy in my heart. I think I'll regret losing this one case all my life."

"If you really did lose it," said Ross.

"What do you mean, 'if I really did lose it'? The man's dead."

"And that, perhaps, was the only victory that Kimura could win." Ross felt a strange comfort in the thought. Perhaps he was attributing to Kimura motives that he had never expressed in life but he could now see the Japanese major's death as an indictment not only of the Japanese system he had served but also of the conquering West. On the one hand, he was apologising for Japanese wrongs without forsaking Japanese ways and, on the other hand, he was reminding the victorious West that absolute power was not to be mistaken for absolute wisdom nor confused with a capacity for error-free judgements.

Ross told Sainsbury about the last game of checkers that he had played with Kimura. The Japanese had had Ross at his mercy but had allowed him to win.

"I think I know now why he did it," said Ross. "It was his way of letting me know how he felt about the strange friendship we had . . . About our different cultures . . . About a war which neither of us had sought . . . About life . . . About everything. He was letting me see that although I was in his power as a result of the war, he felt that moral right was on our side. The only way that he could salvage any moral pride from the situation was to allow me to win. In this way, he could feel that he had done the correct thing. It must have been the same with you and his trial for crimes he had never committed. By staying silent and refusing to defend himself he was asserting moral superiority over those who were sitting in judgement over him – and if they couldn't see it, he wasn't going to enlighten them. If they wanted to play Pontius Pilate, he was going to be quite happy obliging them by playing Christ. The key was that he knew something that they didn't know and you didn't know. And he wanted to die with that knowledge because it was all he had left that was of any value to him. You didn't lose a

311

case, Captain Sainsbury, any more than Kimura lost a moral argument. He won. Or, at least, he won what he wanted to win – and that wasn't an argument, or his life, or even the chance to save face in the eyes of the world. All that he wanted to win . . . to salvage even . . . was his self-respect."

The words had poured out of Ross in a breathless torrent. Sainsbury heard him out, the skin of his forehead corrugated into a frown.

"Perhaps you're right," he said, "but I'm a lawyer by profession, not a philosopher. Your theory doesn't afford me much consolation. Does it make you feel better?"

"Better, no," Ross replied evenly. "Humbler, yes. Sadder, yes . . ."

"And wiser?"

"About life and living? About my fellow-men? No, I feel no wiser. Only more respectful, perhaps, of all those things that I can't understand. I never fully understood Kimura, but I respected him when he was alive. I respect him even more now because, in the end, I think he was able to respect himself."

"We can't bring him back," said Sainsbury wearily. He drained the whisky from his glass and then refilled Ross' and his own. "We can't even get ourselves drunk," he lamented. "Perhaps we should drink to his memory?"

A smile flickered on Ross' face. He raised his glass.

"To absent enemies?" he said, with a glint in his eye.